the
HIDDEN HEIRS

PART ONE

Printed in Australia
Cover and internal design by Shawline Publishing Group Pty Ltd

First printing: October 2023

Shawline Publishing Group Pty Ltd
www.shawlinepublishing.com.au

Paperback ISBN 978-1-9231-0104-3
eBook ISBN 978-1-9231-0107-4

Distributed by Shawline Distribution and Lightning Source Global

 A catalogue record for this work is available from the National Library of Australia

the HIDDEN HEIRS

PART ONE

Simone Kamfonas

To Chris, the man who made it all happen.
I love you immensely

CHAPTER ONE

Ten minutes to go! I was excited for this day to be over.

'Year sevens, before the bell goes, I want you to open your planners and put in your homework. I will be checking it before you leave for the day.'

I heard them all grunting and groaning before opening and doing as I said, as I looked over the room. Year sevens were always wonderful to teach; they were innocent almost, no attitude – that came later when adolescence really kicked in.

'Miss, what are your plans over the weekend?' Sarah asked. She had a doll-like face with her hair always in braids. Her bright blue eyes looked up at me. She had the sweetest nature. If one was to classify her, she was the teacher's pet. Always the student who would fetch whatever a teacher asked and always helped to quieten the class even when the teacher never needed it. I smiled down at her before responding.

'I am going away with some friends, what about you?' I asked her while she followed me around the room as I checked that all the students had written the homework into their planners.

'My history homework,' she said with a smile and walked away. I was in desperate need of a mini holiday, especially on a day like today. Today marked the one-year anniversary of when everything changed for me in a way that I had never expected it to.

I grew up in an orphanage run by nuns. No family ever wanted to adopt me. I wasn't an ugly child but for some reason, I was always looked over. Every weekend the orphanage would open its doors for wannabe parents to come in and view us like we were prizes. I remember once I was adopted but I was sent back after two months; they never gave a reason. I remember it well, the sound of the tyres screeching as they drove away and the feeling of the gravel flicking up and hitting the back of my legs as I looked up at the orphanage. Yeah, I had a rather sad life growing up but I tried to never let it get me down. I was glad the day that I met Toby; it changed the moment that I met him. Despite everything that happened in my life, I never stopped or looked for excuses or reasons to stop. Why did having no family mean that I could not find one in the future with someone else? I kept moving forward because I believed that my biological parents, whoever they were, would want that and especially Toby. In my mind, they were dead because why else would I be left with no answers?

The bell rang, which shook me from my current thoughts. I dismissed the class.

'Have a lovely weekend, year sevens, and don't forget to finish your homework or else you will be spending lunchtime with me next week,' I said to the class with a smile while I waved them out the door.

They left with smiles and laughs, talking loudly with excitement of their plans for the weekend. It was hard being at school today as I closed the door behind me and leaned against it, sighing. It was the first time I had allowed myself to think when I heard my phone ringing. I walked over to my desk, which was messy as it always was after my lessons. I was a good teacher but I had a tendency to be messy. I disliked it but this was who I was. I sat down and smiled seeing the name as I picked it up to answer the phone.

'Hey, Harley.'

'FAITH,' she screamed into the phone as I pulled it away from my ear as she continued yelling with excitement. That was Harley, she gave me hope and joy when I needed it in my darkest moments. When I heard her voice quieten, I put the phone back to my ear.

'I am out the front when you are ready!'

'Hurry up, woman,' Annie yelled in the background.

'Give me about five minutes to pack up and I will meet you guys soon,' they mocked me on the other end of the phone, which made me laugh as I hung up.

I tidied up my desk before grabbing my work bags and my weekend bag. Harley and Annie were two of the most amazing best friends a person could ask for; we called each other soul mates because we were all as crazy as one another. I would not be standing here without them – I loved them, we did everything together. It was their plan this weekend to take me away and hopefully cheer me up and not let my brain overthink and go to the dark place that it had a tendency to do. I knew nothing about where we were going only that it was going to take two hours on the road to the mystery destination.

For the first hour after jumping into Harley's little silver Toyota Yaris, I kept asking, 'So, where are we going?'

I was pestering them about it consistently but they were

used to my annoying traits.

'Just shut up. We are spoiling you for once. Can't you just shut up and enjoy the drive?' Harley replied with her voice showing she was getting annoyed with my pestering. I looked down at my work clothes, which were covered in ink and whiteboard marker.

'Can we at least stop somewhere so I can change out of my work clothes?' I responded with my usual amount of sass as Harley looked in her rear-view mirror at me.

'Yes, Miss Bushanti,' she teased, poking her tongue out at me.

I snorted at her. My name came from the nun who raised me; it was her last name before she married God.

Harley was the youngest out of the three of us. I liked to think she was the most innocent of us, the one with the least life experience. She was always hopeful and optimistic and I adored her for those traits. It was refreshing and helped me to remember what life was like before I became a miserable person and lost my optimistic nature. Harley was quite successful – she ran her own restaurant. She started as a waitress before working her way up to becoming the manager and saved the money to buy the restaurant from the owners. To think that I met her when she was eighteen and how much she had grown. I always felt like a proud big sister around her to see how much she had grown and how much Annie and I had corrupted her over the years.

Annie was the oldest and by oldest, I mean she was only two years older than me but she was the loudest. She was probably the smartest as well (as much as I hated to admit it); she had her master's and was now working on her doctorate in archaeology. She probably had the most life experience. She travelled and lived in Europe for over a year. She loved history as much as I did but her enthusiasm towards it was stronger than my own. I wasn't going to dig in the dirt to find it, I preferred to read about it. Even though she was older than me I still treated her like a little sister. I was the motherly figure of the group and I liked it that way.

We met when we were working at the same restaurant and clicked instantly and have done everything together since. You know how you meet people and you feel like your life would not be complete without each other? The one common element that made us all work together as friends was our immature jokes. It would not matter what type of comment was said, we could all turn it into something dirty and inappropriate. We each bounced off one another and all brought something different to the group: Harley was the optimist, I was the realist and Annie was always full of important information. We never made decisions without consulting each other first. They were my family and I would die for them. I knew they would do the same for me. I smiled as I sat in the back seat watching Harley and Annie talking about some nonsense.

*

We finally pulled over only because we all needed to use the toilet. I was just grateful to get out of my work clothes, they were beginning to itch. It is not fun wearing pants on a summer's afternoon – I ran to the bathroom after grabbing a pair of floral shorts, a black tank top and a bikini top out of my bag in the boot. Walking back to the car, I heard Harley and Annie wolf-whistling. Harley was wearing a floral pink maxi dress that complemented her pale skin and golden-brown hair which was braided off her face, which emphasised her deep brown eyes. We were all around the same height of five foot nine. Annie was wearing black yoga shorts and a green tank top that accentuated her slender figure. Her auburn hair was pulled back into a neat bun which highlighted her petite facial features and hazel eyes. We could all be considered beautiful in our own individual ways even with society's ridiculous standards on beauty.

'Who says we are going to the beach? We haven't told you where we are going. Huh?' Annie said, smugly nudging Harley.

'Well, considering the way we are heading, the only destination we are heading is towards the coast, therefore a beach and hence the bathers. DUH!' I said with a cheeky smile on my face and shrugging at them cockily.

'Yeah, yeah, just because you are a geography teacher, show off,' Annie responded.

'Always,' I said while laughing to myself and jumping back into the car.

Back in the car, we were as immature and fun loving as always. Singing and dancing in the car to the songs of the nineties: Backstreet Boys, Spice Girls, NSYNC. You name it and we were listening to it. Suddenly, Harley turned the volume down on the radio.

'Oh, oh, oh, I almost forgot. How was your date the other night?' she asked, looking at me in the mirror.

'Oh god, please do not remind me. Tinder is definitely not the best place to meet people. I mean, what happened to being a gentleman? Have men changed that much?'

'Yeah, but Faith, the question you need to ask yourself is,

is it the men that have changed or is it you? You have been through a lot and I hope – I am saying this with love, of course – that you are not comparing them to Toby. He was one of a kind and he was your soul mate. You may never find another man like him. He was your perfect match in every way.' Annie always was the most insightful. I sat quietly staring at my fingers after she said that, wondering how much was actually true. It was hard to know how much I had changed and if I was subconsciously comparing them to Toby, which I probably was. Nobody would ever fill that hole and I knew that but I always knew he would want me to be happy despite everything, which was how I honoured him by getting up every morning and just continuing towards my goals.

I finally responded, 'God, you are such a... a... a... a bloody cow, Annie! I don't like how you are my rationality.'

We all started laughing because she wasn't the rationality, we all were to each other. Harley turned the music back up. I didn't keep singing but rather sat alone to my thoughts and processed what Annie had said while staring at the changing landscape around us. Toby left a hole that I struggled to fill and the date reminded me of that hole and if it could ever be filled again.

We finally arrived at our destination; of course, it was a beach. I knew them too well. We pulled up to our cabin, which was almost right on the beach. We all did the same thing: got out of the car and just breathed in the air. We all turned to each other, smiled and had a group hug.

'Thank you, guys. You are awesome. I love you guys,' I said, choking back tears. If there ever was a day I needed friends, today was that day and I realised how much I did mean to my friends and what we did for each other. We started grabbing the bags and taking them into the cabin. It was your typical-looking cabin with dark wood on the outside, a tiny porch and an old rickety rocking chair. Harley found the key above the door frame and unlocked the door, pushing it open as we all peeked into the cabin from a safe distance.

Annie shrugged.

'Fuck it,' she said, walking into the cabin as the floor creaked under her tiny feet. I walked in after her with Harley following hesitantly; she did not like dirty places. I noticed there were three rooms with two beds in one room and one bed in the last room. We picked up the two little beds and brought them into one room. This is what we called a girls' night – you cannot separate us. Annie opened the fridge.

'Oh, Faith, there is another surprise. Come here.'

I walked over and the fridge was full of alcohol with our personal preferences. I liked my red wines; Harley was white and Annie was beer.

'Yeah, I paid an extra two hundred for them to fill the fridge with wine. How much do you love me?'

'Heaps,' I said as I kissed her on the cheek and put my arm around her shoulder, smiling.

'So, what shall we start with?' Annie and I started laughing as we searched through the bottles of alcohol.

Harley yelled from the bedroom, 'We need to eat first. Don't make me be the adult this weekend. I am the youngest, remember?' Annie and I looked at each other and made mocking faces at each other in front of the fridge door.

'Alright, what are we eating then?' I asked, closing the door on Annie and turning around to look for Harley.

We finished eating our juicy pizzas and finished a bottle of pinot noir as well. We were like teenagers again, not a worry in the world. We ventured out to sit down on the beach and watch the sunset. The soft sound of the waves crashing on the shore was relaxing as the colours of red, orange, yellow and some soft purples danced across the sky. It was beautiful. I watched the sun slowly departing with a soft smile. We huddled together as we felt the temperature dropping slowly with the sun descending. Annie started talking about her new dig in Western Australia. She found old Aboriginal tools and something unknown. She was so excited to keep researching and to find out what it was. I was listening but also focusing on the sound of the waves crashing into each other and the crickets chirping away.

They suddenly stopped and it became unnaturally quiet. I searched for a reason; it was strange.

'Did you notice that?' I asked them.

'Notice what?' Annie asked, looking around to understand.

'It just got really quiet. The crickets stopped chirping.' I stood up and looked around. The sky was clouding over quickly and I breathed out, noticing the fog on my breath. I felt a tingle down my spine – something was off.

'I think we had better get inside, without sounding obvious. I think there is a storm coming. Come on, we can keep talking and drinking inside,' I said, worried at how big this storm was going to be.

Seconds later, the rain came pelting down. We all started running towards the cabin. It was hard to run because the rain was coming down so hard and obscuring our view. I had never seen or felt rain this hard before; every droplet stung as it landed on my skin. Thunder started rolling in and I could hear the waves crashing louder in the ocean. There were flashes of light. We all held hands and started running together. I was in front, running and dragging the others with me. Lightning struck within a metre in front of us. We all screamed but I kept dragging them to safety. I had never seen a storm like this before; it wasn't normal. I felt prickles all over my body. I knew what this was – static electricity as I moved quicker dragging the girls with me. The next strike was going to be very close to us. I felt it in my body before I saw the light and...

CHAPTER TWO

Aleksander

It was quiet after the storm. The thunder and lightning had passed and I could smell the fresh air. I raised myself from the bed and looked out the window into the quiet night. The stars were shining brightly in the sky. I sat in the window thinking about how events had come to pass. The man with a disgraced family who was a slave to the king. I heard a small moan behind me – it was the whore I paid for the night to keep up the belief that I belonged to no one. I may have been allowed to keep my title but my family had lost its dignity within the royal families when we renounced the Bouchard family as the rulers of our land and agreed to support the Faulcon family.

The Faulcon family slaughtered any person with Bouchard blood or whoever refused to renounce the Bouchards as the rightful rulers. It had been twenty years since the night the slaughters began. To save my life, my mother agreed to support the Faulcon family and forever be their loyal servant. My father was murdered before my eyes in the dining hall. I did not mourn or at least tried not to mourn as he was a traitor. Since the Faulcon family took power of the country, it was no longer as beautiful as it once was. There was constant infighting, starving citizens and homeless living in the streets within their own filth. Our country was now covered in a dark cloud of misery. There was another moan from the bed. I looked over and her dark hair reminded me of Crystal Bouchard. My childhood friend; we were inseparable. She was a stubborn but spirited princess unlike many other members of royal households. It was hard to remember her face but impossible not to remember the colour of her crystal blue eyes.

I closed my eyes and grabbed my necklace. Crystal gave it to me one night and told me that she would always be mine. She was the one reason that I would never trust the Faulcon family; they killed three innocent children that night. It was a senseless murder that did not need to happen. I was glad that I never saw it happen. I was a slave to the Faulcon and put on my fake smile and followed my orders. I finished my warm wine as I watched the sun slowly rising from beyond the mountains, the colours danced across the sky. It was a new day to prove my loyalty to the Faulcons. A bright light flew across the sky and landed in the distance. Light exploded and filled the sky with white.

'What was that?' I muttered to myself. I knew that someone would be at my door shortly.

I walked over to my bed and nudged the girl, hoping to wake her. She did not wake.

Knock, knock, knock.

'Aleksander, the prince requests your presence,' said the guard outside the door.

'Yes, I will be there soon.'

'No, he requests your presence immediately,' he responded

with a rough voice. I walked over to my bed and grabbed a top throwing it on and adjusting my sleeves moving towards the door when...

Knock, knock, knock.

I threw open the heavy wooden door and heard the wood creak from the sudden movement. I looked down at the guard – it was Miguel. He knew of my dislike for him as he disliked me in return.

'Miguel, I heard your incessant voice the first time, thank you. I received your message. You can escort the lovely lady back home for me. The prince requests my presence,' I said smugly as I pushed past Miguel and started walking down the corridor towards the grand hall. Miguel was a short and arrogant man which reflected in his harsh features which looked to be scrunched and placed upon his face in an awkward manner. He had no appealing characteristics but the prince enjoyed his company.

As I strode into the grand hall, I heard my shoes echoing through the room.

'Your Highness, the Gods shine upon this morning. How can I be of service for you?' I said with a cheerful smile but even I knew that my attitude did not reflect how I truly felt about Prince Sebastian.

'Good morning, Aleksander. Did you see the sky this morning?' he asked with his tone suggesting that I should already know what he was talking about.

I nodded, holding my hands behind my back.

'I want you to retrieve it before any other families have the opportunity,' Sebastian ordered.

The stories about falling stars were said to grant power to

whomever holds it within their hands. Sebastian obviously wanted this power for himself, knowing that his lands were falling into disrepute.

'With pleasure, Your Highness. I shall gather my men and ride with haste.'

I turned with excitement, grateful for any opportunity to leave this poisonous castle. I gathered ten of my most trusted men and we rode in the direction of the explosion. The morning was cool on my face and I felt it through my hair as we rode quicker than we expected. Sebastian was evil incarnate; he enjoyed reminding me of my obligation and loyalty to his family. He was the prince and I was lucky to even be allowed to have my title.

*

The morning turned into night before another day passed us by. We stopped briefly for food and water before continuing. The horses were spooked when we reached the area where the star had fallen; it was unlike any of us had ever seen. We dismounted the horses and walked over to the hole; it was bigger than expected. It was taller than I if I ever stood inside it. I noticed three sets of shoe prints and outlines of shapes inside the hole.

'Dmitirov, can you see this?' I pointed to the shoe prints in the mud, speaking to my most-trusted advisor. He stood beside me and followed my finger to the shoes.

'They are heading in an easterly direction. Are you ready?' I asked, looking up at him.

'My Lord, always.' Dmitirov was back on the horse within moments.

We began riding once more and it was not long till we came across three figures walking in the middle of the road; they heard the horses and turned to see us. They ran into the tree line to hide as Dmitirov and I rode faster.

Dmitirov and I raced to catch them. I dismounted my horse before it came to a halt. I was at a loss for words; what was I to say to three figures that were possibly connected to the falling star?

'My name is Aleksander Marchés. I do not wish to harm you. I swear. Please come out from the trees. We are not the enemy. We want to know about the star.' I waited patiently but there was no response. I turned towards Dmitirov who was still on his horse.

He shrugged his shoulders as I slowly walked towards the trees. Dmitirov, Aidan and Langford all dismounted their horses to follow me into the trees. The rest of the men stayed behind to stand guard. We proceeded into the forest, my hand on the hilt of my sword.

'We are not your enemy. We do not wish to harm you, please...' The floor cracked ahead of me. I hastened my steps and suddenly...

CHAPTER THREE

Faith

Harley, Annie and I had been walking aimlessly for the past two days; we were starving and dehydrated. We had managed to find some berries while walking but it wasn't enough to satisfy our hunger. Our mouths were dry and our lips were beginning to crack. Every step was filled with pain. Surely we had to find a city soon. We were not even sure what had happened. We all felt the lightning coming and the flash before we woke up in a field surrounded by trees. I was trying to stay strong for them – I was the one being optimistic in this moment, not Harley. They needed my strength. It was keeping them going. We managed to find areas to sleep and covered ourselves in fern branches for warmth as well as cuddling each other. Our lack of appropriate clothing was not helping either; we were covered in bug bites from sleeping outdoors.

I was walking ahead dragging Harley and Annie behind me when Annie stopped. I turned to look at her. She had her head tilted with her brown hair messy on top of her head.

'Can you hear that?' she asked as I looked beyond her.

Harley and Annie's eyes followed my own. We all saw the

horses approaching us and they were not approaching slowly. Harley started shaking and Annie's face went paler than usual. Who were these people? I had no idea if we could trust them because I had no idea where the hell we were. My mind went into fight mode.

'Quick, let's hide in those trees,' I shouted at them to get their attention away from the horses that were almost upon us. Once we reached the tree line, I realised that there were not a great many places to hide. We were all exhausted, had very little sleep from our chattering teeth; we needed showers, food and desperately needed water. Harley and Annie could barely stand upright. Keeping myself upright seemed to keep them going.

'Alright, I will stay behind and distract them...' I knew I was the strongest in this moment and I would not be able to forgive myself if they were hurt.

'I want you guys to run in that direction and don't stop. Do you hear me?' I could see their heads moving and I could already anticipate what they were going to say.

'No, there is no argument. I know how to take care of myself. Neither of you have completed self-defence classes and does boxing once a week. Please...' I said, beginning to beg. 'Please, trust me. I am doing this for you. I will find you, run in that direction. I love you guys.' We all hugged each other and they turned and ran.

Shit! Now I was scared. I had no idea what to do. I peeked around the tree and saw a dark figure approaching. I knew that I needed the element of surprise. I heard a twig snap, turned around the tree, swung my fist. It connected to a face and the man dropped. Thank God for the element of surprise.

'Hey, stop right there,' I heard a random man yell and before thinking, I turned and started running in the same direction as Harley and Annie. I could still hear the men yelling after me.

I caught up to Harley and Annie. We were still using the trees as cover. 'We need somewhere to hide,' Annie said with a petrified look on her face. We all looked around and tried to find somewhere to hide.

'Let's climb!' Harley said as she was looking up into the trees. I helped Harley and Annie into two separate trees and saw I was running out of time with the men gaining on us. I quickly ducked into the bottom of a hollowed-out tree and just prayed they would not find me. I wished that I could see Annie and Harley just to make sure they were safe but I was too scared to look out in case I was spotted. I sat for what seemed like hours just waiting and listening intently for any movement approaching in my direction.

I heard shouting and what sounded like metal clanging against one another. I moved to poke my head out of the tree when legs appeared out of nowhere. Black leather boots covered in mud and dirt. They showed wear and tear on the bottom. The man fell to his knees. I bent down to get a closer look when I saw a silver sword go through his torso. I moved back quickly and had to cover my mouth to hold in a gasp. I was in shock; someone was just stabbed in front of me. Where the hell was I?

'Spread out and find them. We are not going home to his loggerhead highness until we have what we came for. They cannot have gone far.'

Whoever this person was, I did not want to be found by them. His voice was angry. I wondered if it was the man that I punched.

'My lord, I found one.'

'I found the other one,' I heard two men yell out.

SHIT, I thought to myself. My friends had been found already; clearly, our plan to hide was not working for us.

'Hi there. Are you going to come down? Or do we need to come up and get you because honestly, I think I can speak for all of us in saying that we really do not wish to. My men are not pleased with you.' There was a pause before he spoke again. 'I think that may be the wise choice, thank you. Where is the third?'

I heard Annie answer, 'We're not sure. She helped us into the trees and ran to find somewhere else to hide.'

'Dmitirov, find her NOW,' he growled at his man.

'Yes, my lord,' the man responded but his voice did not show fear at his boss but more respect. There was no quivering, just the answer of 'yes'.

I stood in the hollowed-out tree, having an internal conflict. Should I keep hiding and wait to be found or just go out now and make it easier? I didn't know what these men were capable of doing but I couldn't leave Annie and Harley alone – what if they were hurt?

'Achoo!'

Well, that answered my question.

'I think the next town heard that sneeze,' I heard the man say.

'Yeah, yeah, yeah,' I said as I crawled out from my hollow tree.

The man grabbed my arm; his fingers dug into my skin. It was going to cause a bruise.

'OUCH! That is hurting me.'

'Yes, you punched me. We are even.'

I looked up at his face and there was dry blood coming out of his nose. I silently congratulated myself and cockily responded, 'I was taught never to trust strangers,' as I resisted the urge to poke my tongue out at him.

I looked over his clothing; it wasn't the usual jeans and dress shirt attire that I was used to. This was something else entirely. We were not in the land of our time. We were in the past.

'Hmm, Aidan, grab some rope and tie her hands up before she hurts anyone else,' he barked more orders at his men.

'There is a compliment somewhere in there I am sure,' I sarcastically retorted. He tightened his grip until Aidan had wrapped one layer of rope around my hands.

'Ouch, it is a bit tight.' I was ignored and led towards the other men and planted beside Annie and Harley. I looked over at them; the fear was obvious on their faces. I moved to stand in front of them. It was my way of ensuring they were safe.

'Ladies,' he said, pointing at Annie and Harley with no emotion on his hard face.

'Tend to my men's wounds.' There was no question; he was simply ordering them to do as he said.

I turned to look back at Annie and Harley; they were staring at each other dumbfounded before looking back at me. I bemusedly smiled to myself – they knew nothing about tending to wounds. After growing up in the orphanage and always helping the nuns to clean any wounds plus being a teacher meant that I had to have a basic first aid knowledge. I was way more qualified than them and we all knew it. Harley shyly turned to the man.

'Excuse me but if I am being honest, we may be female and are expected to know how to tend to a wound but um, yeah, we don't. She is better off helping than the two of us combined.'

Annie chirped up in response after Harley.

'Besides, that is sexist to assume that we would know anyway.'

I laughed to myself because based off the clothing and the way he barked orders, I doubted whether he knew what the term sexist meant.

'Sexist? What is that word you speak? What tongue do you speak in?' he asked, looking at me while I purposely looked away from him. After all, he wasn't asking for my help – he asked for theirs.

'Assist my men to the best of your ability. I am not untying her hands after her actions earlier.' I snorted to myself and had to hold back the smile as he glared in my direction.

Annie and Harley walked in front of me.

'So, what do we do?' they asked in unison.

'Tend to the men, girls,' I said, laughing while holding my hands up.

I walked over to a tree and sat down; I knew this was going to be entertaining. I watched Annie and Harley – they were doing surprisingly okay but it wasn't hard to do basic cleaning of wounds. But it was obvious that there would be infections later down the road. The lord in charge walked over and bent down to my eye level. With the smug look showing through his dark eyes and face, I wanted to punch him again.

'Now, if I untie your hands, do you promise to behave?' he asked, playing with the little knife in his hands.

'Behave? I didn't behave for the nuns – what makes you think I will for you? Besides, I am enjoying the show.'

He growled and stood up to walk away.

'Fine, I will somewhat behave. You have my word,' I said as I held my hands up.

He didn't cut them with the knife. I felt his rough hands on my skin as he untied the ropes and helped me to my feet.

'Alright, Annie, Harley, I need hot to warm water and plenty of spare clothes of some sort that are clean to fix your mess. Some of these wounds are going to need stitches as well. Can you ask what's his name if he has any string – something to... well, you know.'

They ran off to go and find what I needed, while I started tending to the less serious wounds.

It took roughly an hour; at least, I was guessing from watching the sun go down. The man called Dmitirov walked over. He had light brown hair to just below his ears, dark green eyes with olive skin and was almost six feet tall and looked to be in his thirties. He had rope in his hands with a small apologetic smile on his face.

'Wow, that was quick. Am I that untrustworthy and dangerous that you need rope for a girl?'

He laughed at my words – at least he found me funny, unlike his boss.

'For now, yes. I do the lord's bidding and that was not a little punch. For a young lady, you know how to hit someone. I think more than anything, you hurt Aleksander's pride,' he said as he was tying my hands up. 'We are resting here for the night. I will bring you some food over soon. We will be leaving as soon as light breaks through the trees.'

'Thank you, Dmitirov?' I said with doubt but hopeful that I was right in his name.

'You are smarter than you look, milady.' It was an insult at my gender and a compliment as I sank back against the tree.

Annie and Harley walked over with smug looks on their faces; they were bringing food.

'Here you are, milady,' Annie said mockingly with a slight

bow as she sat down beside me. I wanted to throw my spoon at her but it was a little difficult at the moment.

'Yeah, do I even want to know where we are? Or what is in this'—I picked up the spoon and watched the liquid fall back into the bowl—'soup?' I was dubious to try it.

'I can tell you what is in it. I cooked it.' Harley sounded very proud of herself.

'What, Harley? Seriously? Well, I will definitely eat it then because I am sure you won't try and kill me.' I nudged her with my shoulder as she looked out at the men in front of us.

'So, we found out some interesting information while we were tending to the men's wounds,' Annie said with confidence and holding up her hands to show quotation marks.

'Ooohhh, what? Do tell,' I said, straightening while eating my soup and hoping to not drop it on myself.

'Alright, from what I can tell there are five different areas, like, um, states. They all used to be ruled under the one family, until another family – I cannot remember their name – slaughtered the entire family that was ruling and took over control. All the five different states broke away from each other because they did not agree and there has been conflict ever since,' Annie spoke in hushed tones just to make sure no one else heard. Sounded like a normal country spat from historical times; probably over a girl or something.

'So, which, like, state or area are we in?'

With the way Harley and Annie looked at each other, they didn't need to answer and we all went quiet.

To break the silence, I said, 'I am worried – how I am going to sleep with my hands tied up?'

We all started laughing.

CHAPTER FOUR

Aleksander

I sat rubbing my nose when Dmitirov walked over.

'What hurts more? Your nose or your pride from a lady making you fall to the ground?'

'I am removing you from my service,' I said bluntly to him as I winced from the pain in my nose.

'Oh, Alek, you know I am only making light of an interesting situation. Who would have thought that punch could come out of her?' Dmitirov had a point.

I looked over towards the girls and saw them laughing to each other. They were all rather beautiful even if their clothing was not appropriate.

'At first light, we will return to the castle. You will have...' I paused under the sudden realisation that I had yet to learn their names. 'Have we learnt their names yet? Do we know what they are wearing? They look like a common harlot from the streets—'

Dmitirov interjected while I was speaking. 'I believe that is their normal attire, my lord. It cannot be compared to our own and what we believe is normal.'

I shook my head knowing he may have been correct but nevertheless, it was not appropriate for a lady to wear such minimal clothing.

'Regardless, you will take the one in the black pants that are short. Aidan will take the one in the dress and Christoff will take the last one that I believe may be the youngest. She may be the easiest to infiltrate for information.'

'Infiltrate? Alek, they are just girls. I doubt they are an enemy. Relax.'

I moved away from Dmitirov.

'We leave at first light,' I ordered as I stood and walked to my tent. I could not wait till I could deliver these ladies to his royal pain in the behind and get back to my normal life.

I found sleep not long after laying my head for the night when Christoff woke me to take watch. It was a quiet night with the sounds of the bugs and the crackling of the fire the only noises to fill the night air. I walked past the three girls; they were huddled into one another. They looked peaceful, elegant and innocent. I grabbed a blanket from one of the horses and draped it over them. The presumed leader of the group stirred; she looked uncomfortable with her hands tied to her front. I bent down and gently cut the rope holding her hands. A small moan left her lips as I brushed the hair from her face. I heard a noise that distracted me as I walked to investigate.

CHAPTER FIVE

Faith

The melodic sounds of the birds woke me as I opened my eyes to discover that yet again it was not a dream. I stretched my arms out before noticing that my hands were no longer tied together. The cut rope was on the ground before me. I stood up and stretched my legs. The camp was still quiet as I looked at the blood on my skin and clothes.

'I need a shower,' I whispered to myself as I smelt body odour coming from me.

Annie and Harley told me there was a lake just up ahead. I snuck off in that direction when I heard the sound of water running. I could no longer see the campsite and felt a little guilty leaving the girls but I knew the lord would find me; he was too stubborn to let me go. I looked around and saw no one as I removed my top, then walked to the water and dipped my toe in. It was freezing and I quickly pulled it out. The only solution to cold water was to just dive straight in and let my body warm up. I danced around in a circle to try and build my confidence before I walked into the water. The stones were covered in green moss and I made sure my foot was secure before moving on.

I was shivering as I ducked underneath the water and rinsed my hair with the water before grabbing my top and rinsing off the blood and squeezing out the excess water before hanging it off a rock above the water to let it dry slightly. I put my head under again and held my breath for thirty seconds. I wanted peace and quiet to remember the events that had happened over the last three days. I was sitting on a beach with Annie and Harley for a weekend away that they had planned because of my issues when a freak storm happened and we were now in a completely different world. I saw a rock fall into the water and shot out of the water, spinning around to see Lord Aleksander standing with his arms crossed, tapping his foot on a rock and looking rather unimpressed with his dark features.

'Could you pass me my top please?' I said politely, pointing to it on the rock beside him.

I moved towards the water's edge but stayed deep enough so Aleksander and his other guard would not see my half-naked body.

'I knew I should not have cut you loose. I felt compassion for a moment and now I feel regret. Out of the water,' he ordered as he threw my top in my direction.

I was lucky to have caught it as I walked out of the water keeping myself covered before sliding it over my head.

'I have one task assigned to me and that is to return you to the castle. I will be grateful to no longer have to deal with an irresponsible harlot.' He was gritting his teeth in frustration.

'Thank you,' I said, shivering from the top that was still wet but it was clean. I felt better after dipping into the water. I felt more myself as I squeezed the water out of my thick hair.

'With haste,' he growled as he walked up the hill – he was testing my patience now.

'Look, I get it. You don't like me because I punched you but you don't need to be rude. I was protecting my friends. If I wanted to run, I would have but I am still here. I apologise for not alerting you to this but I was covered in blood and wanted to feel clean. Also, I am walking slowly now to ensure that I do not fall back and hit my head on a rock. I am sure you would enjoy thaaatttt—'

It was as if God had planned for my words to ring true in that very moment. I slipped and started to fall backwards. I closed my eyes in preparation for the pain that I was going to feel. I felt a strong muscular arm pull me flush against a solid body. I opened my eyes and saw Aleksander looking down at my face. We were both panting, his warm chocolate eyes were searching my face for something – I couldn't tell you what – as I felt his breath on my face. As I looked at his face now, he had the littlest split of a dimple on his chin. His dark brown hair was down to just below his ears and had a slight wave in it. His skin was a darker shade of olive compared to my own and the lines on his forehead and face showed evidence that he had not had an easy life. His face was covered in stubble but it was kept neat and tidy. He was taller than I thought; if I stood on my tippy toes, he would still tower over me but I would be able to bury my head into his chest and I was not short for a girl. I was almost five foot ten.

Despite his poor attitude, I couldn't deny that he was ruggedly handsome. We continued looking into each other's eyes. I felt a sense of familiarity within them – the warmth in the chocolate colour made me feel safe. I shook my head.

'Are you ready to leave, my lord?'

Aleksander moved away from me quickly before I could even say 'thank you' as he stormed off up the top of the hill. I was confused about what had just happened.

Dmitirov walked over to me with a big smile on his face.

'Are you ready, milady?' he asked, gesturing towards his golden horse.

'Ready?' I asked, making sure I knew what he was asking about.

'Up on the horse. We are riding together for the remainder of the journey till we reach the castle.' Dmitirov walked over to help me onto the horse by bringing his hand close to my leg.

'What are you doing? I can get on a horse myself,' I said bluntly, feeling a little vulnerable to have to share a horse with another person that I did not know. I realised I would have sounded incredibly rude at that moment. I turned back towards him.

'Thank you for offering, Dmitirov,' I said with a soft smile as he nodded and gave me space to get onto the horse. I looked around for Annie and Harley. Annie was safely sitting on a horse and we were both watching Harley struggle to get on a horse before we started laughing at her struggles.

'Thanks for the support, guys,' Harley said sarcastically as Annie responded.

'Well, I am sure all the men enjoyed seeing your bright pink underwear.'

Annie and I could not stop laughing. Harley had turned bright red.

'That is enough, ladies, if you are finished. We would like to proceed.' Aleksander rode past as Annie and I were trying so hard to hold our laughter in.

Annie turned around and yelled out to us. 'I will walk five hundred miles, oh, I will walk five hundred more.'

We rode for a while but there was too much silence; in some circumstances, I didn't like quiet and this was one of those times.

'Dmitirov, tell me about yourself.'

He was kind and I knew I would be able to find out some information from him.

'Excuse me?' He sounded confused. I clarified my question for him.

'Tell me about your life – are you married? Do you have any children? What do you do with your life as a job? Tell me about yourself.'

Dmitirov obliged me.

'I have been married since I was eighteen. My wife was young but my family had wealth and power as did my wife's. We have two children and another on the way. For my job, as you say, I work for the crown and for Aleksander. I am loyal to him and his family; they saved our lives many years ago when the Faulcon family took power from the Bouchards. Any families who supported the past rulers were murdered. I owe Aleksander my life and for this, I would do anything for him.'

I admired his loyalty; it would be something that proved useful when selecting men to serve you but I wondered if Aleksander was always the way that he was. I turned my head to ask.

As if he knew what I was about to ask, Dmitirov said, 'Aleksander might be arrogant and headstrong but he means well – but he finds it hard with his life thus far. His father was beheaded before his eyes at a young age and his mother was sacrificed to allow his family to keep their title. He is cynical but has the best intentions. To put it into perspective for you, all the men here today would fight and die for him. He is very well respected within the castle if not by the king and the prince.'

'That explains his tough exterior,' I said, sighing. 'If Aleksander has a title, is he not a prince as well?' I asked, wondering if he was on the same level as the Faulcon family.

Dmitirov cleared his throat but did not answer my question. We continued to talk but I was wary on the questions he was asking me but it was obvious that he adored Aleksander.

I was beginning to feel tired despite sitting on a horse for hours.

We had been riding since the morning and the sun was now beginning to descend for the day when Aleksander announced, 'We shall rest up ahead for the night and for the horses.'

I exhaled in relief as my legs were cramping. Dmitirov hopped off the horse and put his hand up to me help down. I accepted his gesture on this occasion as my legs were so sore. I dropped into his arms. It was obvious that Dmitirov would easily be able to pick me up and throw me over his shoulder. I walked over to Harley and Annie, shaking my legs occasionally as I went.

'Is it just me or are your legs hurting?' Harley responded curtly.

'Maybe it is karma for you picking on me earlier.' She poked her tongue out.

'I am going to find out what they are doing for food and how I can make it better,' Harley said, walking away.

'Yes, Chef,' I yelled after her in a mocking tone. Annie was playing with my hair, running her fingers through it. I swatted her hand away.

'Where did you go this morning? Obviously, you had a shower because I love your hair when it is natural.' She moved towards my hair again as I swatted her away once more.

'Yes, I bathed in the lake and cleaned the blood from my clothes. My hair is all frizzy. Would you just leave it alone? You know that I don't care and I never have. I wash it – that is the extent of my styling abilities.'

Annie groaned.

'That is only because your hair is always amazing and you don't need to do anything to it. I am always jealous of the softness, the deep chocolate colour and the waves within your hair. It is perfect,' Annie said while looking down at the floor.

She had a hard time lately; her boyfriend broke up with her because she wanted to take the next step but he was not ready for that. She was career driven and willing to sacrifice that for him but he did not believe in marriage.

I put my arms around her and said to her, 'You will always be one of the most beautiful people I have ever seen and I know you will find that person who sees you exactly the way that I do.'

'What the fuck was that?' I asked, looking around and instinctively grabbing Annie's hand.

The men around us had unsheathed their swords and were getting prepared for a fight. I pulled Annie with me to find Harley; if a fight was going to break out, I wanted to know where they were. I took a few steps when I felt arms wrap around my shoulders and pull me back. I screamed as the men turned, looking my direction. Aleksander and Dmitirov were already running towards me. I looked over to Annie – a middle-aged man wearing all black was holding a knife to her throat.

'I recommend not moving unless you want a dagger in your throat,' the man holding me whispered in my ear.

That only seemed to ignite my rage. I didn't want to be a damsel in distress waiting for a man to come and save her. I saw Annie was about to burst into tears from fear alone. I closed my eyes and took a deep breath.

'That is your biggest mistake. These men can attest that I do not do what I am told,' I said as I stomped on his foot.

He was taken aback by the action and dropped his arms on me, which gave me enough room and time to spin around and kick him in the groin. I felt my foot connect as he dropped to the ground, clutching his groin and moaning in pain. He dropped his dagger and I went to pick it up. Aleksander and Dmitirov were now standing beside me, staring at one another in disbelief of my actions.

'I recommend you let her go unless you want to end up like your friend here,' I said as I looked at the man writhing in pain.

Shouting started behind us. I turned around to see more than double the number of men that Aleksander had charging towards us. We were outnumbered and I felt my own fear rise. Where was Harley in all of this?

I screamed at Annie, 'Do something unpredictable,' to get out of his grasp. Dmitirov charged at the man holding Annie as Aleksander grabbed my wrist and dragged me behind him. He turned when we reached a few trees for cover.

'Stay here,' he ordered and as much as I wanted to in that moment, I couldn't.

I had to find Harley; I knew Annie was safe with Dmitirov

now but Harley was nowhere to be seen. I went to move when Aleksander spun back around and grabbed my arm.

'I beg of you, please stay.'

I saw the concern in his chocolate eyes; he genuinely did not want me hurt. It wasn't because of his duty – it was him that didn't want to see me hurt. I nodded at him.

'ARGH,' Aleksander screamed; it was too late.

My actions had caused him to be distracted and miss the man approaching us. Aleksander had been sliced open and blood was gathering across his stomach. He dropped to his knees from the shock as the other man lifted his sword. I didn't even process what I was doing as I grabbed Aleksander's sword and swung it at the man. It landed in his stomach. I felt it stick in him; I felt the flesh part from the sharpness of the sword and the sound and feeling made me want to vomit. I let go of the sword.

'Holy shit,' I said in disbelief at my actions.

The man stood again but Aleksander was faster. He grabbed the sword, pulling it out before plunging it back into the man again. The life left his eyes as I watched him fall to the ground. Aleksander groaned in pain as he grabbed his wound.

'Hold it,' I said to him as I put his arm around my neck and lifted him to walk.

'Come on. I won't let you bleed out. Where the hell is Harley?'

Aleksander chuckled at my orders – I presumed from the fact that I was now ordering him about. Aleksander walked with me but at each step, he let out a little noise. It was obvious he was struggling with the pain. Aidan walked over to protect us, holding his sword out and constantly turning to ensure no one was coming up to us. The men who attacked us started to retreat and I felt eyes on me. That feeling when you know someone is watching you. I looked around and found the source of the eyes. He was off in the distance but I knew his face. He was older than me, old enough to be an uncle. He bowed his head before taking off on his horse with the other men.

Aleksander's men started to cheer as I finally found Harley. She was hiding behind a tree. I smiled with relief upon seeing her. She ran over to me and wrapped her arms around me, crying. It was hard to comfort her at that moment as my arms were preoccupied with holding up Aleksander but I knew words would comfort her at that moment.

'Shh, I've got you. They are gone. You are safe now.'

Annie ran over and pulled her into her arms, knowing that I would be doing it if I could.

'I would never let anything happen to you guys. I love you and I would never leave you or abandon you.' I stood looking at them and listening to them cry. Why did I feel as if this was all my fault? I knew I couldn't tell them the truth about having to stab someone to save Aleksander – they had seen enough. They did not need my emotions on top of that. Aleksander groaned again; his head was hanging down.

'I am going to need your help. I need someone to start a fire. I need clean water, something to wrap the wound with, some stitches and some possible herbs that have medicinal qualities.' I knew Harley would know this and what to look for – even the other men would know.

'I need to stop a possible infection with a wound this deep.' I turned and looked at the other men who were groaning in pain from cuts and scrapes.

'Annie, I need you to triage and see who is the worst.'

Her face said it all but these men just protected us; I wasn't about to let them suffer because I felt as if it was our fault that we were attacked.

'I need to get to the fire. I think I may need to cauterise this wound.'

Aidan had put Aleksander on the ground as he was still holding his stomach. I felt Annie put her hand on my shoulder.

'You can do this. You will be fine,' she said before walking away to get what I had asked for.

I rubbed my face and felt something sticky on my hands; it was Aleksander's blood. This wasn't going to be easy. I breathed out and clapped my hands together.

'Let's get to it.'

Annie had done as I asked and started to sort the men from worst to least wounded; some were capable of looking after themselves, which made it easier. I washed my hands in the water and turned to Aleksander. He was still fully clothed in his tunic.

'I need to take your clothes off.'

Aleksander just looked at me, blinking, his face expressionless. This man was incredibly frustrating.

'Do you want me to fix you or not? I am happy to keep you here bleeding to death while I look after someone who wants to be fixed up. I mean, seriously, I can tell you are in a shit load of pain but if you want to stay in agony—'

'I get the point. There is no need to go on about it. You have to be the most talkative lady I have ever met. Do you ever hold the bluntness of your tongue?' he snapped, moving to a more comfortable position.

'Welcome to a girl from the twenty-first century. We do not shut up—'

'ALRIGHT!' Aleksander yelled and rolled his eyes. I couldn't help but smirk at the fact that I was annoying him.

He started to remove his clothing but I could tell he was struggling and I grabbed the dagger from my back pocket. Aleksander didn't flinch when I held onto his clothes. He moved his hands away and let me cut it down the middle so he could take it off like a jacket. I walked around behind him and pulled it down slowly. He let out little moans in pain.

I threw it away as I looked at his body. It was covered in scars. I couldn't help but run my hands over some of the largest ones before I realised what I was doing.

'Sorry,' I said, clearing my head of the thoughts of what had happened to him.

'They are horrifying, I apologise.'

'Do not apologise – every wound tells a story whether it is on the inside or on the outside,' I said to him with a small smile. He returned it but looked away from me.

'Harley, I am going to need your help,' I yelled out to her. I knew she would come when she could. I turned back to Aleksander.

'I need you to look at me...'

His eyes stared into mine; the colour of them was beautiful – a deep chocolate that had a warmth to them.

'I am going to need to clean the wound before I cauterise it to stop the majority of the bleeding. It is going to hurt like a motherfucker. I will be burning your skin.'

'A motherfucker?' he asked, not taking note of the fact that I said it was going to hurt.

'Don't ask. You may or may not pass out from the pain but I feel like you have a high pain tolerance.'

He snorted at me as Harley joined with me with a bowl of water and herbs and a cloth, and I saw a sword sitting on the fire, getting ready to be used. I felt my hands starting to shake. This was more than just basic first aid. Aleksander grabbed my hands and looked at me.

'I trust you.'

'What, now you do?' I said, snorting a little at his comment.

'You saved my life when you could have run.'

He was right; I had the choice to leave him but I stayed and carried him to safety.

I moved his arm, holding his stomach away. It stuck to him a little as he winced from the pain. I took a deep breath and Harley handed me a cloth as I cleaned it. His breathing became shallow. It was obvious it was hurting him as I tried to hurry to avoid hurting him further. Dmitirov came over and put his hand on my shoulder.

'Ready when you are,' he said softly as I finished cleaning it.

'What is your name?' Aleksander asked as Dmitirov got the sword for me.

'Faith,' I said in response.

'Thank you, Faith,' he said as he moved and lay down.

Harley cleaned up what little blood spilled out as I got into position. I placed the sword on his skin and heard it sizzle as he screamed out in pain. It echoed through the trees and surrounds. He finally passed out from the pain. I cleaned it once again before Dmitirov helped to lift him so I was able to bandage his wound.

I cleaned my hands of the blood and went to tend to the other men but Annie, Harley and Dmitirov had cleaned them all up. I cleaned my face and looked at my top.

'Great, dirty again,' I mumbled to myself as I looked over at Aleksander.

He was still out cold. I sat where I was able to keep an eye on him as Annie sat beside me. Dmitirov asked questions about our lives back home as we tried to explain our modes of transport were no longer horses and carts. The creases in his eyebrows showed his confusion about the items we described to him.

'You are telling me a metal object has the ability to take off and fly in the sky?'

It was entertaining trying to explain how they all worked; he could not understand the concept of power and electricity.

'It is starting to get dark. Aleksander is still out. I need to go check on him,' I said, standing up and feeling the cold. I shivered.

It was in that moment I wished I had not changed out of my work clothes. I walked over to Aleksander and put my hand on his head to check his temperature. He did not have one but he was dripping in sweat. I grabbed a fresh sponge and wiped down his face and checked his wound. It was not too inflamed; it was as I expected it to be. I picked up his jacket and covered him up to keep him warm. For some reason, I sat down and lifted his head onto my lap and leaned against the tree. I wanted to make sure he would be okay during the night. I was watching Harley, who seemed to be having an interesting conversation with Aidan. Everyone was starting to fall asleep and relax for the night.

'Would you like to swap and take turns watching him, if you wanted to get a nap in?' Dmitirov offered as I looked down at his peaceful face.

'No – thank you for the offer but I just want to make sure he is okay myself.' Even if I couldn't understand why I wanted to. I smiled back at him.

After a few hours, Aleksander opened his eyes and started to shiver. I grabbed some water for him. As he drank, I fetched some more before he finished it. He passed out again as his shivering was starting to subside. His men were worried as they woke from their watchers' posts and came over to check on him during the night. Their loyalty was something to be admired; it was the same with Annie, Harley and I.

My eyes were starting to feel heavy. I needed to stretch my legs or I would fall asleep. I walked around for a while to keep myself awake before walking back over. Aleksander started to stir as I stroked his thick dark hair.

'Shh, I have you,' I whispered softly as I started humming softly to him.

Aleksander stopped stirring and fell back into a deep sleep. I noticed his necklace; I ran my fingers over the blue quartz. It was striking. I had never seen a colour like it. I had seen purple, pink and citron but never blue. It was stunning and incredibly smooth but not rounded. It was an irregular shape as if it had not been smoothed out – all the imperfections were present. I could stare into it all day. It was beautiful despite being imperfect. That was the last thing I remembered before waking up the next morning on the ground covered in a blanket.

CHAPTER SIX

Aleksander

The night was restless when I woke and found myself waking on the lap of another. I noticed it was Faith. I moved slowly to not wake her as my abdomen burned with pain. I winced slightly as I stood. I took the blanket and placed it upon her, moving her dark auburn hair from her face. She looked peaceful but she was a puzzle to me. She was unlike most ladies that I had encountered in my life. There was more to her and I knew that for certain. Dmitirov walked over and slapped me hard on the back; it vibrated through my body as the familiar burning sensation returned.

'How are you? I was wrought with worry.'

I felt my wound that was bandaged as I remembered the feeling of the blade cutting through my skin. I shivered.

'Yes, I am alive and unsure how.' I looked at him quizzically for answers.

'Faith saved your life. She cleaned your wound and cauterised it before staying with you all night to ensure you did not become feverish. Do you not remember?' he said as I turned around to look at her. She slept peacefully under the blanket – she had not stirred.

'No, I do not. We shall let her rest before we begin our travels.' If she had stayed with me all night, she would need it before we started our ride.

'What is there to eat?' I asked, knowing that I was not hungry but would need it to recover from my injury.

The men were in good spirits as I picked at my food, keeping my eye on Faith. She was still sleeping peacefully as the hair that I had moved earlier was now falling over her face. I judged her harshly upon our first meeting but she was not the selfish harlot that I believed her to be; the warmth in her crystal blue eyes showed me her compassion. I had not seen a beauty to compare her to.

'Dmitirov, do you know what a "motherfucker" is?'

He shook his head, as confused at the word as I was. I may need her to explain later.

*

'Same as before, my lord?' Dmitirov asked.

I nodded my head in response as I watched Faith, Annie and Harley mount the horses. I did not know where they originated from but I did enjoy the lack of appropriate attire that she wore.

The lady with the shorter hair yelled out, 'Let's play ninety-nine bottles of beer on the wall.'

Faith laughed as the other followed behind her. Her laugh was infectious. I noticed the effect she was having on my men. She continued to laugh till she snorted like a pig. I trotted over to her and Dmitirov.

'Too bad if we needed to be quiet.' Dmitirov smiled at my remark while Faith laughed in response.

'Stealth and being quiet are not my forte, in case you haven't realised that yet. Besides, they say laughter is the best medicine and I got all your men to smile,' she said, beaming at me while a small smile spread across my face.

Dmitirov broke my attention.

'Aleksander, look ahead.'

I followed his eye line.

'Who is that?' I said before discovering the identity of the person; it was Miguel.

It was obvious from the fact that the horse was bigger than him. It was hard to believe that man could be that short, round and arrogant all rolled into one person.

'This cannot be good,' I said to Dmitirov as I straightened as much as I could muster before looking at Faith.

'And you are not to say a word – AND THAT GOES FOR ALL OF YOU. Let me do the talking,' I said with a heavy warning. Faith seemed to understand as the smile disappeared from her face and she adjusted her position on the horse.

'Miguel, how nice to see you venture from the castle. To what do I owe this pleasure?' I said with a smile, keeping up the pretence that I was happy to see him.

'You are late,' he snapped at me. 'His Majesty Samael expected you back yesterday and yet you are still over a day's ride from the castle. Why the delay?'

I shifted in my saddle at the thought of bringing the girls into the devil's castle.

'We ran into some unexpected company. The Arundel family attacked us and we were severely wounded,' I said, holding back the pain from my own wound.

'I cannot see any wounds and there would be no reason for the Arundel family to attack you. We have a treaty,' Miguel retorted back with his snake-like voice that hissed on particular words.

'Are you saying that I am deceiving you?' I said angrily as I tried to keep a level head. I heard a voice in the background.

'I am sorry to say, Miguel, but the lord is correct. I had to dress the wounds myself. I would prefer the lord not to be riding today but he decided against my medical advice to get home to His Majesty Samael. In case you do not believe me, you are welcome to look at my clothes, which are covered in blood.' She spoke with little to no sass and with a different tone in her voice – a gracious tone. She seemed like a completely different person.

I turned my head to look at her in shock and her facial expression was unlike I had ever seen before. She had a prideful look and was not going to back down.

'Of course, milady, I would never suggest that the lord was a deceiver. I was just enquiring as to why it was taking so long,' Miguel answered back nervously as the sweat was obvious on his brow.

'Well, you have your answer, so unless you are going to keep talking, we would like to be on our way,' she said and gestured for Miguel to keep moving.

I saw Dmitirov whisper in her ear and the softness in her face changed to something more serious. I guessed he warned her that this was not a man to cross.

*

Miguel stayed to escort us back to the castle with his sidekick. The atmosphere had changed; the ladies were talking with Miguel. My brows creased with confusion. Could they not see through him and understand that he was a snake? A man who did not deserve their kindness. The sound of their laughter was unnerving; I had never heard a lady laugh in that way. Nightfall was beginning to descend as the sun and warmth were disappearing. I whistled to get everyone's attention.

'We shall camp here for the night. There is enough tree coverage to ensure our safety from further attacks.'

The men seemed to rejoice for the break.

'No, we must return to the king,' Miguel argued as I rolled my eyes out of his sight before turning to him to speak but a sweet voice stopped my words.

'Miguel, it has been a long and arduous journey for us ladies. I would like for us to rest and to ensure that the men are cared for with their wounds. I do believe the king would like for his loyal servants to return to serve him and not be left upon the road to die. I will gladly apologise to the king when we reach our destination.' She spoke with grace and her smile was irresistible as it reached her eyes. She tilted her head to allow her hair to fall slightly leading to her breasts. She was flirting with him.

'As long as we can leave at first light,' he said, dragging his eyes away from her assets.

She nodded in agreement.

The men dismounted and I helped them to set up the camp. One of the girls organised the food for the men for the night. I leaned against the tree, watching everyone complete their job. I watched her walk over with her near-naked legs on display.

She was clutching her hands in front of her.

'I would like to apologise for punching you the other day. I hope you can understand that I was just trying to protect Harley and Annie; it was nothing against you personally. I did not know whether you were a friend or a foe.' She was staring at the floor and in that moment, I craved to look into her blue eyes and feel the warmth they gave me.

I put my hand up to her chin and lifted her head slowly to look at me. I felt instant relief as she looked at me without seeing the scars inside.

'There is nothing to apologise for. You are forgiven, milady.'

Her eyes smiled even if her face did not. She was happy to be forgiven but her attitude towards Miguel was irritating me; I needed to know why.

'Why do you speak to Miguel in a way that you do not speak to others?'

She snorted softly before moving closer towards me and dropping her voice to a whisper.

'It is obvious he is a snake and I would prefer to flirt with a snake for the sake of keeping him on my side, rather than to be on his bad side.'

I grunted in response to her remark; she was right. She did not know Miguel but she could already sense that he was trouble. I extended my hand towards her.

'Aleksander Roberto Marchés.'

She hesitated before sliding her hand into my own. Her skin was soft as it touched my own as I pressed my lips to her skin.

'Faith Maria Bushanti.'

I bowed to her as she tried to curtsy but stumbled on her feet. She couldn't help but let out a little giggle before quietening herself. She knew Miguel would be watching her as I peered over her shoulder to see she was correct. He was watching her intently as I tried to keep my face expressionless.

'We are being watched.'

CHAPTER SEVEN

Faith

I felt relief apologising to Aleksander and felt as if we had formed an alliance especially with Miguel within the ranks. I walked over to Annie and Harley.

'What do we think about Miguel?' Annie responded.

'I think he is a snake – one of those people who will easily stab you in the back but smile to your face.'

'I agree,' Harley said, chirping in response.

'Yes...' I looked around. 'Shall we continue to charm him?' I said, holding in my laughter as we all smiled in response.

We knew that sometimes it was better the devil you knew, especially when he worked closely with the future king. Harley dished up dinner to all of the men before finally sitting down and eating. I looked at our clothing – I wished we had more clothes to wear as I was still covered in dried blood as was Annie, but Harley was covered in food scraps. We stayed close to one another knowing that we were safer next to each other than apart. I looked at Aleksander as he played with his food. I needed to check his wound and felt uneasy at the thought of bringing it up with him. I felt something shift when he introduced himself to me and when I saved his life before he saved mine in return.

I cleared my throat as I walked over to Aleksander.

'Clothes off,' I said without explanation and confusion was written on Aleksander's face. 'I need to check your wound and change your bandage to avoid infection which we have done well so far to avoid.'

Aleksander cleared his throat and stood up, straightening himself. Dmitirov smirked and whispered something to Aleksander, which caught him by surprise as he looked back at him in horror.

'What did Dmitirov say?' I asked, curious what he said to elicit that response from Aleksander.

'Nothing that a lady needs to hear.'

I nodded with a smile.

'I think we both know that I am a lady but not to the standard of your world.'

Aleksander smiled and looked at me. 'He told me to be careful as you might break me.'

I could not help but laugh as I directed for Aleksander to sit down. I would have so many retorts to that comment but it was not worth it with another party present who was watching my every action.

Aleksander removed his clothing. As I looked at his body for the first time, I almost gasped. I had to look away to stop myself from blushing at the sight of him. He was built like a god: strong muscular arms leading to a strong chest and his chiselled abs that led into the v-shape heading into his pants. I wanted more than anything to run my fingers over his abdomen but I needed to focus on his wound. I took a breath and started to remove his bandage slowly. He lay down. As I moved to touch him and check for infection on the wound, he flinched and grabbed my hands.

'I apologise. Your hands were colder than I expected them to be.'

'Oh, harden up because I am going to keep on touching you.' I realised what I had said after the words left my mouth. I felt heat rise in my cheeks as I knew they would be flushing red. I avoided looking at him but I could see him smile for the first time showing his teeth. I needed to keep my mind out of the gutter but it was difficult seeing him in this position and how attractive he was.

'It is healing well. Red as expected but no signs of inflammation or infection. How is it feeling?' I asked, moving away from him slightly to put some space between us.

'It feels acceptable as long as I do not move.'

I grabbed the clean bandage as Aleksander sat up to give me more room to wrap it around him. He took in a deep breath as I started to wrap him.

'Am I hurting you or making you feel uncomfortable?' I was worried.

'No. It has just been a while since I have been this close to a lady dressed in as little clothing as you.'

'I am finished. You can put your clothes on, thank you,' I said, quickly moving away from him.

A man had never made me feel so vulnerable and not in control of myself before. I shook my head, grateful that it was over but the images of his body were not disappearing. It was going to be a long day.

I watched the sun go down by myself on the edge of the

camp. It was peaceful and beautiful as I yearned to return home. I still had no real answers on where I was. Annie and Harley walked over, breaking my thought train.

'Where are you, Faith?' Annie asked, sitting down beside me.

'Sorry, I was in my own little world thinking about home. It feels weird not being so connected to the world anymore. I mean, do we know where we are yet? I feel weird in this world – I feel like it is a dream but also it feels strangely familiar, like I have seen it in a dream before.'

Harley put her arm around my shoulder. 'A dream with ten hot, sweaty, dirty, muscular men all around us. I will admit, I do not quite want to go home.'

Annie and Harley laughed but I couldn't bring myself to laugh in that moment. Dmitirov walked over and handed us a blanket.

'To keep you warm,' he said softly as we accepted it and wrapped it around ourselves.

I could not sleep tonight. I stayed awake to stare at the stars. I stretched my legs, leaving Annie and Harley to keep sleeping as I walked around the edge of the camp.

'Why are you still awake?' the voice said in the dark as Aleksander came into view.

'I couldn't sleep and the stars are quite beautiful tonight.'

He smiled and looked above his head.

'Yes, they are, indeed. You need your rest, Faith. We shall reach the castle tomorrow.'

I smiled softly as I turned to walk away from him.

'Wait,' he said as I felt his hand grasp my wrist.

I stopped and turned back towards him as he moved slowly and reached for my face before grabbing a leaf out of my hair and holding it up with a smile and handing it to me.

'I may have wanted that in there, you know. It may have been my version of a flower.' I crossed my arms at him.

'You do not need any flowers to make you more...' He drifted off and cleared his throat. 'Go to sleep, Faith,' he said, turning back around.

If I wasn't such a loyal person, I would gladly walk and leave Annie and Harley but I could never do that. I sat and just took a breath to gather my thoughts; before I knew it, the sun was coming up. I walked back to the camp and sat down with the girls, closing my eyes. I did not sleep for long before we had to begin the journey to the castle.

I was standing beside Dmitirov's horse, waiting for the sign that I could mount the horse. Aleksander walked over with stealth as I did not hear him but I heard his voice behind me as I turned to look at him.

'Would you like to ride with me today?'

I saw Miguel out of the corner of my eye; he was watching our interaction. I noticed he was watching Aleksander and his actions more than my own. It was obvious that they did not like each other and I did not want to make life more difficult for Aleksander.

'No, I think I will stay with Dmitirov.' Even the words out of my mouth sounded stupid and I grimaced at myself.

Aleksander nodded his head and walked away before I could try and make myself sound better. I wished I could have explained myself. Dmitirov walked over, clapping his hands together.

'Are you ready?' he asked, a smile on his face before it changed. 'Are you unwell? You look not yourself.'

I shook my head at him and put on a smile. I hoped I could explain to Dmitirov why I said no to Aleksander.

'No, I am okay, Dmitirov,' I said as he offered his hand to help me on the horse. I happily accepted his assistance now – our journey together and conversations let me know that I could trust him.

'How long do we have to travel today?' I asked.

'Until midday,' he said, kicking the horse to begin its walk.

The day was dragging on; at least Dmitirov kept me entertained by asking questions about how life was different to life here. I looked around for the sight of Miguel and noticed he was too far in front to be able to hear our conversation.

'Dmitirov, can I ask you a question?'

He responded with a yes softly.

'Miguel is a man not to be trusted. I get the sense that he is quite loyal to the crown and if I spoke out of turn, he would inform His Majesty instantly and there would be severe consequences or punishment.'

'You are right, milady. Aleksander and I keep the peace but we would not shed a tear upon his death.'

I snorted softly at his answer.

'I got that feeling when I heard Aleksander speak to him. He had a different tone and I picked up on that and decided to use my charm,' I said with a smile on my face.

'Yes, we were puzzled on why your tone changed.'

I laughed at his response. 'A lady knows when to use her charm to sway a man.'

'Yes, you do. Ladies certainly do.'

The clouds were growing darker as I felt the wind rush against my exposed skin. A storm was coming, it was obvious.

Dmitirov grabbed his cloak and wrapped it around me. I assumed he could feel me shivering from my lack of clothing.

'Thank you,' I said through chattering teeth.

He moved closer to warm me up as my bare legs were still in the cold.

'I hope the rain holds off,' I said, looking at the darkening sky. I could see quaint little cottages in the distance. The nerd inside me was getting excited; I loved anything old and looked around to Annie and pointed. She looked just as excited.

'Not long now, milady,' Dmitirov muttered as he smelled the air.

I took in a deep breath and could smell salt, the smell you get from being close to the ocean. Aleksander rode up beside us and opened his mouth to speak but no words came out. He stopped and rode off to Harley.

'That was odd.'

'That is Aleksander,' he said under his breath. I wondered what he was talking to Harley about and not me.

We rode over a hill when my eyes lit up from the sight before me. It was a castle; I had seen them back home but most were ruined and this was unlike anything I had ever seen before. It was magnificent and bigger than I thought. The grey stone castle sat on the edge of the ocean; the back of the castle looked out over the crystal blue water. It had four drum towers on each corner with a bell tower at the front. I could hear the bell ringing even from the distance that we still had to travel. It was music to my ears and seemed almost majestic in its tune. The town was at the bottom of the hill before you could make your way to the castle. It was rows and rows of wooden houses with straw roofs. In the front of the castle was a beautiful garden.

There was so much colour it was hard to describe; it took my breath away. I could not wait to reach the walls and see what it looked like in person, up close. We rode past a group of farmers covered in dirt and tending to the garden. They stopped and looked up at the convoy of men riding past. I smiled at them and motioned a little wave.

'You do not smile at peasants. They are beneath us,' Miguel spat towards me but stayed beside me, looking down on the people that we passed.

Aleksander rode beside him and stopped.

'Miguel, I recommend that a few men remove their cloaks to allow the ladies to cover themselves before we walk through the town. I do not believe it would be wise to gather attention from prying eyes.'

Miguel nodded and held up his hand to alert the men to stop. Dmitirov slid off the horse and held his hand up to help me. I fell graciously into his arms. Miguel walked over and handed me his cloak.

'Here you are, milady,' he said, bowing his head slightly.

'You are too kind, Miguel. Your wife is lucky to have you,' I said, batting my eyes at him. I felt sick at my flirting but I needed to keep the peace for my sake and the sake of Aleksander and his men.

'I am unwed.' He blushed.

'Lucky me,' I said as I turned around, looking at Aleksander and Dmitirov, rolling my eyes and showing my disgust out of his eye line. I could tell they were trying not to laugh as they looked away. I turned back around after tying the cord around my neck and performed a little curtsy.

'How do I look?' I said with a girlish laugh.

Annie and Harley were laughing as well. I had always been charming; it was one of my strengths.

We walked through the town and as I felt the mud under my black ballet shoes, I felt sorry for the townspeople. They all looked so dirty and depressed with the streets covered in filth, rotting food and human excrement. I had taught students about the dirt in towns but seeing it first-hand was a little different and a real eye-opener. We were approaching the castle and Dmitirov must have sensed my anxiety as we got closer. Fear and dread were spreading through me; it was as if my body knew what my mind wasn't accepting. I was officially trapped.

'Just take a breath, Faith.'

I smiled, knowing his wife was a lucky girl. I was petrified. I didn't want to know what was beyond the iron gates that stood before me. As we approached, the rattle of the gates being raised echoed through the town. I looked at Annie and Harley; their faces were showing exactly what I was trying to hide. I was an excellent poker player because I could hide my emotions from others. We walked through the gates but I couldn't focus as we looked around. I was too nervous – was this going to be the end of me?

I moved to get closer to Annie and Harley but was cut off from them by the men who started to surround us. I felt a hand around my arm.

'I need to speak with you.' Aleksander's voice was rushed and frantic while I was being rushed towards the door.

I looked at him to continue when Miguel appeared and interrupted us; his eyes drifted to Aleksander's hand as he dropped it before it was discovered.

'His Royal Highness Sebastian Faulcon cannot wait to be introduced to you and your companions.'

I looked behind for Annie and Harley who were a few steps behind, being escorted by Miguel's men. Miguel led me deeper into the castle with a gentle hand behind my back. I turned to look at Aleksander; he looked worried. He knew something that I didn't and he wanted to warn me. In that moment, I wanted to run towards him. He had been my safety net and now I was about to be eaten by sharks. I didn't take my eyes off him until I was escorted through another hall. What was about to happen? And why could Aleksander and Dmitirov not be here?

CHAPTER EIGHT

Aleksander

I watched as Faith was escorted away by Miguel, her face watching me as she disappeared from view. Her wavy brown hair flowed across her face. She may not have looked like she was filled with worry but I could tell that she was. Faith would be hiding her true self for the benefit of Harley and Annie. I knew I was not allowed to be within the room; I was not allowed due to the disgrace of my family but I would be there for her. I felt the need to protect her. I had to find a way into that room. She saved my life but this was more than owing her in repayment. I moved to follow her as I heard Dmitirov calling after me. I knew he would be telling me not to upset the king but I only felt the need to be close to her. Why did I feel this pull?

I walked into the grand hall. The large room echoed with the footsteps on the stone floor, the coloured windows bringing in a variety of colours from the sun beaming against them. King Samael was sitting on his throne with Sebastian leaning on the throne beside him, his usual cocky demeanour showing through. King Samael was looking old and weathered. It would not be long until Sebastian would rule. I worried for that day to become reality.

Sebastian had spoken about his desire to destroy the other ruling families and be the one sole ruler of them all. The Arundel, Fitzhugh, Somneri, Bennett and Ladislas were the remaining royal families. The system worked perfectly until the Faulcon family became greedy and believed the Bouchards betrayed them in the distribution of land.

'Your Majesty, I present to you the lovely ladies who fell from the stars,' Miguel said with an overexaggerated bow. Faith sniggered softly.

'Curtsy,' Miguel growled back at them while he held his bow. Annie and Harley followed Miguel's instructions but Faith stood taller than usual, holding herself with pride. I wasn't sure that I understood her reason behind this – my thoughts believed that she was testing the king.

'Forgive me, Your Highness, but I do not see you as my king. I will bow my head out of respect but I will not curtsy when you are not the ruler that I follow.' She was testing him. I wasn't sure that I understood why.

I looked at Dmitirov, knowing this would only fuel Samael's rage. He shook his head softly. King Samael's face was red with anger as his grey hair was pulled behind his head. Faith's face kept its demeanour. She was not moving on her stance. It was admirable, if not a little stupid.

The two stared each other down before he pushed himself from his golden throne and walked over to her.

'How dare you talk to me in that manner? While you are in my castle, you will show me respect as I rule these lands. Miguel.' He gestured towards him as he walked over with his smug look.

I knew what was about to happen. I moved slightly but Dmitirov grabbed my arm.

'Don't, Aleksander,' he said through his teeth to avoid anyone hearing.

Miguel raised his hand and slapped her face. The noise echoed through the hall. She straightened herself and lowered herself in a curtsy before smiling at him.

Samael smiled.

'Good. Welcome to Zilanta. You will stay here at my leisure. One of you may be lucky enough to marry my son Sebastian and rule over the kingdom.'

I watched Faith; her cheek was flushed from the slap but she wasn't showing how much it hurt. Samael moved between each of the girls, touching their chins and turning their heads to inspect them. Sebastian's eyes were trained solely on Faith – his eyes were dripping with desire.

'I am sure that we do not deserve the treatment you are giving us, Your Majesty. We are eternally grateful and look forward to spending time in your humble abode. We would rather like to wash ourselves and find some appropriate clothing, if that is okay with you?'

He walked away from Harley and towards Faith. I had a feeling that is what she wanted to achieve. She was trying to protect her; it was obvious she was the youngest. He grabbed her hair in his fingers and twirled it around. She did not move or flinch but kept eye contact.

'Of course, milady. Whatever you wish, I will do my best to deliver it to you.'

He turned around.

'Would you please escort the ladies to the south tower and

find them some appropriate clothing? Ladies in my castle do not look like harlots!' He walked towards his throne but before sitting, he turned his attention onto me.

'Aleksander, I would like you to stay and discuss why you were two days late.'

Miguel was ushering the girls outside but I saw Faith look back towards me; her eyes were searching me for something. I could read her face now. She was scared. I wished I'd never brought her to this castle. She was trapped and I would never be able to help her escape.

I knew what was coming. Samael did not say a word but rather sat there and looked at me.

'Aleksander, I am waiting for you to inform me as to why you were so late in arriving back at the castle.'

I could see Prince Sebastian smiling in the corner. He was smug and I wanted to punch the smugness out of him, if I was ever given the opportunity.

'We were ambushed by the Arundel family and my men were wounded. The ladies tended to my men and helped to heal some of their wounds. Faith recommended that we wait before moving on to avoid any further complications.'

'Faith? Do you answer to her? No! You answer to me, Aleksander. I have allowed your mother and you to live despite all the trouble your family has caused. Do not make me regret my decision. When I give an order—'

I cut him off. 'I am deeply remorseful, my king, but I was gravely injured and I was unconscious for over a day trying to recover. Faith had to cauterise my wound; otherwise, I would be dead.'

'I doubt that.' Prince Sebastian scoffed, moving from

his father's throne.

I grabbed my top and pulled it up to show the wound.

'This Faith healed you?' Samael asked, looking at my bandaged wound with his head tilted to one side.

'Yes, Your Majesty,' Dmitirov interrupted. 'The girls have many skills that ladies in this time do not have. If it was not for Aleksander and Faith, none of us would be alive.'

I nodded before lowering my top again.

'In what way?'

Dmitirov had unwillingly given information to the king and his face was showing that.

'Aleksander was attacked protecting Faith. She took his sword and stabbed the man to protect Aleksander before healing his wound. She may be insolent but her intelligence runs deep.'

'Thank you, Aleksander and Dmitirov.' King Samael waved his hand. As we bowed and turned to walk away, I heard Prince Sebastian arguing with his father and I smiled to myself, knowing that Sebastian did not get as he wished – for my punishment to occur.

CHAPTER NINE

Faith

I was terrified and trying not to show my fear was getting harder by the hour. Annie and Harley had no idea how scared I was and I needed to be brave for them. Miguel took us to the south tower. The walls were stone and looked smooth. I wanted to run my hands over the lumps and bumps in the stone but was finding it difficult. We approached a door. The deep-coloured wood was diagonal as it was held together with floral black iron bars. I felt like this room was going to be my prison, my own personal hell with no escape. I felt fear running down my spine with little tingles telling me not to walk through the door – it was telling me to run. I couldn't bring myself to do it. I couldn't leave Annie and Harley. I felt Harley grab my hand. I squeezed it in response. I wasn't going to let them separate us.

Miguel opened the door and gestured for us to move into the room. I hesitated but I knew I needed to walk through the doorway. I hesitantly took a few steps as I saw a large four-poster bed with wood engraved with swirls and various patterns. There were two arched windows with no glass.

I could smell the salt in the air from the ocean. There was a rope with a cover to close the windows at night, a dirty mirror in the corner and a wooden cupboard to store any clothes that needed to be stored. The floor creaked beneath my feet as I looked at my tattered ballet shoes, covered in mud and filth with my feet looking exactly the same. I walked closer to the bed and felt the wolf's fur blanket; it was silky against my fingertips. Annie and Harley were standing in the window. I walked over to them.

The ocean was just outside the window and I could hear the waves crashing against the shore. The water was crystal clear and the golden colour of the sand sparkled as the sun's rays hit it. There were a few columns of sandstone in the water in various shapes that had been eroded over time from the wind and water. It was almost like a Mediterranean island, peaceful and beautiful.

'I will bring some clothing momentarily,' Miguel said as he left the room.

I had almost forgotten he was in here with us. I was grateful when he left us as I looked around the room at the various tiny details that I had missed upon entering. I closed the door to the room and leaned against the back of it. I felt my head hit the iron bars and winced slightly.

Annie and Harley looked at me as I sank to the floor. Their worry was evident as I felt my own façade fading.

'How the hell are we going to escape from here? What and where the hell is Zilanta? I have never even heard of it and I am a geography teacher. We need to get out of here.'

Annie and Harley exchanged a look; they did not seem to share my beliefs.

'What is it, Annie?' I asked, knowing she would be truthful. She always was.

'Honestly, I say we wait this out. Let's see what it is like. I am intrigued and I have nothing important to return to – neither do you guys.'

I felt dread building in my stomach; this wasn't what I wanted. I needed to be away from here. I couldn't be here. I looked at Harley whose face was now showing the same emotion as Annie's.

'If Annie is in, I am. Why the hell not? If we have each other, we will be fine.' She said it so casually that it made the pit in my stomach grow.

How could I say no to them? I was overruled. The only time that I felt like myself was around Aleksander; when he wasn't near, I felt uneasy and unsure. I hated it. I wasn't a girl who depended on a person and yet I felt strange around him; I couldn't explain it.

'Looks like I am overruled,' I said, throwing my hands up in the air while letting my head bang against the door again.

Harley and Annie jumped on me with fits of cheerful laughter. I tried to return it but fell short. Why did I have the feeling this was going to end badly?

Miguel returned to the room with three different costumes; at least, that was what they looked like to me. They were dresses but I felt as if I was in a play and about to walk onto a stage. Annie and Harley walked over to inspect them as I sat in the window and watched the waves crashing into the shoreline. I saw no boats. It was obvious there was no harbour down below; we were literally on a cliff. That would be one way to escape but you would need a boat.

I shook my head as I heard Annie and Harley giggling. There was no point in thinking about it. We had somewhat agreed to stay.

Harley picked up one dress and walked over. 'This is YOUR dress. It matches your eyes.'

The dress was pale blue with golden thread around the neckline and down the sleeves. It looked as if it would sit off the shoulders. I traced the golden thread and its intricately delicate pattern down to the hem. Harley was right about one thing; it would suit me perfectly with my dark features and blue eyes.

I tied the corset up on Annie's dress. I missed zips already – the simple pleasures. I was yet to put on my dress. I didn't want to; it was the final nail in the coffin for me. The one item that would symbolise my prison forever. The knock at the door was a welcome relief to my tired fingers and Annie's corset. Harley was already dressed in her maroon dress. She skipped over rather awkwardly and opened the door.

'Aleksander, please do come in.' She gestured with her curtsy.

Aleksander smiled and chuckled slightly at her actions. 'Harley and Annie, you look spectacular and like well-bred ladies.'

'Mule,' I said under my breath, not looking at Aleksander.

They both giggled like children as I finished the final tie on Annie's dress. Aleksander looked at me.

'May I speak with Faith alone for a moment?'

They both nodded and walked towards the door.

'Please do not go fa—' The door had already closed as I rubbed my forehead and looked up at Aleksander. His face was a welcome relief.

'Are you well?' he asked.

I knew he was referring to the slap I had received earlier. I didn't want to talk about it.

'I'm fine, Aleksander,' I said, shrugging my shoulders and looking at the redness of my fingers.

He moved closer with his hands behind his back in a proper stance. I knew he was going to speak more.

'I should check your wound,' I said, changing the subject.

'My wound is fine, Faith, it does not need to be checked. I am here for you.' The five words seemed to be the realest thing I had heard today. He looked away and cleared his throat as if he had not meant to say them. 'I tried to warn you earlier about the king before Miguel interrupted us. He is a fair king...'

I crossed my arms.

'Fair enough to hit a lady,' I said in objection.

'Faith,' he said in a warning tone.

I motioned for him to keep talking.

'Samael is not the worry. Sebastian is. He has a tendency to kill anyone who defies him. As I know, you're defiant in general. I worry about your reactions to him. He is dangerous – you all need to be careful. Smile and follow his rules. Do not trust him, do not draw attention to yourself.'

'Do you think I have not encountered men like him before? Did you not see how Miguel reacted to my charm?'

He let out the tiniest growl. 'Yes, I did and I did not agree with your methods. There are other ways to handle men.'

'Like how?' I questioned him. I looked into his eyes as their lines looked deeper; he was worried and it was showing. He moved towards the door.

'Get dressed, Faith. I have overstayed my welcome and it is

unbecoming for an unmarried lady to be alone in a room with a man.'

'Pity that ship has already sailed,' I said under my breath as he left. Annie and Harley walked back in and they helped me into my dress.

*

Annie and Harley had already left the room for dinner ahead of me as I paced the bedroom. I wasn't ready to leave. I felt sick as the nausea was getting worse. Aleksander had made me worry. I started to bite my fingernails. The worry in his face, the warning – it was all getting to be too much. I kept trying to calm myself back down but it wasn't working. I was too far in my own head to find a way out now. I was never good like this. I always found the more I thought, the worse that it got.

KNOCK, KNOCK.

The knock managed to give me back some sense as I walked over and opened the heavy door. The snake of a man, Miguel, was waiting with his face that made my skin crawl.

'Are you ready, milady?' he said, offering his arm.

I nodded but refused his arm and started to walk down the passage. The dress was heavy and I heard it rustle behind me. I felt uncomfortable playing this role as I looked down at my breasts clearly on display. It was on purpose. I felt more like a harlot as they called me now than I did in my actual clothing. Outside was growing darker as I could barely see the village now, just the small fires to light the darkness that was approaching. I walked past paintings along the wall of men in crowns and jewels and some of family portraits and others were just single royals. The detail in the faces was incredible; not many artists back home could draw the same now. I stopped as I looked at one painting. He looked to be in his forties and he was handsome with darker features; his dark eyes were piercing along with his deep frown lines. He almost reminded me of Aleksander.

Miguel cleared his throat to tell me to continue. I walked further along the passage and noticed the chandeliers hanging from the dome roof. It was getting cold and if it wasn't for various rooms being lit with fires, I would be colder than I already was.

We approached the banquet hall. I could hear the soft music from outside the closed door. The giant doors opened into the hall. I paused at the sight of the cathedral ceiling and the sheer size of the room. There were three rows of tables, each of them draped in golden fabric with rows of flowers, red roses, carnations and lilies of various different colours. The smell of food and flowers made my stomach grumble for the first time. There were five golden chandeliers throughout the hall, each made of cast iron with candles carefully placed into each of the holders. It was like stepping onto a movie set, where the prince asks the peasant girl for a dance. Purple fabric was covering the royal table which was normal. I was intrigued that the archways that led outside were a different coloured stone to the rest of the castle. It shimmered in the candlelight. I wondered why it was different.

I searched for Annie and Harley's familiar faces. There were more people here than I expected – possibly a hundred if not a few less. I walked further into the hall and felt all eyes fall onto me. A quiet covered the room and I could hear my own heart beating in my chest when a server walked over.

'Libations?' he asked, lowering the tray.

'Yes,' I said, eagerly grabbing a glass and finishing it in one gulp as I looked at the golden chalice.

The wine was bitter with a hint of cherries. It would suffice for now despite the lack of taste within the wine. I found Annie and Harley's faces in the distance and I raised my glass at them. Aleksander came into view and I saw him staring at me with a small smile on his lips. I felt a blush rush to my cheeks as I returned my focus to Annie and Harley.

Harley had placed her mousey brown hair into a high bun with her side fringe gently flowing across her forehead. Her dress was grey down the side with jade covering the middle. Annie's dress was lilac with white cuffed sleeves and a thick white trim down the bottom. Annie had pinned her short hair to the left side and the rest of it was flowing. I looked at Aleksander wearing his shiny black leather pants, not the same tan brown from earlier. His white shirt could be seen through his red and golden threaded vest with it tied together in various places down his front. Annie was trying to get his attention but his eyes had not moved from me as the same concern fell across his face.

I turned to see the reason for his concern as Prince Sebastian joined me. His light brown hair was pulled back into a ponytail. It was longer than it should have been but these were different times. His crooked nose did not flatter his face; he was just taller than me but he had the longest lashes I had seen on a man and it helped to show his hazel eyes. He smiled, which showed the dimples on his cheeks. He wasn't ugly but he almost wasn't a panty dropper either.

'I see the dress that I selected suits you well. It shows your beauty in more words than I could dare to describe, milady,' he said, bowing slightly to me.

'You flatter me, Prince Sebastian,' I said softly to him.

'A lady like yourself deserves to be flattered. Any man would be lucky to have someone of your beauty as a prize.'

I wanted to return with a witty retort but I heard Aleksander's warning in my head. *Be careful!* I almost wanted to slap myself.

'Same to you, Prince Sebastian. Any lady would be lucky to receive affections from a man of your title,' I said with a charming smile, flicking my hair back off my shoulder to show a little skin.

His eyes darted towards it before moving back to my face.

'If it pleases you, Prince Sebastian, I would like to introduce you to my friends.'

Sebastian nodded and gestured for me to walk.

'Annie, Harley, I would like to introduce you to His Royal Highness, Prince Sebastian, King Samael's son.'

Annie and Harley curtsied, flashing their most winning smiles.

'It is a pleasure to meet you, Your Grace,' they said in unison.

I finished my wine and was looking for another goblet when a server walked past and I swapped the glasses over.

'Pleasure to meet you, ladies. My father has asked me to inform you that you will be sitting at the royal table. If you would follow me.'

Annie, Harley and I followed Sebastian to our seats. I was sitting the furthest away from the king and the prince. Thank God for that. I did not want to be near either of them if what

Aleksander was saying was true. I looked around for Dmitirov and Aleksander's faces and could not see them anywhere. I felt lonely again. Where was he?

The room fell silent as King Samael stood up. It was obvious that many feared him and sensed the power that he held. His grey hair was hidden under his golden crown. He had the same nose as Sebastian, obviously a family heirloom. He had a scar along his forehead, which made it seem as if he only had one eyebrow as the other was cut into. I felt like the black tunic almost represented his soul as did the wolf cloak on his back with the head still attached. That would have been heavy and not ideal to wear but obviously it was significant to him. The crown was covered in jewels: rubies, emeralds, sapphires and even diamonds. He raised his hands, which made the smallest whispers stop.

'Welcome, citizens of Zilantrioun. This evening is in celebration of our newest citizens that were delayed yesterday but have finally arrived. Ladies, please stand. Annie Wakchter, Harley Gelden and Faith Bushanti. Let's welcome them to our humble town.'

All eyes were on us, with everyone clapping. Annie and Harley smiled proudly but I only managed a small one. I couldn't fake it; the feeling in my gut wasn't going away.

'Now, let the celebrations begin.' He clapped his hands.

Trays upon trays of food were brought out: chicken, lamb, turkey, pork. Trays of salads, warm bread. I muttered to Harley who was beside me.

'I wonder what the poor people are eating.' She laughed.

'I know right.'

There was enough food to feed an entire village and the

men dug in. I just picked at small items; I wasn't hungry.

The five glasses of wine were starting to take effect due to the fact that I did not each much food. I ate some bread, a few pieces of meat and some salad but I picked at it sparingly. The people had finished eating and the music started to sound a little more lively. I was enjoying the sounds of the violins, flutes and whatever other instruments were around.

'Harley, I am going to go outside and get some air. The wine isn't sitting well with me.' I stood up and walked towards the archways.

I pushed the door open and felt the night air hit me. It wasn't overly cold tonight but I could still feel the chill in the air. It was refreshing as I walked to the balcony and leaned on it. I could hear the waves crashing into the shore; it was peaceful. It was exactly what I needed as I looked up at the stars in the sky. I had always enjoyed watching the sky at night and seeing the stars twinkle. I started humming to myself an old tune that the nuns would sing to me when I was growing up. I could feel my body swaying; the wine was not agreeing with me.

I heard a noise behind me and moved suddenly but stumbled on my dress and feet. I felt arms wrap around me and pull me up from my fall. I opened my eyes and giggled.

'We need to stop meeting like this.' Aleksander smiled and helped me to my feet. 'I apologise for my clumsiness.' He waved his hands up.

'Enjoying the wine, I see.' I snorted and covered my face from embarrassment.

'Yes, it was stronger than I anticipated. My head feels foggy.' I stumbled a little again and Aleksander grabbed my hand. It sent tingles through my fingers as I looked at him touching me.

He stopped instantly and pulled away. 'How about I escort you to your room?'

I raised an eyebrow at him.

'I am a gentleman, Faith. I would never do anything unbecoming of my stature.'

'No, I suppose not. I mean, you did call me a whore for what I was wearing when it was appropriate for my time.'

He laughed and shook his head. 'Yes, it was quite revealing in its nature.'

I looked at my breasts trying not to explode out of this dress before looking back at him.

'I feel more exposed in this than I did my shorts.'

'Yes, those shorts were...' He paused before clenching his fists and moving backwards.

'Aleksander...'

'Goodnight, Faith. I shall see you tomorrow.'

'I thought you were going to escort me to my room?' I said, confused as I moved to him and stumbled a little.

He groaned. 'I can't.'

'Why? Did you want to join me?' Now the wine was talking and I knew it.

He growled and left quickly. Was he angry at me?

I woke the next morning to Annie and Harley laughing in my room.

'Do you guys have to talk so loudly?' I said, covering my head with a pillow from the noise.

'Hey, drunky. How is your hangover? How many glasses did you have in the end?' Annie asked, grabbing my legs under the blankets.

I moved away from her and sat up in the bed as I moved

wild hair from my face.

'I think it was around five but their wine is so much stronger than back home. Did I do anything stupid?' I asked, looking at them.

'Depends on what you call stupid,' Harley said, jumping onto the bed beside me with her usual glee.

'You didn't do anything too bad but you were quite drunk and very flirtatious like you normally are when you drink.'

'Oh, God. Please do not tell me that I flirted with Sebastian or the king.'

They both shook their heads. I felt instant relief and dropped back onto the bed.

'But they certainly were taking notice of you like men always do,' Annie said with a tone of annoyance to her voice.

She went behind the dividers to get dressed. I knew exactly what she meant because when it came to the three of us going out, I did get the extra attention. I couldn't help it but my blue eyes made it difficult to go unnoticed. Annie sometimes resented me for that; she was obviously in one of those grumpy moods.

KNOCK, KNOCK.

Harley leapt from the bed and answered the door. It was only Miguel.

'Good morrow. You are being summoned by the king. He is waiting for you in the throne room. I believe you may have discovered his gifts. Make haste,' he said before leaving the room as quickly as he entered.

'Yes, because we run on your schedule,' I said, rolling out of bed, groaning as I walked over to the mirror and looked into it.

Harley was tying up Annie's dress. I noticed the dark rings

around my eyes; I was tired.

'I think you should be grateful that they haven't killed us yet. It could be worse – we have shelter, food and clothes. Remember our first two days? We had no food, no shelter, nothing. You can be pessimistic sometimes; maybe you should try changing your attitude.' Annie slammed the door behind her as Harley walked over showing me her dress as I tied it up for her.

'What did I do to her last night?' I asked as my fingers screamed from tying up the string again.

'Can you braid my hair?' Harley asked.

I nodded so she could see in the mirror.

'Harley, please tell me what I did to her last night.' I was not above begging for an answer.

Harley sighed and looked at me in the mirror.

'She was with Aleksander last night but you walked into the room and he had no care for her anymore. The same happened with the prince – he was paying attention to her but you started dancing and all the attention was on you again.'

'She knows I did not do that on purpose, right?'

'You know she does, Faith, but it doesn't change the fact that her feelings were hurt.'

I nodded, knowing she was right.

Annie was already in the throne room talking with Sebastian and Samael when Harley and I walked in together.

'Ladies,' the king said with his arms open wide. 'Did you enjoy the celebrations in your honour last night? All of Zilanta agreed that you are now part of our beautiful country. On the condition that you marry any man who requests your hand in marriage or enter a union that is approved by me.'

I heard the door open and turned to see Aleksander and Dmitirov walking into the room. Aleksander bowed.

'Forgive the intrusion, Your Majesty, but an ambassador from the Arundel family is here to speak with you urgently.'

'Thank you, Aleksander. Excuse me, ladies.' The king left quickly.

I noticed that Aleksander was refusing to look at me. Had I insulted him last night? Either that or I flirted too much and have now made him uncomfortable in which case I would be a harlot. Prince Sebastian walked into my eye line.

'Faith,' he said, bowing to me slightly. 'I would like you to accompany me to the garden where we might spend some time together on this beautiful morning.'

This was not going to end well.

'With regret, Your Grace, I would prefer to spend time with my friends but I do appreciate the offer,' I replied with a smile before turning my back on him and putting my arms around Annie and Harley before kissing their cheeks.

'Because nobody is more important than the two of you,' Annie whispered softly.

'I'm sorry.' I hugged her tighter because there was no reason for her to apologise. I didn't need nor did I want it.

We walked up to our rooms. When we opened the door, we noticed three ladies standing inside sorting through a chest of clothing.

'Ah, who the hell are you?' I asked, making sure Harley and Annie were standing behind me.

'Forgive the intrusion. My name is Makenzie; this is Ivy and this is Rosa. We have been appointed to be your lady's maids by Prince Sebastian. He assigned us to help with your every need.

You will each be given your own rooms from now on.'

I looked at Annie and Harley. We were all a bit dumbfounded as Makenzie continued talking.

'Annie, if you would follow Ivy and Harley, if you would follow Rosa.' Makenzie stayed in my room as I watched Annie and Harley leave my room with their maids in tow, carrying a handful of gowns.

She was incredibly short with brown hair and a little on the rounder side. She was wearing rather bland clothing, almost like peasant clothes as she sorted through dresses, shoes and jewels placing them in various places around the room.

'Prince Sebastian organised this?' I asked for clarification again while watching her move about my room. She nodded in response.

'Excuse my bluntness but I don't trust you and I am not comfortable with you going through my room the way that you are.'

She stopped and put a pair of earrings down. 'I understand, Lady Bushanti.'

'Faith,' I corrected her. I felt a little guilty for being rude now.

'There is a garden party this afternoon. The king expects your attendance. It is in celebration of his daughter's betrothal to one of the richest men in the land. You need to change into this dress and I would like to fix your hair.' She didn't seem to care about my rudeness. She was here to do a job and to do it properly. I sat down in the chair for her to do my hair before she could change me into a gown.

The dress was laid out on the bed; it was a black petticoat with a pink lacy overcoat. The sleeves were short and went to the elbow. There was a matching pair of ballet shoes. She pulled my head hard to brush my hair.

'Ow,' I remarked to her. 'I would prefer my hair up. It is a little frizzy at the moment.'

'No,' she said sternly. She wasn't one to be tested.

I sat and waited for her to finish as she brushed through the tangles and pulled the sides back and clipped them behind my head with an ornate golden clip, letting the rest of the hair fall down my back. Makenzie handed me a necklace and some earrings. They were made of crystal and weren't too excessive. The necklace had two rows of hanging crystals and the earrings matched. I put them on and moved to sit up.

'No,' she said forcefully, pushing my shoulders down again. She fixed my hair one last time. 'Now you are ready.'

The person in the mirror, I didn't recognise her. I made the choice that with or without Annie and Harley, I would be leaving tomorrow.

Makenzie wouldn't allow me to walk to Annie and Harley's room but rather escorted me to the garden. It was beautiful; I only recognised one type of flower and that was a rose. The rest of the flowers I had never seen before. This place had its own breed of flowers with colours and smells. There were pink, blue, purple, red, yellow and even rainbow-coloured flowers. I started walking around, looking at all of them closely when a young man walked over.

'Libations, milady.'

I moved to speak.

'I believe the lady has had enough.'

I turned with a smile on my face to see Aleksander standing behind me smugly.

'I think that is a wise choice.' He smiled at me.

'I don't remember what happened last night but I feel the need to apologise for anything that I did that was untoward in any way.'

Aleksander chuckled. His face had a secret that I didn't know. 'We had an interesting conversation before I left you for the night.'

I felt my cheeks flush with embarrassment. 'I am sorry,' I said.

'Faith, it was endearing. Do not fear but if you are available later...'

'As always, Aleksander, you like to reach for the things that you cannot have. You will always fall short to a prince, especially with your title.' Prince Sebastian walked over, standing rather close beside me as he handed me a glass.

I opened my mouth to say something but Aleksander put his hand up to tell me that it was not worth the effort to say anything. Sebastian put his arm around my shoulder, which seemed to annoy Aleksander further as he turned and walked away from Sebastian and me.

'I hope I did not make you feel uncomfortable discussing your beauty so openly. I do find it hard to lie.'

I didn't respond as I took a sip from my glass. Sebastian continued talking as I looked around at the guests.

'Did you like my gift of the lady's maids? A lady like yourself deserves to have someone to tend to their every need, especially if my father picks one of you to be my wife, which I have informed him of my de—'

I spat my wine out from shock as I turned to look at him.

'WHAT?!' I shouted at him.

Sebastian's face turned red from either rage or embarrassment.

'Faith, there is no need for you to raise your voice,' he said, stroking the hair from my face. I shivered from his touch. I didn't want this.

'I will never be your wife. A lady like myself, as you say, would never go for such a pompous asshole, you half-wit idiot. There aren't enough words to describe a person like yourself. I have self-respect for myself and would rather die than deal with a lifetime of you.' I stormed away, throwing the glass onto the ground.

I could hear Annie and Harley calling after me but I just kept walking. I couldn't stop; I couldn't be near him. I could still feel his touch on my skin. It was cold and I still felt my body on edge from it. He was a true... dick.

I walked back into the castle, frustrated as I clenched my fists. Who was Sebastian to assume I wanted a lady's maid? Who was he to want me to be his wife? The thought of having sex with him made me feel physically ill; the man was a prick. He didn't deserve to be anywhere near my vagina. I stopped short when I realised that I had taken a wrong turn. I was lost as I looked around. This part of the castle seemed darker than the rest; it was not as well-lit as the other areas. I saw a dark wooden door and thought I would try to see what was behind the door to see where I was.

The heavy door squeaked open as I coughed instantly. I could smell the mould and dust within the room; it smelt old and musty. I saw the dust on the portraits and furniture that filled the room. What was this? There was a bed, a chest for clothing, portraits and everything. It was almost like a shrine. I walked further into the room.

I noticed a family portrait of the parents, the two sons and the daughter. There were matching portraits for each of the children; at least, I assumed they were the children. I coughed again as I moved around and the dust followed me. I stopped in front of a set of mahogany-coloured drawers. The mirror was thick with dust and I rubbed my finger over it. I pulled open the little drawer that was attached to the mirror and saw jewellery moving around. I picked up a ruby ring and I looked at the massive size of the ruby. It would have been close to two carats and surrounded by tiny little white opals. I slid the gold ring onto my finger; it fit perfectly. I took it off again as I saw the matching earrings and necklace. I recognised it from the woman in the portraits. I continued moving around seeing more images of this mystery family.

The mother in one of the paintings had a sash over her dress. She sat on the chair with the daughter standing beside her and the dark hair flowed far down her back. The sash was embroidered gold with a red 'B'. She was stunning and it was obvious she was born from nobility with her prideful look. She was lighter in colour than the rest of the family with her caramel hair but the bright blue eyes looked similar to my own. The father was darker with black hair and dark brown piercing eyes and an olive complexion; he looked like a stern man with his face and the way he stood. The crown stood atop his head and a scowl was on his face; he was the king and the wrinkles on his face were showing the stress he had endured. The children all had the same dark complexion and the mother's blue eyes and softness to them.

'I am guessing that you are the infamous Bouchard family,' I said to myself, staring at them in wonder. They seemed so normal.

'You would be correct, Faith.' I turned quickly to find the

source of the voice to see Dmitirov standing in the room with me.

'Thank you for calling me my actual name. It feels strange with all of the formalness. When do I get to meet your beautiful wife?'

He smiled and walked closer in a similar stance to Aleksander with his hands clasped behind his back.

'I try to keep them away from the politics inside the castle.'

I raised my eyebrows at him, knowing I would prefer to do the same.

'Now that I can understand and relate to...' I paused, wondering if I should tell him my next thought but Aleksander's words rang through my head. 'I am thinking about running away and finding a way back home. Not sure how but I can't do this, Dmitirov.'

'What of Annie and Harley? Did you think about the consequences for them?'

I looked down at the ground – I was ashamed. I had but I was being selfish.

'I was but this place is not for a girl like me. I am opinionated and stubborn and I don't fit societal norms. I am more likely to be beheaded than to survive.' I looked around the room at the last royal family as a reminder that power can be toppled at any moment.

'I beg to differ. We could use a lady like yourself. You do remind me of Crystal Bouchard. She was the youngest and by far the strongest of all the Bouchards. They went against tradition and made the choice to change the rule of succession but before their change could be implemented the riots started. Crystal was a born ruler – she was fearless. When she was a babe, she was gravely ill and the doctors informed her parents that she would not survive the sickness. Despite all odds, she survived and thrived. Her spirit could barely be contained. Her smile and laugh were the life of the castle.'

'What happened to her?' I said, looking at the picture of the little girl in the painting and I could see the mischief in her eyes.

'She was killed with her family. The whispers were the Faulcons burnt them alive in the family chapel. They say the screams could be heard for miles and those who venture to the chapel on a full moon can hear the screams.'

*

Just after dinner, I was summoned by the king. Makenzie escorted me to the throne room. I knew this was about the repercussions of my tantrum at Sebastian. As we approached the door, she put her hand on my arm.

'Just breathe, Faith.' Her smile was small and soft; she seemed to genuinely care.

I walked into the room and curtsied despite neither wanting to nor thinking that they deserved it.

'Yes, Your Majesty, you summoned me?' I said while batting my eyes and throwing on my charming smile to stop the brunt of the possible attack that I was about to get.

He looked me up and down – I was in the same dress from earlier today when he announced the engagement of his youngest daughter to a man very much older than her. Sebastian had on his usual smug face leaning on his father's throne.

'Faith...' He took in a deep breath. 'I do believe that you owe my son, your prince, an apology.'

I heard the door open behind me and I looked to see Aleksander. It was possibly a blessing in disguise as I was about to come out with a snarky comment on how Sebastian was not my prince. I looked back at Sebastian and Samael.

'My apologies, my prince, I did not realise that my truthful words had caused you so much pain.'

Aleksander coughed behind me; it was a warning or he was holding in a laugh.

'Lords, no encouragement is needed. Faith, my son has picked you to be his wife. You will be the next Queen of Zilanta. Your beauty is already whispered about and your strength seems to be admired by many ladies within the court. I find it to be the ideal choice.'

I bit my lip. 'Yes, a beautiful queen that he would like to show off but he would not respect the words that left my lips. A queen who would have no input in her life or any decisions. I am sorry, King Samael, but I respectfully decline. I will never be able to be a lady who can keep quiet and expect a man to fix the world's problems, especially when all they think about is their penis and how they can make their ego grow. You want a girl to look pretty? Find someone else because over my dead body will I ever marry your son.' I curtsied as I turned to leave.

'If it is not you, who shall it be? I'll select Annie or Harley.'

The words hit me in the gut as I looked at Aleksander before me. I could not subject them to this life. I wouldn't allow them to be abused by Sebastian on a daily basis. I wanted to cry and scream. Aleksander's face showed no pity but simply regret – for what, I didn't know. I stood there for what seemed like forever before I turned around slowly.

'You wouldn't dare,' I said through my teeth.

'Make the choice, Faith. I will give you the night to make your decision.' Samael looked at Sebastian; they both knew they had already won.

I walked out of the room, trying to keep my head held high, trying not to cry until I reached my room. I was trapped more than I ever thought that I would be. How did this happen?

CHAPTER TEN

Aleksander

Faith was never going to be the type of lady who would allow herself to be the property of a man. I admired the strength about her. She just stood up to the king who had slaughtered hundreds of people for less and showed no fear but she did not expect him to threaten Sebastian would marry Annie or Harley. She would never subject her friends to that life.

'She should be beheaded, Father. How dare she speak to you, the king, in that manner?' Sebastian said, filled with rage more from the rejection than the way that Faith spoke to his father.

'If I may interject, Your Majesty, how can you punish a lady from a different world?' I tried to get them to understand that she may have had worse in her life.

'You are right, Aleksander, but if a man can break a horse's spirit to make it obedient, I will find a way to break hers. She already has one weakness and that is her friends. She is too important to let slip through our fingers as I believe her to be...' He trailed off in thought.

I looked at Dmitirov, confused; his face showed the same confusion.

'Your Majesty, if I may, how is she important and who do you believe her to be?' I asked, moving closer. Had I missed something important about Faith?

'None of your concern Aleksander. Your task is to find her weaknesses. Annie and Harley are one but I need more as I will not always be able to dangle them above her head.'

'There are plenty of other appropriate ladies in the land, why not choose them? Would it not be easier?' I did not like the idea of Faith being trapped in a marriage to Sebastian.

'Are you questioning me, Aleksander?'

I knew I had stepped too far with the king.

'No, Your Majesty, I apologise. I will find the information that you require.' I bowed and left the room quickly.

'My lord,' I heard Dmitirov call as I ignored him and kept walking.

'Aleksander,' he tried again.

I kept thinking on who Faith could be – who was she? Why was she important? She had only just arrived, how was she in their sights already?

'ALEK,' Dmitirov yelled as I stopped and turned to look at him. I waited for him to say something, anything but we both stared at each other.

'Aleksander, who is she?' he asked. It was obvious he was trying to figure out the same.

'Dmitirov, I have no idea. I need to see Lady Marchés.' I didn't want to but I knew she may have the answers I sought.

'Is that a wise decision? You have not seen her in over five years.'

'I know.' I nodded as I put my hands on my hips before turning to walk towards Faith's room.

Dmitirov didn't know that I had seen her three years ago when I snuck in but she was beginning to lose her mind. Whether it was wise was not the question; it had to be done. She would have the answers I wanted. She knew everything.

KNOCK, KNOCK.

I reached Faith's room quicker than I expected. Her lady's maid answered.

'Yes, Lord Marchés?' Her eyes bright as they looked at me. I knew she had asked for permission to be courted by me but I rejected her.

'I wish to speak with Lady Bushanti,' I said while putting my hand on the door to open it and walk in. I had no need for propriety at this moment.

'Forgive me, Lord Marchés. She went to the roof. She was quite inconsolable,' she said before closing the door on me.

I am unsure whether I walked or ran to the roof of the tower. She would not be silly enough to leap from it to avoid the marriage to Sebastian. I heard Faith crying as I paused listening to the conversation and peered through the gap in the door.

'Everything will be okay. We will find a way to get home. I promise you,' Harley said, holding her tightly around the shoulders.

'Yeah but I am staying here. I have nothing to return for. I don't want to go home to my life,' Annie said, standing up while looking at Faith and Harley.

'Annie, this is not about what you want. This is only going to get worse. You would prefer to be wed to the prince than return home? How stupid could you be? We are all safer to go home. We need to leave.'

The idea of Faith leaving and never returning again did

not sit well with me.

'Ahem.' I coughed to get their attention.

Annie and Harley spun around quickly but Faith did not bother to move. Her head was leaning on Harley still. They smiled at the sight of me as Harley touched Faith's arm and stood up, leaving her sitting alone as they walked past me and down the tower stairs. I didn't know what to say. I had never encountered a crying lady.

'It is a beautiful night to look at the stars, is it not?'

Faith laughed while wiping the tears from her bright eyes. Even though they were filled with tears, they seemed bluer than usual.

'You don't know how to speak to or comfort a girl, do you?' she said, wiping her nose and looking up at me. Her face was patchy but her beauty was still radiant. The moon was shining upon her face that revealed no imperfections upon her. I stirred as I felt something change – I was a gentleman. I moved and sat down beside her.

'I am speaking the truth, look at the stars. Beautiful lights in the sky to help the lost find their way home. A gift from the gods.'

She giggled as she looked at me. 'You don't know what stars are. Wow, you are a little behind on the times. Stars are exploding balls of gas. They weren't made by the gods; they are helium and hydrogen.'

I looked at her. The words she spoke, I had never heard. I was confused.

'Just call them exploding balls of gas; there are multiple galaxies in the world and the brightest stars are the closest to us and the stars that are the dullest are either further away or about to die and that is how you get a shooting star.'

'Do you ever make shapes out of stars?' I replied, lying down on my back.

She turned and looked at me. 'Uh, duh. Why do you think I came up here? I have always loved looking at the stars.' She lay on her back beside me and we just watched the stars in silence.

I felt Faith move closer. It was the most comfortable I had ever felt with another person in my life. She spoke about her life back home and how she felt teaching was the most rewarding career in the world, inspiring the young minds of tomorrow and helping to shape the future. She spoke about her students with such pride and how much they had grown in a small amount of time. It seemed as if she forgot about her problems.

'Faith, I need to know if the rumour is true. Are you planning on leaving?' I took my eyes from the stars and looked at her.

She looked away from me. I knew the answer. I put my hand on her chin and moved to bring her face back to look at me.

'Do not leave, I beg of you.'

Her eyes welled up again as she pushed my hand away. She stood up. 'Good night, Aleksander.'

'Faith, please. Give me something.'

'If I stay, I have no choice but to marry Sebastian. Aleksander, you are asking for me to stay for selfish reasons. Would I not be trading one cage for another? Please, don't follow me.' She walked away as if her words held no weight to them. She was a beautiful mystery that I wanted to unravel. I would never betray her to the king but I needed to deliver some inside information about her. I felt a need to protect her.

I watched as the night turned to early hours of the morning.

I needed to prepare myself for the visit with Lady Victoria Marchés, my mother. I went to my chambers to rest until the morning but I felt it hard to rest knowing that she knew information that she dared not tell me. I sighed as I looked at the ceiling; it had been three years since I saw my mother. She was charged with practising witchcraft. I had to beg King Samael to spare her life. My price was my life. I had to do whatever he asked of me – I was his slave with a title. I had no choice or it would mean the death of my mother. Part of the condition of her living was that I was forbidden from seeing her again but there were always some who enjoyed the price of gold for their silence. I did not care to see her as I did not agree with her choice in practising witchcraft and how she allowed my father to die.

Victoria would have the answers I needed. She was best friends with Queen Katherine Bouchard. She would know everything; she always did. I was not going to bother asking for permission to see her. I was simply going to buy my way in. I put on my dark cloak and covered my face as I walked down the stairs towards the prison.

'Good morning, Webster. How are you this fine morning?' I said while walking past with a bag full of gold coins, placing it in his hand.

'Very well, my lord,' he said as I continued walking past him and he left his post for an appropriate amount of time.

I continued walking down the stairs and past all of the prisoners, covering my nose as the smell of urine and faeces was strong. I reached the end of the cells to find my mother. Her room was fully furnished as she so rightly believed she deserved.

She smiled upon seeing me. She had lost more weight and the last three years had not boded well with her. I looked nothing like my mother; her hair was golden and her eyes were grey and lifeless.

'Aleksander,' she screamed with delight and ran over to the bars between us.

'Hello, Mother,' I said, squeezing her hand and trying not to vomit from the smell of human excrement that followed her.

'How long has it been, my son?' she asked, her face alight with joy.

'Three years.'

'Oh, how I have missed you. Tell me, how is your life for you?' she said while reaching to fix my hair as I took a step back from her.

'Joyous. I wake up every morning with so much love in my heart.'

She looked at me dubiously but didn't speak for a while.

'Do you not know what I have had to endure for you? To keep you alive? I had to sell my soul.'

'I never asked for that, Aleksander. I would have gladly been burnt at the stake,' she said with venom.

'Was I to live with your death on my conscience?'

She didn't respond.

'That is not the reason for this visit,' I said, pacing the room. She just sat and continued to stare at the sunlight coming through the window. 'MOTHER.'

'Yes, my sweet boy.'

'I need to know what happened to the Bouchards all those years ago.' I squatted on my knees to her level to look her in the eyes.

'You already know what happened. They killed them all,' she said, cupping my face.

I swiped her hands away. 'No, there must be more. Katherine must have told you something. They must have known it was coming and found a way to protect themselves. There have always been rumours on how they died; I need to know exactly how they died.'

She shook her head and her eyes welled up with tears. 'No, I will not revisit those memories.'

'Mother, I need them. Please,' I said on my knees, begging her for the information. 'Were they all killed? They made Father clean up the mess. You would know more than anyone.'

She just kept shaking her head. I grabbed it in my hands.

'Mother, please.' She stood up.

'You know this is a forbidden subject. There were only four bodies that were burnt in that chapel but there were remnants of another but it was hard to know for sure.' She sighed. 'Five days before the attack, Katherine came to see me. They knew it was coming and knew they could not stop it. She begged for the coven to help her. To save her children, she offered to pay through the nose. Every day she came back and begged again. Until Caroline, the coven leader, finally accepted the payment. I never knew what they spoke about and to this day can never be sure but as Katherine was walking out, she simply said, "Just one, Your Majesty, I will only save one." I can only assume to know what she meant. Katherine never spoke to me again until the day of the attack, saying that she could die peacefully knowing that her bloodline would continue.'

I was shocked and stunned. Could Faith, Annie or Harley be a Bouchard heir?

'Aleksander, has the Bouchard heir returned?'

I didn't know how to answer. If Faith was Crystal, she was in even more danger than I had already believed. How could I possibly protect her from this?

'I cannot be sure, Mother.'

'Caroline's last words to me were, "When the star lights up the night sky, the saviour will return."'

I do not remember the rest of the conversation. I was stunned and I could not risk telling anyone this information. I needed to get in contact with the Bennett family; they were my cousins but to do so was treason.

I was at the castle garden and saw Annie, Harley and Faith having one of their lessons. I could not face Faith. She may not be Crystal; Annie or Harley could be descendants of Crystal. My thoughts could not be controlled as they ran through my head as if a horse was running a race.

Two days later

I finally had the chance to speak to Dmitirov when we went out for our monthly hunting trip. He was speechless, as was I when I first found out. I was still trying to process it. How could King Samael have kept this secret for so long? I dismounted my horse and pulled out my bow and arrow.

'I saw you with Faith the other day, Aleksander.'

I turned to look at him. 'She asked for training with a sword. Who am I to deny her some way to protect herself?'

I would never admit to him that being that close to her was

intoxicating, that she smelt like sea air and roses. Her beautiful wavy hair kept flowing in my face but I did not mind. I enjoyed the closeness between us. She had asked for lessons once a week for herself, Annie and Harley.

'Are you telling me that you have no feelings for her?'

'No, Dmitirov, she is not the girl for me. Too much tongue for me,' I said but the words I knew were not true. I did enjoy the candour that Faith had. I worried that one day she would soon disappear forever.

'Oh yes, my lord, not your type at all,' he said smugly.

I just ignored him and took aim for the pronghorn.

DING DING DING DING.

Dmitirov and I looked at each other. That could not be good. When the bells rang from the castle, they alerted either trouble or joy. I jumped back on my horse and we rode towards the castle. The bells were still ringing when we arrived. We ran through the front doors and into the grand hall. It was packed with people. I found Harley.

'Harley, what has happened?' I was frantic; I had yet to see Faith.

'How should I know? Do I look like I can see into the future?'

I ignored her and kept walking around the hall. The room fell silent. Miguel was standing at the front, looking utterly devastated.

'King Samael is dead. Long live King Sebastian.'

The entire room chanted, 'Long live the king! Long live the king!'

I found Faith's face; she already knew everything was about to change. I knew now that I needed to visit my cousins. The only problem I would encounter was trying to leave the castle.

The lords and ladies were in despair at the loss of their king but many were praising Sebastian. He was showing no emotion; he had been looking forward to this day for many years.

'Dmitirov, I need you to send a message for me.'

He looked at me.

I moved closer and whispered in his ear. 'I need to get a message to my cousin, Charlotte Bennett. I know what I am asking you is dangerous but I trust no one else.'

He nodded; he always had my back. 'Of course.'

I saw Faith walking over to me. I smiled and turned away from her. I had more important matters to attend to than to speak with her and how her future would possibly change.

I walked briskly to my chambers to grab the ink and paper.

Dearest Charlotte,

I have missed you, cousin, and wish dearly to see you again.

You must pass this note on to your father as it is too dangerous for me to give it to him directly. King Samael has passed. I fear the rule of his successor Sebastian, as I am sure you will too. Samael was in works to create a treaty between the families but it has always been Sebastian's wish to break the treaty and for the families to follow his rule or else.

I have a new development; I am unsure if you have heard but three ladies landed in our country. They are mysterious and from a different time. It is believed one may be a Bouchard or a descendent of a Bouchard. It is hard to know but if this information is true, we must band together and find a way to protect her.

I await your response,

Aleksander Marchés

I folded the envelope and dripped the hot wax, then placed my family's crest on the paper. It was two horses back-to-back in a shield and surrounded by the national flower: a red rose. I put it into the slip in my top and walked down to the stables. Dmitirov was already waiting.

'Say hello to your wife for me, Dmitirov. Enjoy the rest of the day off.'

If he was captured, we were both dead. I felt sick to my stomach. I had not only risked my life but that of my closest friend. I could not go back to the grand hall; I was not ready to face Faith. I went out to the courtyard and sat down. Ivy walked over.

'Hello, my lord Marchés. You look troubled. Is there anything I can do to help you?' she said seductively.

'No, thank you, Ivy. Have a good day.' I got up and walked away. I wasn't in the mood to keep up appearances with girls at present. I was worried about what Prince Sebastian's first move was going to be.

The day seemed to pass slowly as I waited to hear from Dmitirov. I was pacing the garden waiting to hear from him when I heard her sweet voice behind me.

'Are you avoiding me?'

I turned to look at her and she took my breath away. She was wearing a gold headband with crystals sparkling in the sunlight. It pulled the hair off her face and showed off her blue eyes; they looked brighter than usual. Her black and gold dress hugged her womanly curves and enhanced the view of her breasts. I wanted more than anything to speak with her but I could not.

'Faith, I do not have the time or patience for you today.'

Her face dropped but she walked over and put her hand on my arm.

'I just wanted to make sure that you were okay. I saw your face when news of the king was announced.'

I put both of my hands on her arms. 'Faith, I am sorry.'

I couldn't face her knowing that she may have been the little girl that I had grown up playing with or a descendant of hers. I left her quickly.

The sun was beginning to set as I stopped pacing the garden and wandered through the castle before I ventured down to the stables.

'There you are, Aleksander. King Sebastian has been looking for you all day.' I had never seen Miguel look so happy but knew his master was the king and he would have more opportunities to do whatever he pleased.

'Sorry, I had business that needed my immediate attention.'

Dmitirov rode into the stables. His face was serious. I sighed with relief knowing that he had returned.

'I need to speak with my second in command, then I shall find the king and speak with him.'

Miguel nodded, looking pleased with himself. 'I shall inform the king, Aleksander.'

I was irritated with his lack of propriety.

'It is "my lord" to you, Miguel. I think you forget that I am above your station and as such deserve the respect of my title.' I growled through my teeth.

'For now, Lord Marchés.' He smirked and bowed his head slightly before walking away.

I looked back towards Dmitirov. 'What did my cousin say?' I asked him, speaking in hushed tones, knowing that Miguel may or may not have still been lingering.

'She wants to meet. She will deliver a message when the time is right. Her father said if what you say is true, all the families would unite behind her but he worries that the Bouchard heir returning may be dangerous. You must protect her.'

I was confused on the why. The Bouchards were a loved and adored family. I knew I would have to wait for my cousin before I discovered the reason why it was not desirable.

I felt relief knowing that the Bennetts were still my allies despite my family's betrayal towards the Bouchard family. I climbed the stairs away from the stables, not knowing when my cousin would desire to meet but knowing that it would happen. My letter would have set things in motion that could not be stopped. If one of the girls was a Bouchard heir, she was the rightful leader for the throne and the majority of the families would back her. My thoughts were that it was Faith from the eyes that matched the blue of the Bouchard siblings but I would not know. I walked into the throne room and put on my best smile for Prince-now-King Sebastian.

I opened the oak doors and bowed.

'Your Majesty.' I beamed with fake delight. Sebastian turned and had a scowl on his face. It was not possible for him to have discovered my correspondence with the Bennett family.

'Aleksander, you were told by the late king to discover information on the lady Faith Bushanti. Do you have any news for the king?'

Samael, his father, had just died and yet Sebastian was demanding information that I had not discovered and was hesitant to inform him of what I did know. I was taken aback by his sudden need for this information.

'No, Your Majesty, I have not had the chance to speak with her.'

Sebastian's face turned bright red with anger. 'I would like to announce our engagement before the return of my mother, Aleksander.'

I felt ill at the mention of his mother. My mother was evil but Sebastian's was made from the devil.

'Your mother,' I stuttered to him, forgetting about showing him respect. King Samael had banned his wife from the castle for her misdeeds. Sebastian had received his mother's looks and personality. She was deceiving and controlling and lusted for more power. If she was to return, there would be chaos.

'Where are your manners, Aleksander? The king is above your station; you must show him respect,' Miguel said smugly after my comment from earlier about his respect towards me. I desired to roll my eyes but it would only anger both of them.

'Of course, my apologies, Your Majesty. I was just in shock. It has been about ten years since your mother was banned from the castle for treason,' I said as a reminder for him to remember that she was not a pleasant woman.

'I am aware of that. I am now the king and she has not been treasonous against me. I am her son.'

For now, I thought to myself. A woman like her only lusted for power and could never get enough.

Sebastian dismissed me and ordered for me to discover any information that could be used to manipulate Faith. I returned to my chambers to change and wash myself when I heard a knock. Rosa was standing at my door – it was Harley's lady's maid.

'My lord,' she said softly while curtsying.

'Rosa, I do not expect such things, please. What do you require?' I asked, throwing my shirt on quickly.

'I am worried about one of your men – Aidan. He seems to be taken with Lady Gelden.'

I smiled to myself at the thought of one of my men enjoying themselves rather than the constant training that I asked of them.

'There is no harm in their attraction, Rosa.'

'No, but his parents arranged a match with another woman and he now wishes to end that match to be with Lady Gelden. I worry about the timing of this, knowing that King Sebastian may not desire for his newest attractions to be paired off with other men.'

I crossed my arms, knowing that she was right. Sebastian would have to approve of the relationship between them. He would not be pleased with this at the present time but I wondered if it could be used to my advantage in a way to manipulate Sebastian.

'I will speak to him. Thank you, Rosa.' I closed the door and dropped onto my bed to rest as I was tired from worry.

I woke before the sun started streaming through my windows. It was my duty to train all the young men recruited by the king to join his army. I pulled on my tan leather pants, black boots and simple blouse, tying the strings at my neck loosely and flicked my hair from my face. I grabbed my belt and walked down to the kitchen.

'Good morrow, ladies,' I said as they all blushed before I pinched a delicious red apple to eat on my way out to the courtyard for training.

All the men had their armour on and longswords in hand. Aidan was already present and preparing the men for the manoeuvres. I could hear a female laugh as I turned to see Faith and Langford; they were sword fighting. I stormed over.

'What do you think you are doing?' I looked at Langford's arm around Faith's waist and felt rage flood my body. I clenched my fists as I looked down at her clothing.

She was not wearing a dress; it was strange to see her in men's attire. Her tight pants clung to her legs while her maroon top had short sleeves and a black corset that covered her breasts, unlike her usual gowns. Her hair was plaited with some strands whispering on her face. Langford dropped his arm immediately and Faith lost her smile.

'I am here for my lesson. I think you will notice how much I have improved. Are you ready for a duel, Lord Marchés?' she said while standing on her side with her legs in the appropriate position and holding her sword upright.

I grabbed my sword and swung it at her, knocking it from her hands as she gasped. It landed on the ground and her face was filled with anger, frustrated and shocked that I had used my full strength on her.

Langford made the wise decision to give us some space.

'Faith, I want you to hold your stance the same and your sword.'

She got into position and made sure that it was the same, looking between the both of us.

'No, bend your knee more, like this.' I walked over to her

and put my hand around her waist and pulled her close to me. I put my hand on her leg and slid it down her leather pants to make her knee bend. She breathed in deeply; it was obvious I was making her uncomfortable.

She didn't realise the effect she was having on me. Her perfumed hair smelt like strawberries and her skin smelt like roses; being around her was arousing. I kept her close and instructed Langford to swing his sword. The swords clanged together but she didn't drop it this time. She turned her head and looked at me. Our eyes met and she smiled. They were searching for something. I felt her breath on my face. I saw Miguel out of the corner of my eye and let go of her, instantly knowing he would report this information to Sebastian.

'Raise the gate! Raise the gate!' a young guard yelled as my men stopped their training to see who was arriving.

Two guards rode in through the gate, all dressed in black with black horses and followed by a black carriage. Aidan and I looked at one another; confusion was obvious on his face but I knew who was inside. Sebastian came out into the courtyard wearing a green tunic and black pants, a bright smile on his face with the same smugness as present every day. Queen Yelena stepped out of the carriage. Her strawberry hair was in a high bun with a golden crown sitting perfectly on top of her head. She was no beauty and had plumped up since her exile from the castle. She had always disliked me and made it obvious with her looks and general demeanour. She was covered in jewels to show her station and wealth, which was not needed but she believed a woman should be covered in jewels. Her golden dress was covered in jewels and her chest was not covered as appropriately as a lady should be; she almost looked like a whore. The crowd fell silent and bowed at her arrival.

'Oh, my handsome son, Sebastian. How I have missed you. You have grown into a strong young man like I always knew you to be.' They embraced.

Sebastian did look very happy but I did worry. As she was walking towards the castle, Yelena turned and glared at me. I smiled in response.

Faith turned to look at me. 'That is Sebastian's mother. I assumed she was dead because I had never seen her.'

I shook my head. 'No, she was exiled by the late King Samael for acts of treason against him.'

'Holy shit! What is she doing back here?' she asked but I didn't know and I wanted to know the answer to this. What did Sebastian gain from his mother returning to him and to the castle? Yelena tried to kill her husband to take the throne from him but he loved her too much to kill her. I moved away from Faith and began training the men. I heard her sigh in response.

'My lord, these are the new recruits th—'

I cut him off, knowing the answer already. 'Yes, Aidan,' I said, watching the men attempt to hold a sword correctly and attempt to attack another person.

They were weak but I knew they would be better with time. The messenger came over to Faith and passed a note.

'Can you read, milady?' he asked. He was young and had no knowledge of who Faith was as she stared at him for a few moments before chuckling to herself and grabbing it from him.

'What the? I am being summoned by the king.' She ripped up the note and let it fall to the ground before leaving without saying goodbye. She was upset but I had no time to think about her; I was waiting for news from my cousin.

*

Training had finished as I grew tired of watching the men fail. One of the kitchen ladies smiled at me and handed me a plate of mutton and potatoes.

'Thank you. Aren't you a pretty little girl?'

She looked no older than twelve and her face showed the typical baby features she was yet to grow out of. I felt pity for the peasants as I would never allow a child to work in a castle. Children should be children and playing in the mud. I walked through the castle to change into fresh clothes for the ball tonight that Sebastian would have planned for his mother's return to court. The idea of Yelena being close made me feel ill.

'My lord, my lord.' The messenger was running after me.

'Elric, slow your steps.'

The young boy almost fell over. 'I have a letter for you. I have been told...' He lowered his voice. 'That it must be secret.'

I nodded, grabbed the letter and headed back to my chambers. I tore the wax and read.

Aleksander,

I hope this reaches you.

Meet tonight under the cover of darkness at the old chapel.

Charlotte

I scrunched the letter and threw it into the fire, knowing that there must be no trace of it. I asked one of the ladies to run a bath for me to clean myself for tonight. While two ladies filled the bath, they proceeded to giggle and stare. I covered myself with a blanket and coughed, waiting for them to give me the privacy that I desired.

'My lord, what ails you?' the young blonde said, batting her eyes in my direction.

I didn't answer, just coughed and stepped into the bath. My peace was disturbed shortly after when Yelena burst into my room.

'I see my fool of a husband allowed you to live.'

I nodded my head, feeling vulnerable in my naked position in the bath. She looked at her nails and walked to the mirror to look at her crown, fixing them before turning her glare back towards me.

'I suggest you make yourself unseen if you want to live. I will not be as kind as my husband.'

I could never hold my tongue with Yelena and her spitefulness. 'I never harmed you in any way and I will not be unseen as you demand. What seems to be the reason for your fury?' I asked her, knowing it would only provoke her further. Her face scowled; it was familiar. I had seen it before with Sebastian.

'If it wasn't for your father, none of this would have happened. We were in the talks for Crystal to marry our son but the Bouchards did not listen and agreed to let Crystal marry you.'

My mouth dropped open in shock – I knew our parents desired a match between our families but I had never been told.

'Oh, did you not know? Poor Aleksander,' she said and walked off, smiling to herself before exiting through the door.

I knew that I had to show my face at the ball to keep up the pretence that I was there for the whole evening. I pulled on my tan leather pants and matching tunic. I saw the cross around my neck, picked it up and kissed it, praying for luck. I walked into the grand hall where it was abuzz with noise and laughter.

The music was soft to allow for our traditional dancing as I picked up a goblet of wine. Annie saw my entrance with a small smile and walked towards me.

'You look handsome, my lord.' I smiled at her; she was attractive but not enough to turn my head in her direction but I never dared insult a lady.

'You are looking delightful tonight, Annie.'

Annie was wearing a similar dress to the black and gold dress that Faith wore, but it did not suit her the way that it did with Faith. Faith had a womanly figure compared to Annie who was too skinny, for me at least. I had almost finished the wine in my goblet.

'Annie, will you accompany me for a walk around the hall?' I asked, knowing that I needed to be seen and I would be with one of the new ladies of the court.

She nodded and took my arm. It was a quiet walk with neither Annie nor I speaking. Talking was not needed; it was only to be seen by Yelena and Sebastian to witness that I was present. I noticed Faith on the dancefloor with Langford. She was beaming, her smile lighting up her entire face. It made her skin appear to glow. Her light pink dress brought out the darkness of her skin and hair, as her hair was up in a bun with a braid hanging down from the side. I felt eyes on me and noticed Yelena was watching me like a hawk. Annie must have noticed.

'She is beautiful, isn't she?'

I did not respond to the question; I worried about the repercussions of mentioning her beauty.

'Don't hurt her, Aleksander. She has been through enough. I haven't seen her smile as much as she has since Toby.'

I looked at her; I had heard that name before when they were on the roof. Who was Toby? Annie moved to walk away.

'Annie, wait...' I said as I untied the cross around my neck. 'Could you hand this to Faith?'

I wanted her to have some form of protection and it had given me that since Crystal and her family were slaughtered. Annie took it with a small smile and walked away.

I looked out over the grand hall before taking my leave.

'Leaving so soon, Aleksander?' Miguel said, leaning against the door and stuffing his face with food. I knew he purposely forgot my station as always.

'I am feeling unwell, Miguel. I will be resting for the remainder of the night,' I said as I snuck away into the darkness of the castle.

I knew the places to hide; I had lived here my entire life. I found Dmitirov hiding out the back of the stables with two horses already waiting. He handed me the reins as I mounted my horse. We rode off into the dark. We could not risk using light to help us see as we may have been exposed to any watchful eyes. We needed the cover of darkness to avoid being discovered. It did not take us long to reach the chapel – or what was left of it after being burnt down. It was unsettling being at this place, knowing what had occurred all those years ago but no one dared to venture here for the fear of ghosts haunting the area. I shivered, thinking of the Bouchard family and their terror as they were killed.

Dmitirov walked around the area in search of wood to start a fire. He grabbed his sword and a rock to create sparks. I watched them take hold of the wood and cause a small fire to take place. It wasn't long before Charlotte walked in. She was paler than I remembered with her shiny blonde hair and brown eyes. She was taller than I remembered but it had been years since we had seen one another. She walked over and embraced me. She barely reached my chest as I embraced her in return.

'Cousin, I did not expect to see you here tonight,' I said, looking at her father Cedric as he entered.

'Why not, Aleksander? She is my only heir and will rule when I reach my untimely demise,' he said with a slight smirk. He was not aging well. His blonde hair was now grey. He was taller than Charlotte but still did not reach my height. He walked over and brought me into him, holding me tight.

'My, you have grown into a strapping young lad,' he said as I heard a laugh in the background. I peered into the dark to see Marcus Arundel. I reached for my sword but Cedric put his hand over mine.

'Be still, Aleksander. I invited Marcus here,' Cedric said softly to bring down the rage I felt from our last meet.

'Yes, my apologies for our last interaction,' Marcus said without any emotion.

I never liked or trusted the Arundel family. They had been in the pocket of the Faulcons for years. They were one of the families who helped to betray the Bouchards. Marcus was just shorter than myself but his hair was perfectly cropped and the obvious greys peeked through. He had well-defined cheekbones and a rather large nose that he attempted to hide with his beard.

'It was not my intention to hurt or harm you in any way. I merely wanted the prize for myself,' Marcus said with no remorse as he looked at his fingers in the dark light as if this was beneath him.

Dougal Fitzhugh arrived in his boisterous manner.

'I bet the wee young man to win,' he said with his thick, distinct accent. He was a man who was hard to miss; he towered over my own height with his broad shoulders and large muscles but he stood out more due to his bright red hair and thick red beard.

'Come on now, laddie, you wanted us here'. What you got, boy?' he asked while sitting on a fallen log.

'Are the Somneri and Ladislas families not coming?' I asked but I feared that I knew the answer.

'No,' Marcus said sternly. 'The Ladislas are too far away to get here in the limited notice that was given and the Somneri were and still are the biggest allies of the Faulcons. You should know never to trust them. They helped with the death of your father,' he said, biting into an apple but making sure that he stayed hidden in the shadows.

'Were you not in the pocket of the Faulcons?' Cedric asked, looking at him with a warning.

'I ally with those who can benefit my family the most,' he said with a sly smile.

I drank some water to clear my throat in preparation for what I was about to say. I feared that they would not believe me or that it would cause more separation between the families. Our lands did not need any more fighting; it needed peace and Faith or Crystal or whoever she was may bring exactly that. I breathed in deeply as I heard Dmitirov shuffle behind me.

'We have been told lies by the Faulcons. Days before the castle was overrun, Katherine Bouchard paid one of the witches in town to save her children. They promised to only save one child. I do not know which child was saved but one of the ladies who arrived by the stars is a Bouchard. One of them may be Crystal Bouchard or they may be the child of the Bouchard sons.' I paused, waiting for the questions but it was quiet; it was as if I could hear their thoughts churning.

'How can you be sure, Aleksander?' Cedric asked, rubbing his chin with contemplation on his face.

'Where is the proof? I have seen the girls but how can we be certain?' Marcus questioned, coming out of the shadows.

'How can the lassies be a child of the Bouchard?' Dougal asked.

'You are foolish, Dougal. It is a different time from the rumours that I have heard,' Cedric responded.

'My father collected what was left in this very chapel all those years ago and only found the remains of four bodies,' I said, running my fingers through my hair with nerves. I had never thought about the numbers before.

'Ye father was killed for treason,' Dougal said while spitting at the ground.

'Or to cover up the truth.' Marcus sneered back. All of the men agreed in unison.

'I wanted to meet in hopes that you may stand behind her and allow the Bouchards to reign again,' I said in hope.

'Behind a girl,' Marcus spat out.

'Hush, Marcus, we know the real reason why the Bouchards were killed,' Cedric said, snapping his head to glare at him.

The men erupted in arguments, shouting at one another for their claim to the throne or whatever they thought was good enough.

'No, my family is next in line. They took the crown from me.' 'What if she does not want to rule?' 'How can we trust

Aleksander?' 'How do we know that he does not want the power for himself?' It continued for a long time until silence came over the men. They had shouted until they had no more arguments.

'I did not convene this meeting for you to battle. I do not want the crown; I want someone just to run our country the way that it should be. The Bouchards cared about the people; they did not care about money or power. I do not care who rules. I only care that the last living Bouchard is protected. You can believe me or not. It does not ail me but I am behind her and I will do whatever it takes to protect her. Let me know what you decide.' I walked over into the darkness with Dmitirov as we found our way to our horses. I heard footsteps behind us; they were determined.

'Wee lad,' I heard Dougal call out. I stopped to give him time to speak. 'Ye pa was a friend of meen. If ye arr like him, which I thenk ye arr, you have me family behind ye.' Dougal put his arm out as a gesture of good faith. I grabbed it and held on tight.

'Thank you, Dougal. I will stay in touch.'

'Wait, before ye go. Ye families wee wante to see herr. Try and convince ye king to head round ye country wit her.' Dougal had a point, the heir needed to be seen.

She could no longer be hidden. If they saw any of those girls, they would remember her face more than I. It would persuade them to join behind me and ultimately her. I did not want to rule; I never had a desire for the crown. I only wanted the rightful heir to be back on the throne. That was why I would try my hardest to protect those girls. I saw something different in them; whatever it was would change our lands for the better.

Dmitirov and I mounted our horses and made the journey back to the castle.

'Dmitirov, who do you think it is?' I asked him, knowing that I had yet to ask him this question.

'I am not sure, Aleksander, but you are right in what you said to them. We must protect them and we are going to need the founding families' help.' His words did not sound hopeful but neither was I.

'Let us hope that we can get it,' I said as we snuck back into the castle.

It was quieter than usual, it was eerie; something had happened tonight. I climbed the tower to Faith's room and stopped myself from knocking on the door. I saw a wedge on the ground to my right. I walked quietly up the stairs and heard a voice softly speaking.

'Toby, I do not know if you can hear me anymore. I don't even know where I am right now – I could be in some form of heaven or hell, more than likely hell...' I could hear the sadness in her voice and the soft weeping in her pauses. 'I miss you so much. It has been so hard without you. If I ever had a bad day, I could call you up and listen to your voice on voicemail and talk to you. I have nothing here to remind me of you – no photos, no videos, not even the sound of your voice. I miss looking into your green eyes... and hearing you tell me that everything is going to be alright. I need you. Where are you? I hate that you left me. It wasn't your time. It should have been me. I am so lost without you. I need you back. God, bring him back to me... I want to go home. I do not deserve this life – haven't I had enough happen? Don't I deserve something more, something better? I lost the love of my life when you died and a piece of me died too. I cannot...' There was a long pause. 'God, why did you do this to me? Why do you make me suffer?'

Faith was on her knees, sobbing. She was vulnerable but it wasn't right for me to interrupt her. I made the choice to leave her alone as I snuck back down the stairs.

CHAPTER ELEVEN

Faith

I started to watch the sun coming over the mountains. I didn't sleep much last night. I knew it had to be now or never if I was to leave. I had no idea how to get home but I would figure it out. I needed to escape this castle; something about being here felt wrong. I couldn't understand the feeling that I didn't belong here but it wasn't that – I couldn't explain it. I looked in the mirror at my face. It was still bruised from last night. My lip had a small cut in it and it was slightly puffy from last night. Yelena had struck me for talking back to her. Alas, I was wrong but she had no right to call me a common whore. I was being polite to the lords of the room and I was called a whore as I was not paying enough attention to her son. She sure was classy – I understood why Aleksander had no time for her and why her own husband had exiled her.

I dressed myself in a boring brown dress that seemed to blend in with those who had no titles. It had red along the sleeves, across the waist and at the bottom. It was perfect in my plan to not draw attention to myself. I looked at the cross Annie gave me from Aleksander. It was beautiful. It was silver with etching all over it but the centre of the cross was a rose with a royal blue stone. I grabbed some black ribbon from one of my dresses and tied it around my neck. I don't know why he gave it to me or what the significance of this type of present meant in this time. I only wore it as I had lost my own cross and I felt that as much as I hated God in this moment, I needed him close to me as well. I wanted his protection despite feeling as if I did not deserve it.

I placed the letter that I wrote to Annie and Harley on my dresser:

> *My dearest friends,*
>
> *I am sorry I cannot do this. I am not built for this world. I cannot sit by and let someone order me around and expect me to be a person that I am not.*
>
> *I hate to leave you but I gave you the chance. You guys are stronger together and will be safer together.*
>
> *I thank you for everything you have done for me and I hope you guys find all the happiness that you both deserve.*
>
> *I love you and always will.*
>
> *Faith*

I knew Makenzie would see it when she came in to wake me up within the next hour. I knew from watching every morning that the prostitutes who were paid for the night left at about this time in the morning and I just needed to blend in with them as I snuck out of the castle. I walked through the kitchen and gestured for the ladies to be quiet by putting my finger to my lips and letting out a 'shhh'. I saw the flock of women and ran quickly to catch up with them. The guards opened the gate and two of them smiled.

'Hello, ladies,' they said, checking all of us out. I walked beside another girl with blonde curly hair.

'Oh, my. I know you. You're Faith,' she said with glee, a little too loud for my liking.

I shook my head. 'No, you are mistaken.'

We were getting closer to the gate. She kept trying to look at me, to see my whole face. I let her and grabbed her arm. I could understand why she was a whore; she was beautiful and would easily have access to any man that she would desire. Her blonde hair made her stand out but the small features on her face made her attractive and her green eyes.

'Please help me!' I begged of her. She nodded and put me between her and another girl.

'Keep your head down,' she said softly. I held my breath as I was walking through the gate.

'WAIT!' I heard one of the guards shout. All of the girls stopped and turned. The guard pointed at me.

'How much for a night with you?' he asked as I kept trying to hide my entire face from view.

'You could not afford me and a guard is beneath me.'

The girls all laughed as we kept walking. Once we were at a safe distance, I looked at the girl.

'Thank you, I am eternally grateful for your help.' I looked at the bracelet on my wrist and started to take it off in an effort to pay her for her help.

'No, I could not accept that. You will repay me in time. I am Elizabeth, Lizzie for short.'

I smiled at her. 'Faith,' I said, which was obvious she already knew.

'Where are you off to this early in the day?' she asked, looking around the town, which I had barely noticed.

'Trying to find a way home,' I said, looking down at the black cobblestone path. I could see rubbish on the ground and it smelt like human faeces and rotting food. The smell was so bad that I started to hold my breath in an attempt to stop myself from dry retching. Lizzie grabbed my hand.

'Follow me. I will show you the way out and give you some things to help your journey.'

Before I could tell her no, she pulled me into a house. There was no room between the houses; they were all packed tightly in the streets. They were made from wood, wattle and mud to make the walls hard. They only had one door and no windows. The house was stuffy and smelt damp and dirty but it smelt better than outside. There was just one room with everything in it – a bed, a bucket for the toilet, an area to cook and a chimney. I felt like I needed a shower or even some hand sanitiser if I touched anything around me. She walked over to the cooking area and moved some of the firewood around to make sure the fire was still alight before she leaned up into the chimney and grabbed a pouch. She opened it and counted the coins before giving them all to me.

'I cannot accept this,' I said, taking a step back.

'I know that in time, you will repay me for this kindness. I never wanted to be a whore but after everything that happened, it is the only way to keep my family alive and fed.'

I felt pity for her; she was sacrificing herself for those she loved.

'I am so sorry, Lizzie. I cannot accept this.' I handed the pouch back to her.

'Please do not insult me.' She put her hand into her dress and pulled out coins. 'I earned plenty last night and the lord booked me again for this evening.' She laughed. 'Now, come here. If you want to pass as a lady without money or class, we need to change a few things.'

I walked over and sat on the bed; she apologised before rubbing dirt into the bottom of my dress and my shoes and a patch on my neck. She took off my headband and put my neat, wavy hair into a plait. She removed my earrings and put them into the coin pouch along with my bracelet. She went to remove my cross.

'No,' I said, putting my hand up to protect it. 'I can hide this in here.' I put the cross between my breasts.

'Now you look like a peasant.' Lizzie smiled and seemed rather pleased with her efforts and what she had accomplished.

'The money should be enough to pay for a horse and to pay for your way out of the gates.' She walked towards the door and motioned for me to follow her. I stood and walked over. She pointed.

'See the big grey wall with the guards on top? Just keep walking towards that wall. I wish you luck, milady,' Lizzie said while she curtsied at me. I smiled and pulled her into a hug.

'Thank you. I am eternally grateful and I will find a way to repay you,' I said before putting on my coat and leaving her tiny little home. Despite the smell, it did feel like a home even though it did not consist of much.

I walked towards the wall as Lizzie had said all the while wondering how long it would take them to notice that I had left the castle. I felt like I was betraying Annie and Harley but it was what I needed to do. Sebastian had already made his intentions clear that it was either me or them. I was willing to accept that he would be my husband but with Yelena last night, I couldn't. What abuse would I receive from her in the future and if she was willing to hit, what would Sebastian possibly do? I felt a pinch of guilt as I knew Sebastian would take Annie or Harley as his wife but I couldn't, not after losing Toby. I shook the thoughts from my head and started to take in the sights – if I returned home, I would never see them again. I had always wondered as a history teacher what it would be like to walk through a town like this; the smells, the sounds and the cleanliness. It was everything I had imagined and despite the filth, the townspeople seemed happy. Every person was going about their business and smiling. There were merchants and blacksmiths, you name it and I saw it. The fruit markets were wheelbarrows with hay over the top to protect them from the weather. I was hungry and the apples looked ripe and delicious.

'How much for four apples?' I asked the merchant who was old enough to be my father with his aging looks.

'Four silver.'

I looked inside the pouch. I did not have any silver coins – it was only gold. I was hoping that gold was worth more than silver here but who knew? I grabbed out two gold coins – half of what he expected with the silver – and held them up in anticipation. He grabbed one gold coin and smiled.

'I would never steal from a lady as lovely as you.'

'Thank you, good sir,' I said, smiled and walked off, eating the apple. It was so crisp and juicy; it wasn't covered in wax like the ones at home were. I was very happy with myself for my first purchase.

I watched as one young man maybe just shy of eighteen walked past with his wheelbarrow. Two guards walked over and bumped into him on purpose as they sniggered. He and his wheelbarrow fell over and crashed into the ground. He landed in poo. The guards proceeded to laugh.

I couldn't just sit there and watch this happen. I ran over immediately and helped the young man pick up his wheelbarrow. One of the guards grabbed my arm. I knew I needed to avoid attention right now but I had walked right into trouble.

'Who are you to help him?' he growled at me.

'Someone who will not put up with bullies,' I said as I shrugged my arm out of his grasp.

I continued to help the young boy as one of the guards pushed me over. He was younger and possibly in his thirties, if not a little older. He had a receding hairline and a long fat nose with eyes that were too close together. I bit my tongue to avoid attracting any more attention, as I knew I was known in the town but didn't know how much was known. The young poor looked terrified and oh so innocent. His face was covered in dirt and his sad brown eyes looked at me with promise. I pushed his hair out of his face.

'We are almost done,' I said as we picked up the last bit of fruit.

'Thank you very much, milady. I am much too little for this place.'

I laughed at him knowing he was still young.

'One day you will be big and strong. Give it time and don't ever let anyone tell you otherwise.' I put my hand on his shoulder as reassurance. 'Do you know where I can buy a horse?' I asked him sincerely.

He nodded and pointed towards the blacksmith, I kissed him on the cheek and ran off towards the blacksmith giving him a quick wave over my shoulder.

I knew I needed to sound slightly less twenty-first-century and more like a woman who was scared of men. I reached the man; it was impossible to tell his age as he was covered in soot and charcoal from the constant burning fire that he was under. He was barely taller than myself and seemed to have rather bushy eyebrows but the colour seemed black with specks of grey. It was impossible to tell from his dirty appearance but his rather large gut was clear and present. Someone enjoyed their beer.

'Good morrow, good sir,' I said with a smile and a batting of my eyes.

'Ye, how can I help ya?' he said with a gruff voice as he rubbed his nose.

'I was told you may be able to assist me in acquiring a horse.'

'Nothing is for free, missy. Do not go batting your eyes,' he said, looking me up and down.

'How much?' I asked, which made him chuckle in response. This was going to be fun.

'Twenty silver coins. Not one less.'

What a little bugger. I knew he was trying to rip me off from my obviously poor appearance. Thank you, Lizzie. I went into my pouch and pulled out eight gold coins and walked over before handing them to him.

'I believe this may be more than enough.'

His eyes lit up instantly as he adjusted his shoulders.

'Follow me, milady.' He led me through his dusty and dirty workshop to the stables out the back.

There were four horses all tied up.

'For that amount, take your pick. You may even have two if you desire, milady.'

I knew nothing about horses. There were two black ones and one chocolate brown and one light brown. I picked the chocolate horse. He saddled the horse up for me and went to help me onto the horse as I shook my head. I didn't want him to touch me and I didn't want to ride through town when I could walk until I reached the gate. I smiled and nodded at him.

'Thank you for your assistance, good sir.'

He nodded his head and walked off.

I walked off holding onto the horse's reins. I knew how to ride horses and knew them to be intelligent creatures but that was about it. I thought I should let him hear my voice.

'I wonder, what should I call you? Hmmm, what about Max?'

The horse looked at me and nickered.

'Nope, sorry,' I said with a small chuckle at the horse's response.

'Honey? Coco? Romeo? Prince? Charlie?' There was no response to any of the names. 'Wow, you are one picky horse. Oh, how about Milo?'

The horse nodded his head and neighed.

'Finally. I thought I was stubborn but it seems that I met my match in a horse.'

Milo rubbed his head on my shoulder as we walked closer to the gate. I grabbed another apple and my dagger from my cloak pocket and cut the apple into pieces before handing them to Milo. We walked past a sword fight in a little arena.

The men's clothes were ripped and covered in blood. I did not think it would be this savage; I walked over to investigate further but Milo would not budge. I kept walking towards the gate as it finally appeared. There was hay all around the edges of the walls and women and men were shovelling up horse poo and putting it into a cart. They were literally covered in poo and looked generally unhappy. How times had changed. Thank God for sewerage. Why had my world advanced and why was this world so far behind the times?

As I approached the gate, I looked around at the guards to see which one would be in charge. There were young men, middle-aged men and one older man. The older man would not be in charge; at least, that was my assumption. I believed one of the middle-aged men would be. I looked for the man with the stern and serious face. I knew a man in charge would show it on his face. It did not take long – there he was with his light brown hair, pulled back into a ponytail and constantly looking around and not talking like all the other guards. I walked over to him with a sweet smile.

'Good morrow, kind sire. It looks like the gods have blessed this day. The sun is shining and the birds are singing.' I felt sick even saying these words as I continued towards the gate.

'Where do you think you are off to?' he said in a grumpy tone and grabbed my arm.

What was with the men and grabbing women with so much force? I knew I would have a bruise on my arm, possibly to match the one on my face.

'Somebody bought this wonderful creature and I was asked to deliver it to the new owner,' I said with a tone of certainty.

'A lady travelling by herself. Do you think me to be a fool?'

I grabbed some coins from my pouch and slid them into his hand.

'There is no fool in front of me, just a guard trying to do his job.'

He opened his hand and smiled. 'The gate is locked once the sun is down.'

I nodded and walked out of the gate. I felt freedom already. I felt relief – I was one step closer to freedom.

After walking a few metres, I put my foot into the stirrup and pulled myself onto Milo. I grabbed the brown leather straps and clicked my tongue while adding some small amount of pressure into Milo's side. He started to trot; bells rang behind me. I looked back, knowing what that meant and kicked into Milo hard. He started galloping. We rode up the hill and there were two paths: one heading east and one heading west. I couldn't remember which way we came. I was too tired and exhausted. I looked to the sky and motioned for Milo to ride west. He galloped for what seemed like hours. I looked up in the sky. It was past midday and I was still on the same path. I knew they may be tracking the hooves or I was just being paranoid. I pulled on the reins.

'Good boy,' I said, patting his side as I pulled him off the path and into the forest in hopes of hiding his steps.

The sun was still shining through the trees. They were thick but there was still plenty of room to walk through while on Milo. The ground was muddy and covered with fallen trunks, leaves, ferns and plenty more plants and bugs. I shivered at the thought.

The sun was starting to set. I needed somewhere to rest for the night. This time there was no Annie or Harley to keep me warm, just me. I knew that I still had a couple more hours before there would be no more light in the sky. I clicked at Milo to start galloping again as I smelled the air for signs of life: food or fire.

It wasn't long until I smelt a fire and I searched for signs of its direction. I kept riding until I saw what looked like smoke. I turned Milo in the direction of the smoke. I didn't know who the people were and I didn't think I could trust them; I was now a fugitive from the king. There were two houses – I assumed one was a house and the other to be a barn. They looked only slightly different with the doors to the barn being bigger than the doors to the house.

The sun was now completely gone. I clicked for Milo to trot slowly towards the barn. I jumped off Milo and grabbed the reins, walking into the barn slowly and hesitantly. There was a metre-wide opening and the same mud walls all around. There were wooden posts for each of the different stables – pigs, cows, sheep and two horses. I looked around for a place to sleep; there was one stable that was empty. I opened the one pen and lay down on the ground. I was glad I had my cloak but it was still going to be cold tonight. I started eating another apple and gave the other half to Milo. I put my knees up into my chest, tucked my arms in and closed my eyes.

I do not know how long I fell asleep for when I felt someone poking my arm. I had brushed it away, thinking it was just part of a dream when I felt it again. I opened one of my eyes and saw a dark figure standing over me. I went to let out a scream as I started to move away but they put a hand over my mouth to stop any noise from coming out. I could barely make out any features.

'Shhh, my masters will hear you,' the stranger said.

I felt his hand slowly moving away from my mouth.

'My name is Sonny. How are you, milady?' His voice was kind.

'I am fine, I suppose...' I looked around and it was still dark. 'The sun isn't out yet. I had better keep moving. If you are awake, it will not be long until your masters are awake.' I got up to move but he pulled me back down beside him.

'No, the king's men are outside. They are looking for a lady named Faith.'

I gasped. How did they catch me so quickly? Had they been riding all night?

'If you are running from the king, I can only presume one of two things. You have stolen or you escaped?' Sonny said, asking the question.

I knew he was trying to pry for information but I didn't respond to him. I mean, what could I honestly say? I was trying to run back home to a completely different country, place, time. How could I even put that into words? I just shook my head, avoiding answering his question.

'Do not fear, I will hide you,' Sonny said and grabbed my hand, yanking me to a location within the stable. 'Over here.'

Sonny put me behind the bales of hay. He knew they would search this area as he grabbed one bale and shook it to cover me in the hay. I was already imagining how itchy I was going to be after a couple of minutes but I knew that I would have to hold it in otherwise I would give away my position.

'Do NOT move,' Sonny emphasised before running off.

I heard Sonny yelling from afar.

'The stables are clear, Master.' His voice was cheerful as if his response would please his master.

'My lord, I think it would be wise for you to check them yourselves. Sonny is not too bright.'

I was beginning to feel the itchiness building. Now was not the time to move but when you have an itch, you have to scratch it. I started to bite my lip in an effort to distract from the itch but I forgot about the cut on my lip. It hurt more than I expected but it was distracting me from the itchy feeling on my skin. I heard footsteps crunching on the hay around me. I started to take longer pauses between my breathing. If they were too shallow, they would be able to see the hay move; if there were more pauses between them I knew it would be harder to notice. At least, I was hoping that would be the case.

'See, Master. The stable is empty,' Sonny said again with his cheerful voice.

I could tell from the voices that they were close.

'My apologies, you did not find what you were looking for, Lord Marchés,' the master said, sounding rather defeated. I wondered if there was a reward for finding me.

'No need to apologise... for your troubles and if you do see a young lady with crystal blue eyes, be sure to let us know with haste. She is very important to King Sebastian and others.' Aleksander sounded different – he sounded more proper and like a lord.

I felt guilty hiding from Aleksander after he had been nothing but a genuine and caring person but I wanted to return home.

I heard the footsteps retreating but I did not move until Sonny walked over and moved the hay off and away from me.

'Thank you,' I said with a smile as I pushed it off my face.

'With pleasure, milady.'

I extended my hand and said, 'Faith,' as I introduced myself with a gentle smile.

'Ah, you are the lady they are looking for.'

I chuckled at him.

'Guilty as charged.'

Sonny turned his head in confusion. I laughed in response. The sun was starting to come up.

'Do you happen to have any food? I am starving and haven't eaten anything but an apple since yesterday.'

Sonny nodded and walked away. He returned with a bowl of food. I didn't ask what it was; I was too hungry.

'Why are you helping me instead of turning me over? If your master finds me, you will be punished.' I felt sorry for Sonny. I was glad that slavery was not as prevalent in my time anymore. We had only evolved somewhat slightly – racism was still a big problem but slavery was non-existent in first-world countries but not in all third-world countries. 'Do you have a family?'

He didn't answer and after I saw a grimace on his face, I decided not to pursue the matter. The bowl of food was delicious – it was a porridge with fruit. It was tasty. After I finished my food, he took my bowl away.

'The master will be leaving soon. You will have the opportunity to leave after that.'

'Thank you, Sonny. I am very grateful.' I went to open my coin pouch but he put his hands over mine and shook his head.

'No, I will not accept. If I can change a person's circumstances, the same will come back to me,' Sonny said with a smile.

'Like karma?' I asked eagerly.

'What is this karma you speak about?'

I sniggered at the thought of some of my words not making

any sense. 'If you do something good for someone, something good will come to you.' I explained to him what karma meant for me.

'Yes, that is what I am saying. "Karma." I enjoy the sound of that word.' He chuckled and moved around the stables.

Sonny went about his chores for the morning while I sat down and watched him. I did offer to help as payment for the food and shelter he had given me but he would not accept any help. Sonny spoke about his home town in Kagarnt. He described it as being incredibly hot but he preferred the warmth to the cold. He talked about the girl he loved and how he was only working to earn enough money for them to be together. He dreamed of building a life for them. The way his face lit up from talking about her made me smile. I wished someone would speak about me that way.

As the sun was coming up, I could make out his features a little better. He had shiny black skin; it looked so smooth that I was tempted to touch its almost velvet-like appearance. He had long black hair pulled back roughly into a ponytail with a few strands that he would occasionally blow out of his way while he was shovelling his hay. His clothing was too big for him and had rips and tears all over them. They were covered in dirt and filth and his boots were beginning to wear thin but he did not seem to mind. His dark piercing eyes brought light to him and made his appearance rather striking. He spoke about Stresina. He described her as being the most beautiful girl in the world and no one could compare. It was exactly how any girl would dream that her man would describe her in the same way.

'Faith, quickly, with haste. The master is coming,' he said, sounding stressed and looking terrified.

I grabbed my dress and ran behind the hay. I sat quietly waiting and listening to the footsteps entering the barn.

'Hello, Master,' Sonny said meekly.

I felt pity for him to fear the man he worked for so much but he did it for love.

'Is my horse ready?' The master responded with little emotion.

'Yes, Master,' Sonny replied.

I could hear a horse's footsteps walking around. There was a pause and no sound from the horse, Master or Sonny. I was becoming increasingly worried about the silence; it can never be a good thing. There was no rattle of the saddle and no sound of his foot sliding in the stirrup.

'Did we buy a new horse?' the master questioned, obviously seeing Milo standing in the stables. I closed my eyes knowing that I was about to be discovered and returned to Sebastian.

'Who is the owner of this horse?' The master raised his voice and Sonny whimpered.

'No, Master, I found it just outside the stable. I was going to ask you what we should do with the animal.' He sounded like he was crying. He knew what was coming. The master must have been beating him.

I heard footsteps growing closer by the crunching on the hay. I moved slowly and quietly to walk to the other side of the hay and sat out of the master's sight.

I breathed a sigh of relief when I heard the horse ride off. I walked around and saw Sonny on the ground. He was bent over with his head in his hands. I rushed over to him but he put his hand up to stop me.

'Please let me help you, Sonny,' I said, moving closer at a slow pace.

He sat upright and looked at me. I grabbed the pail of water and wiped his face.

'I owe you for all your kindness. I am sorry to have put you into this situation.'

There was a small cut on his cheek. He did all of this for love. Sonny put his hand on mine and looked at me.

'I will be fine, Faith. You should be on your way.' He stood up and walked over to Milo. He untied him and walked him over to me. I was still on the ground and as I stood and opened my mouth, he cut me off. 'No, you need to be off before it gets any later.'

I threw my arms around him; I felt his body go stiff from the shock of me holding him but he softened and returned the embrace.

'Thank you for everything, Sonny.' I put my foot into the stirrup and pulled myself onto Milo and looked down at Sonny. 'I will find a way to repay you for this.'

I knew if I asked him to come with me that he would not accept it because of his love for Stresina and saving the money for her. I smiled at him and rode off.

The ride was quiet. I never liked it being too quiet so I started to sing softly to myself.

'I'll be your dream, I'll be your wish, I'll be your fantasy. I'll be your hope, I'll be your love, I don't know the rest of the verse. I want to stand with you on a mountain, I want to bathe with you in the sea, I want to lay like this forever, until the sky falls down on me.'

I had never been the best singer and it was completely off key and possibly like hearing nails on a chalkboard but nobody was around to hear it. I kept trotting along with Milo in the same direction as I tried to see anything familiar. I knew I was possibly lost. It looked like the same scenery over and over again with a path in the forest. I stopped worrying about leaving horse marks on the ground as Aleksander had possibly already ridden past where I currently was. I looked into the sky; it was becoming overcast and the clouds were no longer light and fluffy. A storm was approaching. I had not felt the temperature drop yet but it was on its way.

'Well, Milo, hate to admit it but I am, um, lost in case you didn't realise and yep, I am talking to a horse. I am a completely sane person.' I needed a rest.

I pulled on Milo's reins and directed him into the forest for a fallen log to sit on. I jumped down from Milo and sat on a log that luckily was not covered in too much moss. I was starving; breakfast had obviously passed through me. I had no idea how long I had been riding for. Milo began to graze on the ground for grass. I watched him while he ate and thought about this being either a good decision or a bad one. The one thing that I missed more than anything and could not wait to get home to was a toilet. I was not a squatting-over-a-hole-in-the-ground girl and it was made even more difficult by the length and weight of this dress.

I jumped back onto Milo and continued trotting around. My hair was all over my face. I wished I had a tie of some sort. Milo slowed down suddenly and walked towards some water on the ground. I thought about having some of it but I didn't know if it had any bugs or how my stomach would handle it.

An hour later, we were still trotting along when I noticed what looked like an ocean in the distance. We approached it slowly but I was right, the water looked beautiful. As we got closer, I noticed it was a cliff. There were no trees around, just bright green grass. There was a house and barn off in the distance that I would try and sneak into to sleep in tonight.

I walked to the edge and looked over it; the drop was massive. If anyone fell down it, they would not survive the fall. The cliff was ragged and you could tell this place was rather old from the evidence of the eroded cliff face. The waves could barely reach where I was but I could feel the sea mist on my face. There was a rock tower in the shape of an 'M' a distance away but not too far that you couldn't see it clearly. It was covered in trees and something that was white. I couldn't make it out but it certainly added to my confusion. The rocks were a different colour not as dark; it looked more like sandstone. How amazing was nature? I sat down and decided to enjoy the view while I figured out where I was going from here.

The sound of the waves on the cliff was so peaceful. I lost track of time and noticed the sun was setting. I turned around and jumped onto Milo. I looked at the house in the distance and turned and looked back at the trees. I could stay in there until the sun went down and sleep in the stables again. I was feeling so proud that I still hadn't been found yet.

'Clearly, you aren't that good at tracking, are you, Aleksander?' I made a fart noise with my mouth.

Milo and I started towards the trees slowly. It started spitting; the grey clouds had caught up to me. I reached the trees and my hair was wet enough to wrap around my finger and put into a bun. It was finally off my face. I was standing in the trees waiting for the sun to go down before I snuck into the stables to sleep.

I started biting my nails in anticipation and leaned back

against a tree. The trees created an umbrella – only a few drips were getting through. I started humming to myself and patting Milo who was leaning his head on my shoulder. I started thinking about Toby and waking up and finding him dead in our bed. I grabbed the cross from Aleksander and looked at it. I started thinking about him. I wondered how he was right now. He genuinely cared for me and I didn't know why. I didn't deserve that and I didn't deserve this gift from him. I went to take it off and started to yank on it but I stopped myself. Why was I scared to take it off?

It was still raining. The sun had not fully gone down yet but it was hard to see anything because of the storm. Should I take the risk or wait until it was darker? If I waited until it was darker, knowing my luck, I may fall off the cliff. It might be safer if I started to ride out now. I jumped back onto Milo and we walked to the tree line so I could see up and down and make sure no one else was around. I couldn't see anyone or anything for that matter; the rain was too thick.

'Alright, Milo, let's go.' I directed Milo to walk along the tree line, hoping that we would be hard to spot from the house.

The rain was so cold. I was worried more about Milo than myself. I had no blanket to cover him with. We had walked as far as we could and now just had to head straight towards the stable. I heard a twig snap in the tree line beside me. I stopped and looked but couldn't see past my wet cloak. I dropped the hood and looked. I couldn't see anything apart from trees. It was getting too dark. I could barely see; I turned Milo towards the stable. I clicked my tongue and kicked him in the side for him to start galloping. He was so fast; before I knew it, we were at the stables.

The smell was unbearable but I knew that I was going to need to bite my tongue and deal with it. There was no spare pen; I would have to sleep in the corner against the wall. I heard noises from outside. I stood up to go and have a look. I poked my head out and saw nothing but I could hear the sound of hooves on the ground. I walked out of the stable and poked my head around the corner. There were four men on horses riding in this direction. The speed they were coming, I knew that I could not outrun them. I ran back into the stable and looked for a place to hide. There was nothing around. I was trapped.

'Fuck,' I shouted.

The men had reached the stable. I could hear them talking outside. I kept looking around and noticed the beams above my head; if I stood on Milo, I would be able to pull myself up and hide up there. I knew it was worth a shot, better than nothing. I climbed onto Milo and reached the beam and I pulled myself up with what little upper body strength I had. The wood was rough; I could feel splinters in my hands. I pulled my hands back and looked at them. There were tiny cuts and some were bleeding.

'Ow,' I said as I pulled out a splinter. My hands were equally throbbing and cold from the rain. 'Come on, Faith.'

I tried again and was successful. I walked across the beams slowly to the darkest corner, which was just on the inside, and wrapped my dark cloak around me, grabbing the parts that were hanging down. I crossed my fingers and hoped that the master of the house was stupid enough to not notice a new horse in his stable.

Voices were growing louder as I could start to hear a little better.

'With pleasure, Lord Marchés,' I heard a man say.

Aleksander was here. A part of me was happy but I grew worried knowing that he may recognise Milo from the other stable. He had an eye for that. I wondered what direction he went in if he had just managed to catch up to me again. How big was this country? I heard the crunching of footsteps on the ground. I held my breath and hoped that I wouldn't be noticed.

'As you can see, Lord Marchés, there are only my animals within my stable,' the short plump man said in a rather high-pitched tone.

I kept my eye on Aleksander to see what was happening. I watched as he walked over in his tight black pants to Milo.

'Whose horse is this?' he said, sounding rather angry.

It brought a small smile to my face. I enjoyed the fact that I enraged him sometimes. The short man stuttered.

'I... am... I...'

'ENOUGH,' Aleksander shouted at him. 'Find her. She cannot have gone too far.'

I heard multiple steps retreating out of the stable. I heard the short man speak again.

'My lord, please, I beg your forgiveness. I was not aware that she—'

Aleksander cut him off with his hand. 'Dawson, she is intelligent and rather sly. I have no argument with you. I only wish to find her.'

'Yes, I can imagine the king would not be happy to have his future queen disappear.'

Aleksander cleared his throat and shifted; he did not respond. I wasn't sure how I felt about the sly comment. I would have taken crafty or sneaky. I continued to watch him moving around Milo as if searching for a clue.

I heard a set of footsteps walk away as I took a shallow breath. I lost sight of Aleksander but it sounded as if he was right near me.

'Hello, boy. Where is she? You are quite a magnificent horse and she is feeding you well. Always caring for others.' Aleksander clicked his tongue as I smiled, knowing he knew me rather well already. I heard his steps moving around.

'Faith, Faith, Faith, Faith,' he said my name continuously but his tone changed.

I looked up from my knees and saw him staring straight at me. I smiled at him cheekily.

'I was never the best at hide and seek,' I said, crooking my eyebrow at him. He shook his head.

'I am interested in how you got up there,' he said, looking for a ladder of some type.

'I have skills that you don't.' He stamped his foot. His hair was soaked and his clothing. He looked rather rugged, not as put together as usual.

CHAPTER TWELVE

Aleksander

I waited patiently for her to come down.

'I am waiting, Faith,' I said while tapping my foot.

'How the hell am I supposed to get down? Do you have a ladder?' she asked, looking around the stable.

'I thought you had skills that I do not.' I chuckled slightly.

'Ha, ha Aleksander.' She was not impressed; she was shaking her head. 'Bloody useless place, no technology, no common sense—'

I cut off her mini-rant. 'Have you finished?'

She muttered something that I did not hear. I noticed that she was looking between Milo and the beam. I walked over and grabbed the horse's reins and held him still. I looked up to see how she was doing. She had lifted her dress and I saw her bare legs. I turned away quickly.

'I apologise, Faith.'

'For what?' she asked, confused.

'I saw under your dress.' I cleared my throat.

'Oh, Aleksander, you saw me in a small top and shorts when we first met. I forgive you.' She laughed at me, which I did not agree with and I groaned at her.

I looked around the stables when I heard Faith's voice.

'Can you guide my foot onto Milo, please? I cannot see over my skirt.'

I coughed and cleared my throat as I looked up briefly to still see underneath Faith's dress.

'Would you mind... if you... put your dress down?'

She giggled.

'Sorry for making you uncomfortable,' she said softly and allowed her dress to fall down again and slowly lifted herself off the post.

'A little further... a little more... I have you, Faith,' I said, reaching out and grabbing her foot and guiding it onto the horse saddle.

She was still holding onto the post above her head. I walked around to the side and put my arms up for her to jump into them. She looked at me, confused.

'I will not bite,' I said with a smile and pushed the hair from my eyes.

She bent her knees and fell into my arms. She still smelled like roses. Her hair came loose and parts of it fell into my face but it did not bother me. My arms held her tightly against me. She looked down at me; her blue eyes were so distracting and enticing. It was hard to look away from her beauty.

'Aleksander, you can put me down.' Her laugh had a nervous tinge.

I lowered her gently to the ground and she took a few steps back and flattened her dress back down. I moved towards her and moved her hair from her face. I noticed a cut on her lip. As I reached for it, Faith froze and her eyebrows crinkled.

'What the hell are you doing?' She sounded insulted.

'My apologies,' I said and took a step back. I walked towards the door to look for my men. I turned to check on her and watched as she was trying to put her hair back up again.

'Dammit,' she swore and walked towards the door.

I put my arm out to block her path. 'Where do you think you are going?' I eyed her suspiciously.

'I just want to step outside quickly and get my hair wet again. I need a little water to put it up and off my face. It is filthy.'

I stood in front of her and did not let her pass.

'I promise I am not going to run away again.'

I looked at her. She smiled, showing her teeth.

'No. I will not be letting you out of my sight again. You are too smart.' I stepped to turn around and paused. 'And your hair looks better down anyway.'

I searched for my men out the door but the rain was making it harder for anything to be visible. It was getting colder and I heard the chatter of Faith's teeth behind me. I looked at her. She was shaking. I walked over to her and offered my arm.

'May I escort you into the house?'

She looked at me and laughed before sliding her arm into mine. I shook my head at her as I grabbed her hand and put it on top of mine.

'This is how a lady such as yourself is escorted by a male companion.'

'Oh, sorry,' she said, looking away from me, her cheeks slightly flushed. I walked her along the edge of the stable out of the rain and under the shelter of the roof.

'Am I walking correctly or is it too casual?'

I ignored her, knowing she was mocking me. 'Come, Faith,

before the rain changes direction.'

We walked through the rain in the gap between the house and the stable. She moved closer to block the rain from hitting her. I knocked on the door to the house and Dawson opened it.

'She was hiding in the stables. It is too late to travel home with this weather. May I request an invitation to stay at your home for the night?'

Dawson looked at Faith and smiled; his look was unnerving. 'Yes, the lady may sleep in my bed for the night.'

Faith responded quickly. 'Not necessary. I will sleep next to the fireplace.' She pushed her way into the house.

I looked at Dawson and shrugged my shoulders. He was incredibly short and an odd-looking man. His hair was thinning on the top and he had irregular lumps on his nose. His left leg was crooked and dragged behind him when he walked. He followed Faith into the house. The way he looked at her made me uncomfortable.

Faith sat down in front of the fire. She removed her cloak and folded it into a pillow and put it beside her. Dawson walked over and handed Faith a drink.

'Thank you, sir.' She took it in her hands. 'How close was I, Aleksander?' she asked but she did not turn around to look at me. I noticed she was holding the cup to her face. I walked over to her.

'Another half a day's ride.'

I heard her whisper under her breath. 'I was so close.'

I knelt beside her and put my hand under her chin. I turned her face to look at me. She put her hand up to block me.

'No. I am too tired and wish to sleep,' she said.

'Faith, please,' I begged of her.

I did not want to see it but I knew that I had to. I stood up and walked to stand in front of her. I dropped to my knees and put my hand on her cheek and as I moved it again to look at me, she flinched. I saw the tears roll down her cheek. The bruise on her cheek was beginning to fade as the colours changed from purple to yellow. The cut in the centre of her lip was deep. She was hit hard. I opened my mouth to ask her who but my men returned and walked into the room. I stood instantly as Faith subtly wiped her face and stood up to say hello.

'Have a nice ride, boys?' All of her emotion disappeared and her candour had returned.

I was beginning to understand her now; she used it to cover her pain. Dawson brought my men something to drink as they sat around the house.

I left Faith to sit by the fire as I walked over to my men for information that they said was important.

'What time will we leave in the morning?' Aidan asked.

I knew why he asked – he would want to return Faith to her friends.

'Once the sun rises.'

He was Dmitirov's nephew and the second youngest man in my legion. He shared a close resemblance to Dmitirov but was taller than him – he was also just as loyal. Langford walked over to Faith and spoke with her. I watched their interaction; she was reserved with Langford as she kept her head down when speaking with him. She kept shifting her position and seemed uncomfortable. Dawson walked over to speak with her. He put his hand on her arm. She pulled back, startled.

I stood. 'Men, we have a long journey tomorrow. We should retire for the night.'

Dawson walked to me. 'I am happy to share the room with the lady. I will sleep on the floor and make sure she is comfortable.'

The idea of Dawson in the room with Faith did not agree with me as my body shivered from the thought of him being so close to her.

'NO,' I said abruptly. 'That will not be needed, Dawson. I thank you for the hospitality.'

The men found a spot on the floor for the night and settled. The rain was pelting down on the roof and the waves were crashing into the side of the cliff. I made sure all the men were resting before I found a spot; it was close to Faith. She was asleep. It was obvious from her steady deep breaths. I lay on my back and stared at the roof. Faith woke suddenly.

'Toby,' she said before rolling over, her eyes locked onto mine.

I rolled to look at her. I wanted to ask who hurt her.

'It was Yelena. She said something I did not agree with and as you know, I am incapable of keeping my mouth shut and this was the consequence. Lucky me.' She was holding back her tears.

'Why did you run?' I asked her, moving the hair from her face. It was dry now from the warmth of the fire. The bruise was larger than I expected from a woman hitting another woman.

She stuttered. 'I am not built for this place, Aleksander. Your world is built for men and isn't ready for a woman with an opinion. I was never one to dress up and play nice – it is not the person that I am.'

I saw the cross around her neck. I smiled. 'I think you may be surprised. You have more power over men than you know.

I believe you could get Sebastian to bow to your will if you tried. You may even convince him to remove Yelena.'

She smiled at me.

'You told me on the roof that night that you wanted to inspire people. You can do that here but you need to play the game. You need patience.'

Faith snorted. 'You are always so kind to me. I don't think Harley and Annie will be quite as forgiving as you.'

I smiled and wiped my face. I was tired from the travels.

Faith sat up quickly and went to untie the ribbon around her neck that held the cross.

'No. It was a gift and it suits you.'

A shiver ran through my hand and body as it touched hers – if Faith felt this, she did not let on.

'Why did you give it to me?'

I struggled to find the answer and changed the subject.

'It is warm in here, is it not?' I hoped this would distract her from wanting to know why.

'Yes, it is, but I normally sleep in a top and underwear and not a full-length dress. I am not the biggest fan of dresses this length. Most of my clothing back home is shorter in length and more colourful.'

I looked at her, confused. Why would she want a shorter dress? I assumed that was how they dressed in her world – I remembered her shorts on the day that we met.

'Goodnight, Faith,' I said, kissing her hand and letting her rest.

She reached for my hand again. 'Night, Aleksander. I am glad it was you.'

We fell asleep holding each other's hands and facing one another.

Dmitirov woke me by shaking my shoulder.

'Aleksander,' he said as I sat up and looked around the room, suddenly alerted to my surroundings.

'Yes, what has happened?' I asked.

'Nothing – it is morning. The men are already getting ready for the day.'

I shook my head to wake myself and smoothed my hair back down. I sat up and straightened my clothes. I noticed the smile on Dmitirov's face.

'What do you find so amusing?' I asked him.

'Nothing, my lord,' he said, still smirking to himself.

'Not a word, Dmitirov,' I said, walking out the front door. I paused to look back at her but left her to rest.

The clouds were grey but the rain had passed for now. Dawson offered the men food before the journey; they sat and ate. Faith did not. She walked outside to check on her horse. I followed her, unsure if she would try and run again. She patted him and offered him her hand with fruit. I leaned against the doorframe and watched her.

'What did you name him?' I asked her, watching her gentle nature with the horse.

'Milo, as he looks like chocolate.'

I chuckled at her.

'I suppose he does but what is "Milo"?' I asked her as I walked over to be closer to her. Her brown hair was hanging down her back with her waves framing her feminine features.

'Milo is this chocolate powder that you add to milk to make it a chocolate milk. It melts in your mouth.'

It sounded delicious.

'Why not just name him Chocolate?'

She chuckled at me and turned to look at me.

'It didn't suit him, Milo does,' she said, crossing her arms as Milo put his head on her shoulder.

I had never seen a horse be so attentive to a human; he cared for her, which was not difficult to understand why. Faith smiled in return. I walked back towards the house but stopped and looked back at her.

'I want you to know that you can trust me, Faith. I would never do anything to hurt you. I wish I was there for you that night, I would hav—'

'I know, Aleksander. Other than Harley and Annie, you are the only person I trust. You are a gentleman and any lady would be lucky to have a man like you.'

She smiled and turned away from me.

*

We were halfway back to the castle when Faith turned around.

'Aidan, how annoyed is Harley at me?'

I turned and looked at him. He was stunned and shocked at her question.

'What? Girls talk!' Aidan was lost for words.

'How long have you known for?' I asked Faith softly to avoid many of the other men hearing.

'Ah, since the beginning. The very first night. I always suspected because he came and visited her most nights. Aidan, I am waiting for an answer,' she shouted at him.

'She is upset but I cannot say her true feelings as I do not know.'

Her head sank.

'Thank you,' she said softly but loud enough for him to hear. 'If you hurt her, I will personally remove your manhood.'

I laughed at her threat; she snapped her head in my direction.

'What?' she asked, almost offended.

'I would pay good money to see that.'

Aidan came up beside me. 'You knew, my lord.' He stumbled in his speech.

'Yes, and I only wish to say to be careful. You never know who may be watching and the king would like the ladies to have their innocence.'

Aidan and Faith started to laugh.

'What is so humorous, Aidan?' I asked him with frustration.

'It is funny that you tell me to be careful but you pay for ladies to spend the night with you to keep up appearances but you have never felt the touch of a woman.'

I shifted in my saddle as I felt Faith's eyes on me. 'Yes, I believe such an intimate moment should be filled with love and not lust.'

'Oh, Aleksander, that is admirable. You should not laugh at him, Aidan, that is cruel. How many times have you been in love, Aidan?' She paused briefly. 'Also, the king needs to know that all of our innocence is long gone – different time, gentlemen,' she said plainly as if it meant nothing.

I was shocked that Miguel had not been sent out to find us or to escort us home like last time. I wished I had the courage to tell Faith who I thought she was related to but I needed some form of proof before I could be sure of her true identity. I did not think it was Annie or Harley purely from the colour of their eyes. Faith's eyes were like Crystal's but I could barely remember her face, it had been so long. They seemed to share the same spirit but it was eating me up inside not knowing if it was her or her daughter. She was talking with Langford as I walked up beside Dmitirov.

'Has she mentioned anyone by the name of Toby to you?' I asked him, wondering who this stranger was.

'No, Aleksander. Are you envious of this person who has her affections?' he said with a sly smile.

'No, I wonder who he is. She has spoken his name twice now.'

'Ask her, Aleksander. She speaks to you with great respect. I believe she will answer your question.'

I knew he was right but would she expect answers that I could not give her in return?

'Aleksander,' she called out to me. 'Can we stop briefly?' she asked.

I turned toward her. 'No.'

We were travelling slower than usual and I would not risk upsetting Sebastian this time.

'But I need to use the little girls' room.'

'The little girls' room?' I asked her in confusion.

'I need to pee,' she said, almost embarrassed. Her candour flustered me.

'Men, take a quick break and stretch your legs.'

All the men stopped as Faith jumped from her horse and ran into the nearest set of trees for shelter. After a few moments, she did not return. I began to pace and hoped that she had not run off again; she promised she would not. I heard a scream and ran into the forest after her before I thought about the consequences. I stopped suddenly to survey my surroundings and put my hand on my sword as I walked softly on the crunching ground. Dmitirov and Langford caught up to me as I pointed in two different directions for them. I continued slowly and spoke softly.

'Faith.' I looked up in the trees for a possible enemy hidden.

'Aleksander.' I heard her voice but it was shaky. 'Aleksander, help, please. I am slipping.'

I heard her voice clearer now and ran in that direction. She was holding on to a root on the ground and her face showed her fear. She had fallen into a trap; if she lost her grip she would be impaled.

I ran over and grabbed her hand. 'I have you.'

Her face was white from fear. She had never looked so scared.

'Pull me up, please.' She was worried this was her end.

'I just need to get my footing,' I said, adjusting my stance to lift her up.

I put one foot in front of the other and grabbed both of her hands and pulled her up quickly. I stepped back but lost my footing on a log and fell backwards. My head hit the soft ground; it hurt but I was lucky it was not solid. I opened my eyes to look at her and was shocked to see her perky chest in my face; it was not how I desired to see her at this moment. I thought of how soft they would feel in my hands. She noticed and stood up quickly.

'Oh my God, I am so sorry. Ah, thanks for saving my life.' She tapped me on the shoulder. 'We had better keep going.' She turned and walked back to the horses.

I took a moment to calm myself down from the excitement of having her breasts so close to touch that I could almost feel the softness of them. I fixed myself as I stood up and returned to the horses. Faith was already back on Milo and ready to continue on the journey before I even left the forest. I mounted my horse and waited for Dmitirov and Langford to mount their horses before we headed off again. Faith and I did not speak after that incident but I listened to the conversation of my men around me.

We were close to the castle as we approached the last hill.

I looked at Faith. 'Remember what I told you. You have the power to make change.'

She nodded and smiled as we rode off towards the castle. This was going to be entertaining. We rode through the iron gates before entering the castle. Harley ran towards Aidan but he shook his head at her in a warning motion. She stopped and took a few steps back. Neither Harley nor Annie spoke to Faith; they glared at her as she rode past them. She did not seem to mind their change in attitude. She kept her head held high. Miguel approached her with a sour look on his face.

'Where is King Sebastian? I would like an audience with him.' Faith spoke loud enough for all to hear and her voice was determined.

Miguel nodded and led her inside the castle. She threw her head back and winked at me before walking inside.

I walked over to Harley and Annie. Annie was comforting Harley.

'My apologies, Harley. I have told Aidan to be careful of your interactions.' I moved to walk inside the castle. 'He does care for you deeply.'

They did not speak to me but glared at me with distaste. What had I done wrong? I walked into the throne room where Sebastian was sitting with his mother.

'Your Majesty, Lady Bushanti would like a moment to speak with you?' Miguel said, bowing deeply for him.

Sebastian nodded and gestured for Faith to move forward. She did so elegantly without taking her eyes off him. Yelena opened her mouth.

'She is a whore, I forbid yo—'

Faith cut her off. 'Oh, I am sorry are you the queen or the Queen Mother? Just making sure I understand royal protocol as I believe I was speaking with your son who is the king and I doubt he needs his mother to hold his hand. He does have a rather strong voice and he can use it himself.' She was blunt and graceful all at the same time as she continued to stare at Yelena before speaking again. 'Your Majesty, I would like to request a private audience with you so we may discuss any grievances we may share.'

King Sebastian responded with a smile. 'Yes, Lady Bushanti, as you wish. Please follow me.' He led her into the private dining hall. Yelena went to follow.

'I believe she requested a PRIVATE audience, Mother.'

The room fell silent as they left. The lords and the ladies in the hall were stunned by what had just unfolded before them. I smiled, knowing Faith had returned.

CHAPTER THIRTEEN

Faith

I had not seen the inside of the private dining hall. The table could seat around twelve people and was made out of a dark, near black wood with a silver tablecloth covering it down the centre from end to end. There were blue carnations in pots, perfectly placed the same space apart. The grey bricks of the wall made the room look smaller than what it was. There was no window to the outside world, only two doors. The fireplace had yet to be lit but it was the largest that I had seen in the castle. It looked to be over a metre wide and easily more than a metre in height; it was very grandiose. There was a portrait hanging above the fireplace of King Samael and Sebastian as a teenager with a little girl. He was a chubby kid growing up and had the type of cheeks that grandparents would have loved to pinch. I heard Sebastian clear his throat behind me. I became so swept up in the details of the room that I had forgotten that I was not alone here. I smoothed out my dirty dress and turned to look at him with a charming smile.

'Your Majesty, I hope you will forgive me for the way I spoke with your mother. It was not my intention to be rude but rather I wished so desperately to speak with you alone.' I felt sick from the fakeness of my words but I bit my lip, hoping to draw his attention to the cut that his mother had given me.

'You requested a private audience, Lady Bushanti. Please, the floor is yours,' he said as he grabbed a chair and sat down at the head of the table.

'Please, call me Faith, Your Majesty, at least for this meeting.' I grabbed a chair beside him and sat down. He moved his hand as a gesture for me to begin talking.

'I am coming to terms with the fact that I may never be able to return to my home. This will become my new home and I believe it is imperative for us to come to some conditions where we make it as comfortable as possible for the both of us,' I said as I moved my hands continuously out of nerves.

'Are you accepting my hand for marriage?' he asked, sitting upright and looking rather happy with himself. I wanted to slap his face but I chuckled nervously.

'Ah ha... ha... no. BUT, I would like to start by saying that Annie, Harley and myself all come from a different place where dressing in these items is a little uncomfortable for us. We appreciate your generosity in paying for them and we thank you kindly but would we be able to design future dresses with some slight alterations? If we are spending too much of the crown's money, we will happily stop.' I looked at him eagerly, awaiting his response.

'That seems fair. What do I get in return?' He wanted me to say 'me' but I wasn't going to give him that satisfaction.

'Forgive me, Your Majesty but I am not finished with my requests...' I paused, waiting for his approval to continue. Sebastian nodded. 'I would like a personal guard for each of us – one of our choosing as we need to feel comfortable around them.'

Sebastian nodded again to allow me to keep talking as he listened to my requests or demands as I thought of them in my head.

'We would also like to be able to move around the castle and not feel as though we had a leash attached to us. For myself personally, I would love to head down to the local orphanage and play, and teach the children. I cannot speak for Annie and Harley on their desires. Finally, I want a pet for each of us. A dog or ca—'

Sebastian interrupted my sentence.

'Do you not already own a horse, Faith?' he said, raising his eyebrow.

I bit the inside of my lip. 'Yes, that is true but I will consider Milo a donation to the crown. I am sure you are always in need of reliable horses.'

He chuckled silently and continued to look at me with his finger on his temple and the rest of his hand down his face and under his chin. I knew the pet was silly but I wanted to see how far I could push him.

I finished speaking and waited for Sebastian.

'Is that all of your requests?' he asked.

'Yes, Your Majesty,' I said, batting my eyes at him and pressing my hands together and drawing his attention to my breasts.

Subtle flirting is always easy to do. Sebastian stood up and walked towards the fireplace. He looked up at the painting of him and his family. 'I will allow all of them but I want something in return.'

I knew he would ask this; he had already said that he wanted me to be his wife and if it wasn't me that he would take Annie or Harley. I waited and moved to show more of my cleavage again. Sebastian's head dropped to look directly at it as he cleared his throat. I smiled internally; mission accomplished.

'I would like Annie, Harley and yourself to attend... let's call them "ladies' lessons". They will comprise of dancing lessons, posture, arts, academics and anything else that I desire for you to learn.' He looked at me for a response.

'That seems more than fair, Your Majesty.' I nodded at him with a smile.

'Good, good. You will also accept my hand in marriage.'

I walked over to him and took a deep breath. I grabbed his hands and put them close to my chest; I wanted him to listen but not fully in hopes of him accepting what I was about to say.

'I believe it is only fair for you to try and woo us. No, that is not the word – ah, what is it called? Yes, I think you should court us. We will all agree to spend a day with you each week and we will do what you please but there is to be no intimacy. It is only fair for you to get to know all of us, as you may find that you enjoy the company of another over me.'

He smirked and nodded. I was hoping this would buy some time before I had to accept his hand in marriage. I knew he didn't want Annie or Harley; he wanted me more than anything. It was obvious in more ways than one.

'Yes, that seems fair.'

'Is it a deal, Your Majesty?' I said with hope in my voice as I held out my hand. He looked at it, confused.

'What is this?' he asked.

'Oh, it is what is an acceptance of a deal – a handshake to

say that it is all sorted.'

He slid his calloused hand into mine and we shook on it.

Sebastian smiled as did I knowing that I just manipulated him into more time and more opportunities for me within the castle. I moved towards the door and looked back at him after our conversation; maybe I judged him too harshly. I did have a tendency of judging people too quickly but it was from my past.

'Oh, yes, my personal guard. His name is Sonny and he lives with a master not far from here and he comes from Kagarnt.' I knew if I selected Sonny, I may be able to bring his Stresina here for them to be together.

'I will ensure he is found with haste, Faith.' He looked up at the portrait of his family.

I wondered what he was thinking as I watched him for a few moments. 'Thank you, Your Majesty.'

He turned his head to look at me and smiled. 'Faith, I always get what I want. It would do you best to remember that.'

I swallowed hard. He knew I had manipulated him but I wasn't worried or scared. I had dated worse men than him in the past. I left him alone in the room as I made my way back to my own.

I walked into my room. Nothing had been moved; nothing had been changed. It was as if I had not been gone for the past two days. Makenzie was lying on the bed. She jumped up and ran over.

'I hope you were not punished for my escape,' I said to her as she threw her arms around me.

'No. I was just worried about your safety.' She pulled back and sniffed the air. 'I will run you a bath.'

I chuckled at her. I knew I would smell from sleeping in stables two nights in a row.

'Wow, thanks. I didn't think I smelt that bad,' I said, removing my shoes and cloak. We started to discuss my conversation with Sebastian and what deal had been made. She was shocked that he had agreed so easily.

'He may be a better king than anyone expected.'

'Who knows,' I said to her as the bath was finally full.

Makenzie helped me out of my dirty dress as it had to be peeled off my body from being stuck to me in the rain. Makenzie left me alone to give me some privacy. It was relaxing and I enjoyed the rose aromas in the bath. I could almost fall asleep. I was dreading speaking to Annie and Harley. The glare I received was evident enough of their unhappiness with me. At least I could trust Makenzie; she was added to my list of allies.

I must have nodded off in the bath because I woke suddenly to the noise of someone knocking on the door.

'Just a second,' I shouted in response and grabbed the towel, ready to jump out of the bath and answer the door. I looked around for clothes but it was going to take too long to get dressed properly. I pulled myself into the dress and only opened the door slightly to see who it was. It was Miguel. I groaned but put on a smile before he could notice.

'Hello, Miguel. You have come at a bad time. Can you possibly come back later?'

He tried to look around the door with a stern face. 'No, do you have company?'

Before I could answer, he pushed the door open. I stumbled and almost fell over.

'Do you mind?' I screeched. 'I just got out of the bath and

I am not quite fully dressed yet. GET OUT!' I yelled at him furiously.

How dare he barge in while I was washing myself and with his accusations that someone was in my room? He stuttered and walked out.

'My apologies, milady.'

I slammed the door shut behind him. It was not long until another knock sounded on the door.

'That had better not be you, Miguel.' I put my hand on my dress to hold it up and flung the door open.

'Oh, thank God,' I said with relief, seeing Makenzie standing in the doorway.

'What happened?' she asked, concerned and ran around behind me to help do up my dress. She looked stressed.

'Miguel just stormed into my room because he thought I had company.'

She laughed at what had happened.

'What is so funny?' I asked, frustrated and flustered.

'Nothing, Faith. Miguel is a creep and it does not shock me but you need to remember he is also the king's man on the side. He will be cautious of you.'

I rolled my eyes at her answer.

Knock, knock.

'Can you answer that? I think I already know who it is,' I said as I walked away to the window and looked out.

The clouds were grey; another storm was brewing. It would be a cold night tonight. At least I was not in the stables again. I felt the chill in my bones. I zoned out temporarily and started to think of home again. I felt Makenzie tap me on the shoulder.

'Sorry, I zoned out.'

'The king is requesting your presence for dinner tonight.'

I let my head fall back. I thought he would have at least given me a reprieve for tonight and it would start tomorrow. I guess I was wrong. I nodded my head and Makenzie walked back to give Miguel my answer. I had at least a couple of hours before dinner. I lay on the bed before Makenzie walked over.

'What do you think you are doing?'

I looked up at her and poked my tongue out. 'I am being lazy. I barely slept for about two days. Go away, Mum.'

She walked over and slapped my arm; it was not gentle. 'No, get up. You will be going to speak with Annie and Harley.'

I grabbed the pillow and screamed into it and popped my head up. I rolled over the bed to the other side and stood up. I smoothed down my blue dress and looked in the mirror. I fluffed my hair and walked out the door. I stood there for a moment. Which one should I go see first? I knew Annie was strong-minded like me and Harley was the softer and gentler one compared to Annie and myself. But if I went to Harley first that would annoy Annie more. I started biting my nail and swaying my dress.

I heard a laugh from behind; I turned around quickly to see Aleksander leaning against the wall and watching me.

'I figured you would have had enough of me by now. Some people can only handle me in small doses.'

He looked down at the ground and back up again with a smile plastered on his face. He had a beautiful smile, the type of smile that makes others smile.

'I will admit, I do enjoy your candour and find it'—he clapped his hands together—'refreshing.'

I snorted at him. 'That is a nice way of saying that everyone else around here is stiff. What can I do to help you?'

He walked closer and spoke softer.

'How was your audience with the king?' He walked around me as if he was stalking his prey.

Before I had a chance to answer him, I heard a door open behind me. It was Annie and Harley; they were both coming out of Harley's room. I caught sight of Harley's face and rushed over to her immediately and wrapped my arms around her. She started sobbing. I turned to look back for Aleksander but he was already gone.

'Oh, now you care.' Annie scoffed.

I turned and glared at her; now was not the time to start a fight when Harley was this upset and she knew it. I kept my arm around her and walked her to my room. She had come to like it better because of the view of the ocean. Harley sat down on my bed. I walked over and wiped her face clean.

'What happened?' She was sobbing and I could barely put a sentence together.

I looked to Annie for help to interpret her right now.

'She went to run towards Aidan when you guys got back and he told her not to. She went to speak with him later and he told her that they need to slow things down.'

I felt my stomach knotting; I knew what this was about but I didn't know how to break it to Harley without upsetting her more.

'Harley... ah... Aleksander has asked Aidan to take a step back – not to hurt you but to simply protect the both of you. We are being watched and your relationship with Aidan has been noticed and not in a good way. The king believes that he owns us and we should be indebted to him for his kindness.

Aidan is taking things slow to protect you. He cares for you. I know it from how he spoke about you on the ride home.' The last part was a lie but I wanted her to understand that he did care for her but we were all in a difficult position and needed to play along until I accepted Sebastian as my husband.

I pushed a few strands of Harley's hair from her face and looked at her. 'I mean, honestly, how could anyone resist your pretty face? Even I want to kiss it right now.'

Harley laughed and wiped away a few of the tears on her face.

'Thank you, Faith,' she said as she squeezed my hand.

I stood up from my position and walked over to Annie who was standing in the window.

'I am truly sorry for leaving. I did try and tell you that I wanted to leave but you didn't listen and look at my face and lip. Do any of us deserve this? I could have kept running when I was caught but I didn't. I came back for you guys. I swear on my life that I will never leave you again and we will not lose ourselves in this place. I was scared after Yelena hit me. Sebastian has told me he wants me to be his wife. I feel trapped in more ways than one. I regretted leaving you but it was what I needed to do until a friend told me that I was better than this place.' I smiled, remembering my conversation with Aleksander.

Annie looked at me without anger; her eyes were watery.

'As long as we stick together, we can stay alive and trust only our closest circle,' Annie said as she reached for me. I grabbed her hand and held it tightly.

It wasn't long till Harley walked over and grabbed my other hand and Annie's other hand.

'We need to stick together, the three amigos,' Harley said as we all laughed at the comment.

'But Harley must be careful with Aidan. What about you and Aleksander?' Annie said with a big cheeky smile on her face.

'Ha, ha, you are so funny. He is like my guardian angel,' I said while pulling away from her and moving to avoid this topic completely.

'A super-sexy guardian angel. If you don't want him, can I?' she said. I knew she was prodding me for a response.

'Yep, go for it. He isn't my type, too serious all the time,' I said quickly before I changed the topic. 'So, while you guys are here. I did something kind of sneaky and I don't know if you may hate me again after it. I negotiated with the king on a few different things upon my return.'

'WHAT,' they shouted in unison.

I backed away to put space between us before I explained. 'We are allowed a personal guard, a pet of some sort, we can design our own clothes with a few stipulations and we can move about the castle freely and out to the grounds within reason.'

'Faith, how did you manage that?' Harley asked, seeming genuinely happy but Annie screwed up her face in suspicion.

'Yes, Faith, how? What do we have to give in return?' Annie crossed her arms, waiting for my response.

'Yes, there is a catch. We have to have lessons on how to be a lady and...' I closed my eyes in preparation for their response. 'We will have a sit down with him at least once a week but that is only so I can hold off on his proposal for a little longer. Sorry, I know it was selfish,' I said as I moved closer to the door, ready to run.

Annie and Harley ran over to me.

'Ouch, I said I was sorry. I don't want to marry him but...'

I couldn't tell them the truth that it was me or them; I needed to make light of the situation for them. 'I mean, what will my kids look like, blue-eyed with a messed up crooked nose?'

Annie and Harley laughed. I breathed in relief, knowing they had no idea how close they had been to becoming his wife.

'Beauty and the Beast was always your favourite,' Annie said as she poked her tongue out.

'Screw you, it is not funny.'

*

Knock, knock.

Makenzie was in the middle of fastening my dress for me. She walked over to answer the door. I waited with my hands on my hips; it was a messenger. She handed me the note and a small wooden box.

Lady Bushanti,

It will give me great honour if you would wear this bracelet to dinner.

I am waiting with anticipation to see your beautiful face.

King Sebastian

I scrunched up the note and threw it into the fireplace before opening the wooden container etched with the initials 'S.F.' The bracelet inside was stunning with two rows of pearls joining up to a pear-shaped purple amethyst. It did not match my silver dress in any way but it made me giddy with excitement. I had never seen a bracelet so immaculate. I let Makenzie finish tying up my dress – too tight, as she usually did – before she latched up the bracelet on my right wrist and helped put my hair to the side before pinning it. Makenzie pinched my cheeks while I bit my lips a few times to bring out the red and give the illusion of wearing lipstick. I will admit that I did not miss makeup; I found it annoying to wear and worse to remove it after. It was all about natural beauty here. I opened the door just as Annie was about to knock.

'Oh, I see you girls are invited to dinner as well,' I said smugly.

'Yeah, thanks,' Harley said, looking unimpressed.

They both looked gorgeous. Harley wore a cream dress with a lace pattern on the front and her hair loosely out and put up on one side. Annie was wearing a green dress; it had short sleeves and gold trimming on the edges. Green suited her skin tone and created a contrast between that and her brown hair.

We walked together to Sebastian's private dining hall. I did not bother to knock because Sebastian would make a grand entrance as he had since the beginning. The table still looked the same as it did earlier that day but the candles had now been lit around the room.

'I wonder, do you think there is a secret passage in here?' Harley asked as she started to search around the room. She looked in every nook and cranny for a clue.

Annie walked over to the table and sat down looking deflated and unimpressed. I walked around the room and took in the details. I stood beside the fireplace and looked up at the picture on the wall that I saw earlier. Sebastian looked rather mischievous with a cheeky smile on his face. I bet he would have been a horrible spoilt brat growing up, knowing he would rule one day.

I felt a hand on my lower back. I didn't move but I felt breath on my neck.

'Not a lot has changed since that was painted. I am still as pleasing to the eyes.' He was as smug as usual.

'Forgive me, Your Majesty. I did not hear you enter.'

He shook his head to alert me that it was not an issue. He walked to the head of the table and stretched his arms out on either side as a way of saying, time to take your seats. I purposely pushed Annie and Harley to sit closest to him. I sat beside Harley and smiled at Annie on the other side of the table. She pulled a face, which showed the deep lines on her forehead; she was worried.

'Ladies, while in this room, I would prefer to be called Sebastian. Let us avoid the formalities.'

We nodded and smiled to agree with him as he clapped his hands. The noise echoed through the room. The doors sprung open with servers holding their trays.

Plates were brought from the kitchen and placed in front of us. I grabbed my fork and moved the food around to see exactly what I was eating. I thought it was chicken but it looked way too small to be a chicken. The roasted potatoes were covered in some herbs with carrots and chickpeas. I was not a fan of chickpeas on their own but I would try them in hopes of not being rude. But more than anything I wanted nothing more than a juicy burger.

'It is quail; it is a delicacy here and I require only the best for my future wife and her friends,' Sebastian said, not looking at us while he cut into the quail. He was in his element tonight, surrounded by three beautiful women; it would be an interesting night.

I cut my potato into quarters with my silverware before popping a piece into my mouth. It was covered with thyme – not my favourite herb but it still tasted amazing. I looked back down at my plate at the chickpeas. I made the decision to mash the potatoes and chickpeas together to dull the bitter taste of chickpeas. I looked up after feeling eyes on me; I had an audience.

'Oh sorry, I forgot about all of you. I am not a fan of chickpeas – I do not enjoy the taste. I apologise, Sebastian.'

Annie smirked at me. I knew she would say something given the chance. Sebastian chuckled and continued to eat his dinner.

'Annie, Harley. Did Faith inform you of our negotiations?'

Annie and Harley nodded and let Sebastian continue to talk.

'Good, good. Tomorrow, you will meet with Royston – he designs the royal wardrobe. You will spend the day with him designing the clothes that you desire. The day after that you will partake in dancing lessons, working on your posture and academics. I will select one of you to share lunch together in a few days. I will send a messenger to inform you when and where it will take place. Yes, Faith, I added a... let us call it, a protection, that if any of you try to leave, I will have you all executed.'

BOINK.

My fork dropped on the plate and bounced to the floor. My mouth fell open in shock.

'Now that I have your attention, we will be travelling to the other cities within the country, where you will meet and greet other royal families. One of you will be my wife while the others will be married off to appropriate suitors to your titles.'

'Sebastian, we do not have any titles. We live by your generosity.' Harley spoke quickly, her nerves evident. Sebastian stood from his seat.

'No...' He walked over to the chest on the fireplace and opened it to grab some papers. 'I have given you all a title and land.'

Annie started to choke on her mouthful of food. We all looked at each other; we knew we were now trapped. Sebastian sat back down and continued to eat but 'eating' was not an appropriate word for it – it was more shovelling of food.

As we all finished the main course, Sebastian clapped his hands together. The sound echoed through the room as a flurry of people came to collect our plates and fill our goblets of wine. They were never allowed to be empty; I had to stop drinking. I was beginning to feel unsteady and light-headed. I had possibly only finished maybe two glasses in full. I knew I was not drunk; this was different.

'Sebastian, may I request some water?'

He looked at me and turned his head. 'Is there something the matter with the wine?'

'No, I am just feeling a little bit woozy.'

He must not have understood my word as he looked confused.

'She means unsteady and light-headed,' Annie clarified and moved closer to me.

'Yes, water please.'

He shouted for someone to collect for me. One of the servants rushed from the room to reappear with three goblets filled with water. I don't know what colour the water was but it did not taste clean. Here comes the dysentery! I felt a little better after the water but Harley could see I was not right and handed me her goblet.

The servants returned with dessert; it was fruit covered with honey. Strawberries, blueberries, apples, pears and figs. I was grateful I had no allergies or intolerances. Sebastian spoke about his life growing up as we ate our dessert.

'I had servants to wait on my every need. I never had to ask; everything was done for me. I was blessed.'

There was a knock at the door to distract us from the boring conversation about Sebastian.

'Come in,' he boomed out.

Miguel walked into the room. He was carrying a large wooden crate. Sebastian finished his food and walked to collect the crate from Miguel and nodded at him to leave. Sebastian placed the crate on the table.

'Faith, as discussed, a royal companion for you.'

Annie and Harley stood instantly and walked to the crate. I put my hands upon my stomach. My nausea and cramping were getting worse. He opened the crate; Annie and Harley squealed with delight.

'Oh, they are adorable,' Annie said, putting her hands over her mouth.

'Pick one.' They looked at me.

'I will have whichever one is left after you guys make your decision. I am not picky, you know that.'

Harley dived in first and picked out the golden puppy. I had no idea what the breed of the dog was but it was floppy and adorable. Harley walked away as Annie picked up the next and did the same, sitting down and holding him. I stood and walked slowly to avoid falling over.

'I believe this is the runt of the litter,' Sebastian said as I looked down at him. He looked up at me and yapped.

'Oh, come here,' I said as I scooped him into my arms and stroked his black and white fur. All three of us were laughing with delight at the gorgeous creatures in our laps.

'They are now your responsibility. I am off for the night. I have enjoyed the company.'

Annie, Harley and I started to walk back to our rooms. I did not want to put down my little puppy until I got to my room. We did not speak to one another as we were too engrossed with our newest additions.

'Goodnight,' I shouted to them as I walked into my room. 'You are so little, did you know that? Oh, yes you are.'

He started to yap at me. I put him down and watched as he ran around the room to get his bearings of the room. I pulled my dress up and crossed my legs, sitting on the floor. He ran over with his blue, silver coat. His brown eyes looked up at me with a yearning.

'What can I call you?' I asked him while patting him behind the ears. A knock broke my focus on him as I called out for Makenzie. 'You can come in, Makenzie.'

She had yet to speak after I heard the door creak open. I did not look back at her; I assumed she was busy readying everything for bed.

'Hey Makenzie, can I call you Mak or Kenzie? Have you seen this little cutie as well?' I said as I picked him up and held him tightly.

'Have you chosen a name?' The voice was definitely not feminine; it was Sebastian.

I stood and pulled my dress down to cover my legs.

'Shit, my apologies, Seb... Your Majesty,' I said while almost falling over. My brain had yet to catch up with my movement to stand. Sebastian rushed over and grabbed my arm to stop me from falling.

'I wanted to see if you were feeling any better. You said at dinner that you felt unwell.' He put my arm on his shoulder and held it tightly as he walked me to my bed to sit down. It was a move I had not expected from him but I knew I was to be his wife and in order for me to open my legs, he would have to be a little charming, at least.

'I am fine, Your Majesty,' I said as I sat on the bed.

'When we are alone, I would prefer if you called me Sebastian.'

I looked up at him; I had decided on a name. 'Toby.'

Sebastian felt my forehead. 'No, I am Sebastian.' Concern filled his face.

I chuckled. 'No, my puppy is called Toby.'

A wave of exhaustion hit me and I attempted to stand. Sebastian did not move as he looked me over and felt my cheeks.

'Good night, Sebastian,' I said sternly at him with a gentle push to let him know that I would be retiring for the night.

'I wish you the sweetest of dreams, Faith.' He walked from my room.

Sebastian opened the door to reveal Aleksander standing, holding his hand ready to knock.

'Why are you visiting a lady so late, Aleksander? She is not one of your whores or usual conquests.'

I cleared my throat at Sebastian; it was obvious from his

tone that he was worried and possibly jealous.

'Ah... goodnight, Your Majesty...' I said as I smiled at him before I looked at Aleksander. 'How can I help you, Lord Marchés? Have you seen Toby, a gift from the king?'

Aleksander entered my room as Sebastian stormed out. He looked me over and he was filled with concern.

'Are you unwell, Faith? You do not look right,' he asked as he moved closer.

'Yeah, I am sweet, just not feeling my best,' I said as I stumbled to my feet.

Aleksander reached me in two strides and put out his arm for assistance. I grabbed hold of it when I felt my stomach turn.

'I am going to be sick.' I looked for a bucket but stumbled to the window and stuck my head out and vomited. I hoped nobody was down there. I became very warm and remembered falling but seeing Aleksander's face before I blacked out.

*

I woke the next day; I was covered in sweat from the night and felt lethargic. My head was pounding. I had never felt this before. My eyes would not focus; everything was blurred. I heard voices but I could not focus on any one voice. I moved to sit up and felt a hand on my shoulder.

'Faith, you must rest. Do not try and move.' It sounded like Harley, possibly, but I could not be sure.

'What happened?' My voice croaked; I was not sure if I even spoke any words. I rubbed my eyes as I hoped my eyesight would return shortly as some clarity was returning.

'The doctor believes you were poisoned.'

'What?' I shouted. 'That is impossible. By whom? And why?' I moved too quick and winced from the pain in my stomach; it was like little knives poking at it. I had annoyed maybe one or two people but not enough to be poisoned, surely.

I heard a thud that I assumed to be a knock at the door. I looked up and could make out the figure that leaned on the door frame. It was Aleksander and as he came into focus, I rubbed my eyes a little more and saw his gaunt face filled with worry.

'I am fine, Aleksander,' I said as he grabbed a wet cloth and dabbed my forehead. 'Should a female not be tending to a man more than a man tending to a female?'

He chuckled softly at my remark as he moved my hair from my face.

'Aleksander has not slept and has not left your room for long periods of time. If it weren't for him, we may have lost you.'

I put my hand up and touched his face; he settled into the cup of my hand.

'You are my guardian angel. You have saved me twice in one week.'

He looked away. 'You have been out for days, Faith.' His voice broke as he spoke.

I inspected his face closely as I saw the dark rings under his eyes. I grabbed his hands and squeezed them tightly as he looked back at me. 'Thank you, Aleksander. Truly, thank you.'

He smiled and nodded. Another knock revealed a new guest. Aleksander turned and stood up instantly.

'Your Majesty,' he said as he bowed his head. Everyone followed the action.

'How are you, Faith?' Sebastian asked as he looked over the

guests in the room. He was dressed within his usual adornment of gold and obscenely thick dark-coloured tunic, which did nothing for his complexion.

'Doing much better, Your Majesty. I would show my respect but I cannot move currently,' I said with a laugh.

'May I have the room?' Sebastian asked, looking at the guests. It emptied quickly. He walked over and sat on my bed as he reached for my hand.

'I was worried you may not survive, Faith.' He looked away and I heard a slight sniffle from his nose. I tried to sit up and look at him better. His eyes were filled with water.

'Sebastian, I am alive. There is no need to be upset.'

Before I knew it, Sebastian put his arms around me and brought me close to his body.

'Sebastian, I hurt,' I said struggling with the pain of the sudden movement.

He pulled away and shook his head before he stood. 'I apologise, Faith.'

I reached for his hand to provide comfort. He squeezed it in response.

Another knock interrupted the conversation. I felt popular with all my guests.

'Your Majesty, there is an urgent matter that needs your attention,' Miguel said as he poked his head around the door.

'Yes, I will come at once,' Sebastian responded as he moved to leave the room before he stopped and looked back at me. 'I would like to take a walk around the garden with you tomorrow. At your pace, if you are well enough,' Sebastian said before he left my room.

I kept feeling as if I had judged him too harshly from the

beginning. Was he sweeter than he seemed? Maybe his father was the royal prick and influenced his son to follow in his arrogant steps. Or maybe his death had changed his attitude. I shook my head from the thoughts. Why did I care? I knew he was to be my husband but... Annie and Harley entered to drag me from the bottomless pit of my thoughts.

'Where is Toby?' I asked them, anxious to know if he was alright.

Annie and Harley looked at one another.

'Really, you called him Toby?' Annie said as she crossed her arms.

'Yeah and?' I asked, knowing I did not expect a response.

'Of course, she did. This way she knows he is watching out for her,' Harley said as she picked up Toby and put him on the bed.

Was I that transparent? Toby ran up the bed and I held him tight.

'Hello, precious. How are you?'

I was licked in response and kissed his head.

'What did Sebastian want?' Annie asked as she sat on the edge of the bed.

I looked up at her. 'Wanted to make sure I was ok and he started to tear up slightly. It was strange. I did not expect that from him.'

They both nodded but the look on Annie's face felt different; it made unease creep through my body.

The doctor returned after a few hours. I sat upright in bed as I tried to teach Toby a few tricks. He looked at me and tilted his head.

'We will get there eventually,' I said as I looked up at the doctor. He smiled.

'Your colour has returned, milady,' he said as he felt my forehead.

'I am feeling heaps better. Whatever was in that tea, despite the horrible taste, has certainly done the trick,' I said, perking up and returning his smile. My stomach was no longer hurting and I could move a little more with less pain.

'There was no trick. It was medicine, milady.'

I took another sip and giggled at him for his lack of understanding of what I meant with 'trick'.

'No, I did not mean trick in that way. I mean, it seems to be making me better. It is an expression – I apologise for the confusion.'

'No need to apologise. I will have to adjust to this new language,' he said, packing up the instruments in his bag and bowing as he left the room.

'There is no need to bow,' I said but he had already left the room. I doubted that he heard me.

I moved to wash my face as I needed to get out of bed and move. I was going a little stir-crazy; I swung my legs off the edge of the bed in preparation to walk to my table.

I sat and edged myself off the bed till my feet touched the ground. Toby barked at me. I looked down and smirked.

'What? I was never the best at core work.'

He growled and grabbed my dress while on the bed. I moved him away. I did not want him hurt while I attempted to move.

'I can do this. It is only two metres away, give or take.' I felt my sweat beginning to collect on my forehead and various other areas. I put my hands on the bedpost and pulled myself up to stand.

'I did it,' I said but even I could tell it was a rather weak tone. I put one hand on the bed and moved it to shuffle my feet around to get myself to stand in the direction that I needed to head. Toby continued to bark at me while I moved ever so slowly to avoid the stabbing pain in my stomach returning.

'Toby, shush, you will draw attention to the room.' I slowly shuffled one foot at a time towards the bowl.

Toby began to bark louder and jumped off the bed and scratched at the door. I paused halfway to the bowl. I was out of breath and my legs were still weak and were starting to buckle. I knew I could not stop. Toby had intensified his attack on my door.

I heard it open and paused to see who had entered without knocking.

'Aleksander, to what do I owe the pleasure?' My voice was shaky and my knees were wobbling as Aleksander looked me over.

I lifted my foot to take another step when I felt my knee buckle under me. I felt Aleksander's arms snake around my waist to stop my fall to the ground. He pulled me upright slightly before sliding his other arm under my knees and lifting me into his arms as if I weighed nothing but from what I had seen, he could certainly lift heavy things.

'Ah, thank you,' I said as I looked at his face. His concern was obvious but I was worried about the dark rings around his eyes. 'You can put me down now. I don't want to break anything on you.'

Aleksander laughed. 'You are not heavy, Faith,' he said as he carried me to the bed and laid me down gently.

I almost did not want to let go of him; it was a strange feeling deep inside.

He took two steps backwards. 'Now why were you out of bed?' He crossed his arms over his chest and put a look of disapproval on his face.

'I wanted to clean myself up. I feel dirty.'

He walked to the bowl and brought it over to me.

'Was that hard?' he said with a smirk covering his face.

'Ha, ha, ha, Aleksander. You are so funny that I may die from laughter,' I said sarcastically as I moved to bring the bowl a little closer to me.

'You look healthier, your colour has returned. Your skin was dull yesterday.'

'I cannot remember if I said it or not but thank you for saving my life again. You always seem to be in the right spot at the right time.'

He grabbed my hand and brought it to his mouth and kissed it. 'For you, always.'

He brushed my hair from my face while I put my hands into the water. I wasn't sure I deserved this from him.

Aleksander stood up to leave but I didn't want him to leave yet.

'You don't have to go. You can stay if you like. I am a little lonely. I don't like quiet. The doctor wanted me to rest but I have never liked...'

'Doing what you are told,' Aleksander finished my sentence and ran his fingers through his hair. He walked to the other side of the bed and lay down next to me while he picked up Toby. He seemed to enjoy licking his face. There was silence between us.

'How was life for you growing up?' I turned and asked him as I wiped down my face.

'That is a conversation for another time,' he said, shifting on the bed to show his uncomfortableness with the question.

'Sorry. How was your day?' I thought of a simple question instead.

He laughed. He had a beautiful laugh; it was deep and roared through his chest.

'I did not sleep last night. The floor outside your door is rather uncomfortable. After I woke, I ventured for some food before I checked on the men and how their training was going. The young men are hopeless – you would do better at disarming. I checked for any messages before I made my way to your chambers after I heard Toby barking at the door and found you falling over.'

I didn't say anything for a while because it sounded rather uneventful.

'Wow, what a boring day,' I said while laughing. 'Why did you not sleep on the couch in my room?' I said, pointing at the lounge in my room.

'Oh, that is not appropriate,' he said sternly.

'You lying on my bed isn't either?' I asked him as I gestured to where he lay.

Aleksander went to move but I put my arm across him to stop him from moving.

'I didn't say it for that reason. I was trying to prove the point that people will always talk but as long as you know the truth, there is no point worrying about it,' I said as I wiped the back of my neck.

Aleksander was quiet for a while as he patted Toby and scratched behind his ears. He stood up.

'May I ask you a question?' He sounded shy as he took the

bowl back over to the table. Toby jumped up and cuddled into my arms.

'Of course,' I said as I nodded my head and wondered what he could possibly ask.

'Who is Toby?' Aleksander walked back to the bed. I did not expect the question.

'He is my dog,' I said as I avoided his eyes.

He shook his head. I noticed his shoulders sink. He could tell I was lying.

'He is, sorry – *was* my fiancé. He passed away. We were together for eight years.'

'You were not married to him? Was he an immature man?' Aleksander asked, rather confused on the situation.

'No.' I chuckled. 'We were too young to get married and we waited until we had enough money. We were a month from getting married when he passed away.'

I held back my tears. I did not like to talk about the situation and was not sure why I felt comfortable enough to discuss it with Aleksander but I always felt at ease with him.

'My apologies, Faith. I did not mean to upset you.'

I waved my hand away from him. 'I will be fine. There are people starving in the world. What about you? No special lady in your life, huh?' I said as I nudged his arm.

His cheeks blushed.

'Oh, you are blushing. She must be rather beautiful,' I said as he rubbed his hands together before standing and fixing his clothes.

'There are many beautiful ladies. It is hard to find one that is suitable to a man like me.' He avoided the subject as I eyed him suspiciously.

CHAPTER FOURTEEN

Aleksander

How could I reveal that I found her to be the most beautiful lady in the lands? She would never be interested in a man like myself. I had a tainted reputation and terrible family background. I was lucky to be alive. I wished I could find someone who could love me even with my tumultuous past.

'Annie likes you. You should court her for the day,' she said with a smile brightening her face.

I felt my cheek inside. I wanted to say that I could court Faith but I knew she would pull herself away from me.

'Yes, she is rather pleasing to the eye, as are you. I may need some time to think this through.'

I wanted to be away from this conversation as I stood. It felt like we were avoiding speaking our truths.

'You should be resting, Faith,' I said as I walked from her room and closed the door behind me.

I knew Faith was right as I walked to Annie's room. I was not sure what to expect or if this was wise. I halted, took a breath and knocked twice.

'One moment,' I heard Annie yell behind the door. It was

not long until it opened to reveal her face smiling. 'Aleksander, to what do I owe the pleasure?'

She was rather beautiful, her hair pushed to the side with a golden butterfly clip that matched her red dress. She had little breasts to display but the gown was pushing up whatever it could. I had to take my eyes away from her assets to look at her.

'It is a rather nice day outside. I wondered if you would like to accompany me for a walk around the castle gardens?'

Annie looked stunned at my question.

'I would love to,' she said while attempting to curtsy.

'My title is not high enough to warrant a curtsy, Annie.' It was awkward as I moved to walk towards the garden before I discovered that I had walked off on Annie. I walked back to her.

'Right, my apologies, Annie. This is—'

She held up her hand to silence me. 'Your first time asking a girl to escort you?'

I nodded. 'Yes.' I scratched the back of my neck.

I extended my arm for her as she put her arm around the same way that Faith had. I did not bother to correct her; it was a norm for them. I believe she enjoyed grabbing a hold of my arm and squeezing it tightly to feel my muscles move underneath her hand.

No words were spoken between us as we walked through the garden. It was a beautiful day; the sun was high in the sky and there were few clouds in existence.

'Wow, look at all the colours. This garden is amazing,' she said cheerfully.

'Hmm,' I responded. I was not sure what to say. Annie spoke of what she did as a job in her world.

'You dug around in the dirt?' I asked her, unsure if I heard incorrectly.

'Yes, I find artefacts from different times in the world. It is amazing to see the history of the world beneath our feet.' Annie was filled with joy as she spoke, much like Faith was when she spoke of inspiring students. It was understandable why they were friends.

'It seems rather dirty,' I said, thinking of her digging in her dress. It was foreign to me. 'How did you meet Faith?' I asked curiously. I wanted to know about her. I wanted to know if she was a Bouchard.

Annie scratched her head and looked away from me. 'We were working together in a restaurant. We would serve drinks and food to people. She was Harley's and my boss for a period of time before she finished her degree and became a teacher full-time.'

'You have access to higher education?' I asked.

'Yes, we have access to everything that a man does. It is somewhat equal between the sexes,' she said.

I wanted to know more about the difference in our worlds to gain a better understanding of them.

'Aleksander, be honest. You want to ask more questions about Faith, don't you?' Annie asked.

I stuttered, not sure how to respond. The answer was yes, I did want to know more about her. She was a marvel to me. I wanted to understand her; she seemed to be hiding part of her. I opened my mouth to answer when Annie spoke.

'Aleksander, I can see you care for her and the chemistry between you is strong. I can gather why you asked me to walk on this lovely day but you will not see me as you see her. Please do not deny it, just don't. I will always protect her as she will with me. She hides her pain, especially since the death of Toby. She changed. She lost her spark and retreated into herself and hid from the world. Her childhood was not easy, she never knew her parents and she was bounced around different homes but never found one to suit. Toby taught her to be strong. They were soul mates; you would never find a couple more in tune or in love as they were. She wants to move on but she isn't sure how to move past the pain. If you care for her, be patient. She is not the type to talk about her true emotions. Enjoy the rest of your day, Aleksander.' She tapped my shoulder and walked away.

I could not deny my attraction to Faith but did I feel something more than simple protectiveness to ensure her safety? That was only due to her possible bloodline. I looked around the garden as my eyes drifted to Aidan and Harley beside one another. They made sure to keep a safe distance between them. I smiled at their attempt to seem neutral.

'Aidan, if you walk around that corner, there are some high trees that block the sun.'

He nodded at my statement and walked quickly with Harley around the corner. There were plenty of places to hide in this castle; I grew up here and knew all of them. I remembered running through the garden with Crystal and her brothers. They always picked on her, pushed her over and hid from her. I remembered watching her one day; her eldest brother pushed her into the rose bushes and a thorn pierced the skin on her back. They tried for days to remove it but couldn't. Her screams filled the castle; everyone felt her pain. It took three days for them to remove it and it left a star-shaped scar on her back.

I stood quickly from the same rose bush. The scar. If it was Crystal, she would have the same scar on her left shoulder. I knew Makenzie would have the answer. I ran through the castle to find her. She was washing Faith's clothes, in the room near the kitchen. It smelt damp as the clothes hung from various lines around the room. I slipped on a puddle of water and gained my balance.

'Makenzie,' I said abruptly. 'I must speak with you urgently.'

She wiped her hands on her apron and stood.

'What can I help you with, Lord Marchés?' she asked with her innocent eyes, reading my face.

I was out of breath and paused to fill my lungs. 'I need to know if Faith has a scar on her left shoulder.'

She stared at me blankly. I gently placed both of my hands on her arms and shook softly.

'Makenzie, I beg of you to answer me.'

She finally opened her mouth to answer.

CHAPTER FIFTEEN

Faith

Annie and Harley stayed with me all night. We all slept in the same room and in the same bed. Thankfully they were big enough to hold all three of us but it was still tight; we all slept on the side spooning one another. I woke up early to the sounds of the birds singing outside. I looked over to see Harley was lightly snoring. I lifted her arm, which was across my stomach, and slowly started to shuffle off the bed. My stomach didn't hurt as much today and my legs were no longer wobbling from the weight of my body. I was still rather weak but there was a definite improvement since yesterday.

I sat on the windowsill and looked out at the ocean. The sound of the waves was relaxing as they crashed into the shoreline. I took a deep breath; as much as I wanted to know who wanted me dead, I was also too scared to know or find out the answer. I had a feeling who it might have been and if it was her, I knew that my life would constantly be in danger. I would always be looking over my shoulder. Toby walked over and nipped at my feet. I bent down slowly and picked him up. I knew that if I moved too quickly that it would hurt my achy body more than I wanted it to.

'Hi big boy, how are you?'

He started to chew my finger. I knew what this meant.

'Right, you are hungry. Let me get some clothes on and I will organise some food for you.' I kissed his head and put him back down while I searched for some clothing that would be easy to put on before I walked to the kitchen.

I left Toby in the room with Harley and Annie as I started to walk to the kitchen. I walked down through the arches in the corridor and rubbed my hand along the stones as I walked. They were smooth and rough to the touch. I felt the wind coming through the open windows; it was cold from the ocean. The stairs were a little difficult to walk down. There was not a lot to them; you could barely put your entire foot on the stair. I lifted my dress up a little and leaned against the wall as I walked down the stairs; I knew if I could see my feet that I would be less likely to fall. I stopped at the end of the fifteen stairs. I was out of breath; my pants were erratic. I held my side before I continued towards the kitchen.

'Toby had better appreciate the food that I have scoured for him,' I said to myself.

I heard someone speaking from around the corner but I could not make out the voice. They came around the corner quickly and smacked into my already weak body but I managed to hold my ground.

'I beg your pardon,' I said as I gritted my teeth together in pain.

'My apologies, Lady Bushanti,' Yelena said, holding her hands in front of her in a shocked way. 'I am pleased that you are up and around after your sudden illness,' Yelena said with contempt but a smile on her face. She stepped beside me and started to walk away; her cocky demeanour had built a small rage inside me.

'Yelena, I think it would be best if you were honest because we both know that it was not an illness. You are the only person in this castle who had the means and motive to want to harm me... especially after your son chose me over you in the throne room. That must have stung a little,' I said, holding my hand up to cover my mouth in a fake shocked expression. After I saw her, I made the decision to no longer hold back what I wanted to say to her, especially in close private quarters.

'My son will never marry you and I will make sure of that,' she said with a smirk, showing her joy at her belief of causing me displeasure.

'Oh, yes, because I want to marry your son. He is so... desirable and I cannot wait to be his queen and bear his children. Oh, please, do not take my dream away, Yelena...' I paused as I waited for her to register what I had said. 'Go for it, Yelena. I have no desire to be queen, whatsoever,' I said with a smile as I walked away from her.

Her stunned expression would be the highlight of my day. I turned another corner to bump into Langford. I gritted my teeth once again from the small spurt of pain that jolted through my body.

'Good morrow, milady,' he said as he bowed his head.

'Please, Langford, I am Faith and you do not need to bow to me. I do not care for it. We are equal in my own eyes,' I said as I continued to walk past him.

'May I escort you?' he asked.

I turned around and looked at him; he was being kind.

I could not fault him for this.

'No, but you can walk with me.' I would not take his arm; I was too proud.

Langford strode over to catch me. We walked in silence until we reached the kitchen.

I searched for a familiar face. I noticed Makenzie.

'Makenzie,' I shouted at her as I walked down the four steps into the kitchen. She spun around with a look of horror on her face.

'What are you doing out of bed? You should be resting,' she said as she rushed over.

'Toby wanted food and I am feeling refreshed.'

'How did you manage to dress yourself?' she asked as she looked over my clothes that may not have been the most presentable.

'With my hands,' I said as I waved them in front of her face.

She glared at me in response.

'Was that the wrong answer?' I asked her.

'Get back to your room now. I will bring Toby some food. The king has requested all of you ladies for breakfast this morning.'

I stared at her, dumbfounded that I had to dress up this morning.

'Now, Faith,' she said, putting her hands on her hips.

'Yes, Mother,' I said sarcastically as Langford burst out laughing at my comment. At least he was entertained but Makenzie showed her frustration with a simple look. She had serious facial expressions.

Langford and I started to walk back to my chambers. I noticed his eyes continually look in my direction before he darted them away again.

'What's the matter? What do you want to ask?' I said with a concerned look on my face. I was exhausted but I was trying not to show it.

He turned to look at me. 'I find your friend Annie to be rather lovely to look at and I would like to spend some time alone with her.'

The statement brought a smile to my face. Annie deserved to be treasured.

'Why are you asking me this? You do not need my permission; she is her own person. Just make sure you tell her what you said to me.'

He smiled at my response. I laughed at him; he was adorable. His cheeks began to blush. I hoped Annie was not witty towards him like I was towards everybody. She knew when to tone it down more than I did. Langford put his arm out to help me up the stairs to my chambers. I slid my arm around his and held on. He must have seen that I was in pain with my struggle to walk. He walked slower to allow me time to get a secure footing before I attempted the next step.

I looked up and saw Aleksander standing at the top of the stairs, looking rather unimpressed.

'Good... morning... Alek... sander,' I said, panting between each word.

Langford withdrew his arm too fast and I almost lost my balance and tumbled backward. He bowed towards Aleksander.

'Forgive me, Aleksander. I was escorting Fai... Lady Bushanti back to her chambers.' Langford's voice was trembling. Why was he scared?

Aleksander nodded but the look did not disappear from his face.

'I have a message to deliver to the ladies, if I may leave?'

Aleksander nodded once more. Aleksander did not move to help me, he just looked at me with disapproval.

'What have I... done now?' I said as I looked at him. He walked down and offered his arm as if he had an internal battle before doing so.

'You should be resting,' he said with a peek in my direction.

'I am feeling better today,' I said back to him.

'Then why are you out of breath?' he snapped back at me.

'What is your problem? Did you wake up on the wrong side of the bed?' I said, rather annoyed at his attitude.

'No, you are just a rather stubborn woman and you frustrate me.'

We arrived at my chamber door.

'And what, you think you are so peachy to be around sometimes? You can be just as stubborn as me. Did you ever think you may be looking into a mirror?' I said as I opened my door and walked in before closing it behind me. He was so high and mighty sometimes. I don't think he realised it.

Annie and Harley were no longer in my chambers. I assumed that Langford had passed on the message about our breakfast with King Sebastian. I walked over to the dusty mirror; it missed the clarity of the mirrors back home. This mirror was patchy with an almost rust-like colour but it was not rust. I grabbed the washcloth and wiped my face over with the warm water. It was the best way to wake without having a warm drink in your hands. I grabbed one of my headbands and put it on to pull my hair back from my face. I waited for Makenzie because I did not know how to plait. I had two styles: out and wild or in a ponytail. I was not a typical girly girl, unfortunately. I preferred to get my hands dirty. I preferred being more active than looking like a doll. I would happily prefer a punching bag over a manicure or a spa day.

I sat down on the floor and played with Toby until Makenzie came. She had more style than me. She had a better idea of what the king would expect me to wear. I was attempting to teach Toby how to sit. He would tilt his head at me with confusion. The puppy dog eyes made me laugh.

'Oh, we will get there, won't we?' I scratched the top of his head.

I heard the door open. I turned to see Makenzie with her warm smile.

'Good morning, Mak,' I said while taking it slow to stand.

'You have more colour in your cheeks today. I am glad you are feeling well.' She walked over to Toby and placed a bowl of food in the corner. Toby ran over excitedly to eat.

'Yeah, you know how to stuff your face. Typical male.'

Makenzie giggled as I turned to her and clapped my hands together.

'What am I wearing today?'

She responded with a kind remark. 'What would you like to wear?'

I didn't respond. I knew it was a trick. I had asked in the past or pointed to a different gown but she would simply shake her head. I walked over and sat on the bed; it was my cue for her to pick whatever she desired for me to wear today. She walked over to the cupboard with a winning smile on her face. I rolled my eyes as I watched her tap her chin as she decided what was best for me to wear. She grabbed out a silver gown before placing it back again. She grabbed out a maroon dress with white sleeves and white lace with flowers at the bottom. I loved the shoes more than anything: black lace-up boots.

It was more of a casual dress rather than a ball gown. She started to lace up the back of the dress while I tied the white belt across the front. She walked me over to the mirror and sat me down. She played with my hair before she plaited it and pinned it up into a bun. She pinched my cheeks for the rosy cheek look.

'You are ready, mi... Faith.'

'Thank you, Mak,' I said as I looked in the mirror at her.

She had skill while she worked with hair and she took care of me, more than I generally would myself. I stood and straightened my dress before I opened the door to make my way to the dining room. I had heard Annie and Harley leave earlier. I lifted my dress and started to walk down the stairs, slowly. I stopped to lean against the wall for a few minutes to catch my breath; as much as I was healed, I still was not at full health. Aleksander came around the corner. He was walking rather quickly. Had he come to give me more attitude?

He walked over and offered his arm for me to grab a hold of.

'Are you in a better mood now?' I said as I pushed his arm away. I did not want to accept it on principle.

'My apologies. I just need you to understand how important you are,' he said with a serious look that showed the deep crease in his forehead.

'Important to who? The only people I am important to are Annie and Harley. That's it. I don't care about anyone else. I wish you would stop with your cryptic shit,' I said as I walked away from him. I heard his steps increase as he ran to catch me; he offered his arm once again.

'Just promise me, you will take care of yourself,' he said as he touched my arm softly.

I knew Aleksander cared for me but I found him to be incredibly frustrating. He walked me to the door and kissed my forehead before he left as quickly as he had appeared. I was surprised by his affection, especially in front of the two guards in front of the dining hall.

I walked into the room; Annie, Harley, Sebastian and Yelena were all seated at the table. I smiled and made eye contact with all of them but one. I am sure we can guess which one.

'Sorry for my lateness; it takes me a little longer to walk than usual.' I moved slowly into the room.

Sebastian stood up and walked over. He pulled out my chair.

'Thank you, Seb... Your Majesty.'

He smiled at my mishap and it was not one of anger; it was kindness. Sebastian clapped his hands together and food was brought out instantly.

I turned towards Annie. 'I would kill for some coffee.'

She laughed at my remark. 'I know, right.'

We both loved our coffee but I was grateful that neither of us went through withdrawals from the lack of our normal morning cup. The servants brought out five bowls filled with food. They placed them in front of each of us. It was a bowl of porridge with fresh berries; the aromas of the strawberries hit my nose as my stomach growled in anticipation. I picked up the silver spoon and placed small amounts to avoid upsetting my healing body. There was no talking while everyone ate. It was so quiet you could hear a pin drop in the room. Yelena would, on occasion, look up and glare in my direction. I smiled at her as I knew it would only piss her off more.

'Is it not to your standards, Lady Bushanti?' Yelena asked as she noticed that I had not finished the entire bowl.

'No, it was delicious. My stomach has not fully healed just yet. The culprits must have used a potent poison but obviously not strong enough to cause permanent damage or even death,' I said with a slight smirk on my face. She was not the type of woman who would easily be tripped up into a confession, but that did not stop my attempt.

'Yes,' was her only response.

Harley spoke up. 'I am just glad that we did not lose you.'

'Hear, hear,' Sebastian said as he raised his glass.

We all followed his direction and raised our own; hesitation still ran through my body at the prospect of another poisoning that may occur.

There was a knock at the dining hall door. We all turned and looked as we placed our glasses on the table. Sebastian waved for the doors to open. He stood up and walked over to the man.

'Good morrow, Lord Carmelide.'

The man bowed. He had a rather stern and confronting face. His clothes were too tight and he just appeared as a generally unappealing person. He had short black hair with patches of grey and his beard did not suit his face; his jawline was too long for a beard.

Sebastian turned towards Annie, Harley and I. 'Ladies, it is my honour to introduce Lord Gareth Carmelide. He will be creating your elegant gowns.'

I raised my hand to ask the question. 'Was he not here the other day?'

I was confused why he was here again.

'Yes, Faith, but you were unwell and it was postponed

for another day,' Sebastian responded as he held his hands together behind him. His self-assured stance let me know that I was not to question further.

'Yes, I apologise, Your Majesty.' I looked back at my bowl of uneaten food.

'It is a pleasure to meet you, ladies. I am thrilled to work with you and to assist in designing and making your gowns,' Lord Carmelide said. His voice did not match his face or demeanour.

Annie, Harley and I exchanged a look to say as much to one another as we tried not to laugh. His voice was so squeaky like a dog's chew toy.

I stood up to speak. 'It is a pleasure to meet you, Lord Carmelide. I do apologise for the reschedule of your visit.'

I heard Annie make a remark to Harley. 'Do you think he is so squeaky because of how tight his pants are? Is it squishing his package?'

I snorted and covered it with a cough to pull together a smile.

'Come on, girls,' I said as I gestured for them to stand up and join us.

Yelena was being rather quiet in the background while we all introduced ourselves. I turned around and noticed Yelena and Sebastian in what looked like a heated discussion. I tried to listen to what was being said but I only heard the end when Sebastian spoke over her.

'This is my decision, Mother. I am king.' He was flushed in the face and looked upset.

Yelena huffed and left the room with speed. Harley turned to me.

'What just happened?'

'I don't know,' I said back to her as I walked over to Sebastian. He looked devastated and had his head in his hands.

I bent down beside him and placed my hand on his shoulder.

'Is everything alright, Your Majesty?' I asked as he turned to look down at me.

He put his hand on my face and smiled. 'You are exquisite, Faith.'

'If that is a distraction tactic, it won't work with me. Are you alright?'

He nodded at me and sighed. 'Yes, just my mother trying to rule my kingdom.' He kissed the top of my head and walked toward the dining hall entrance. 'I will leave you ladies to your dresses.' He left the room.

Annie spoke first. 'Did he tell you what was wrong?'

'Yes and no – he said his mother was trying to rule his kingdom.'

Harley walked over to join us. 'She seems like that typical kind of bitch who wants everything for herself. You have to wonder why she was excommunicated, no?' she said as she crossed her arms and looked at the door as Annie and I already were.

'I think we can all understand why?' Annie went to open her mouth but closed it again. I waited for her to ask. 'Do you think she poisoned you?'

I nodded my head at her. 'Without a doubt. I said it to her face this morning.'

'YOU WHAT?' they said in unison in horror.

'Look, I am stuck here but I won't change who I am for this place. You guys know that. This is me, deal with it. I just said to her that I wish her luck in the future when she tries again.'

'Do you honestly think she will try again?' Harley asked as she held her face in worry.

'Without a doubt. I am her Snow White.'

We heard a cough behind us. We had completely forgotten that Lord Carmelide was in the room.

'Please, ladies, sit.' He gestured toward the table as he pulled out a selection of fabrics from his bag with some paper, ink and a quill.

The paper looked so delicate that I wanted to touch it. I knew that it would be made out of amate, which was a type of bark they used in historical times.

'I would like you to decide from the fabric selection and tell me the lengths and any details you would like.'

Annie jumped in first to my surprise. 'I want this colour and I want a design like this,' she said as she pointed to various areas and explained it to him.

I zoned out; I was not fussed with what I wore. I sat down again and watched Annie as she talked; she looked excited. Her hands were constantly moving as she explained everything. She picked up lighter colours to wear and design that would flatter her figure. Harley picked up a few darker colours and selected lighter colours and did the same as Annie and designed dresses that flattered her figure.

When it came to me, I looked at Annie and Harley.

'Faith can wear any colour – her tanned skin helps with that,' Annie said before Harley interrupted.

'She will want a dress that shows some breasts but not too much to look tacky and she will want it to be pulled in at the waist before flaring out. She prefers that as it flatters her figure.'

I looked at both of them.

'Anything else you want to add?' I said with a smirk.

Lord Carmelide looked at me. 'Did you have any more to add, milady?' He seemed genuine.

'No, I think they covered it, apart from pants. Can we get a few pairs of pants and some tops that go with them? Some days, I do not desire to wear a dress.'

He stood up. 'I will have to confirm with the king on these designs before I start to work.' He walked out of the room.

I was glad to hear the door close as he left. His squeaky voice hurt my ears and his clothes were nice but just too tight.

I looked at Annie and Harley. 'So, what do we do now?'

I looked around stupidly for a clock and shook my head at the thought. I stood up and walked around the room; I ran my hands over the grey bricks and put the cupped blue carnations on the table. They were still alive from a few days ago.

Annie and Harley were still at the table talking when I heard Annie loudly say, 'Oh my God, I almost forgot.'

Harley started to slap her arm gently with excitement. 'What, what, what?'

I walked over to find out.

'One of Aleksander's men, Langford, asked me out in his own way.'

I laughed as I remembered him asking me for permission. 'What do you mean in his own way?'

'He said, I would enjoy the pleasure of your company as I do checks through the town later in the day,' Annie said, beaming with happiness.

Harley and I looked at one another and nodded. We both threw our arms around Annie and squeaked at her.

'We are so excited for you. That is amazing,' I said as I pulled back. 'He is a cutie pie as well, you deserve someone who is sweet like him.'

She smiled and asked, 'What do I wear?' Her nerves showed.

'Well, why are we sitting here? Come on, let's go and have a look,' Harley said as she jumped up and headed for the door.

'Are we allowed to leave?' Annie asked as she looked at us.

'Oh, stuff it, we are leaving,' Harley said as she opened the door.

We all popped our heads out of the door, one by one. We didn't see anyone apart from the guards standing at their posts. Harley took the first step out and looked around again. We were all holding our hands; I felt like we were children sneaking out of detention. We walked slowly out of the room as we held in our giggles. Miguel came round the corner and saw us freeze in place.

He shook his head. 'Ladies, may I escort you to your next lesson?'

'Next lesson?' I asked him, confused on what he may be talking about. I knew Sebastian said we would have lessons but for them to start so suddenly, I was a bit confused.

'Yes Lady Bushanti, you have lessons with the Queen Mother. She will teach you how to present yourself in the correct manner.'

'What?' Annie said as she shook her head.

Miguel did not bother to respond but rather looked at us unimpressed.

'If you will follow me,' he said as he turned around to walk off.

We all looked at each other and refused to move.

'Are you kidding me?' Harley said with a glare in my direction.

'Do we not present ourselves in the correct manner now?' Annie responded as she crossed her arms.

'Oh, fuck no. We are bloody horrible.' I laughed. Maybe we did need lessons due to our vulgar language; it was certainly not ladylike.

Could they honestly expect to change everything about us? We had grown up differently and they could not expect us to change overnight – we were who we were.

Miguel came back with a flushed face because we did not follow him as he had requested. Why did it have to be with Yelena?

Annie whispered to me under her breath, 'Don't worry. We will make it difficult for her.'

'What, you want her to hate us more than she already does? Why is she even doing it? She has no class anyway – she was excommunicated,' I said back to her.

Miguel turned and glared at us. I did not care; he was just as bad as her.

'Shh, ladies.' Harley turned around and smiled jokingly.

I started to get tired again. Annie noticed and put her arm through mine to help me walk.

'Thank you,' I said softly to her.

'At least you are looking more like yourself today. You were very pale yesterday,' Annie said as Harley started to hum to herself. Annie saw my face. 'Miguel, is it much further? Faith is still not back to her old self.'

Miguel ignored her and kept walking.

'He must have a new master to follow. He sucked up to Sebastian, now he is king. There is someone else to suck up to. Such a loyal man you are, Miguel,' I said, breathless.

He stopped in front of an arched doorway and opened the door.

'Your lesson awaits.' He bowed and walked away.

We all stood still – none of us wanted to be around Yelena but if Sebastian wanted me as queen, I had to do this, in order to survive.

'Jolly,' Harley said.

'Alright, here goes,' I said as I walked into the room without Annie's help. I could not show her my weakness right now.

Yelena was sitting at the table with her hands on her lap; she looked rather annoyed with us or that could have been her face in general.

'Good morning, Yelena. What a mighty fine day it is today.'

She looked up. 'It is "Your Highness" to someone of your social strata.'

I thought of the sarcastic remarks I could make as I smirked to myself.

'My deepest apologies, Your Highness. I will ensure that it never happens again.' I sat down on the chair next to her.

She shifted in her seat. Annie and Harley walked over and sat beside me. Neither of them wanted to sit next to her on the other side of the table.

She raised one eyebrow and looked at each of us. 'You are not fit for your titles.'

Annie grabbed my hand as a warning to not respond and to just let her be. I looked at Annie and pulled a face but I knew Annie was right. As was Yelena – none of us were fit for a title. We had no money and no land and certainly did not come from a good family.

She stood up and grabbed a book for each of us.

'A lady with a title must be able to walk with grace and poise.' She placed the book on her head and cupped her hands in front of her. She began to walk back and forth all while the book did not move. 'See as the book does not move.'

She did not tell us to move but rather just stood there and glared at us before we realised what she was after. Harley started to laugh but that only awarded her a murderous glare.

'Is something the matter?' she asked.

'We used to do this for fun when we were at work except we used dinner plates.' Harley could not contain her laughter as she held her sides.

'Oh my God, we did too.' Annie joined in on the memory as she looked at me. 'Do you remember?'

'Of course I do but I am lost on why you are laughing,' I said with confusion.

They stopped as I grabbed the book on the table and stood up. I placed it atop of my head and cupped my hands in front of my stomach as I walked back and forth.

'Am I doing it correctly, Your Highness?'

She did not answer me but rather nodded her head. Annie and Harley followed my lead and did it as well.

'If you really wanted to challenge us, you should try giving us more books,' I said as I giggled to myself with the book still stationary on my head.

Yelena put her hands up. 'That is all for today.' She stormed out of the room.

'Should we keep practising?' I called after her but we all started to laugh.

We sat back down and pulled the books from our heads. I put my head in my hands and sighed deeply.

'Let me guess what you are thinking about,' Harley teased. 'Hmmm, I think you are saying, did I make the wrong deal with the king because I have to work with his darling mother?' Harley poked my side.

'Yeah, yeah. I get it. It was not the best decision – you know I am not always the smartest one here,' I said back to her with my head on my arms on the table.

'On the contrary, it was a smart decision. We are going to meet a whole bunch of new people and we are all charming young women. I say we use it to our advantage.' Harley and I looked at Annie.

'How the hell do we use this to our advantage? Remember feminism? That was the point of equal rights,' Harley asked.

'Yeah, I second that.' I looked at Annie.

She walked around the table and sat opposite me. Harley sat beside me.

'Look, we have no idea where we are, some Zilan... whatever it is called. We have no idea how to get home. I mean, Faith, you looked for two days and couldn't quite find it and had no idea what to do when you got there. You made a friend on the road in Sonny. People will find us charming because we are fresh and new. We are smart and witty and some may find that charming. We need to play this game in order to stay alive. The king seems dead set on marrying you, Faith. During our date, he reminded me as such that this was for your benefit but you were already to be wed...'

I went to interrupt that she had a date with him but she put her hand up to stop me.

'One of us needs to make that sacrifice. He is not an unattractive man but his personality makes him ugly. He is a smug son of a bitch but if we use our beauty, we can sway him to make certain decisions and use it to our advantage.'

'Yeah because that worked out so well for the Boleyn family,' I said back to her.

'Yes, but we are smarter. We have read about historical people and their mistakes. But this place is not Earth nor is it medieval Europe or England. We don't know the rules nor understand them.'

'We are having lessons to learn the rules. We have Aleksander and his men on our side.' Annie raised her voice slightly; she was half right but it was hard to know because we did not understand this place at all.

'How do we even know we can trust Aleksander? How do we know he is not paid by Sebastian? The only people I trust are you and Harley. I did trust Aleksander but not anymore. He is hiding something and I am over it,' I said in response while I also raised my voice at her.

Annie banged her fists on the table, which made Harley jump. 'No. You are not trusting Aleksander for another reason and you know it.'

I saw her frustration.

'What the fuck does that mean?' I snapped back at her as I leaned back in the chair and crossed my arms.

'You know exactly what that means.'

'No, please do explain, Annie. Enlighten me.'

'You won't let Aleksander in. You will refuse to trust him because you shut down whenever someone starts to cross that line. You did the same thing with Toby when you first met him. You prefer not to let people in and you do it to Harley and I as well. You just shut down. You have never changed, and it is not easy being your friend and you know it.'

'How DARE you talk about Toby? You have no right – you did not understand our relationship and you know I never let Toby in for another reason. You try being abused by nearly every male who entered your life. Screw you, Annie,' I said as I walked from the room.

I walked around the corner and broke down in tears. She knew that I found it hard to trust people, males in particular. I had been bounced around foster homes and abused in one way or another. I was always made to feel like it was my fault and it took a long time for me to come to terms with the fact that I didn't do anything wrong. I didn't trust Aleksander because I knew that he was hiding something and I just wanted him to tell me what was on his mind.

I slowly started to make my way out to the garden for some fresh air. I didn't struggle to walk this time; I think it was because I was so annoyed and pumped full of adrenaline. I reached the garden and found a concrete seat to sit on. I reached up and pulled my hair out. It was too tight and hurt my head. It fell out in its natural waves and I ran my fingers through it to smooth it out. The sun was out in the cloudy sky; it felt a little cold but the breeze was warm, which made it more comfortable. I just sat there and looked at the cherry blossom tree as it swayed in the distance. I was relaxed being out in the garden; so far, it was my second favourite place in this castle. I loved looking at the moss growing on the outside walls, in so many colours. White, green, black, some in bigger chunks and others just small spots. It gave the castle character. I would love to know how old it was and if this place co-existed on another plane with our world how has it not evolved, like we have?

I sat there and thought about what Annie said. Why did she keep coming back to Aleksander? Did she have feelings for him? Because she could have him. She could be so frustrating but then again, we were incredibly similar and that was the only reason we got into such heated arguments. I closed my eyes and just tried to relax. I was a quick-tempered person and especially when confronted in an awkward situation. I knew I would have to apologise to her but I expected one back as well. She stepped over the line with the trust issue remark. I walked back to the castle, through the garden and all of the colourful roses. As many colours as you could imagine. I loved the blue – they matched the blue in the cross that Aleksander gave me. I turned the round latch handle to get back into the castle. I lifted my dress slightly as I walked back up the stairs. I assumed that they were still in that room or they had returned to their chambers. I walked back to the room where we had our lessons with Yelena. They weren't there. I kept walking around the tower and headed towards the stairs that led to our chambers. I slowly walked up them; I was tired and hungry. I reached the top and knocked on Annie's door.

KNOCK, KNOCK, KNOCK.

I heard footsteps as she walked over to the door. She opened it with her grumpy face directed solely at me.

'So what's new?' She crossed her arms and waited.

'Yes, I am sorry. I lost my temper and it got heated too quickly. I am sorry – you just hit a nerve and you know not to bring that up.'

She put her arms around me and cried. 'I am sorry too. I don't know what came over me. I shouldn't have said what I said with your history. It was insensitive and over the top.'

I held her close. 'It is fine. I should have listened to you rather than losing my temper.'

She stood rather abruptly in the doorway as if she did not want to let me in.

'Can I come in and we can talk and strategise on how we are going to survive?'

She shifted uncomfortably. She scratched her head and looked like she wanted to speak but did not know the words.

'Oh, you're not alone, are you?' I asked and she nodded her head and grinned at me. 'I am... just... going this way. Have fun,' I said softly before I left her alone with Langford.

I walked down the corridor and noticed King Sebastian in my chamber doorway. He was wearing black leather pants with a cream long-sleeve top and a green and gold tunic over the top. His long hair was pulled back into a ponytail, which never flattered his nose. I noticed him speaking with Makenzie.

'I requested her presence today. Where is she at this moment?'

'I am unaware, Your Majesty. She should be back by now. She may be with one of her lady friends.'

Sebastian looked rather upset. I snuck up behind him.

'Are you looking for me, Your Majesty?'

He jumped and placed his hand on his chest as he spun to look at me. 'You gave me a fright, Faith. Did you forget about the time that we had planned for today?'

Makenzie closed the door with a smile. I looked at Sebastian and made it obvious when I eyed him up and down. I needed him to be besotted with me.

'How could I forget? I have been looking forward to it all day.' I fluttered my eyes at him and touched his arm.

Sebastian smiled and put his arm out for me to grab.

'I must warn you, Sebastian, I am still quite weak and you may need to take it slow with me,' I said before I grabbed his arm the way that Aleksander had taught me.

'Where are you taking me, Sebastian?' I asked as he had not spoken a word in five minutes. We seemed to be wandering around the castle with no clear room in sight.

'To my favourite place within the castle. I go here when I want some alone time,' he answered my question but did not look in my direction.

It was too silent and I had never liked the quiet. I started to bite my lips to pass the time between the no-talking and the mystery destination.

We finally stopped in front of an arched brass door. This was the only door in the castle thus far that was not made out of wood. You could tell this castle was old from the cracks in the stones and the moss that came through the windowsills. Whenever it was windy, you could hear the wind pushing its way through the cracks and making that irritating whistling sound – that always reminded me of horror movies. The door had no handle, had no lock and did not look like it actually opened. I peered up at Sebastian, confused on how we were going to get through this door. Sebastian looked back at me with a grin that bared all of his teeth. He removed his arm from mine and walked towards the door. He walked over to the stones beside the edge of the door and started to count to five from the bottom and three across before he pushed that stone beside it.

'It's a fake stone? That is awesome,' I said and walked closer to see what was in the hole in the wall.

He bent down; I did the same. I could see the solid gold

arched lever handle; there were no marks or imperfections on the handle. Sebastian put his hand up and turned the handle to the side. I could hear what sounded like gears turning behind the stones before the stone wall slid open to the side.

Sebastian gestured for me to walk in through the door. 'After you, milady.'

I walked in slowly, almost tripping over my feet. I lifted up my dress and noticed that my laces were undone on one of my boots.

'Oopsy daisy,' I said and began to bend down to tie up my laces.

Sebastian walked over.

'Allow me, Faith.' Sebastian bent down and looked at me in anticipation.

I lifted my dress slightly for him to be able to tie them back up. It was an awkward silence; when he had finished tying up my boot, he ran his hand up my leg and pulled my dress back down. I looked at him.

'That was inappropriate,' I said sternly.

He simply grinned in response and stood up. I thought men would be more respectful in this place but they seemed as inappropriate as back home. Any chance to perve on a girl.

I continued to slowly walk into the round room and looked up at the gold and marble dome roof. It was in a checker pattern with different black symbols in each box. They looked like a cross between Ancient Greek and Japanese symbols. There was only one window and it had glass; this confused me a little as all the other windows in the castle did not have any glass. It was dark wood timber flooring with what looked like a wolf's skin rug. There was only a desk and a chair in the centre of the room. There were about six different paintings spread evenly around the room.

One looked like his father King Samael; another was a painting of what looked like the cliff I was on a few days ago. They were all different landscapes: one desert, another a rainforest, mountain ranges and lastly a waterfall. I walked over to the rainforest and went to put my hand up to touch it. I felt Sebastian slide his hand into mine. I turned around and saw the painting of his father.

'You did not seem to care after your father passed.'

He sighed and sat in the chair.

'That painting used to be another one. I replaced it with my father. This is the room I come into to speak with him. You are correct; I have not been able to show my emotions. It shows weakness. I cannot be weak taking over a kingdom.' He put his head in his hands.

I felt sorry for him; it must have been hard to want to show emotions but knowing that if you did you would be portrayed as a weak person.

'There is nothing wrong with showing your emotions. I believe it makes you look stronger rather than weaker.'

'Hmmm,' was his only response as he did not make eye contact.

I decided to drop the matter.

'Are these paintings of different landscapes around here?' I said, making a circle with my finger in the air. I knew that hand gesture would be lost on him but hey, he was going to have to get used to it.

'Yes, they are of different regions around our world.'

I was surprised he understood my gesture. He walked over

and put his arm around my waist and with his other arm, gestured to the desert paintings.

'That is Kagarnt. It is a desolate land and the people are not always friendly. It is run by the Ladislas family.' He pointed to the waterfall. 'This one is from Ayrthian. The entire region is always covered in green; it is the most beautiful of all the regions. It is run by the Fitzhugh family.'

'I'm sorry, how did you pronounce that? Aertoan?'

He chuckled at my poor pronunciation of the word. 'No, Ayrthian. I am not saying it appropriately. The people in that region have a distinct way of speaking.'

'Right,' I said and pointed to the rainforest. 'Where is this one from?'

'Oh, the rainforest is from Nharabalu, another beautiful region. It is run by the Arundell family and this painting of the mountains is from Mourwest. It is run by the Bennett family. The last one is from Zilanta.'

'Does it snow on the mountains? They are a little bland in this photo.'

'Yes, it does.' He did not remove his hand but just stayed there standing close to me.

I did not feel comfortable with him but I did not want to move him away. I stepped away from him and walked towards the window to see if it opened in a way to create distance but to not offend.

'I see why you come here when you want to be alone. It is nice and peaceful here,' I said to him as I leaned against the wall beside the window with my hands placed gently in front of me.

'I have one more surprise for you,' he said and walked over

to grab my hand but before he could grab it, I walked past him and out the door.

I didn't want him to think I would be too easy.

Sebastian escorted me back to my chambers and it took me a while to figure out who was standing outside my chamber door. I ran towards him.

'Sonny,' I shouted.

He pulled back, rather afraid. I put my hand out to shake and he grabbed it.

'Pleasure to see you again, Faith. It is my belief that you now own me.'

Before I responded to him, I turned around and walked back to Sebastian and put my arms around his neck and gave him a hug.

'Thank you,' I said.

Sebastian lifted his arms and put them around me. 'My pleasure.'

I pulled away and walked back to Sonny.

'Come in, Sonny,' I said, opening my door.

I did not close the door but left it open ajar. Makenzie was in the room.

'Makenzie, Sonny. Sonny, Makenzie,' I introduced them to one another.

Sonny looked at me. 'I do not know why I am here?'

I was taken aback by this question. I thought he would have wanted to be away from his master and with someone who could give him the opportunity to have his own house and to bring his girl over. I stared at him blankly, unsure what to say in response.

'Makenzie, can you excuse us for a moment?'

'Of course.' She curtsied and walked from the room and

closed the door behind her.

I turned to look at Sonny.

'I thought you would want to be away from your master. He did not seem to treat you with the respect that you deserve. I asked for the king to appoint you my personal guard. I will ensure that you get paid and a have a room to sleep in and I will do everything in my power to bring your love here to be with you. I need someone I can trust and I trusted you from that first day. You helped me hide from the king and his men. I need someone who understands and who cannot be bought and who works out of the goodness of your heart.'

Sonny paced the room with his hand on his chin. He was speechless; I knew I was taking a big risk. I could sense from his eyes that he was someone I could trust and from how he helped to hide me when we ran into each other. I did make the assumption that he would want to be somewhere else and away from his master but who else could I use as my personal guard? Sonny still had his back to me when he started speaking.

'Will you promise to bring Stresina to me and my freedom?'

I walked over and grabbed both of his hands and looked at his face. 'I promise I will do everything within my power to do this for you. If you scratch my back, I will scratch yours,' I said but noticed that Sonny was confused.

'I do not need a scratch,' he responded with creases in his forehead.

I looked at him and just started laughing; I needed to remember that the people here did not always know what I was saying.

'It is an old saying where I come from.' I could not contain my laughter.

Sonny straightened himself and simply responded, 'I would be honoured to accept the position. Even if I have to live in the most corrupt town in Hisadalgon.'

'I'm sorry. Hisa what?'

Sonny looked at me, confused, as if I should know this information. 'Hisadalgon is what our country is called and it is split into seven different towns. We are currently in the capital where the king resides in Zilanta.'

I turned around and thought to myself, *Was everyone drunk when they named the towns in this place Hisadalgon? They speak English like we do but the names of their towns make absolutely no sense at all.*

Sonny and I continued talking about his role and how he would be given a weapon and I would organise some nice clothes for him. He was happy because he knew I would do everything I could to give him his freedom and I would treat him right. He would be fed every day and treated with the same respect that he gave me. Makenzie came back into the room and escorted Sonny to his new chambers. I went out of my room to organise to sit down with Annie and Harley; we needed to finish our conversation from earlier. How were we going to play this game?

I knocked on Harley's door. She did not answer straight away.

I said through the door, 'Do not make me open it and see something I do not want to see, please. We need to finish our discussion from earlier today.'

I heard a fumble in the room and Harley responded, 'Give me five minutes.'

'Fine,' I said and walked towards Annie's room and knocked on the door. I heard her walk towards the door. She opened it.

'Hey, what's up?' she asked.

'I wanted to finish that conversation we started earlier; we need to figure out how to play along with the game here.'

'Yes, right. Where did you want to talk?' Annie asked.

She did not seriously have company again, that little whore. Just kidding!

'I was hoping in your room because Harley is preoccupied at the moment,' I said as I held my hands together in front of me like I was praying she was going to say yes.

Annie opened the door. 'Come in.'

Oh, thank God. She did not have anyone in here. I was relieved; my face must have shown it.

'What, did you think I had company?' Annie asked.

I just looked at her and smiled.

'Not at all, you are a respectable young lady.'

Annie had been with the most people out of all of us. She was a year older than me and three years older than Harley. She had struggled to find what she called 'The One'; she had experimented with everything. I had always admired her strength and determination that even after every heartbreak and every time she had been hurt, she just kept going. She believed in true love and envied my relationship with Toby.

Annie sat down on the bed and picked up her book.

'Where did you get that from?' I wanted a book I hadn't read in a week.

'Langford gave it to me,' she said with a big smile on her face.

'Oh, receiving gifts already? Aren't you a lucky girl?' I said as I walked over to sit down on her bed.

She lowered her book slowly and peeked over it at me and just smiled. She looked really happy; it made me happy. I was never a person to judge someone on their decisions; whatever made them happy would make me happy.

'I haven't slept with him yet,' she said putting her book down and facing me.

'No? Good on you.' I didn't pressure her to talk and had always waited for her to talk about it to me.

'Yeah, I don't know how Harley jumped into it so quickly. I am being really hesitant and I am not sure why. I feel so comfortable around him and he makes me incredibly happy but I am just unsure about this place.'

I was worried about her saying this. 'Why are you unsure? Talk to me Annie, what are your reservations?'

She pushed her brown hair behind her ear. 'Are we honestly going to be here forever? As much as I love it here, I do not want to be here forever.'

This made me even more concerned. What the hell had made her so scared? What had happened?

'Annie, you love it here. What has made you so scared?' I asked, putting my hand on top of hers to make her feel as though I was there for her.

Harley walked into the room and interrupted our conversation. I knew Annie would shut down now. I would try and talk to her later.

'Hello, ladies,' Harley said with a big smile on her face.

'I thought Aleksander and I told you and Aidan to slow it down. People have noticed the closeness between the two of you. You had better hope you don't get yourself pregnant.' I glared at Harley, really unimpressed with her behaviour.

'I still have the rod implant in my arm.' She pointed towards her right arm.

'It only lasts for a couple of years, just remember that,' Annie mentioned from experience; she had one a few years ago before she had it removed. Annie changed the subject quickly.

'Anyway, moving on and onto more important topics. What is our game plan?'

Annie and Harley both looked at me.

'Don't look at me. I have no idea where to even start.'

We all sat silently staring at each other; none of us knew how we were going to survive this and where to start.

Annie piped up. 'Okay, we need to act like this is a game. We need to start with who we trust.'

Annie was right; before we could figure out how to survive, we needed to know who we could trust.

Harley responded with, 'Aidan and you guys.' Harley looked at me and waited for me to respond.

'Makenzie, Sonny and Dmitirov and of course you guys.'

Annie raised her eyebrows.

'I trust Aleksander and I am quite shocked you did not say it, Faith.'

'I know he is hiding something and until he tells one of us, I do not trust him,' I said back to Annie. She nodded her head and understood what I was saying and did not pursue the matter further, almost too suspiciously.

One of the things I hated was people who hid things from me. I preferred honesty, even if that honesty would hurt me in some way. I did not like people who kept things from me.

'One person we cannot trust for sure: Yelena.'

We all nodded our heads in agreement. Annie was taking control of the conversation today.

'We need to get the king on our side. One of us must have his affections so to speak. If we have some influence with him, we should be able to survive a little longer.'

'Yes, I agree but only to a certain point. From what we have all heard, the king is not the most liked man in the country. We need to be wary of that. What if he loses favour?' I said in response to what Annie had just said.

She looked at me, stumped for words.

'If what you are saying is true, we need to play both sides. That is even worse. How do you propose we do that?' I said to Annie. I was growing increasingly worried with each second.

'I already have the king's affections. He is a really genuine person but he was just raised the wrong way.'

Harley turned her head and looked at me. 'Are you falling for him?'

I looked at her and laughed. 'God, no. I just feel sorry for him and he is not unattractive. I would do anything for you guys and this is my sacrifice. But one of us needs to gain the affections of the lovely Miguel,' I said sarcastically, batting my eyelids. I would prefer the king to the snivelling Miguel.

'Faith is right. Miguel has changed alliances. He is now around Yelena all the time.' Harley nodded while she picked at her fingers; it was her nervous tic.

I looked at Annie and made eye contact and raised one eyebrow at her. She shook her head.

'Alright, fine but only because I cannot imagine corrupting Harley.'

Annie and I had always seen Harley as the innocent little sister and it had not changed in years and I did not think it would anytime soon. Even though she was spending most of her time having sex with Aidan.

'Alright, we need to play along with these lessons and try and understand as much information as we can about this place. I will keep playing along with the king and Annie will start working on Miguel.'

'What are the three of you ladies planning?' It was Aleksander behind us.

I turned around to look at him. He looked unimpressed, standing there with his arms crossed. I did not want to answer; I stood up.

'Makenzie is expecting me,' I said and walked out of the room. It was a lie but until he could tell me what he was hiding, I did not want to speak to him.

CHAPTER SIXTEEN

Annie

I watched Faith walk out of the room. She had been through so much in her life and if someone broke her trust it was so hard for her to trust that person again. Yes, we had our arguments but I had never broken her trust and I would always do whatever I could to protect her and help her find her happy ending. I wished I could tell her that she could stop sacrificing herself for Harley and I and just focus on herself for once in her life. She was the type of person who deserved happiness and after every obstacle, she never stopped believing that she would find it in the end. She knew she had no choice in keeping King Sebastian's affections. I looked at Aleksander; it was quite obvious that he was attracted to her as he watched her walk out of the room. The way he looked at her was how I wanted someone to look at me. Langford was sweet but I was not sure if he was the man for me.

'Aleksander, to what do we owe the pleasure of your company?' I asked while sitting on the bed.

I realised that he would be able to look straight up my dress and quickly pulled it down. Harley stood up and left the room. She was probably going back to her room or going to find Aidan. Faith was right; she was being irresponsible. It was unlike her. Aleksander took a couple of steps towards me.

'I am of the assumption that we are acquaintances,' he said rather uncomfortably. I wondered what was bothering him.

'Yeah, I consider you to be a friend. I trust you, Aleksander. What is the matter?' I stood up and walked over to him.

'I must confide some information to you.'

I wondered if this was what Faith was talking about. Why would he tell me if that was the case?

'You have heard the tales of the Bouchard family. There have always been whispers that one of the Bouchards survived. Since Faith has returned, the whispers have started again. The Bouchards were one of the founding families and were always known for their olive skin and now their blue eyes from the queen. I asked Makenzie this question but she did not know the answer. I shall ask you the same question. Does Faith have a scar on her left shoulder?' He paced the room, waiting for me to respond.

I was dumbfounded; I stood there with my mouth open. I knew the answer to the question but I was too afraid to say it out loud. Aleksander started running his hands through his hair; he was becoming impatient.

'I... um... I... oh God, why is this so hard to say?' I said as I walked to the window to look out. I took a breath and turned to look at Aleksander. His face looked like how I was feeling inside. Sick and worried because once I said the answer, I knew everything would change.

'Yes, it looks like a demented star. I always tell her it reminds me of her demented personality. She never knew how she got it but has had it as long as she can remember.'

Aleksander let out a big breath and fell to his knees. I walked over and put my hand out to help him up. He grabbed it.

'This changes everything. She must be protected; Crystal Bouchard must be protected.' Aleksander turned to walk out of the room.

'You cannot do that. We have to tell her. She deserves to know the truth. She walked out of here because she knows you are hiding something. I cannot hide this from her.'

Aleksander walked back over. 'You CANNOT tell her. She does not remember anything and it is better to keep it that way. A spell sent her away and I believe it removed her memories.'

The serious nature of this was written on his face.

'Faith is Crystal but she does not remember anything. Aleksander, I can't hide information from her. She is like my sister,' I begged him.

He turned and looked at me. 'Promise me, not yet. When the time is right.'

I agreed and nodded my head. I had just asked my best friend who was technically the rightful heir to the throne to seduce the king, who wanted her anyway. We were not going to win this game.

CHAPTER SEVENTEEN

Faith

KNOCK, KNOCK.

Makenzie walked over to the door. It was the messenger.

'The king has asked me to inform the ladies that dinner is served.'

I rolled my eyes and lay back on the bed. Makenzie nodded and closed the door.

'Faith, that is not the way a lady should act. If you are going to make the king fall for you, you must act appropriately.'

I pulled a face at her. While I turned around, I heard her chuckle. I was grateful that I told her about our plan; she had her own insight into the king and explained more on how her world worked. I sat up and walked over to the mirror as I fluffed my hair before heading to the door.

'Wait.' She grabbed the bracelet the king had given me.

'You must always wear this in his presence. It will show that you respect him.'

I nodded and held out my wrist for her. She pushed the clasps together and straightened it before I walked down the stairs. I saw Annie in front of me.

'Annie,' I shouted to her.

She ignored me or maybe she was in her own world. I knew this was not ladylike and decided against yelling louder.

Harley caught up to me.

'Hey, Harley. I wish you would take my advice seriously,' I said to her.

Harley glanced at me. 'I am but it is hard. Have you ever felt an intense connection to someone and found it hard to be apart from them?'

I nodded to her. 'Yes, I did with Toby but the difference here is nobody would try and kill us for sleeping with the wrong person. We must be vigilant.' I wanted her to understand the warning.

'I know. I am just finding it difficult.'

I put my arm around her and pulled her close and before letting her go, I gave her a kiss on the head. I loved her and I would always protect her; she was my little sister. We arrived at the arched doorway and Annie was already waiting. Harley snuck up behind her to scare her but before she could...

'Harley, do not even think about it,' Annie warned.

'Since when do you have eyes in the back of your head?' Harley chuckled.

'Since I have known you.' She smiled back. Annie walked over and grabbed my hand. 'I am beginning to have doubts. Maybe it is not the best idea for you to befriend the king.'

I looked at her, confused, and asked her, 'Why the sudden change of heart?'

She pulled back. 'I just don't want you to push yourself to do something you may not be ready to do.'

I could see the care in her eyes but I could also see something else but wasn't sure what it was exactly.

The doors opened; Annie and Harley walked in before me. I sat down next to the king. Harley started speaking with Yelena while I turned my attention to Sebastian. The night ran smoothly; Sebastian and I talked and I laughed at his ridiculous jokes. Only a few evil glares from Yelena but Harley kept her entertained most of the night.

'Faith, would you mind staying a little longer?' Sebastian asked, placing his hand on mine.

'Of course, Your Majesty.' I bowed my head at him.

Yelena, Annie and Harley all got up. I heard Annie start to speak while walking out the door.

'Hello, Miguel. My, don't you look handsome today?'

I smiled to myself. It was a horrible line but for a person like Miguel, it would easily work. I turned my attention back towards Sebastian. I was intrigued to discover what he wanted to talk to me about. I didn't think I had done anything wrong. Sebastian got up from his chair.

'Your Majesty, what is the matter?' I asked him. I was worried about what was going on.

'I have asked you to remove the formalities when we are alone,' Sebastian said as he looked me over. 'Tomorrow, you have lessons with a scholar to teach you the ways of our world before I allow you to leave and visit the local orphanage. Not without extra guards, I would recommend Miguel—'

I cut him off; there was no way I would allow Miguel as a guard. I didn't trust that he wouldn't wander off. I stood up from my chair to look at Sebastian.

'Excuse the interruption but I would prefer not to have Miguel as an extra guard. May I recommend Aleksander? I understand that you do not like him but he has done a good job of protecting me so far and is in your service.'

Sebastian rubbed his chin, pondering my suggestion. I knew in order for him to consider my decision I would need to use my charm. I started walking towards him. I put one hand on his chest and looked up into his face.

'I mean, I would prefer if you would come with me but I understand that you are a busy king, so I can settle for the second-best man for the job: Aleksander. Miguel is not very talented with a sword and I just want to be safe for you and ease your stress.'

He looked down at me. His breathing increased and he started to move his face towards mine. I stepped back and turned around before he could do anything else. What was that old saying? Treat them mean, keep them keen. It was not always the best move but I was not ready to commit to another person, even if I felt a little spark between us. Sebastian sighed.

'Yes, I enjoy your honesty. Aleksander is the best choice. I will not see you tomorrow – may I call on you in the evening?' he asked and looked like a lost puppy.

'As you wish, my king. Enjoy the rest of your evening,' I said as I curtsied and walked out of the room.

I walked with haste to Aleksander's room to let him know that he would be busy in the afternoon and stuck with me. I knew he could only handle my annoying personality in small doses. I enjoyed annoying him; it was a form of entertainment for me. I reached Aleksander's door and straightened my dress and hair before knocking on the door.

KNOCK, KNOCK.

I heard Aleksander say something on the other side of the

door but I couldn't tell. I turned the door handle and walked into the room.

'Aleksander, the king requires you to... HOLY SHIT.'

I finally looked up and saw Aleksander; he was standing in his tub naked. His face was stunned and I just couldn't stop looking at his incredibly sexy body, the irresistible 'v' down to his large package. He was statuesque. I hadn't seen many in my life but I had not seen one quite that perfect. I couldn't help but stare; he was so ruggedly handsome and Aleksander had to interrupt while my mind was racing and I couldn't stop looking at him.

'FAITH,' he said loudly.

'Shit, right, sorry.' I turned and walked out of the room. 'Let me know when you're dressed.' I closed the door behind me.

Oh my God. I was trying to remove that image from my head but it was rather difficult. He was like fresh meat on a beach that you just could not take your eyes off. I was leaning against the door when Aleksander opened it. I fell backwards and hit my head on the ground.

'Ow,' I said opening my eyes and looking up at Aleksander.

He was smiling and wearing different clothes than usual; they were more laid back and he seemed more relaxed than his usual uptight attitude.

'That was not funny, it bloody hurt,' I said as he pushed his black hair off his face and offered his hand to help me up. I rubbed the back of my head.

He started to laugh; he had a beautiful smile. I smiled back at him and playfully hit him on the shoulder.

'Ha ha, this was all your fault. Stop smiling,' I said, getting annoyed.

He put his hand on his stomach and stopped laughing quickly. 'How may I assist you, Faith?' he asked.

I couldn't help but look down at his package. I blushed before clearing my throat.

'Yes, the king would like you to guard me while I go to the local orphanage because my new guard, Sonny, is a little new and not quite as trained and skilled as you in some areas,' I said, thinking about his package again. I needed to get my mind out of the gutter. I walked away so I wasn't standing face-to-face with him.

'Yes, it would be my pleasure, Faith. I will speak with Sonny tomorrow,' Aleksander said, walking around to try and face me.

'Yep, thank you. Bye,' I said and couldn't walk out of that room fast enough.

I began to walk back to my chambers when Makenzie ran into me. 'Where have you been?' she said as she grabbed my hand and dragged me back to my room.

'Ouch, you are hurting me. Makenzie, what is the matter?'

We got in the room and she closed the door behind me. She stood in front of me and looked me up and down.

'Why are you flustered?'

'No reason.' I avoided eye contact and walked over to my mirror to take my jewellery off.

I could see her standing behind me in the reflection; she had her arms crossed and was tapping her foot on the floor. I knew she was waiting for me to respond but I was ignoring her and trying to remove the image from my head, even if it was a desirable one. I closed my eyes and sighed.

'I had an awkward encounter with Aleksander and I saw him naked.'

Makenzie walked over and sat on her knees beside me.

'You did not give him your precious gift, did you?'

I threw my head back in laughter; it took me a couple of minutes to contain myself again. 'Makenzie, my precious gift has been gone for a while but thank you for caring. I am not the type of person to be intimate with someone I barely know.'

She nodded her head and started undoing my dress.

'Why did you need to find me so badly?' I asked her.

'I was getting worried that you were still alone with the king.'

'Oh, you care about me. That is so cute,' I said as I touched my chest in a heartfelt gesture.

I lifted Toby onto the bed and pulled the cover over me. Makenzie left the room. Toby walked around in a circle continuously until finally sitting down. I rolled over and blew out the candles. The fireplace was still lit and left the room nice and snug.

I must have slept in. Makenzie was shaking me on the bed to wake me up. 'Faith, Faith.'

I swiped my arms at her to make her stop. I opened my eyes. 'What?' I said while I yawned.

'You are late. You have missed breakfast and your scholar is waiting on you.'

I jumped up quickly and ran over to the bowl to wash my face quickly and started to brush my hair while Makenzie was organising clothes for me to wear today. Toby hadn't moved on my bed; he was still snuggled up in a little ball. I picked up a pair of earrings and Makenzie smacked them out of my hand and picked up another set. They were golden drop earrings with red rubies; they were plain and simple but elegant. I picked up Aleksander's cross and put it on. I grabbed a golden clip and pulled my hair back on both sides before putting it where the hair gathered at the back. She opened the dress in order for me to step into it. I pulled it up; it was a simple dress, no elegance to it. I pulled it onto my shoulders and tied the string near my breasts. I pulled it down slightly to make it sit properly. Makenzie placed the black boots on the floor near the bed. I sat down and she helped me put them on. I looked in the mirror quickly; the red dress looked fantastic against my tanned skin. She quickly fluffed my hair before opening the door.

'Good morning, Sonny. How was your sleep?' I asked as he escorted me to the room where I would be hopefully educated about this land.

'It was peaceful. You look lovely, milady,' Sonny said.

'Please, call me Faith. We are on the same level and I do not want formalities.'

Sonny nodded his head in agreement.

'Do you need my assistance inside the room?' Sonny asked.

'No, please go enjoy yourself. I will see you in the afternoon,' I said as I closed the door and turned around.

Annie and Harley were already sitting down. They were laughing over some gossip. I walked between them and bent down.

'What did I miss?' I asked, looking from side to side at them. Harley was chuckling under her breath.

'I will tell you later, I promise,' Annie said and nodded to the man standing at the front of the room.

'Good morrow, fair lady. If you would please take a seat.' He gestured towards a spare chair at the front of the classroom.

He was an elderly man, possibly in his sixties. His grey hair was turning white and he had a receding hairline. He had a massive scar on the right side of his chin and down his neck. He had deep wrinkles on his forehead and eyes. He was not aging well and needed to lean on objects in order to stand up straight. He was wearing a black tunic that went all the way to the floor, with only a belt around his big stomach, which looked like he had enjoyed way too much food and drink in his lifetime. He leaned against the desk at the front of the room and started talking. I was a teacher by trade and listening to this man talk was making me want to fall asleep. I knew the king wanted us to know his world but couldn't he at least find someone who would not put me to sleep?

My stomach was starting to grumble; not the best idea missing breakfast. I wondered why I slept in. I saw a bird out the window; it was a beautiful green and red and was tweeting in the window. The man walked in front of my desk and stopped.

'Milady,' he said sternly.

I had a tendency to get distracted easily. It wasn't the best trait for a teacher but it made for some interesting lessons sometimes.

'Yes, um, sir?' I hadn't even heard his name. Served me right for getting distracted.

I shuffled to make sure I was sitting in the chair with my back straight and started listening. Their world was measured differently to ours. Instead of it being year two-thousand-and-something, it was the first year of King Sebastian Nikolav Faulcon. It had previously been the twenty-first year of King Samael Sebastian Faulcon. There was no way to tell how old this place was unless you were to literally sit down and count the numerous ruling kings. They still had seven days in a week and twelve months in a year but were a little lost on how many hours were in a day. Annie piped up.

'Wow, you are so intelligent. I mean, it is really hard to know how many hours are in a day. I have always guessed twenty-four – it just seems like a good number.' She had a huge smile on her face. Harley and I choked down a laugh.

'That is preposterous. It would never be such a large number.' The man looked outraged.

I turned to Harley. 'Oi, what is his name?' I asked and she shrugged her shoulders. He had his back to us at the moment. I quickly turned around and asked Annie the same question.

'How the hell should I know?' she responded.

I put my hand up; I felt like a teenager sitting in a classroom again. The man turned around and nodded his head at me. I opened my mouth to speak but before I could say anything...

'You do not have permission to speak.'

I closed my mouth instantly. What a little butthead. I turned to Harley and even she was taken aback. I ignored what he said and asked the question anyway.

'Sorry but I have no idea what your name is and I did not want to be rude.' I may have spoken a little rudely but seriously, I just wanted to know his name; otherwise, I would have spent the entire session making up names for him. Bobby, Richard, Neil, Neville and so many other dorky names.

'My apologies, fair lady. My name is Farak Jwanak.' He bowed his head and placed his hand on his chest.

'It is a pleasure to meet you,' I said while secretly thinking what a mouthful of a name that was.

'There are seven days in a week and they are Murkdae, Terndae, Wurjidae, Thaffdae, Frashdae, Sawlodae, Zondae.'

Before I could even think about what I was about to say, I blurted out, 'What the fuck?'

I quickly covered my mouth in disbelief. Farak looked furious before he opened his mouth to scold me.

'My deepest apologies, Farak. I am just a bit shocked because your days just do not sound normal to me. I mean, back home we have Monday, Tuesday, Wednesday and I won't go through them all but you speak English but your days are not English-sounding. I am just lost on the translation and how this is all working.' I spoke so fast I didn't think anyone could comprehend what I just said.

'Repeat after me,' was all he said in response to my fast talking.

'Murrrckdaee.' He was spelling them out as if we were slow.

Annie, Harley and I all repeated, 'Murkdae.'

'Terrnndaee.'

'Terndae.'

'Wurijeedaee.'

'Wurjidae.'

'Thrafffdaee.'

'Thaffdae.' I was beginning to feel like I was in prep again.

'Frasshhhdaee.'

'Frashdae.'

'Sawloaddaee.'

'Sawlodae.'

'Zunndaee.'

'Zondae.'

Farak clapped his hands after that. I felt like my IQ had just dropped ten points. They must have spoken a different language back in their however many years of living and converted to English but even then, how had they learnt English? They all spoke with soft accents but nothing heavily European, Asian, African or American. Where was this place located on a world map?

Farak went on to explain that the twelve months in a year were represented by each of the twelve founding families. I raised my hand immediately.

'Begging your pardon, Farak, but it is my understanding that there are only seven founding families: Faulcon, Arundel, Fitzhugh, Somneri, Bennett, Ladislas and the Bouchard family.'

I looked at him quizzically. He sat down in the chair at the front of the room.

'And the Marchés family.'

Annie, Harley and I all looked at each other. Aleksander's family was one of the founding families? He had never mentioned that. We knew he had a title but never assumed he was that important in the hierarchy.

'The remaining four families were wiped out from centuries of in-fighting. The Bouchard family brought peace but...' Farak just stopped talking suddenly and changed the subject.

Annie interjected. 'Wait, wait go back. What happened with the Bouchards? We had never found out. We knew the entire family was slaughtered but had never found out the real reason.'

'It is not something to be discussed.'

Annie pushed him. 'No, I believe this is your history and we should know as much as possible.'

She was giving him the stare down and when Annie wanted to know something, she never gave up until she found out.

Farak stuttered. He walked over to the door. He opened it and peered out before closing it again and walking over to the three of us. He looked petrified; he started speaking in hushed tones.

'There have been many whispers over the years but the loudest whisper has always been that the Bouchard family were in the process of finding their youngest child a husband. It was between the Marchés and Faulcon families. It is believed that the Bouchards chose the Marchés, which was an insult to the Faulcons who helped the Bouchards rise to power. Yelena Faulcon gathered support from the Somneri family to take back power from the Bouchards. Instead of removing them from power, the entire family was slaughtered.'

I needed to pick my jaw up from the ground; an entire family was wiped out because they did not pick their son for marriage. Annie asked a further question.

'Are you saying that if it was not for Yelena, the Bouchards would still be alive?'

Farak nodded his head in agreement. If she organised it all to take power, why did Samael banish his wife? Farak didn't tell us all of the months; he was flustered after telling us that story.

Farak continued on with the lesson; I started paying close attention. There were so many mysteries surrounding this land. We would need a pinboard and some string to decipher them all. Farak spoke of the religion surrounding the land; they worshipped five gods. All of the gods ruled over different areas. Sea, land, sky, underworld and the people. I didn't catch the names of the gods because of the complexity of the pronunciation. They worshipped the gods once a month and had a feast and a ritual sacrifice once a year to celebrate their birth. He spoke of the greatest leaders of all time and how they changed the world under their reign. He spoke of King Arthur

Bouchard, the man who stopped the war that spanned over three hundred years and instilled peace in Hisadalgon and helped to rebuild all of the nations under it. Five generations of Bouchards ruled before the Faulcons wiped them out.

I was so thirsty and glad for the lesson to be over. I walked over to Farak and thanked him with kisses on both of his cheeks. He smiled.

'It is a pleasure to meet you, Faith, Annie and Harley. I look forward to more moments together.'

We all walked out of the room. I could not see Sonny anywhere. I did tell him to venture off and didn't quite give him a definitive time to be back. We walked back to Annie's room and all sat on the bed.

'You are quite plain today, Faith,' Harley said to me.

'I know, I prefer it compared to the other dresses. They are just too formal. I would love to put on a pair of shorts and a singlet top.' I looked down at the dress; it was one of my favourites. Annie put her hand up and looked at my earrings.

'These are gorgeous, where did you get them?' she asked and I blushed.

'Um, Sebastian gave me a whole bunch of jewellery. Did he not give you any?'

Both Annie and Harley shook their heads. Well, this was awkward. I scratched my head.

'Anyway, how did we find the lessons?'

'No, no, no, no, go back.' Annie shook her hands in a gesture to go back to the jewellery.

'Yeah, I am with Annie,' Harley said. They were not happy.

'Come on then,' I said as I stood up and walked towards the door and headed to my room to show them my jewellery.

CHAPTER EIGHTEEN

Aleksander

I approached Faith's chambers; her new guard was standing outside the door. He stood in front of me and stared at me.

'Begging your pardon,' I said as I pointed towards the door. He was not moving. 'I am not a patient man. I will not ask again. I have a meeting with Faith,' I repeated again.

He did not speak but stared at me.

'Are you a mute?' I asked.

He shook his head. I was not in the mood for stupidness and turned to walk away before realising I was being rude and had not introduced myself. I walked back.

'My name is Aleksander Marchés. I am one of the king's men and have been tasked with escorting Faith into the village. Who am I speaking with?' I said and gave a little bow to the man. He was frightfully tall and I felt incredibly small next to the giant. The man bowed.

'Pleasure to make your acquaintance, my lord. I am Sonny, the new personal guard to Faith. It is my belief that I am to assist in escorting you to the village. It will be a part of my training and I look forward to learning from a man of your reputation,' Sonny said. He was a polite man and seemed incredibly gentle. It was difficult for me to understand why Faith picked him. I had no knowledge of where they had even met.

After we exchanged pleasantries, Sonny turned and knocked on the door. I heard her sweet voice through the door.

'Come in.'

I nodded towards Sonny as he opened the door and walked into Faith's chambers. She was giggling with Annie and Harley. They were playing around with her jewellery. I looked at the vast array of jewellery – where had she gathered all of it from? Annie walked over.

'King Sebastian is being unfair and spoiling Faith over Harley and myself. Are we not enchanting enough?' she asked, batting her eyes at me.

I smirked. 'Yes, it is my understanding that he prefers her affections over others', but I do believe that you have some acquaintances of mine rather fond of you ladies.'

Annie smiled and walked away. Langford spoke to me about Annie and he was besotted with her.

Faith turned and smiled at me.

'One moment, my lord.' She checked her face in the mirror and fixed her hair clip before walking over. 'I am ready when you are. Do I get to carry a weapon?' she asked.

I ignored her request and turned to walk out of the room. She was obviously in her childish frame of mind and I would need to ignore her to protect her to the best of my ability. She grabbed my arm from behind. I turned and looked at her.

'Are you walking off without me?'

I shrugged my arm away from her and looked into her face.

'I am your protection. I will not be your male escort to a function.'

She smiled and held back a giggle. Annie and Harley were laughing behind her.

'What did I say?'

She shook her head.

'A male escort in my time would translate more or less to a whore. Someone who sleeps with people for money. I am sorry, we occasionally have dirty and immature minds.' She turned and glared at Annie and Harley.

I shook my head and pondered what she had just said. What type of land did she come from? Where a male is paid and not a female?

She moved her body forward and back and clapped her hands in front of her. 'So?'

Sonny opened his mouth to speak. I talked over him before he could talk.

'Sonny, you will walk at the front and look out for dangers and I will walk beside Faith and watch for dangers behind her. I do not believe we will encounter any but it is better to be safe than to risk any accidents in the future.'

Sonny nodded and started to walk off down the hall. Faith walked past me and after Sonny but quickly turned.

'Have fun and take whatever you want. Just not the bracelet that I mentioned... Also, spend some time with your men. At least two out of the three of us have found someone to make us smile.' She looked to Annie and Harley and ran off down the hall after Sonny with Toby following behind her.

'A lady does not run,' I said, quickening my pace to catch up with her. She stopped suddenly and called out to Sonny.

'I would like to tell the king I am leaving the castle,' she said as she portrayed a ladylike attitude.

'Why?' I asked suddenly, not even thinking before I spoke. She turned and looked at me, confused.

'Because it is the right thing to do. If you generally show someone respect, they show it back.'

I nodded and just agreed with her because I was aware that she would easily win this argument. I had to learn when to pick my battles with her. She was incredibly stubborn.

I escorted her to the king's chambers and watched her knock on the door.

'Faith, it is a pleasure to see your face on this beautiful day.'

I wanted to heave; he was a false person.

'Your Majesty, I just wanted to let you know that I will be out of the castle for a few hours as planned with Sonny and Aleksander. In case you wanted to spend some time with me this afternoon but could not find me.' She was using a different tone while speaking with him.

'I will look forward to seeing your face at dinner,' King Sebastian responded.

'As will I, Your Majesty,' she said as she leaned in and gave him a kiss on the cheek.

The king blushed and she turned and had a manipulative look on her face.

We started walking through the village on the cobblestones. She was not lifting her dress to keep it from getting ruined; it was odd for a female to not care about her attire.

'Faith, may I ask you a question?'

'Technically, you already have,' she said with a big smile on her face.

I was constantly checking the surroundings and making

sure that we were not being followed. I looked at her.

'Do you have affections for the king?' I asked her timidly.

She laughed. 'Why in heaven's name would you ask that question?'

'You showed him affection back at the castle.'

She stopped and looked at me. 'Aleksander, I do not have affections for him. It is complicated but Annie, Harley and I discussed how best to survive and they have already found men. He seems to be taken by me and we are using that to our advantage. We do not feel safe and are trying to find our footing.'

I grabbed her hands. 'That is a dangerous path.'

She pulled her hands away. 'I am a big girl and I can take care of myself. Are you worried or jealous?' she asked me, crossing her arms over her chest and exposing her breasts.

I avoided eye contact.

'I am not jealous; I am worried that you are not aware of the game you are playing,' I pleaded with her to understand.

'If you were honest with me about some things, I would possibly trust you more and listen to what you are saying now. But I do not like people who keep things from me.' She turned and continued to walk down the cobblestone path.

She caught up to Sonny. I was not jealous. I was just worried about her safety and did not want to see her get hurt. I stayed behind and let Sonny take the lead. I thought it was appropriate to allow Faith some space to herself after our confrontation. She was smiling and laughing while speaking with Sonny. I hastened my pace to catch up and attempt to overhear their discussion. We arrived at the orphanage; she stopped at the front and looked at the door. I saw a tear run down her face. Sonny handed her a handkerchief; she accepted it and dried her eyes. I touched her arm.

'It just brings back memories of my birth parents leaving me out the front of an orphanage with no note to help me find them in the future. Was I that horrible?' Her tears flowed more rapidly. She shook her head and wiped her face and walked in the door. Faith and Toby walked in unison.

'I will stand guard at the entrance. You can watch her inside and we will swap later,' I said to Sonny and he nodded and walked in after Faith.

I checked the perimeter constantly. I was not worried about a threat but I just wanted her to be safe and could not bear the thought of her being injured. The sun was starting to descend in the sky; it was time to return to the castle. I walked into the orphanage and saw Faith sitting on the ground with children sitting around her. I was enthralled with watching her. Her smile was spread across her whole face and her laugh was so enchanting. The children were hypnotised by her. I could not take my eyes off of her; she was angelic.

'Oh, look who walked in. The legendary Aleksander Marchés. Shall we challenge him to a duel?'

All the children jumped up and ran up to me. 'Please, Lord Marchés.'

I looked at Faith disapprovingly; she just returned with a cheeky smile.

'If I must,' I said to the children. Who could turn down their adorable faces?

Faith walked over to Sonny and asked for his sword.

'I do not believe you are wearing appropriate attire for a duel, milady.' I bowed to her.

She smiled and walked over to grab the dagger out of my belt. She bent down and cut into her dress all the way to her knee on both sides.

'Are you worried or scared that I may actually beat you?' she said, winking at me.

I laughed. 'I am trembling.'

Sonny cleared an appropriate space for us.

'Ready when you are, my lord.'

I knew I would have to go easy on her; she was quite clumsy during the lessons. She swung her sword at me up high. I blocked up; she spun around and swiped down low.

'Who has been training you?' I was worried; she was not holding back.

She was spinning around and ducking. Where had this talent come from? She spun around; I put my arm out to grab her and pulled her in close and put the sword up to her throat.

'I believe this means I win.' She stomped on my foot and turned around and put her sword up to my throat. I dropped my sword and allowed her to win this round.

The children ran out and surrounded her. She smiled and put her hand up for the children to smack it. I would have to ask her about that later. A little girl with red hair walked over.

'Disgraceful,' she said and walked off.

She did not realise that I was holding back because I could not harm her. One of the children handed her flowers. She smiled and put her arm around them.

'Faith, we need to head back to the castle,' I whispered into her ear.

'Of course.' She nodded towards me and turned to the children.

'Alright, thank you for spending the afternoon with me but I best be off towards my home. I will come and see you soon, I promise.'

All of the children moaned at her and she pulled an unhappy face.

'Sorry.' I pulled her out of the crowd.

Sonny requested to be at the back with Faith and for me to guard the front.

'No, you will learn more at the front,' I said sternly. Sonny walked off.

'Meeeeooowww, hissssssss,' she said and moved her hand like she was going to scratch me.

'What was that?'

She laughed at my question. 'You were being feisty like a cat so I imitated a cat.'

I looked at her, confused. 'Do not repeat that action.'

'Why?' she teased.

I avoided looking at her because I knew she was going to be doing something silly. She got in front of me and started walking backwards. She was licking her hand and rubbing it over her shiny brown hair and meowing in between each lick.

'Oh, would you desist?'

She laughed at me and tripped over her feet. I lunged forward and wrapped my arm around her waist and pulled her against my body. I almost dropped her but bent my leg and put my other arm around her and took her full weight. Sonny noticed and ran over to assist me. He stood behind Faith and put his hands underneath her back. She wrapped her arms around my neck as I slowly started to pull her up.

We were standing upright and I noticed her eyes were closed.

I removed one hand from her back and brushed her hair out of her face. She opened her eyes; I could stare into her blue eyes all day. I felt her move backwards and I removed my arm.

'Thank you. I will make sure that I watch where I am walking in the future.' She continued toward the castle.

'I believe that for every time I save you, I should receive a present in return.'

She turned and smiled. 'Who are you and what have you done to Aleksander? He is never this cheeky.' She poked me in the stomach.

'I would like to request an opportunity from you,' I suggested to her. I wanted to spend more time with her and to understand her world. She nodded her head and waited for me to respond.

'I seek to spend more time with you, if possible, at the end of your day and we can converse and observe the stars and I would like to understand your world.' I stuttered and scrambled my words together.

She pushed a loose strand of hair behind her ear and smiled.

'I would love to because you could help me understand your world and all of this because the lessons with Farak are rather boring.'

That was odd that Sebastian chose Farak to educate the ladies; his father disliked him for his views.

I walked Faith to her chambers and kissed her hand.

'I look forward to tonight. I will be waiting when the moon is high in the sky.'

She walked into the room. Sonny gave me a disapproving look.

'Thank you for your assistance today. I have training at first light and you are welcome to join to improve your skills.'

I walked away and was excited to speak with Faith later that night. I walked back towards my chambers and Miguel was waiting at my door.

'Good evening, Miguel.'

'King Sebastian has requested your presence,' Miguel said and walked away.

I had not done anything untoward today from memory. I followed Miguel to Sebastian's chambers. Miguel opened the door. Sebastian was sitting in his chair by the fireplace. This was the first time I had been invited into his chambers. He was in his night robes and stood up as soon as he saw me.

'Aleksander, I heard some disturbing news of the venture into town with Faith.' Sebastian crossed his arms and was fuming at me. He just kept looking at me as if waiting for me to respond.

I looked at him.

'Are you not going to admit your fault?' Sebastian yelled at me.

'I am unaware of any faults,' I responded, trying to remember the events of the day. Sebastian lowered his voice but I could hear the anger in his tone.

'You became entangled with Faith and shared a moment of passion. I thought I had been clear in my intentions with her. She is mine and this action is punishable by death—'

I put my hand up to silence Sebastian. 'Before you continue, my king, I would like to clarify this fault. Faith stumbled over her own feet and I had to wrap my arm around her waist in an inappropriate manner to stop her from hurting herself. There was no moment of passion. She is a beautiful lady but I find her to be abrupt and abrasive and her language is disgraceful for a lady.' I was frustrated at the connotations of this conversation.

Sebastian was taken aback at the bluntness of my voice.

'My apologies, Aleksander. I know we have bad blood between us and I should not have assumed.' Sebastian was apologetic and sat back down on the chair next to the fireplace and motioned for me to sit in the chair opposite him.

Sebastian stood up from the chair and poured himself a glass of wine before pouring and handing me a glass and sitting back down.

'I am finding it difficult to run a kingdom. There is more turmoil in Hisadalgon than my father ever informed me. Several of the founding families would like to see the Faulcons fall and I feel that with Faith by my side, her spark will warm the other families' hearts. Are you truthful in your feelings?'

I nodded my head. 'Yes, I prefer my women to not have so much fight.'

Sebastian chuckled. 'As do I but I believe with the lessons, she will understand her place.'

This was the first time Sebastian and I had had a candid conversation. I doubted that Faith would ever be the type of woman to sit quietly in a corner and supply the king with children. She was too independent and outspoken.

'Have you discovered any information about Faith, as you were tasked with earlier?' Sebastian asked. Sebastian wanted to know the truth behind Faith's parentage. I did not want to answer. I felt as if I was betraying Faith.

'No, I have found no new information. I have discovered that she is unaware of her parentage. The only similarity between Crystal and Faith is their blue eyes. I am still endeavouring to discover more information.'

'Yes, those eyes are hypnotising. Keep at your task. Can you tell me what her likes are? I feel that she does not find me sustainable enough for her affections. She warms my heart.' Sebastian looked at his cup and swirled the wine inside. I had never seen him this vulnerable before.

'I cannot say for sure, my king, but you did receive some affection from her earlier.'

Sebastian blushed and smiled. 'Yes, I did indeed.'

I finished my wine and got up to leave before turning around. 'She will not be easy to win over, my king, but she enjoys the smaller things in life. Take her to the water and walk together. Do not buy her with gifts.'

Sebastian nodded and I left the room.

I walked back to my chambers and I pondered the discussion with Sebastian. He had affections for Faith; I was not sure if that was good or bad. I may have misjudged Sebastian. He may be nothing like his father and may genuinely care for the kingdom and for Faith. I had my reservations and I would always protect her at all costs. I walked into my chambers and saw Annie sitting on my bed. It was not appropriate for a lady to be waiting in a man's chambers.

'What do you believe you are doing? You cannot walk into my chambers and not expect whispers that will damage your reputation.'

Annie did not seem fazed. She stood up and walked over.

'I cannot keep this secret from Faith. She deserves to know the truth – she cannot remember anything from when she was a little girl and she has felt like her family abandoned her. She should know that is not the case; they were murdered. They sent her off to another place to save her life,' Annie pleaded with me.

I understood what she was saying but I was not ready to tell her. 'Annie, I understand that I have placed you in a predicament but I beg of you, not at this moment. I believe, in time, she will remember.'

Annie went to open her mouth again.

'My decision is final, Lady Wakchter,' I said abruptly.

Annie stormed past me and stopped at the door. 'Of course, Aleksander,' she said and slammed the door behind her.

I walked over to the window and noticed the moon was bright in the sky. I hoped that she was there waiting. It was a warm night and there was no need for formalities in clothing. I took off the brown leather vest and family belt. I pushed my hair behind my ears and headed off to meet Faith. I did not have affections for her but rather enjoyed her company. I found joy when I was in her presence and was beginning to form a relationship with her. I climbed the stairs slowly and quietly. I pushed the door open and Faith was sitting on the ground. I could barely see her from her dark coat covering her face and skin. I stood on something on the ground and it snapped under my foot.

'Good evening, Lord Marchés,' she said without turning around.

I sat down beside her and put my hands on the ground behind me. 'Good evening, Lady Bushanti.'

'Erk, I so hate being called that,' she said with disgust in her voice. 'I would prefer to be called Queen Bitch.' She giggled. I noticed that she was holding a cup of wine.

I took it away from her and drank some; I wiped my mouth. 'How much have you had to drink tonight?'

'You make me sound like an alcoholic. It was a

looooooonnnnnnggggg day,' she said while letting herself fall flat onto the ground.

'Oh my God, I just remembered I found out something interesting about you today. You had previously mentioned the founding families and all that...' She stumbled upright. 'Yours is one of the founding families – you are like pretty much royalty.' She pointed at me and looked triumphant. I bowed my head.

'Yes, mine was one of the founding families but we were removed after our loyalty to the Bouchard family. Our castle and lands were destroyed and taken away.'

'Yeah, that was because you were supposed to marry the daughter of the Bouchards and apparently, Yelena was super pissed off and the rest is history.'

I was shocked she knew that I was to marry Crystal, her. I shifted on the ground. 'What did you think of Farak?'

'No, I don't want to talk about me. I want you to tell me about your life growing up. Tell me more about this place, please,' she said, dropping to the ground and leaning her head on my chest. I lay down on the ground and put my hand on her shoulder.

'Tell me, please.' Faith lifted her head and looked into my eyes. I moved to touch her face but froze.

'Before the tyranny of the Faulcon rule, Hisadalgon was a peaceful land and the Bouchards ruled as fairly as they could. Charles fell in love with Katherine who had no title and no significant land. Charles broke the law in marrying her but after the founding families saw her and her presence, they accepted her instantly. She had a grace to her that could not be explained; she was born to rule and Charles let her make negotiations for trade and gave her plenty of power. They had three children: Edgar, Victor and Crystal. Edgar never wanted to be king, Victor was too soft and did not have the temperament to rule. Crystal was... ha-ha, she had a fire like her mother. She wanted to be one of the boys and would be the first to challenge anyone to a duel; she always lost but she never gave up the idea that one day she would be unstoppable. She was stubborn and had such spirit. She was born to rule and without a doubt would have made an excellent queen. I was a few years older than her but she followed my every step and said one day I would love her...' I stopped and took a drink of wine.

'I like her – she sounds tough. What happened after that?' she asked, nestling into my chest. I pulled her closer.

'The Faulcons, with the Somneris' support, overthrew the Bouchards with the help of my father. They were trapped in the chapel while it was set alight. After the fire, my father was executed. I still remember the day they came; he was taken away and they placed him on the block and beheaded him. I was only in my eighth year and begged for my mother to be spared by offering my services for life. I have come to regret this decision; my mother is peculiar. She is spending the remainder of her life in a dungeon.' I breathed a sigh of relief. I did not open up to many people but I felt so comfortable with her.

'I have always said "Never regret anything because at one stage it was exactly what you wanted".'

'Are you saying you have no regrets?' I asked her, pondering what she had said.

'No, regret takes away happiness. I have not had an easy life and I made it my mission to be happy and to keep going no matter what. Toby gave me the strength but after he passed,

I realised I had it all along; he just helped me to grow up essentially.'

I started stroking her hair.

'You are going to put me to sleep if you keep doing that.' She laughed.

'Shhh,' I said softly. I was relaxed with her in my arms; I could feel her breath through my shirt. She leaned her whole body against me for warmth. She moved her hand from under her chin to my stomach.

'You are so warm and you smell nice. Tell me about your mother,' she said; her voice was faltering.

She was almost asleep; I did not have the heart to move her. She drifted off to sleep and I looked up into the sky and watched the stars. I did not have the heart to tell her that she was Crystal. I was afraid of her response. She moaned in her sleep. I moved slowly to not wake her. I put my arms around her legs and lifted her up. I walked down the stairs slowly and back to her chambers. Sonny was outside her door; he nodded and opened her chamber door. He walked in and pulled back the covers. I put my knee on the bed and slowly put her down. She stirred slightly and grabbed my shirt.

'Don't go,' she said softly in her dream. I unclenched her hand and tucked her in the covers. I turned to Sonny on the way out of the room.

'This never happened.'

He nodded. I returned to my chambers and fell into bed.

CHAPTER NINETEEN

Faith

It took me a while to realise why I was still dressed and had my cloak on. Aleksander must have carried me back to bed and he even tucked me in. He was such a gentleman; how had he never found a woman to marry? I admired him for his virginity; he wanted to wait for the right girl. Other men would deem that to be feminine but I found it to be an admirable trait. I got out of bed and Makenzie had already drawn the bath and had my clothes draped across the chair next to my mirror. Toby was nowhere to be seen – I assumed Makenzie had taken him for a walk. There was a knock at the door; I took off my cloak. I did not bother to look in the mirror or wipe my face. I opened the door. It was Sebastian. I closed it again quickly.

'Oh shit,' I said to myself. I ran over to the mirror and flicked my hair and ran my fingers through it before I pushed it to one side and placed the butterfly clasp in my hair. I ran back over to the door and opened it again. 'Good morning, Your Majesty.'

Sebastian laughed. 'You looked beautiful before the clip, Faith. I wanted to ask you if I may escort you to the shore later. You have dancing lessons and I shall come and collect you after,'

Sebastian said, leaning against the door. He was becoming more casual with me.

'You are welcome to join me during the lessons but I would love to spend more time with you.'

'I look forward to seeing your beautiful face later,' Sebastian said and walked away.

He was so sweet lately and I was enjoying spending time with him. I struggled to get out of my dress and step into the bath. It was still and smelt like roses and lavender. I put my hair over the edge of the bath and closed my eyes. It was so relaxing until Makenzie walked into the room with Toby. He stood at the side of the bath and started barking at me.

'Alright, I will get out,' I said to Toby. Makenzie was waiting with a towel; I was surprised that I was so comfortable around her.

'You have a glow about you, Faith. I came to check on you during the night and you were not in your chambers.'

I blushed and did not know how to respond. I avoided eye contact with her.

'Did you spend the night with the king?'

'No, I did not spend the night with anyone,' I responded defensively.

'You were in your bed in full attire.' Makenzie was not going to let up without an answer.

'That is enough. I was in my bed last night and that is all there is to it,' I said and walked over to the mirror to grab the clothes and put them on. She offered to help but I brushed her hand away. Why was I hiding what happened last night? Aleksander and I were just friends and we spent half the night talking with each other. There was no harm in that.

Miguel knocked on my door; he was here to collect me for dancing lessons. I walked into the room. Annie and Harley were already waiting. They were talking in the corner. Aleksander walked into the room and I turned away. I did not think I could face him. Harley noticed.

'Um, what happened there?'

'What are you talking about, Harley? What did I miss?' I acted dumb and hoped they would drop it.

Annie noticed and changed the topic. 'This should be interesting. Can any one of us actually dance?'

'Twerking?' Harley said, laughing. 'Shake your booty.' Harley put her backside against mine and started shaking it.

'How old are we? Act your age. Gosh, you are children,' I said poking my tongue out at them. My back was turned towards everyone else. I pulled faces and watched Annie and Harley struggle to keep a straight face.

'That is not very ladylike.' I heard Aleksander behind me. I jumped from being startled and turned around.

'Um,' was the only word that came out of my mouth. I did not know what to say.

'May I converse with you privately?' Aleksander asked, standing with his hands behind his back. I noticed Sebastian walk into the room.

'Later,' was the only word I could speak before I walked away from him. I was nervous around him – what had changed overnight?

Dancing lessons, I did not look forward to these. I had two left feet and no rhythm. It was like trying to watch a cat swim. I was so nervous and my stomach was all in knots. I wanted to vomit but I just kept smiling and waiting for the dance teacher to come into the room. Annie picked up on my nerves from my hands constantly moving. She put her hands on mine and whispered in my ear.

'You will be fine. We are right here with you and if you look bad, I will purposely trip over for you.' She was so sweet.

'Then you might be tripping over quite a bit.' I chuckled.

I was calming down slowly but knew this was going to be a disaster. A man walked into the room. His golden hair was short; it was different because a lot of men had longer hair. They had clearly never heard of a hairbrush or scissors but hey, I was being judgmental. His beard did not match his hair; it was a dark brown. Even though they were two different colours, they created a beautiful contrast. He was not wearing fancy clothes but rather just tan leather pants and a loose-fitting cream shirt. It looked more like he was about to go dig out in the garden rather than teach ladies how to dance. He had a beaming smile and seemed incredibly cheerful.

'Good morrow, lords and ladies.'

Annie and Harley curtsied behind me. I quickly followed.

'What a lovely day to dance,' he said cheerfully. He was too happy for my liking. He was scanning around the room until his eyes lay on Annie, Harley and myself.

'Ah, ladies, you are ravishing. What beauty you have,' he said as he touched each of our faces. Sebastian did not look happy with this display and cleared his throat. Aleksander looked at the ground and shuffled his feet. He was a peculiar man.

'I am Gustavo,' he said, bowing in front of us. Sebastian glared at the man. Gustavo noticed and became cautious in his actions.

'We shall be learning two separate dances for the day.

The only two dances we have here in Zilanta. If you will follow my lead.'

Annie and Harley stood beside me; I was still entwining my fingers with each other out of nerves. Annie grabbed my hand and I grabbed Harley's hand. We followed his steps – he was not counting; this did not help. Back with the right, the left, the right, the left. To the side, four steps crossing over your feet and moving forward again four steps alternating between the left and right feet. Gustavo went through the steps once more before he grabbed Harley's hand and led her into the dance. It ended in a twirl.

'After the twirl, the lord and ladies will come together in a circle, all touching their left hands and moving their right arm in and out of the circle,' he said, showing us an example of what it was supposed to look like.

Gustavo grabbed Annie's hand and did the steps. I was so nervous and hoped he was not going to go through the steps with me. I was not confident enough even though they were simple steps. I was so uncoordinated and petrified that I would fall over. Gustavo grabbed my hand and led me over to an open space in the room. He put his hand on my lower back and the other clasped around my hand. He noticed my breathing was really quick and I was slouched. He moved closer.

'Take a breath, milady, and stand up straight. A lady must always have her poise about her or they sense your fear and you will be eaten alive by the court,' he whispered in my ear.

I stood up straight, closed my eyes and took a deep breath. He moved and I was not prepared; he stood on my foot.

'Ouch,' I said and winced in pain. It was more like a stamp than accidentally standing on my foot.

'My apologies,' he said, laughing.

Gustavo looked at me before taking his next step; I was very slow in moving and making sure I was not going to trip over my own two feet. We completed the dance once.

'Again,' Gustavo said, dragging me back to the middle of the room. He didn't stand on my foot this time but I stood on the back of my dress; it ripped.

Luckily, it was only small and it did not reveal anything that I did not want. I went bright red in the face; I was so embarrassed. It was typical me. I always stumbled over my two feet. Gustavo moved on to the second dance. This one involved more movements; I did not master it all. I kept tripping over my feet and forgetting the steps. Sebastian glared at me; I did not think he was impressed. I noticed Aleksander cover his mouth, hiding a snigger. At least he was enjoying himself. Gustavo stopped trying to teach me – yep, I was that hopeless.

I retired back to my room. Toby greeted me at the door.

'Hello, handsome, how are you?' I said, picking him up and walking over to the window. I sat on the edge and looked out the window. Toby sat on my lap, licking my hand. I was feeling sick in the stomach at how much I was struggling to dance a few simple steps.

'Dancing is not for everyone, is it?' I said to Toby who tilted his head to the side. 'Oh, you are too cute.' I put him down and he started gnawing at my feet; he was in a playful mood.

I stomped my feet and started running around my room with Toby chasing me and barking at me. 'Ah, sit.'

Toby stopped instantly and sat down.

'Who is a good boy?' I said, bending down and picking him up. I held him up in the air and twirled around. He was heavy but not so heavy that I could not lift him. Luckily, he was still a puppy and was nowhere near full grown yet. I lay down on the bed and started reading a book from Annie's collection.

KNOCK, KNOCK.

'Oh, I wonder who that is,' I said to Toby, putting the book down.

Toby put his paw on my side; he did not want me to move. I kissed his paw and got up to answer the door.

'You Majesty,' I said while curtsying.

'No need for formalities, Faith, no one is close,' he said, walking into the room and closing the door. Toby growled at him.

'Toby,' I scolded him.

Toby whimpered and stood behind my legs. Sebastian grabbed my hand and walked us over to the bed and sat down. I was feeling slightly uncomfortable; this was the closest we had ever been alone. He moved a strand of my hair out of my face and placed his hand on my leg. I shifted uncomfortably but held the smile on my face. He stood up again.

'As you are aware, it is my coronation in two days. I would like to ask for a favour.'

I nodded my head and waited for his response. He paced the room.

'I am grateful for my mother in planning the coronation. The procession will consist of representatives of all the founding families. I would like you to stand beside me as I take the crown.'

My mouth dropped open; I did not know what to say.

'Sebastian, we may be spending some lovely time together but I worry that sends the wrong message to the people. I enjoy spending time with you and I am aware of your intentions but...'

Sebastian raised his hand to cut me off. He bent down on his knees in front of me.

'I will wait for you to be ready. It is difficult for you to adjust to this country and I do not want to rush you.'

I put my hand on his face; he was a sweet man. 'May I have some time to think this over?'

'Yes, of course. We shall speak of it again tomorrow. For now, I believe we are to spend some time together on the shore.' He smiled and stood up, offering his hand.

Aleksander knocked on the door as we were about to head out.

'Aleksander, is everything alright?' I asked. He nodded.

'Nothing serious. I will come and speak with you later,' he said and turned away.

'He is a peculiar fellow, is he not?' I asked Sebastian.

'Yes, indeed.' I held onto his arm as we walked down the stairs. We walked past so many people; I did not recognise their faces.

He had a huge smile across his face; it seemed like he was proud that I was on his arm. I looked at him and he looked back at me. It was stupid of me to look at him; of course I tripped but Sebastian tightened his grip and moved in front of me to stop me from falling.

'Thank you,' I said as I fixed my hair, which was all over the place. He laughed. 'Why does everyone feel the need to laugh at me when I fall?'

He smirked.

'It is entertaining – you never know what to expect from a person such as yourself.'

'What, a klutz?'

'I am unaware of the meaning of that word.' His brow was furrowed.

'It means someone clumsy, who always falls over and cannot dance.'

'Yes, that is accurate for you,' he said as we continued walking. We went through a side door of the castle that led us to the edge of the shoreline; there was still grass. I noticed that there were two guards following us. Sebastian saw my concern.

'It is just for our protection; I am the king after all.'

He was right. I shrugged and bent down to untie my shoes.

'What are you doing?' he asked.

'One of my pet hates is getting sand in my shoes. Do you not just love the feeling of sand between your toes?' I said, continuing to untie my boots.

He seemed confused but decided to copy what I was doing. Sebastian was still untying his shoes while I ran off into the sand.

'Woooooohoooooooooooo,' I shouted at the top of my lungs.

Sebastian shook his head at me as he caught up.

'The sun is in our favour today and I believe it is because of your beauty,' Sebastian said.

I wanted to laugh at the corniness of that line but he was trying. I did feel myself softening towards him; I was still wary of his intentions. I will admit I was an attractive young lady but so were Annie and Harley. Sebastian seemed to make a beeline straight for me. Instead of wrapping my arm around his, he grabbed my hand and held it. We walked along the beach; the sun was amazing on my face. I wished my sleeves were shorter.

'Faith, I would like to speak honestly,' Sebastian said.

'Of course, what is the matter?'

He stopped and looked at me.

'I find it difficult to be away from you and if possible, I would like to spend time with you every day.'

I smirked. 'I am sure I can make some time in my day for you.'

'If it is too difficult—'

I cut him off. 'I was playing with you. That is not an issue.'

The water swallowed my feet. It was freezing. I let out a little scream. Sebastian laughed; the water did not reach him and he wandered off, laughing.

'Oh really?!' I said and bent down and splashed water on him. I was beaming with satisfaction – that was for laughing at me, I thought to myself.

Sebastian turned around, looking rather displeased but his eyes were not saying the same thing. I bent down to go and flick the water again.

'Faith, do not—'

I splashed him again. He ran into the water and started splashing me. We were both laughing; he ran towards me and wrapped his arms around me from behind. He picked me up.

'No, no, no, no, no, no, please,' I said, begging.

He put me down and turned me around. 'What did you think I was going to do?' He moved more hair out of my face.

'I thought you were going to drop me in the water.'

'Oh, heavens, no.' He kept looking into my eyes and I saw him moving closer.

I felt his arms move around my waist. I pulled away and splashed through the water.

'Why do you pull away when I move to kiss you?' I heard him ask from behind.

'It is not because I don't enjoy your company. I just

have issues of my own. I lost my fiancé and it has been hard adjusting to the thought of another man. I know it sounds silly but he was my everything. Just give me some time.'

I mean, I barely knew him; I had only been here about a week and he expected me to perform an act of intimacy so quickly. My body was feeling the need to be intimate as it was missing a man's touch but I did not want to rush into anything and regret it. If he truly cared about me and respected me, there should be no problem with waiting.

Sebastian reached for my hands and stood in front of me. 'My affection grows for you daily. I shall wait because I feel we are matched for one another. I shall wait till more time has passed.'

I put my hand on his face; it was so smooth. He had no prickles like Aleksander. He grabbed my hand and kissed it. I smiled. It was obvious he did have feelings for me but I was yet to open my heart. I knew I would need to do it like a Band-Aid: hard and fast.

'I wish for information about your betrothed,' Sebastian said while we continued to walk along the beach.

'His name was Toby. He was a few years older than myself. He had an old soul and he had the unique ability of making me laugh all the time. I was convinced he understood my emotions more than myself. He inspired me to challenge myself and to never give up. I believe he was my soul mate as we were so alike in many ways. But that was also one of our downfalls – when we argued we were both as stubborn as each other and rarely admitted when we were wrong.' I could not contain my smile, thinking about him again.

Sebastian noticed. 'It is evident, the care you had for him.'

'I remember one time an argument started over something little, I think it was a name or colour of something. A few hours later, we were not talking because neither wanted to admit their fault. We started laughing when we realised we had lost half the day over something so trivial. It was not the first or last time that had happened.'

'He would have to have been a strong man to counteract your strong will.'

I nodded and smiled. I had spoken to Aleksander briefly about Toby but not in this much detail. It was like a weight lifting off my shoulders; it was a relief to speak of him again.

Sebastian escorted me back to my chambers where he kissed my hand before turning and leaving. I ran to Annie's room and knocked; she did not answer. I proceeded to Harley's room and knocked. I heard footsteps and the door opened. She saw my face.

'What's wrong?'

I walked past her into the room and sat down on her bed. I didn't know how to start the conversation; I was stuttering before Harley stopped and wrapped her arms around me. She pulled back and looked at me.

'I think I may be developing feelings for someone. It feels wrong – has enough time gone by that I can now feel for another?'

'Faith, you are always harshest on yourself compared to any others. Toby would be glad that you are opening your heart again. Especially to the likes of Aleksander – you two have a unique chemistry. I see the looks you share when you believe no one is watching.'

I put my hand up and the other on my stomach.

'I was not talking about Aleksander. I was talking about Sebastian,' I said, clarifying.

'Oh, did I say Aleksander? I meant Sebastian. Silly me! Sebastian seems like an interesting person to get to know.' Harley avoided eye contact with me. I knew exactly what she meant.

'Aleksander is my friend – he is my protector, my knight in shining armour without the romance. Whereas Sebastian, I think I misjudged him. He seems so genuine and sweet and cares for me. Today he told me he was finding it difficult to go the day without seeing my face. I still have reservations and I don't know if it is from being scared that if I move on, will I forget Toby? What if he is nothing like Toby? I was with him for so long, I don't know how to take the next step. I am scared,' I said, holding back tears. It was hard for me to open up.

I held emotions in and never opened up. I always referred to myself as emotionally damaged. Harley had a tear running down her cheek; she was crying for me.

'Faith, nobody will ever measure up to Toby for you. He was your everything and the love you had for him was like no other love in the world. You two were so in sync with each other. You can open your heart again – baby steps. I know it's hard from your past. You never knew your parents or siblings, you were raised by nuns in an orphanage and he was the first person to understand you. Someone else will see beyond your walls and break them down again. Someone will be worthy of your love and I guarantee you Toby will be jumping with joy in heaven just seeing you smile again. I want to have my old sister back. You have been consumed with grief and closed off. I want you to be happy again. If Sebastian makes you happy then go for it, don't hold back. You want to break down that wall next time you see him? Push through the fear and kiss him. Open yourself back up to joy.'

I cried. I knew she was right and it hurt to hear the pain in her voice. I put my arms around her.

'I'm sorry.'

We both let go of our emotions and sobbed in each other's arms.

The moon was in the sky; I could see it from my window. The stars were not as bright as yesterday; there were clouds in the sky today but the moon was overpowering the vastness of the sky. It was the brightest moon I had seen so far here in Zilanta. I walked up the stairs. Aleksander was already waiting.

'I do not appreciate you picking on me earlier today at my dancing lessons.'

He turned around with a smirk on his face. 'I felt the need to pay you for the entertainment.'

'Ha, ha. You are so funny, you should be a comedian. I thought you of all people would understand how clumsy and accident-prone I am.'

'Indeed. I heard whispers of Sebastian's decision to ask for you to join in the royal coronation in two days. I have decided to take on the burden of refining your dancing technique.'

'What, no talking today? Straight to work, huh?' I said while slowly moving towards the ground to sit down.

'Up, up. I have a feeling he will ask you to dance with him on that night. It will be his way of solidifying you as his companion and you will be untouchable.'

'That is one meaningful dance,' I said as Aleksander dragged me over to him.

'Your sass is not necessary. Come now.'

I poked my tongue out, thankful he did not see this gesture.

Aleksander grabbed my right hand in his and moved his other arm around my side and pulled for me to move closer.

'Is this really the smartest decision – to dance on a roof with very little room? I am seeing graphic images in my mind of us dancing and falling off and splattering our brains all over the ground. I am sure the rodents would enjoy a meal.'

Aleksander cleared his throat – in his own words, it was a way of him saying 'pay attention'. He lifted my arm onto his shoulder and pulled me even closer. I could feel his breath on my face. I just wanted to lay my head on him like last night. I had never fallen asleep more peacefully than that night. Before we started, he spoke.

'I have always believed that only with a strong partner can a female truly shine in her dancing.'

'Oh, is that so? Are you that cocky that you are saying you are the best dancer around?'

'I do not believe I uttered those words.'

Without even realising it, we were dancing. He made me feel so relaxed that I was not counting but following his lead.

'You overthink, Faith. You need to relax. Now, again,' Aleksander said with a knowing smile. It was funny, him telling me to relax. We spent hours going through all of the twelve dances.

'Which one is your family's dance?' I asked him.

He put his head down and shook it.

'I'm sorry, did I insult you in some way?'

'No, not at all. It was the fifth dance and the Bouchards' was the last one.'

'What dance will the king and I dance? I am worried – I have yet to agree to his proposition,' I said, moving my hands in front of me out of nerves. He put his hand on top of my two.

'May I speak candidly?'

'No, you may not. How dare you ask that question?'

Aleksander looked taken aback. I smiled and laughed.

'I was only kidding. I am always candid with you. You do not need to ask me at all.'

'Right, I believe you should take the proposition.' That was all he said before kissing me on the forehead and walking down the stairs.

Curious – why would he ask me to do that? Would it not be better if I was unknown to the people? These were questions for another day. I looked at the moon in the sky. It would have to be early morning, time for bed. Sonny was outside my chamber door.

'Sonny, why are you still up this late? Go on, off to bed,' I said.

'I wanted to ensure that you were safe after your venture earlier tonight.'

'Thank you, Sonny. Goodnight,' I said and closed the door on him. I pulled back the wolf fur doona and jumped into bed. I blew out the candle and fell asleep before I even had time to count sheep.

There was a dove in the window when I woke up. It did not look to be fully grown as its feathers were fluffy and not smooth like an adult's. It was just cooing in the window. I slowly moved my legs under the blankets and got out of bed. I moved slowly over to the window. It just continued to look at me and coo.

'Hello, munchkin.' I put my hand up to pat the dove but it

flew away before I could even touch it. I sat on the window's ledge; it was not a beautiful day like yesterday.

The clouds were grey in the sky and you could not see the sun. I took a breath and pondered the conversation I had with Harley. It was difficult to think about but I knew she was right. I needed to suck it up and just bite the bullet, so to speak. I heard a knock at the door; I knew it would be Makenzie. I did not respond and just simply waited for her to enter the room.

'You are awake, Faith. Are you prepared for your day?' Makenzie asked.

'What are the plans for today, Makenzie?' I asked her as I turned around and looked at her. She had bags under her eyes and before she could answer, I said, 'Is everything alright, Makenzie?'

She avoided eye contact with me. I walked over and grabbed her arm before she could move away from me.

'It is not appropriate to discuss these matters with my lady,' she said.

'Oh, shut up and just tell me. I am not your lady and you are not my lady's maid. You are my friend and I am here for you. Please, tell me.'

Makenzie turned and looked at me; she had a black eye. I put my hand up to move her hair but she turned away again.

'Who did it?'

'No one,' was her only response.

'Well, no one deserves a back-hand and a kick up the arse,' I said back to Makenzie as she continued walking around the room, completing her chores.

'Makenzie, I order you to tell me who marked your face,' I said in a stern voice and I knew I was abusing my power in ordering her but I wanted to know because she deserved better than that. I didn't care if it was the norm in Zilanta. I would not tolerate it.

Yes, slightly hypocritical because I had let someone hit me not long ago but they would never strike me again because I promised myself I would hit them back in the future.

Makenzie turned around; tears were beginning to well in her eyes.

'You cannot make me answer,' she said with her voice crackling.

'I will. Makenzie, I order you to tell me who has hit you because that is never the answer,' I said, crossing my arms and staring at her intently.

'Lord Kestrel. He has been courting me for a while and inquired about you and wanted information. I refused.'

I could feel my anger rising in my stomach; it was never good because I was prone to making irrational decisions. I tried to remain calm but instead I picked up the dress off the bed and put it on before walking out of the room. I stormed over to Sebastian's room and knocked on the door. I had no idea what I was going to say but I knew something had to be done. Who was this Lord Kestrel and why was he trying to find out information on me and what gave him the right to hit my lady's maid? Little prick, I would get him. Sebastian answered the door and was not wearing a top. He was simply wearing black tan pants and had his hair pulled back into a ponytail. I was momentarily distracted at his toned pectoral muscles and the hair that trailed down his stomach. I shook my head and noticed he was smiling at my distraction.

'Good morning, Your Majesty. May I request an audience?'

I asked in the sweetest voice I possibly could.

'Good morning, Lady Bushanti. Please, come in.'

I walked into Sebastian's chambers; it was the first time I had been in his room. It was massive and it made my chambers look tiny. There was enough room for about ten beds. There were two paintings in the room. One was of his family and the second I was assuming was of Zilanta, as the landscape looked like what I had ventured across to get to the castle. I marvelled at the ceiling; there were gold pictures of flowers that looked strangely familiar. I had always drawn this flower for as long as I could remember – people would often say it reminded them of leaves. It was five leaves that created one flower and I started drawing it when I was about seven or eight. The bed was still not made but the bath was full of water.

'Did I catch you at a bad time, Sebastian?' I felt uncomfortable for a moment.

'No, I always have time for you, Faith. What is the purpose of this visit?' he asked. I was not sure how to broach this subject.

'I am aware that I am not necessarily a citizen of your country and you are allowing myself and my friends to live in your castle by your good graces. I appreciate that and the compromise we have come to. I am also aware that I am young in understanding how your society runs but I believe that when a man strikes a woman to retrieve information about myself, this is important as my—'

Sebastian interrupted me, his face no longer friendly. 'Who was trying to retrieve information about you, Faith?' Sebastian asked, looking at me firmly. That was all he'd heard.

'Lord Kestrel – he struck Makenzie, my lady's maid. That is disgraceful and I would appreciate if he could apologise or possibly receive a punishment of some sort. Men and women are equal. No one man can be placed above another in my eyes.' I did not want to back down. I knew I had to tread carefully.

I crossed my arms and Sebastian had a smirk on his face.

'You are a strong lady, Faith. I understand what you are discussing but I cannot punish him for striking a female. I will, however, have an urgent conversation with him to discuss why he was endeavouring to discover information about my lady.'

I smiled without realising at him calling me his lady. I felt protected but was also worried because I would not be his property. I would always be my own person and never ruled by anyone. Even Toby knew that and always allowed me to do whatever I pleased. I walked over to Sebastian and wrapped my arms around him in an embrace.

'Thank you, Sebastian,' I said and kissed him on the cheek. His body stiffened as I stepped backwards. His cheeks were red and he shuffled around; I had made him uncomfortable.

'I am pleased that you came to see me this morning as I have some bad news. I cannot spend some quality time with you later in the afternoon. I have some final planning for my upcoming coronation.' He pulled on his second shirt and I walked over to make sure it was on properly.

'I completely understand. I am sure I will survive one day without you. Dinner, at least?' I asked.

'I cannot last one day without seeing your beauty.'

I smiled.

'You are too kind,' I said, walking out of his chambers.

I closed the door behind me and bumped into Aleksander. He looked at me with such disappointment.

'What is the matter?' I asked him. A vein in his neck was beginning to show.

'Am I to assume that you spent the night in the king's chambers?'

I was insulted by this question. 'I do not believe that it is any of your business but no, I did not. I am glad you think so highly of me,' I said and walked away.

He could be so insulting sometimes when he spoke; I don't think he understood different tones in a person's voice. I walked back to my room. Makenzie was no longer in my room but rather Yelena was sitting on my bed. I had not seen her in a few days.

'Good morning.' I did not feel the need to give her a title or anything. I felt uncomfortable in her presence and wished for her to disappear.

'No formalities. I should not expect any better from a commoner like you.'

'Ouch. Was that supposed to sting? Because I could not give a shit, if I am being honest.'

She stood up and glared at me. 'A lady of my ranking deserves more than your abrupt attitude,' she sniped at me.

'What is the purpose of your visit, Yelena?' I said, walking over to my mirror to fix my hair, as I had not fixed it before leaving the room.

'You are beautiful to the human eye but you seem to have my son bewitched and I would like to know how when you speak in a common tongue and have no standing.'

I turned around and laughed at her.

'How am I to answer that question? Go bother someone else with your pointless conversation,' I said and turned back around and brushed my hair.

'You have power, Lady Bushanti, but power can dwindle. You should sleep with both eyes open,' she said, standing and walking towards my door.

'I have missed the taste of poison. Will I get to try it again soon?' I giggled and she slammed the door behind her. She really did not like me and I wasn't sure if it was because I was a smartass or because her son was slowly being wrapped around my little finger.

I wanted to know more than anything who Lord Kestrel was. Why was this person trying to find out information about me? Makenzie entered the room and wrapped her arms around me to embrace me.

'Is everything alright?' I asked.

She looked up. 'Thank you and I apologise.'

'What on Earth are you apologising for?' I asked and pulled back from her. What had she done wrong?

'I am apologising because I may have judged you too soon. I assumed you were nothing more than a lady with no thought process. I was wrong – you are not who I expected. I understand why the king has fallen for you,' she said and walked me over to fix my hair.

I had obviously done a horrible job. I picked up a clip and she smacked it out of my hand.

'The king came and spoke to me. He requested I take the day off to rest and told me that the matter was being handled.'

I smiled. 'I think the king may surprise Zilanta. He seems to be a better man than I had originally thought and yeah, I feel like there could be a future for us. That is if I am to be stuck in this place forever.'

Makenzie did not comment after that. She fixed my hair and pinched my cheeks to make them blush. I hated when she did this; it always hurt. I had a pimple on my forehead this morning. I knew what that meant – my monthly treat was coming. YEAH, said no girl ever.

I walked over and looked out the window. I missed home. Toby ran over and started biting the bottom of my dress.

'You little rascal.' I picked him up and he started to lick my face. I hated being licked and pulled him away. Toby started whining.

'Such a typical male.' I put him down and bent to start rubbing his tummy. Toby nibbled on my hand. Thank God his teeth were not sharp enough to pierce the skin.

'I will take you for a walk later when I go into town, how does that sound?' I said, making kissing sounds with my mouth. I must have sounded like an idiot because I heard someone clear their throat. It was Aleksander.

'Have you come to apologise for your lovely comment this morning?' I said, not even looking at him.

'Lovely comment? Why would I apologise for a lovely comment?' he asked. He looked confused and the lines on his forehead deepened as he pondered what I was talking about.

I smiled to myself; he did not pick up on sarcasm. It was a pity and annoying at the same time.

'Let me rephrase, your insinuation that I spent the night with the king,' I said, standing up and leaving Toby on his back waiting to be scratched.

'I will not apologise. It was within my rights to ask that question,' he said, glaring at me.

'Yep, it sure was. What are you doing here?' I asked bluntly and started helping Makenzie with making the bed.

'I have been tasked to collect the ladies for your music lesson and to discuss the plan for the afternoon.' He was straight to business.

'I am yet to eat breakfast. Sonny will escort me to the music lesson,' I said.

Aleksander huffed in frustration and walked out the room.

Makenzie shook her head at me.

'What have I done now?' I asked, throwing my arms up at her in irritation.

'Lord Marchés is a good man and he cares about your safety, Faith. You need to let up on him – you are particularly callous towards him at times and he does not deserve that attitude,' she said.

I sighed and I walked down to the kitchen; there was not much breakfast food. I was starving; my stomach was growling. I grabbed a piece of black bread and an apple and walked back to my room. Sonny appeared in front of me.

'Oh, shit, sorry, I forgot about you. Can you escort me to my music lesson, please?' I said with a sweet smile to try and win him over.

Sonny turned and walked off, leading the way to the music room. I was excited to venture into another room inside the castle. There would have to be hundreds of rooms inside this place. The only rooms I did not want to visit would have to be the prison's. I hated to imagine how dirty they would be and even the smell.

I had finished eating my black bread when Sonny escorted me to the door. I started biting into my apple as I knocked on the door. Miguel answered while I had half of the apple in my mouth. That must have looked attractive. I quickly chewed and swallowed.

'Good morning, Miguel.' There was still some food in my mouth and no doubt in my teeth.

Miguel simply moved to the side to allow me to walk into the room.

'Good morning, Annie, Harley,' I said and walked over to hug them.

Sebastian and Aleksander walked into the room in what looked like an intense discussion; both looked displeased with one another. I wondered why Sebastian was at the lesson today when he spoke this morning and said he would not be able to see me as often. I doubted I was that good at manipulating a man into falling in love with me.

I felt a twinge of guilt at attacking Aleksander this morning after seeing his face now. What news had Sebastian delivered to make him look that unhappy? Sebastian smiled in my direction and walked out of the room. I wanted to walk over and speak to Aleksander but Annie grabbed my arm.

'No, leave him be.'

I saw the piano in the corner of the room and walked over to it. I rubbed my hand across the wood panels. I couldn't believe there was a piano in a place like this. It was like the Middle Ages. I had only seen recorders, guitars and violins. It did not have the pedals at the bottom but I lifted the lid to inspect the keys. They were not soft like normal keys I had come across. They were coarse but not coarse enough to give you blisters. I had not even noticed the man walk into the room and introduce himself. I grew up playing the piano in the orphanage and Toby bought me one for my twenty-first birthday. He spent over a year saving for it.

I sat down and put my fingers across the keys. Before I knew it, I was playing a tune I created when I was a little girl. I couldn't stop smiling. I had not felt like myself much while I was here but sitting down now and playing, I had felt my inner strength and confidence coming back. I felt like I could do this without anything holding me back. I oversaw my own fate and I would be damned if anybody wanted to take that away from me.

I remember the day I created my own little tune. The nuns at the orphanage described it as hauntingly beautiful. They always used to call me their dark little angel because in their eyes, I was an angel but they believed I had a hidden past that was filled with darkness. I found that to be quite insulting coming from nuns but nevertheless, I loved them all the same and missed them when I was pushed through the foster care system and never had a stable home. My fondest memories were with Sister Mary, Sister Agnes and Father James. I finished playing and had completely zoned out on the fact that I had just randomly started playing.

'Sorry,' I said and stood up from the piano and walked over beside Annie who smiled and pinched my cheek. I pinched her back and we laughed. Sometimes words could not explain the love we had for each other.

'Lady Bushanti, it is an honour to be standing in your presence. I am Lord Flowerdale.' He bowed and walked over to kiss my hand.

I pulled away in disgust; I didn't know where his mouth had been. 'It is a pleasure to meet you, Lord Flowerdale. I hope you are not expecting me to sing. I am afraid my voice is like a cat's nails on a chalkboard.'

He turned his head in confusion. I cleared my throat and before I could speak Harley turned around and said, 'She will make your ears bleed in pain. I am not exaggerating, she is that bad.'

He still looked confused.

'You are too kind, Harley,' I said, pushing my shoulder into her back.

I inspected Lord Flowerdale; he did not look to be much older than myself. He had a scar across his nose, which was hidden beneath his green eyes and had an amazing moustache. I wondered how the lines were so straight. He had a few freckles on his cheeks. He was the same height as myself and was quite slender; there did not seem to be many muscles to the man at all. He looked weak and frail in frame but his face said otherwise, as he carried himself with pride. I watched him waiting for an explanation of what we were saying.

'I cannot sing, my lord. It is painful to hear,' I said plainly, hoping he would understand.

'Annie, however, has a beautiful voice and it is soft and gentle enough to put you to sleep.'

'Oh, shut up, it is not that good.'

I looked at her sideways.

'And when do I ever lie?' I said and poked my tongue out at her.

Lord Flowerdale clapped his hands. 'Ladies.'

We stopped and looked at each other. We were all holding our sides in laughter – I still prayed daily that we would never grow up. 'Sometimes life is meant to be lived with laughter otherwise it is too dull' – this was Harley's line. I looked towards the floor, trying to contain my laughter. I was on the borderline of falling onto the floor in a giggling fit. I heard Aleksander clear his throat and I looked up with a smile, showing my teeth. Lord Flowerdale handed us some paper with words for us to sing.

I looked at Annie and whispered, 'He is not expecting me to sing, is he? You may need earmuffs.'

Flowerdale picked up a violin and started playing – only Annie was musically inclined and we waited for her to start before we followed. Before Miguel walked out of the room, he turned and looked at all of us. He was up to something. Annie started singing. I mouthed the words to pretend I was singing. He stopped after the first verse.

'Lady Bushanti, I do not appreciate your deceitful actions,' he said sternly. I clicked my tongue in my mouth and rolled my eyes.

'I do not appreciate the fact that I informed you of my lack of skill in the voice department. So yeah, I shall refuse to sing. I am happy to play an instrument,' I said, pointing over towards the piano.

'NO,' he said raising his voice.

Aleksander turned and put his hand on Lord Flowerdale's shoulder.

'That is no way to speak to a lady. Faith has spoken her grievances and you should respect her decision.'

I noticed Aleksander was slowly clenching his hand on Flowerdale's shoulder. Flowerdale turned.

'Yes, Lord Marchés,' he said in a squeaky tone.

Lord Flowerdale picked up another violin and handed it to me. I looked at Aleksander; I had not asked or signalled for him to step in for me and speak. I didn't know where that had come from. I had no idea how to play the violin; I was hoping more for the piano. I was getting over these lessons the king had organised. I would play the part he asked me to but I would never become the girl he wanted. I would never be the perfect lady – I think the only one who understood that was Aleksander. The lesson was dismissed and I walked out of there so fast, I didn't get a chance to say goodbye. I made a mental note to thank and apologise to Aleksander later when I saw him.

'You play the piano beautifully. How long did it take for you to learn the Bushka song?' Sonny asked as we were walking back to my chambers.

'What song?' I asked confused on what the Bushka song was. Annie and Harley were walking behind me.

'The Bushka is the national song of Bushka where the Bouchard family originate from.'

'You are shitting me,' Harley and I said together, completely shocked. I had never been to this place before yet I knew the national song for one of the cities.

'I am unaware of the meaning behind "shitting me".'

Annie and Harley laughed. My mind was spinning. I was trying to remember where I had learnt the tune from. I had known it for as long as I could remember. I didn't remember much from my childhood. Not where I got my scar from, a photo of my parents or anything. I remembered more from living with the nuns than the beginning of my life. I was aware that you lost memories the older you got and might not necessarily remember stuff from being a child but to remember nothing had always seemed strange to me.

CHAPTER TWENTY

Annie

I hadn't had the chance to sing for a while; it felt good. My ex never allowed me to sing because I was more talented – the green bug of jealousy. Faith and Harley came back to my chambers. I sighed and lay down on the bed. Harley followed.

'Do we know when we will be getting our new dresses?' Harley asked Faith.

'Yeah, sounds good,' was her response.

Harley looked at me and I shrugged. 'I don't know,' I mouthed to her.

'Faith... Hello, Earth to Faith,' Harley said, waving her arms in the air.

'Do you guys have memories from your early childhood? Like four or five years old,' she asked, pacing around the room. She looked stressed out and kept fidgeting and brushing her hair off her face. Had Sonny triggered something inside her to realise who she may be?

'How can you expect to know memories from over twenty years ago? Faith, you will drive yourself insane. What is this about?' Harley said.

I was trying to think of something to change the subject.

'They say you can remember your mother's voice and smell, even if you spend a minute or less together. I cannot remember anything and have never been able to. Do you not find that weird?' Faith was really beginning to stress out. Her pace was quick and she was speaking so quickly. 'I have the same eyes as the Bouchard family. I saw their family portrait in one of the rooms somewhere in this castle. I know the anthem of Bushka where the Bouchards originate from. Am I Crystal? But if that is the case, how did I survive? The whole family was slaughtered – there are no Bouchards left to even question. Oh my God! Is that why I have always been different because I was not born on Earth but here? Holy shit. My brain is exploding. Why can I not remember anything?' She sat down in my chair and started hyperventilating.

Harley and I looked at each other; we knew we couldn't tell her. I walked over and sat down beside her.

'Yes, you have always said you felt you were born in a different era. That does not mean that you are this person. It is normal for you not to remember anything – you are twenty-six years old. You cannot expect yourself to remember memories from your early childhood. You are jumping to conclusions. Until you find out more facts, there is no reason for you to freak yourself out. You know you finally managed to control your panic attacks. You cannot go back there again. You were dangerous.'

She had a tear trickling down her face.

'Harley and I will always have your back as you have ours,' I said. I stood up and walked behind her and wrapped my arms around her. Harley ran over and did the same.

'We will stick together forever. We are the only three people we can absolutely trust.'

Faith's shoulders softened and she took a deep breath.

'Now if you don't mind, I am expecting someone shortly so can you, like, piss off now?' I said, fixing my dress.

'Oooohhhh, who are you waiting for?' Harley asked, walking over and fluffing my hair.

'Have you guys done it yet?' Faith queried.

I stuttered before answering, 'No.'

'Oh, you are so cute,' Faith said and walked to the back of my dress.

'One thing we need to fix, if you don't mind. Hold on to the bedpost.' She undid my corset and tightened it in one particular area. She walked around to the front and looked at Harley.

'Yep, much better,' Harley said and they both started nodding. I looked down and my boobs looked fantastic. I barely had a handful.

'You look absolutely stunning. Can I mount you?' Faith poked her tongue out. I felt guilt over the secret that I knew about her.

KNOCK, KNOCK.

My guilt towards Faith was beginning to fade away after I heard Langford knock at the door. I started pushing Harley and Faith towards the door. 'Go, please.'

'Alright, we are going.' Faith opened the door.

'Why, hello, Langford, fancy seeing you here. You look especially fit today, fit enough to run a marathon.'

'Oh, piss off, would you?' Harley and Faith giggled and walked away together. Langford walked into the room.

'A marathone?' he asked. He said the word incorrectly as he

looked extremely confused.

'Never mind. Faith was just playing around like she normally does. You will learn not to take her too seriously. She is not always literal.' By the time I finished my sentence, I realised that he would not understand what I had just said.

'She makes a lot of jokes,' I said to simplify what I had just said.

'Hmmm,' Langford responded. He still wasn't sure what I was talking about and felt as if I should just drop the matter.

'I have obtained a present for you,' Langford said.

I had not even noticed that he was standing with his hands behind his back. He looked handsome today. It looked as if he had brushed his light hair, which made his hazel eyes stand out; he was wearing black leather pants and a maroon tunic-like top with black stitching. He was dressed up today and was not wearing his training uniform but more formal attire. His clothing made him seem taller than usual. He was obviously over six feet. He walked over and handed the book to me.

'If you give me any more books, I may drown in them,' I said, smiling to myself at my little joke.

'There is no water for you to drown,' he said. I smirked.

'It is just a saying. Thank you,' I said and hugged him. I buried my head into his firm chest. I let my imagination run wild thinking about it. I knew Faith, Harley and I enjoyed thinking about the muscular frames of nearly all the men, compared to back home, where they did not always take care of themselves and work as hard as they did here.

I walked over to my bed, sat down and opened *The Trials of Fruthark*. The pages were so rough and not like at home; the writing was in cursive. I did not want to smell the book, as I had no idea what it would have been made of.

'It is about Fruthark Somneri and his rule of Zilanta. It was not a peaceful time in our history.'

'Was there ever a peaceful time?' I asked, not really wanting to know the answer because it seemed that this place rarely had a peaceful history. There was always something going on. Langford sat next to me.

'I find your beauty to be overpowering and would like to court you, if you find the same interest in someone of my stature. I understand it will put us in a precarious position but I am willing if you are,' he said.

I had hesitations since the warning from Aleksander. He was incredibly handsome and seemed to really care about me. I nodded my head in agreement; I did deserve some special treatment.

I leant over to kiss him on the cheek but he turned his head at the worst moment. Our lips locked. I pulled back instantly in shock. Langford smirked and moved forward again. I was more prepared this time. I closed my eyes and waited to feel his soft lips against mine. He opened his mouth and I followed. He lifted his hand up to my face and slid it to the back of my head and brought his body closer. I felt him slowly lowering my body onto the bed and shifting across on top of me. He must have realised what he did and stood up quickly. It took a while for me to catch my breath before I sat up.

'I apologise for my behaviour. It was not appropriate and—'

I stood up and put my finger on his mouth to make him stop talking. He looked at me. I wanted to kiss him again but I was feeling nervous. It was not like me to lose control in passion but I found him to be incredibly sexy. I stood on my tippy toes and moved in for another kiss. He put both of his hands on my face and brought me in closer. He moved his hands around to behind me and pulled me in closer. I let him take control; I was losing track of my thoughts. He was so intoxicating and his kisses were making me melt. He lifted me up and I wrapped my legs around his waist. I could feel his bulging package between my legs; he put his leg on the bed and dropped me gently onto the bed. I felt his hand move up my leg. It felt so good to be wanted.

'No, stop. Sorry, I am not ready for that just yet,' I said, moving away from underneath him on the bed.

He stood up and straightened his clothes. 'Yes, would you like to take a walk around the castle gardens?' he asked, fixing his hair and putting on his stoic façade.

I smiled and nodded; he was more genuine than I assumed he was. Most other men I had met would have been annoyed at a female stopping in the middle of that but he wasn't. Langford and I walked slowly out into the garden. I was so anxious about the conversation with Faith; I knew I needed to talk to Aleksander. She deserved to know the truth about who she was and know her parents did love her and she was not abandoned at an orphanage but rather saved because they loved her so much to rescue her from the horrible death that the rest of her family endured.

CHAPTER TWENTY-ONE

Faith

I was reading one of the books that Annie had been given. I did not find them interesting but rather exaggerated in the plot line. I waited patiently for Aleksander to take me to town. I stood up and thought I would practice the different dances that Aleksander had taught me a few nights ago. I started dancing around the room and humming to myself. I had not even heard Aleksander knock and open the door.

'It astonishes me how you manage to entertain yourself with the smallest of things.'

I stumbled and fell on the floor. 'Oh, shit. Does it astonish you also how easily I can fall over my own two feet?'

He laughed and offered his arm to help me up.

'Thank you. Are you ready? It feels as if I have been waiting forever,' I said.

'I have a present for you,' Aleksander said, walking into the room. 'You must wait till you are outside to receive it.'

'Aleksander, you are a tease – that is so not fair,' I said, stomping my feet out of the room but I was excited to know what I was getting from him.

I walked quickly to the door of the castle. I stepped out and smiled at Aleksander. I must have looked so cheeky. I was technically outside and waiting patiently for my gift. I put my hands out and closed my eyes with the cheeky smile still spread across my face. I felt his hands on top of mine, dropping a cold rectangular object into my hand.

'Can I open my eyes?' I asked him.

He put both his hands on my arms and slowly turned me around.

'Yes, you are allowed to open your eyes now,' he said. He was walking in front of me. I looked down at the object. It was my phone; I thought I had lost it when we arrived here. I had not seen it since. I wanted to cry.

'How long have you had this?' I asked, running to catch up to him.

'Since the day I found your landing area,' he said, not looking at me but continuing to walk with both of his hands behind his back. Sonny was a couple of metres in front.

'You make me sound like an alien landing a spaceship. "I found it at Area 51",' I said in a deep mocking voice. I was not sure whether to attempt to try and turn it on. I had been here a little over two weeks. My phone was good on battery but I doubted that it would be that good.

'What is it?' Aleksander asked as he slowed down his pace.

I pushed my finger on the side button to turn it on. I felt it vibrate in my hands; it was turning on. I started jumping up and down and giggling to myself. I didn't know what turning it on was going to accomplish – there weren't any phone towers around but still, it was something from home. The screen lit up; it was a photo of Toby and myself. Aleksander walked over and looked at the object in my hand.

'How did you put a painting onto that black rectangular brick?'

I laughed. 'Funny you say that; this is not even what is considered a brick now. This is super light compared to the first ones ever created. It is a phone, a way of communicating with other people in the world. I could call them or send a message and they would instantly receive it. Unlike here, there is not much letter writing nowadays. It is all through this technology. You can take photos and listen to music. Look, come here,' I said.

Aleksander moved to stand behind me. I opened the camera app and held the phone up to the surroundings.

'How is that possible? Is it a mirror?' His mind was blown. It was like having a little kid around.

'Not a mirror, it is called a photo. Wait, look at this,' I said, lowering the phone and pushing the button that made the camera move onto selfie mode and holding the phone up again. He looked into the phone and lifted his finger to touch the screen. He took a photo.

'What was that noise?' he asked, looking around.

'It is called a camera shutter, the noise it makes when a photo is taken. Look, watch. We will take one together.' I held the phone up again and he looked into it. I turned and looked at him; his face was adorable. I kissed him on the cheek and took the photo. He turned to look at me. I was staring back at the camera. His face was saying it all; he genuinely cared for me. I took the photo instantly. I went back into the album and showed him the three photos.

'That is beyond words,' he said, shaken about this technology.

'This is the future. I haven't even shown you the best part,' I said, opening the music player and flicking through all of my four hundred songs. We continued to walk together. I put on a dance techno song.

'Ouch, that rumpus hurts my ears,' Aleksander said. I laughed and had to stop to catch my breath.

'Hahaha, this is what I would dance to at a club,' I said, still laughing while talking.

'How do you dance to that?' Aleksander asked.

I quickly ran a few steps in front of him and started dancing. The shopping trolley, the lawn mower and the running man. He looked so confused; I loved it. His face was like watching a child discover a parent's face behind a peekaboo.

'Come now, we will be late,' Aleksander said. He wanted to drop the subject.

I continued to flick through my phone and went into the album. I was beginning to forget Toby's features. I smiled to myself and found a photo of my car.

'Look, look, this is my car. It is what we use to get to different destinations. No more horses, we use these,' I said, showing him. He touched the phone and made it zoom in.

'Argh.' He stood backwards.

I ran ahead laughing and caught up to Sonny. I walked beside him before Sonny realised.

'Why are you not beside Lord Marchés?' he asked, vigilant of his surroundings.

'I think I scared or overwhelmed him a little. He needs a timeout.'

We were around the corner from the orphanage. I saw some children and they ran up to me.

'Lady Bushanti, with haste.' They grabbed my hands and I ran with them. I walked into the room; it was different than last week. It was cleaner and more open. There was a board at the front. They had set it up for me. I was in awe.

'Do you doubt your power over people?' Aleksander asked before standing in the doorway.

'Alright, I am guessing you missed my pretty face,' I said cheekily and started laughing. I felt at home in front of a room. 'Okay, today I have a little object that plays music. I want us to dance today. I will show you the steps and you will follow. We will go through it twice before I play the music and we all do it together. Trust me, it will be enormously fun.'

CHAPTER TWENTY-TWO

Aleksander

I watched her speak to the children. Her smile was hypnotising and being in her presence gave me a sense of peace and tranquillity. I wanted to uncover more information about the deal her mother made to send her to another place.

'Sonny, I have other matters that require my attention. Are you capable enough to protect Faith?'

I did not have fond feelings towards Sonny but Faith had seen something in him that made her trust him. Sonny simply nodded in response – was he a mute? I had no idea who was in command of the coven now; it was a risk but a risk worth it to find out more information. I walked through the poor and filthy area of the town. I reached the outskirts; the rats ran the town more than the humans. I thanked my stars that I did not have to live this life. Two children ran past, they were laughing and smiling. They knew no better and were still incredibly happy. How I wished to find that same peace one day.

My mother always told me the house had a star above the door. I stumbled upon the door; I hesitated to knock. The door opened before I could gather the courage to knock.

'Come in, Lord Marchés.' The woman was terrifying; she had warts all over her face and her grey hair was tied up.

'Thank you,' I said, placing my hand on my chest and nodding in appreciation.

The room was exceptionally dark; there were no windows and it was only lit by candles strategically placed around the room. It smelt like flowers. The roof was covered in a fish net with a variety of trinkets attached to it. I could see no other women around. An object scratched my head. I looked up; it was a chicken's foot. I covered my mouth in disgust and coughed. I had grown up with this but always wanted to pretend that it never happened. I walked deeper into the room; it grew darker and the smell of flowers was dissipating and was being consumed by the smell of rot.

A woman was stirring her cauldron when she looked up.

'Lord Marchés, we have been expecting your presence. You have questions about the Bouchards,' the woman said. She looked deceivingly young from what little light was in the room. She was unbelievably small in her stature; it looked as if the cauldron could swallow her whole. Her brown hair was draped down her shoulders. She had no warts on her face but her eyes were terrifying; they were black and I felt as if they were piercing into my soul. The warty woman placed a chair behind me to sit down on. I hesitated to sit down; I was out of my comfort zone and felt a twinge of worry for Faith. I had just left her and hoped she would be safe with Sonny.

'Please sit, my lord. I am Millicent.'

I nodded my head and draped my cloak over my knees.

'Yes, I believe that the previous leader of the coven struck a deal with Katherine Bouchard. I have discovered that the youngest daughter Crystal Bouchard has since returned but she has no memories of her previous life or her parents. Was this part of the spell or a simple backfire?' I said, understanding that magic can be a precarious thing in nature and you could not always trust that it would work in your favour.

'Yes, Katherine came to Caroline our previous leader, may she rest in peace...' She spoke so gently, it was hypnotic. 'The spell almost broke the coven and she lost her life a few months after that spell. I never understood why she wanted to protect Crystal when she was the youngest and not the rightful heir to the throne. As to why she has no memories, I have no answers as to why this is the case. It was spelled that when she returned to her rightful home, she would remember her previous life. This is not the case?' she asked.

'No, she does not feel like this is home and is quite scared and unsure. She has had so much pain in her life that I fear that it may be blocking her memories from returning. Is there no spell that you can cast to make her remember? I feel as if it would make her safer. I am happy to pay whatever amount is necessary,' I pleaded with Millicent for her help. I needed Faith to remember her life. To remember how important she was and who she was.

'Do you care for her, my lord?' she asked, leaning forward over the cauldron.

'Yes, her family were superb rulers and deserve to regain their title and bring peace across the land,' I said, wanting to stand up from my chair.

'Hmmm,' was all that came out of her mouth as she looked me up and down.

'I should confer with my coven before a decision is made

but I leave you with one question. Crystal returning does not make her the rightful heir to the throne. Another Bouchard was saved and has been living on Trikeque Island. Farewell, Lord Marchés,' Millicent said, stepping into the shadows and disappearing.

'Wait...' I did not get a chance to finish my sentence.

As I walked out, I could not even see the old lady. I shivered from the eeriness of the house. I pondered what Millicent had just said. Who else could possibly be alive? Why were they on Trikeque Island? Trikeque Island was for outlaws and those who had been excommunicated. It was not accessible by horse and was always surrounded in mystery. There were stories of strange music on a full moon and bright lights. If another Bouchard was alive, why had they allowed the Faulcons to continue their rule? The other founding families would support an uprising. I heard music coming from the orphanage. I walked up the stairs.

Faith was dancing with music playing through her brick. All the children were following her movements and the room was filled with joyous laughter. Faith looked at me and smiled. I wished I was oblivious to the dangers as she was. Her smile spread across her whole face and her hair was bouncing around. She looked immaculate; she had no flaws. I knew I had to tell her about the conversation I had with King Sebastian. She ran over and dragged me to the front to follow her movements. This was not dancing but rather having the intention of looking foolish, like a court jester. I followed her steps stumbling after a few tries. She laughed.

'Now you are like me – not able to dance on two feet.'

I glared at her but could not hold it for long. My face

softened and a smile grew. I would miss her while I was away for the next two months.

I noticed the sun was at its peak in the sky. It was time to head back to the castle. Sonny walked in front to guard whilst Faith and I walked together. I could not think of how to approach the conversation I had had with King Sebastian.

'I...' I said and closed my mouth again.

'What is the matter, Aleksander? You have seemed off all day,' Faith asked.

Off? What was she trying to convey? I decided to leave it and try and speak again. I would never understand what she meant half the time. She spoke in a different language.

'I wanted to discuss the conversation I had with the king this morning. He sent a messenger for an urgent matter. He has forged a union between myself and Rohesia Arundel, the only daughter of Marcus Arundel – you encountered him after the attack in the woods, a few days after we met. He has required myself and a few of my men to organise some protective measures for the king on his royal tour. That will begin in two months and I believe you are accompanying him.' I finished speaking and waited for her to talk.

'Well, that is the first I have heard of it. Sometimes I regret making a deal with him. I thought I had control but apparently, I was blind-sided. Stupid me. Anyway, that is exciting that you will be married. I am sure she will be stunning and...'

She continued talking as I thought to myself, *Not in comparison to your beauty.*

'I am very excited for you. Oh my God!! You will finally pop your cherry and be with a woman on an intimate level. Oh, do you need pointers? I am assuming you know where to put your little Aleksander.'

'Who is little Aleksander? I do not have a son,' I said, awfully confused on what she meant. She giggled and pointed to my crotch.

'Oh,' I said and kept walking. 'I am worried about your safety while I am away. I need you to promise me that you will behave and not upset the king or the Queen Mother and just do as you are asked.' I knew she would not listen to my request but I was shocked by her response.

'On one condition. That you swear to tell me the truth on the question that I am about to ask,' Faith said, not looking at me but watching where she was placing her delicate feet.

'I swear,' I said, holding up my hand and wondering what this could be about.

'After this morning, where I played the piano – brilliantly, I might add – the only artistic skill I have apart from falling over my two feet – I noticed that Miguel left suddenly and Sonny informed me that I played the Bouchard song. Annie, Harley and I have heard rumours about this Bouchard girl – cannot remember her name. I have been treated rather well for a stranger from an outside world and had this weird feeling since being here that's hard to explain. Am I the daughter of Charles and Katherine Bouchard? I only ask you because I trust you and I hope you will give me the correct answer but also because you told me you knew her growing up but this doesn't make sense because if I was from here then I should remember something but I don't and nothing looks familiar at all.' Faith finally took a breath and stopped talking.

I didn't know how to answer; I wanted to wait until I knew

how to trigger her memory from the witches.

'No, you are not Crystal Bouchard. Yes, I would tell you the truth.' I felt nauseous in my stomach. I did not want to lie but felt as if I must to protect her.

CHAPTER TWENTY-THREE

Faith

I was ecstatic after my chat with Aleksander. I hoped he had not lied to me but I have felt a warmness towards him since the day we met. Maybe that was why I was so hard on him? I had the tendency to expect too much from people. I plopped onto my bed and started playing with Toby before Annie and Harley barged into my room.

'Where have you been all afternoon?' Harley asked, jumping on the bed and almost hitting me. She looked really, really excited about something.

'I was at the orphanage. Oh my God! Did you know Aleksander is getting married? The king has organised it and ordered him to comply pretty much. He is not very happy and I got my phone,' I said, pulling it out of my cleavage.

'Same,' they said in unison.

'It still has battery – what the fuck?' Annie said, pulling hers out of her pocket.

'I know, right? I was super confused as well,' I said back to her.

'Wait, backtrack a bit. Aleksander is getting married? Why?' Harley looked pissed off.

'To Rh... something Arundel. It is for a union between the Faulcon and Arundel families. Sebastian has ordered it and asked him to oversee protective measures for the royal tour that I am supposed to attend with the king in the next couple of months. Thanks for telling me, Sebastian. I am glad I can count on you guys and Aleksander for not keeping me in the dark.'

'I cannot believe he is marrying him off. I think it is out of jealousy.' Annie looked towards Harley.

'Jealously over what?' As soon as I said that, I knew what her response would be.

'Duh, over you. Sebastian spoke to Aleksander a few days ago about his behaviour with you and requested that he stop manhandling his prized possession or he would pretty much kill him,' Annie said, sounding really excited. She was disturbing sometimes.

'How the hell did you find that out? It sounds ludicrous.' I sat up and leaned against the wall.

'From Langford.'

'I heard the same from Aidan too,' Harley said. Bloody pillow talk.

'We all know Aleksander has no interest in me. That is just stupid of Sebastian to think that. I am no one's prized possession either. The little shit. Still thinks he owns me. Yeah, good luck.' I was annoyed and I spoke rather abruptly. I smiled after I finished the sentence to reassure them that I would not be cracking it anytime soon.

I felt as if I was losing control and was desperately trying to hold on to my independence and who I was before I came here. I looked forward to spending more time with Aleksander later tonight. We chatted for what seemed like hours about anything and everything. To be honest, it was mainly myself talking and Aleksander just taking everything in. I got up and pulled both of them into a hug. I didn't want to let go. I had a sickening feeling in my stomach that it was all about to change. I was genuinely scared for myself and for them but I would not abandon them again and I would hide my fear for them.

'Alright, get out. I am tired; I was dancing all afternoon and I want a nap. You know, I am getting old,' I said with a big smile on my face. They laughed.

'Yeah, twenty-six is so old. Half of fifty. Yep – oh, look, is that a grey hair?' Annie said playfully, slowly walking out of the room.

'Hate you,' I said, laughing. I lay down on the bed; my attempt to nap was not going to happen. My brain was going in overdrive.

I turned my phone back on. My battery was on fifty-six per cent. I opened the gallery and started flicking through pictures of Toby, my car, my wedding dress, my wedding venue and stopped on the photo of Aleksander and me. I had not looked at it properly until now. The first photo he was looking at the screen confused. In the third photo, he was not looking at me but he was actually kissing my head with his eyes closed. His face was relaxed and seemed at peace with crinkles around his mouth that showed remnants of a smile. He did care for me; I didn't understand but it made me smile. I started humming a tune, 'Hmm, hm, hm, hm, hmmmm. Bop bop boooop,' and giggled to myself. I changed it to the lock screen on my phone. I started deleting photos of Toby and I but kept only five. I smiled and turned the phone off again and smiled. I closed my eyes and drifted off to a peaceful sleep.

*

I woke up suddenly because I felt another presence in the room. I jumped up.

'Who the hell are you?' It wasn't Makenzie or anyone else I recognised. She just stood still and didn't move.

'Yes, hi, hello. I can see you and it is rude not to answer someone. Who the hell are you?' I spoke louder this time.

Sonny burst into the room. 'Lady Bushanti, who are you speaking to?' he said, looking around the room. I looked over at the girl in the corner and she was smiling.

'Nobody, I was dreaming. I am alright. Thank you, Sonny.'

Sonny walked out of the room.

'It is official then. I have snapped and I am now seeing shit but if this place has witches, then it obviously has magic. If you wanted to see me, you must want to speak with me and I would appreciate the respect instead of you standing in a corner staring at me.' I tried not to speak too loud to avoid bringing Sonny into the room again.

'Lady Bushanti, I am Millicent, the leader of the coven.' She curtsied.

'To what do I owe the pleasure of your visit?' I felt as if I needed to be polite, in case she hexed me. She was quite pretty for a witch. Yes, I am well aware that I was stereotyping her.

'I was curious about the beautiful girl with the hypnotic blue eyes,' Millicent said, walking towards me.

'So, you decided to appear in a ghost form? How come I can see you but my guard, Sonny, could not?' I said curiously as I walked closer to her as well. I had the feeling that I wanted to swipe my hand through her ghostly figure. It was so tempting.

She picked up on what I wanted to do and disappeared again. I needed a drink after that – pity they didn't have any vodka around. My brain was going into overdrive. How could I see her and not Sonny? Why was a witch astral projecting to see me? Aleksander said I was not Crystal but why were so many little clues adding up to the conclusion that I was?

I sat on the window's edge and watched the waves crash against the sand and retreat into the ocean. I opened the door to my room. Sonny turned and looked at me.

'Yes, Lady Bushanti?'

'Sorry, Sonny, I was just going to wander down to the beach with my thoughts,' I said, attempting to walk around him.

'Not possible. Dinner will be served shortly,' Sonny said sternly. I was still trying to get around him. I sighed.

'Fine, can I at least head to the dining hall now?' I was frustrated; I hated the restrictions placed upon me.

I walked down to the dining hall with Sonny. I didn't want to talk to him because I was annoyed for trivial reasons.

'Faith, wait up,' I heard Harley shout out. I turned and stopped for her. She ran up and put her arm around my shoulder.

'How are you? You have that look on your face that says you want to punch something.'

'Wow, am I that obvious? I am just frustrated; I was not allowed to walk to the beach. I just want to clear my head. It is fuzzy right now. I hope there is some good wine because I feel like I need a drink,' I said, putting my other arm around her shoulder. I didn't want to tell her about my strange visitor. I decided I would tell Aleksander later.

I shook my hair and fixed it up. It got caught on the cross from Aleksander and pulled some hair out.

'Ow,' I said under my breath.

I examined the scratchings on the back of the cross. I should ask him to translate it. I wasn't looking where I was going and almost ran into a wall. Luckily, Harley pulled me out of the way and saved me some embarrassment.

'How is Aidan?' I asked Harley.

'Good. I know it sounds stupid but have you ever just clicked with someone and felt like you knew them like the back of your hand? He makes me feel safe.' She paused briefly.

'And it helps that the sex is amazing – he does this trick that is so hard to explain but it makes me shake with excitement and causes an instant orgasm.' Her face lit up with a smile.

'And that escalated. I am glad you are happy but I do not want to know about what you and Aidan do between the sheets, please. Do not forget it has been over a year since I have had sex. I have forgotten what it actually feels like to be intimate with someone. What I wouldn't give to have a man simply throw me against a wall and just give it to me hard.' I looked up and noticed Aleksander standing there.

I looked at him and felt my cheeks instantly blush. He cleared his throat. Yep, he definitely heard what I was just saying. I had no words and simply walked past him into the dining hall.

'Sebastian,' I said, walking over and giving him a kiss on the cheek.

'Faith, I have a present for you...' he said, smiling. 'But dinner is first.' He pulled the chair out for me to sit in.

'And I get called a tease,' I whispered to Harley, who was sitting beside me.

Aleksander was sitting directly across from me and Annie grabbed a seat beside him. I wondered why he had been invited to sit at the table. The same question could be asked on why Annie, Harley and I were invited to dine with the king every night as well. One of the servants walked over and poured a glass of wine. I grabbed it, possibly too quickly, and if Aleksander and Sebastian knew about Alcoholics Anonymous, I am sure they would both be taking me there instantly. I restrained myself from drinking the entire glass but I was still thinking about Millicent and how I could possibly see her and the likely chances that I was Crystal Bouchard but I had amnesia apparently and had no memory of anything.

Sebastian and Aleksander were talking business about his upcoming marriage and his trip to secure protective measures before the king's royal tour. I was trying not to eavesdrop but I was never very good at that. I wanted to find out more information about the royal tour.

'Faith.'

I looked up.

'Yes, Your Majesty,' I said politely.

'During the ceremony, you will walk in with Aleksander at the back but with your permission, I would like us to exit the room together.' Sebastian spoke politely yet bluntly at the same time, giving me no choice to reject him but rather to just agree with him.

'As you wish, Your Majesty.'

The servant brought out plates of food. The first course was a green soup. I could not identify what flavour it was. I just scooped it up and swallowed. It was not the best tasting but it would do the job. There was not much taste; it would taste better with a bit of garlic. Once our soup was finished, they cleared the plates away.

Harley nudged me. 'Faith, that is your third glass.'

I looked from her to the glass; I did not even realise.

'Thank you,' I said, pushing my glass closer to Aleksander's side of the table.

The king motioned for the servants. He leaned forward and grabbed my glass for it to be refilled. I smiled politely but was seething on the inside. I would pretend to drink it from now on.

The second course came out; it was quail eggs with vegetables. I did not want to think about what I was eating and was just hoping that they were like normal chicken eggs in taste. I just realised that Yelena was not in the room.

'Your Majesty, where is the Queen Mother?' I asked, grabbing my glass and pretending to drink by simply mimicking the swallowing action.

'She does not agree with my decisions about political matters and has removed herself from my advisors,' Sebastian said, not looking at me but cutting into his food.

I glanced at Aleksander who shook his head. Was he on the advisory board? I dropped the topic and asked a stupid question that I already knew the answer to.

'What types of eggs are these? I like them, they have more – um, what's it called? – yolk than normal chicken eggs.' I looked around the table; they were a chatty group tonight.

'They are quail,' a server answered me. I did not turn around and look at them.

'Thank you,' I said.

'You do not thank the servers. They are to be seen and not heard. Guards,' Sebastian called out.

'What are you doing?' I asked with no formalities.

Sebastian glared at me. 'Take that server away to the

dungeons, where I will decide his proper punishment for speaking. I am liking the idea of removing his tongue,' Sebastian said, twirling his hands in front of him.

'WHAT?' I shouted and stood up from the table to walk over to the young man.

'That is callous – he is young and deserves a second chance,' I said, slapping the guard's hand away and pulling the young man behind me to protect him.

Sebastian banged his hands on the table.

'Who are you to overrule me? I am the king. I MAKE THE DECISIONS and I say TAKE HIM AWAY.' His forehead was creased and he looked enraged. The guard snatched the boy out of my hands.

I saw Annie's face; she looked terrified. I had crossed a line with Sebastian. I went and sat back down.

'I apologise for my behaviour, Your Majesty,' I said and continued eating my food. This time I did finish my glass of wine. I sat quietly after that and avoided eye contact with everyone. I felt Aleksander's eyes on me but I avoided him at all costs. I hoped that young man would not lose his tongue. I finished my food and sat quietly in my chair, waiting to be dismissed by Sebastian. I was twiddling my thumbs under the table. Sebastian moved my glass closer to me.

'No, thank you, Your Majesty. I think I have had enough for the night.'

Sebastian nodded. 'Aleksander, may you ask the two guards outside the door to assist Lady Wakchter and Lady Gelden with their new attire?'

Aleksander did not speak but stood up from his chair and walked to ask for the guards' help. I noticed he did not ask for a guard to help me. The guards walked into the room. Annie and Harley stood up. I followed but Sebastian grabbed my arm and pulled me back down. I pulled my arm away and sat down again.

'I need to speak with you,' Sebastian said, moving in.

I wanted to tell him to stick it but thought I had better stay quiet after earlier. He was not pleased with my outburst. Annie, Harley and Aleksander left the room.

I smiled at Sebastian awkwardly. He stood up and walked over to the fireplace. He put his arm on the ledge and leaned his body against the wall.

'What's the matter, Sebastian? You seem not yourself.' I got up from the chair and walked over to the other side of the fireplace. I did not want to get too close; I watched the glow from the fire on his face. He was an attractive man but he had a harsh look to his face that made him look older and unattractive and his personality did not help.

'Since I have taken the throne, there has been animosity from the other leading families and with you three ladies appearing, it has made my position as king difficult.' He looked really worried and it began to stress me out. I waited patiently for him to keep talking.

'I believe when some of the founding families see your face tomorrow, it will strengthen my position and I hope it will begin the unification of all the families.'

I took a step backwards. I knew what he was going to say but I did not want to hear the words.

'There have been discussions on your parentage and birthright but I had doubts over whether you were Crystal or shared a resemblance to her. After today, I can officially declare that you are Crystal Bouchard. I have no answers as to how you are still alive but regardless, with our union soon enough, we will become the strongest rulers in history.' Sebastian started moving towards me. I was in shock. I kept walking backwards until I hit the wall, hard.

'You are wrong. I am not Crystal. I was not born here. I think I would remember or have some memories or anything. You have been given the wrong information,' I said, pushing myself off the wall and walking away from Sebastian.

'I am positive. Aleksander was tasked with finding out more information. Your eyes were the first piece of evidence, then discovering the scar on your back, then your attitude and the last piece was your playing the Bouchard anthem.' Sebastian grabbed my hand to stop me from pacing the room.

'No, you're wrong. It is not possible.' My voice cracked and I could feel tears well in my eyes. Aleksander had sworn that I was not Crystal earlier today; he lied.

Sebastian spoke softly. 'Shh.' He pulled me into his embrace.

I started crying. I was not abandoned like I had thought my whole life. My parents sent me away to save my life and I never had the chance to meet them. My mother was the beautiful woman in the painting I had seen weeks ago – the jewellery I played with was hers. Sebastian caressed my hair; he was trying to soothe me. I buried my head into his chest. I could smell his strong perfume. It was like mint mixed with apples. Very strong but I enjoyed it. Sebastian pulled me in closer and I let him. I knew he had yelled at me before but I needed to learn to keep my mouth shut. Had I really judged him too harshly? He had always been honest with me and to date had not lied, unlike Aleksander.

I looked up at him. I placed my hand on his face and moved onto my tippy toes. Sebastian leant down; I felt his warm lips meet mine. He was soft and gentle. He moved one of his hands to my cheek and the other behind my head. I opened my mouth slightly, as he slowly moved his tongue and massaged it against mine. He put both his hands down to my backside and lifted me up onto the table. We kept kissing; he moved his hand over my breast and started down to between my legs.

'No, stop,' I said, pushing him off. 'Sorry, I am not ready for that,' I said, getting off the table and pulling my dress down.

Sebastian walked over to the wall, putting his hands on his hips and sighing. I saw him brush his hair off his face.

'I am...' I attempted to speak.

'No, there is no need to apologise. I got swept up and should have stopped before taking it further. I apologise for my actions, Faith, they were not the actions of a gentleman or a king.' Sebastian finally turned around and looked at me.

I smiled and he chuckled to himself.

'I am glad that you are comfortable around me.' He laughed. 'I want to apologise for raising my voice at you before. I am trying to show my strength and if others saw this, they would lose their belief that I could be king.' Sebastian seemed really sincere.

'I understand but it was still mean. You need to understand that I will not be the type of girl to just sit quietly when I see something I do not agree with,' I said, walking back over to him and putting my hands in his.

I peeked over his shoulder at the boxes; he smiled.

'I almost forgot about your present.' Sebastian walked over and picked up the box.

'Come now, I shall show you in your chambers,' he said, walking off before me.

That was not fair. I quickly ran to keep up with him. I was excited. I had a feeling they were my dresses. I had no idea why I was so excited but I wanted to see them. I didn't give Lord Carmelide much direction on what to create; here's hoping he was good at his job. I walked quicker than Sebastian and reached my room and opened the door for him. I went inside and was so excited. I could hear Annie and Harley screaming; they must have been going through their packages. Sebastian put it down on my bed and stepped backwards. I looked at him.

'You can open them. I made some suggestions to the designer on your behalf. I hope you approve.' Sebastian spoke with his hands behind his back, looking nervous.

I opened the wooden box; there would have been about twenty or more dresses in the box with so many colours: black, blue, silver, green, pink, red, gold and brown. There were silky, lacy, short-sleeved, long-sleeved and one-shouldered dresses. There was a small black felt-like box at the bottom. It was the size of a purse. I rubbed my fingers over it. It was rough but silky at the same time. I picked it up and looked over to Sebastian.

'Open it. I designed it with you in my thoughts,' Sebastian said, leaning against the window.

I opened the box; it was a headpiece. It was crown-like, with a clear rectangular blue crystal sticking up but not too much, about two centimetres in length. It had a matching necklace; it was longer than the crown – more like five centimetres long.

I looked at him and smiled. 'They are beautiful. Thank you.'

He walked over. 'May I?'

I nodded. Sebastian grabbed the crown and placed it on my head. He brushed my hair behind my ears.

'Now you look like a queen or how I imagined my future queen would look like.'

Wow, that was corny. I laughed internally. Sebastian led me over to the mirror.

'It would honour me if you would wear this tomorrow with the silver and blue dress. I designed it to bring out the colour of your eyes.'

I turned around and kissed him.

'I am sorry, Sebastian,' I said taking the crown off and putting it back in the box.

'What for?' he asked, creasing his forehead and looking confused on what I was talking about.

'For judging you. I thought you were a spoilt brat the first day we met but you are kind and caring. I think you will make an excellent king.'

Sebastian pulled me in for a hug and kissed my forehead.

'It is best if we part for the night. We have a big day tomorrow.' Sebastian kissed me on the lips and left for the night.

I looked out the window; it was around the time I was supposed to meet Aleksander but I was not going to see him tonight. He lied to me. I thought the best decision was to wait to talk to him before I said something I regretted. He may have had good intentions for all I knew in not telling me. I started putting my dresses into my cupboard. I picked up the silver dress I was to wear tomorrow and put it against me and started twirling around the room. I loved the blue ribbon that was around the waist and the blue trim at the bottom; it had a sweetheart neckline, so it would make my boobs look fantastic. I wondered what Annie and Harley's dresses looked like.

KNOCK, KNOCK.

Who on Earth would be knocking on my door this late? I hoped it wasn't Sebastian trying to convince me to sleep with him. Even though the kiss was passionate, I didn't feel a spark between us. He was sweet but I think that was as far as my attraction went. I ran over to the door and opened it.

'Annie, OH MY GOD. How beautiful are the dresses? Come se—' I stopped talking instantly when Aleksander appeared behind her.

'I am sorry to come see you so late but we both needed to talk to you,' Annie said, walking into the room.

Why did Annie need to speak with me? Aleksander walked past me and I glared at him. I wanted to punch him in the face so hard that I would break his perfect nose. I slammed the door behind me.

'I think I already know what this is about,' I said, sitting down on my bed, waiting for their explanation. Annie opened her mouth to speak.

'NO, I want you to explain it to me after you lied to my face this afternoon,' I said, pointing at Aleksander.

'Faith, I apologise for lying but I could not bring myself to tell you. I had every intention of telling you but I did not think you were ready to find out. I was protecting you.'

'NO, that is not an excuse. I trusted you to tell me.' I walked over and slapped him across the face. 'Screw you, I thought you were my friend. I knew you were keeping something from me but I thought you would tell it to me straight when I asked you.

You are not the person I thought you were.'

'HEY, he does not deserve that.' Annie raised her voice at me.

'What the hell are you even doing in the room? Did you know before I did?' I asked, feeling tear begin to well up in my eyes. She knew the pain I felt growing up.

'Yes, Aleksander asked me about the scar on your back.'

'You fucking bitch. You knew and wouldn't tell me. You knew the pain I felt growing up, not knowing my parents and feeling as if I had been abandoned, as if something was wrong with me. I was never normal and you knew that. GET OUT,' I shouted at her.

I wanted to slap her too but I would never hit Annie. Annie had tears in her eyes and walked out crying.

'Annie did not deserve that,' Aleksander said, raising his voice.

I turned and looked at him. I must have had my bitch face on because he stepped backwards. I was livid with him.

'I am waiting for your explanation. You have known since the beginning, haven't you?' I asked, trying to calm myself down.

'Yes, I had my suspicions that you were Crystal. The eyes, the attitude, the candour, the beauty like your mother. After discovering the existence of your scar, I knew it was you but I told Annie that I wanted to wait to tell you until you remembered.' He seemed genuine in the way he spoke.

'You have no idea how angry I am with you; I trusted you. I only came back because you asked me to. It was for no other reason – you made me feel safe. You made me feel as if I had an ally here but now I don't. You may have had good intentions but it doesn't change the fact you lied and kept it from me. I am glad you are leaving because I do not want to see your face again,' I said, taking off the cross from him and throwing it at him.

'Faith, I am pleading with you. Everything I have done has been to protect you. I care for you more than words can express.'

I looked at Aleksander's face. He was about to cry as well.

'Fuck you, Aleksander. I am done. Get out,' I said, walking over to the door, opening it and waiting for him to leave. I did not want to look at his face. He stopped to look at me. He put the cross back on the table.

'It will protect you while I cannot,' he said and left the room.

I slammed the door and cried myself to sleep. I knew I would be puffy tomorrow for the coronation but I didn't care. I felt betrayed and hurt. Two people I trusted and cared for kept something from me. Something that changed everything – I knew now I was trapped forever and I could never leave. Sebastian would hunt me to the ends of the world before he would let me slip away. I felt so alone, more alone than I had in my entire life. I cuddled Toby and eventually fell asleep. I dreamed of a chapel burning and hearing people screaming. I wanted to run inside and save them but Aleksander was holding me back.

'Let me go,' I screamed at him.

'You're not ready,' was all he kept saying before I woke up covered in sweat.

I looked out the window; the sun was about to come up. I knew Sonny wouldn't be at his post yet. I quickly changed out of my dress from yesterday and into a fresh one, quickly cleaning my face. I left a note for Makenzie telling her where I was and ran down to the beach. I put on my shitty brown dress, which was bland and I didn't care if it got ruined.

The castle was so quiet. I snuck out the side door that Sebastian took me through last time and ran down to the beach. I sat down on the sand near the ocean; the waves were coming up to my feet. Toby was running around in the waves; he looked so happy. I sat there and looked out. It blew my mind that I had grown up here right next to an ocean. Did my parents bring me down here to play? A tear rolled down my cheek. I sniffed and wiped it away.

I wished I could speak to my parents – and brothers, from what Aleksander had told me. I wanted to remember but how could I possibly start? I would speak to Annie later today. I was annoyed with her but not as much as Aleksander; he had asked her to keep it from me. That was not fair of him. I watched the sunrise over the clouds. The orange and red colours spread across the ocean and lit up the sky. I watched it slowly get bigger as the colours changed from a light orange to a darker, the red changing to a purple and the blue sky appearing. Someone tapped my shoulder; it was Makenzie. She sat down beside me. I looked at her and she knew. She wrapped her arms around me and let me cry.

'Come now. You have a big day ahead of you,' Makenzie said, standing up and offering her hand.

I welcomed her assistance and stood up.

'Did you know I had the pleasure of meeting your parents once?'

I looked at her.

'What were they like?' I asked in anticipation.

'Your mother was the most beautiful person in Hisadalgon. People would travel to marvel at her beauty – your father adored her. She spoke to me once and said, "A girl is only as powerful as she believes herself to be." I never understood what she meant.'

I smiled because I did. I always said that to myself growing up and never knew where I got it from.

Makenzie continued to tell me stories she had heard about the Bouchards. I was happy hearing about them; it was my way of connecting with them without ever having the chance of meeting them. We got back to my room.

'Sebastian wants me to wear this dress, with the crown and necklace, but no idea how you want to do my hair.'

She looked me up and down. 'Where is your cross?'

I didn't answer and sat down for her to do my hair. She grabbed some charcoal.

'What are you doing?' I asked, moving away from her.

'To highlight your eyes, I am going to draw a thin line on your top lid,' she said while demonstrating what she was going to do.

'Oh, eyeliner, okay.' I closed my eyes and let her work.

She fixed my hair and put the crown on, then tied the necklace around my neck. She opened the dress while I stepped into it. I held on to the pole as she did up the corset; it was nice and tight. I turned around.

'How do I look?' I said nervously.

'I am honoured to be your lady's maid, Faith,' she said, crying. It got really awkward real fast.

'I enjoy waking up every day to your help.' I was at a loss for words and just walked over to hug her. There was a knock at the door.

'If that is Aleksander, I am not here,' I said, getting out of view of the door.

'Good morning, Makenzie. I have come to escort Faith to the grand hall,' Aleksander said.

Are you bloody kidding me? I thought to myself.

Makenzie looked over.

'I can escort myself, thank you,' I said bluntly to Aleksander from behind the door.

'King's orders, Lady Bushanti,' Aleksander said as he walked into the room and looked at me. He stopped and his mouth opened. 'You look like an angel.'

'No, you do not get to compliment me anymore. I will walk behind you and we will not talk. You can wait outside.'

Aleksander walked out of the room. I looked back at Makenzie.

'Am I ready?' I asked.

She nodded and kissed me on the cheek. I walked out of the room and did not look at Aleksander. He kept trying to walk beside me and wanting to talk to me. I stopped dead.

'Just stop. I don't want to talk to you or listen to your voice. Please, just stop. I will be glad when you leave tomorrow. Two months without seeing you will be fantastic,' I said, walking off. I knew that would have hurt him but I didn't care; I was hurt and I wanted him to hurt.

I walked into the grand hall. It was decorated with so many flowers and the throne was placed strategically in the middle of the room. I was in awe; it was like a movie scene with flowers placed everywhere, the red carpet leading to the throne. I saw Yelena speaking to the priest guy. She saw me and made a beeline over. I was scared; I could not ask Aleksander for help with how I was treating him.

'My, you look regal. Who did you steal that dress from?' she said, spitting in my face. I did not flinch.

'It was made for me by Lord Carmelide, specifically for today,'

I said, trying to sound proper and regal to shut her up.

'Who gave you permission to wear a crown?' Yelena said, grabbing it from my head. 'You are not a princess – you are a peasant.'

I was restraining myself with all the people in the room. I felt an arm around my side.

'Mother, you are embarrassing yourself. I gave Faith the crown to wear because she is a princess in her own right. Do not make me remove you from the room,' he said, hissing at his mother.

I smugly looked down and smiled. Sebastian snatched the crown back and stepped in front of his mother.

'There it is. That is my Faith, the unwavering beauty.'

I smiled and leaned in for a kiss. He put his hands on my cheeks and kissed me. It wasn't as long as last night but rather quick. Sebastian put my arm around his and we walked away. I looked back at Aleksander, who looked rather unimpressed.

'I will walk into the room. You will follow behind me with members from some of the other founding families and you will bow and declare that I am the one true king and swear loyalty.'

I felt sick in my stomach. I didn't want to say that at all in front of a whole room. I felt my body heat rising; I was beginning to have a panic attack. This was all too much.

'Can you excuse me?' I said, walking away and out of the room. I leaned against the wall outside the hall. I was trying to catch my breath. I was beginning to black out. I was trying everything I could to stay awake.

'Faith, Faith. Hey, stay with me. Breathe, in through your

nose out through your mouth. Nice deep breaths. Good girl.'
It was Annie.

I looked into her eyes; she was worried about me. I was starting to catch my breath again. She grabbed my hand and led me to another room.

'Come, sit down.'

I sat on the chair and was still trying to get my breath back. I felt my temperature starting to decrease. Harley walked into the room.

'I couldn't find any water,' she said, handing me a glass. It was wine but I drank the whole glass quickly.

'Oh, that is better. My mouth was so dry,' I said, panting.

Harley left the room. Annie stood up.

'Don't. Please, just don't,' I said not looking at her but looking at the floor.

I heard her let out a sigh.

'I get it, you wanted to protect me. Aleksander asked you not to tell me until he was ready. You thought it was the right thing to do. I am still pissed at you but I can forgive you, not him. He lied to my face after he knew and please do not try and justify his actions. I am not in the mood.' I looked up at her and her face was covered in tears.

'I am sorry.' She sobbed and walked over to hug me.

'Shhhh, it's okay. You will ruin your face if you keep crying,' I said, laughing and trying to calm her down.

There was a knock at the door. I turned around, not letting go of Annie and looked at who was entering the room.

'Dmitirov,' I said, running over and hugging him. 'I have not seen you in ages. Where have you been?' I was so excited to see him.

'Faith, you look well-adjusted,' he said, keeping a straight face. 'Aleksander sent for me to find you. The coronation is about to start.'

Annie pulled back and wiped her face out of Dmitirov's sight.

'Yes, of course. Annie?' I turned and asked before leaving the room.

'I am fine. I will be in shortly.' I could hear in her voice she was still upset. I didn't want to leave her. I looked at Dmitirov, showing my concern.

'I will stay with her,' he said, walking back into the room.

'Thank you,' I said, walking quickly back to the grand hall.

I almost tripped over my dress; it was longer than usual and heavier. I found Sebastian waiting nervously outside the doors to the grand hall. I didn't have a chance to look at him earlier; he looked rather handsome. He was wearing black leather pants with a black and gold tunic that matched his cloak. The cloak had a train roughly a metre long; it reminded me of a wedding dress. I smiled when he looked at me. I could tell he was nervous. His hands kept moving and he was bobbing up and down. He seemed to relax when he saw my face. I walked over, put my hands on top of his and kissed his cheek.

'You will be fine,' I said before walking over to my position, standing behind Aleksander. I was glaring into the back of his head; if my eyes were lasers, they would be burning a hole in his head.

I waited for everyone in front of me to start moving; that was the only way I knew what to do. I heard the trumpets sound as the doors to the grand hall opened. I took a deep breath. I saw the seven people in front of me start walking and I followed slowly behind them. Four of them stood on the right of the room about a metre and a half away from the throne. Aleksander, myself and one other stood on the left side. I turned around and saw Sebastian walking down the carpet. He had no crown or staff, just walked slowly and with pride. He looked petrified but proud at the same time. He reached the throne and turned around and waited before being instructed to sit down.

The priest stood in front of him; he was wearing a purple and white uniform with a golden sash going around his neck and down his shoulders. He walked over and grabbed the crown off the red pillow from his assistant who was wearing similar robes but no golden sash.

'Do you, Sebastian Faulcon, swear to protect the northern seas of Hisadalgon?' the priest asked.

'I swear.'

'Do you swear to protect the eastern forests of Hisadalgon?'

'I swear.'

'Do you swear to protect the southern mountains of Hisadalgon?'

'I swear.'

'Do you swear to protect the western plains of Hisadalgon?'

'I swear,' Sebastian said, taking one final sigh of relief.

'By the power given to me by the gods, I pronounce you the King of Hisadalgon. Long live the king.' The priest lowered the crown onto his head.

It was a relatively simple crown, just gold with a large red ruby at the front and spikes the whole way around. The entire crowd was chanting. 'Long live the king! Long live the king!'

I mouthed the words but did not let them come out. He was not my king but I would play the part I was given. I glanced at

Aleksander; he was doing the same as me. He glanced at me and looked away instantly. He knew I was still annoyed and I would not forgive him easily.

'Now, all of the founding families shall swear allegiance to the new king,' the priest said, looking around at all the family members. This was obviously Sebastian's way of presenting me back into the world of Hisadalgon.

The first man on the left stepped forward and knelt before Sebastian. I wanted to reach for Aleksander's hand. I was scared. I didn't know what to do but out of my own pride, I would not grab his hand. I closed my eyes and took a deep breath and smiled.

I heard the man say, 'The Arundels swear allegiance to the new king, Sebastian Faulcon.'

I watched Sebastian nod and the man stood back.

Aleksander stood forward. 'The Marchéses swear allegiance to the new king, Sebastian Faulcon.'

Sebastian nodded and Aleksander stood back up and stepped backwards.

'Introducing the last remaining Bouchard,' the priest said.

I could hear the crowd behind me start whispering and murmuring. I looked down and stepped forward. I did not kneel but curtsied.

'The Bouchards swear allegiance to the new king, Sebastian Faulcon,' I said and looked at Sebastian.

He smiled and nodded. I stood back up and stepped backwards. The remaining members of the founding families all pledged allegiance. My feet were beginning to get sore; I had been standing for a few hours now and was starting to wobble. How much longer would this take?

Aleksander whispered under his breath, 'Stop moving.'

I snapped a quick look at him and stopped moving. The priest started talking again.

'Sebastian Faulcon, may the grace of the gods be with you in your journey as king. May you be a fair and just ruler and protect Hisadalgon against all enemies. Now rise and take your first steps as king.'

Sebastian stood up and took the staff off the priest's assistant and started walking back down the red carpet. I noticed people beginning to bow and curtsy. I followed and went as slow as I possibly could in this dress. I was really itchy and irritable. The people started following him out of the room; I felt Aleksander's hand push against my back to start moving. I started walking. He walked beside me but we didn't talk nor look at each other. I noticed Sebastian was heading out into the garden. As the people of Hisadalgon were walking into the garden, each of them was handed a glass of wine. I grabbed a glass and looked for Annie and Harley. Aleksander tapped me on the shoulder and pointed to where they were. I did not thank him but walked off in that direction. I felt so many pairs of eyes on me as I walked through the crowds.

I gritted my teeth as I reached them.

'Well, that was fun, wasn't it?' I said, shaking off what had happened.

'Sure thing, Miss Bouchard,' Harley said, poking my shoulder.

'You know that is not my name and it will never be my name,' I said, shutting her down instantly.

Annie wasn't speaking. I looked at Harley and nodded my head in her direction.

'Just leave her be. She is having an off day.'

I nodded and turned around. 'Is it me or are there like a hundred eyes on me right now?' I asked Harley as I looked at her and smiled even though I didn't want to.

'No, it is not just you. Everyone is watching,' Harley said, forcing a smile as well. I raised my eyebrows.

'I did not want to do that,' I said to Harley, looking at her and trying not to focus on all the eyes that were on me.

'I know but you had to,' she said. 'Someone is walking over,' she said. I did not want to turn around.

'Lady Bouchard, it is a pleasure to meet you. I had the pleasure of meeting your mother and father many years ago.'

I smiled and put my hand up.

'Thank you, Lord...' I said, pausing, waiting for him to respond.

He kissed my hand.

'Lord Marchés,' he said after kissing my hand.

'Oh, you are related to Aleksander. I did not think he had any other relatives.'

The lady that was standing beside him scoffed.

'I am sorry, did I say something wrong?' I said as I glanced at her.

'He is not our relative – we disowned him and his family when they were charged with treason against the king. We chose the side of the Faulcons and they chose the Bouchards'. It disgraced our family,' she said.

My fist clenched. Harley grabbed my hand.

'That is such a kind thing for you to say to the last remaining family member of the Bouchards. I am glad you chose a side but Aleksander did not pick a side. His parents did. You have no right to judge him based on the actions of his parents – he was a little boy. I am glad you do not associate with Aleksander because you're beneath him and, I believe, in the social hierarchy, you are beneath me and I am tired of your face. You can leave now. Enjoy the rest of your evening, you judgmental bitch,' I said, turning around and giving my back to her.

'Meow,' Harley said. 'Very protective of someone you are not talking to.'

I rolled my eyes at her and turned back around. I saw Sebastian looking over towards me and smiling. He was surrounded by sycophants and seemed to be loving the attention. He nodded and excused himself before walking over to me.

'My beautiful lady,' he said, smiling.

I had never seen him looking this happy.

'My king,' I said, curtsying. 'You look incredibly powerful,' I said, rubbing my hands over his shoulders. The cloak was so soft; it felt like sheep's wool but softer. I did not want to know what it was made of.

'I wanted to request a dance with you later this evening, to show off my future queen.'

I shivered, not wanting to think about the prospect of marrying him just yet. He must have seen the fear on my face.

'When you are ready to be my queen,' he said, taking my hand in his.

'You are so patient Seb... Your Majesty,' I said, covering my mouth over my mistake.

He raised one eyebrow at me. I couldn't interpret what that meant but I just smiled sweetly. Sebastian leaned in to kiss me on the cheek before walking off to meet and greet the numerous other people. I just stood with Annie and Harley. I did not want to leave them and I felt out of my depth with everyone looking at me.

Miguel walked over.

'Lady Wakchter, may I request a moment alone?'

She smiled.

'Of course, my lord,' she said, walking off with him.

'How is Annie going with trying to get Miguel on her side?' I asked Harley behind my cup so people could not read my lips.

'Better than she expected. You and Annie were always the best at seducing. Me, not so much. He comes to see her nearly every day now and no, he does not suspect Langford and Annie. How is everything with Sebastian? I am assuming well,' she asked, rubbing her shoulder against mine. I blushed.

'Yeah, things got a little out of hand the other day. I think it was the mixture of the alcohol and being rather upset and vulnerable but um, yeah... we made out. It got to the point where he was on top of me on the dining table before I had to ask him to stop.' I was not looking at her but continuing to smile at the guests.

'WHAT?' Harley shouted in shock.

Nearly all the guests turned around and looked at us. I just started laughing and pointing at Harley. She copied what I was doing; they eventually stopped looking and continued with their conversations. Servers were bringing around food – thank GOD, I was starving. There was a platter of fruit. I grabbed a handful of grapes.

I saw Aleksander speaking with a lady. She looked quite beautiful from where I was standing. Her red hair went mid-way down her back. She was wearing a beautiful red dress with a massive gold and ruby necklace that looked like it swallowed her neck. She had no boobs but a rather large backside.

'Harley, who is the girl Aleksander is speaking with?' I asked her, not taking my eyes off them. I saw the girl look over and speak to Aleksander before he put his arm out to escort her over.

'I have no idea but she is quite pretty for a redhead. An Isla Fisher-type pretty,' she said, speaking over my shoulder.

'Hmm, yep. Time to smile and be pleasant,' I said, flashing a pleasant smile.

Harley smirked over my shoulder.

'Oh, shut your face. I am trying to be a nice person,' I said, giving her a scalding look. The girl with Aleksander broke away from his arm and ran over to me. She embraced me.

'Crystal, you have not changed,' she said.

I had a good look at her; she was beautiful. Her red hair was soft and thick, and she was shorter than me but her green eyes were the highlight of her face.

I stood, not moving, shocked. She had just embraced me.

'I am sorry – I have no idea who you are and please, my name is not Crystal, it is Faith,' I said, smiling.

'Yes, Aleksander said you had no memories of your previous life. We knew each other as children.'

I snapped a quick look at Aleksander. 'Oh, okay. Aleksander can speak to others but not to me. Well, I suppose it is fantastic to see you again but I believe I have missed your name,' I said politely.

'My apologies. I am Rohesia Arundel, the daughter of Marcus Arundel from the Nharabalu region,' she said, curtsying.

I could get used to this special treatment. *That's right, bitches, I am special,* I thought to myself.

'Nharahbalue region? I think I said that wrong but that is where the rainforests are, correct?' I asked her.

'Yes,' she said, smiling.

'You're going to be Aleksander's future wife. Where will you live? I am assuming away from Zilanta,' I said, wanting to know if I would still have to see his face every day.

Aleksander snapped his head in my direction.

'That has not been decided. Rohesia, we must speak to your father about our wedding,' he said and walked off. Rohesia waved and walked off after Aleksander.

'I wish you and Aleksander would just bone and get rid of the sexual tension between the two of you,' Harley said. I looked at her.

'Argh,' I said and sculled my wine before walking off.

I walked into the castle and saw the servants changing the room around for the feast later. I grabbed another glass and leaned against the wall, watching them. Sonny appeared beside me.

'You look beautiful today, Lady Bushanti,' he said, nodding.

'Thank you, Sonny. I see you got a new uniform as well. You look rather smart, don't you?' I said, straightening his jacket.

'What does intelligence have to do with looks?' He turned his head in confusion.

'No, no, not intelligence. It is more like cute, handsome, well-dressed.'

I wanted to find the room where all the Bouchard items were in storage. I could never remember that corridor I went down. I knew Dmitirov would remember. I would have to find him later. I continued to watch the servants assemble the room. They all seemed so unhappy. I just wanted to walk into the room and start making jokes but I knew that would not be the best decision to make.

'FAITH.' I heard someone yell my name.

I finished my wine and turned around; it was Aleksander. Oh, great, what did he want now?

'You have no right to be rude to Rohesia. She may not understand what you were saying but I can,' he said, fuming. His face was flushed.

'Sorry, not my fault she is not that intelligent. I expected a little better for the trustworthy Aleksander,' I said, turning my back on him. He grabbed my arm.

'When are you going to realise how important you are and how dangerous this place is?'

I looked down at his hand; he must have realised what he had done and let go instantly and took a step backwards.

'I am safe. Sebastian wants to marry me,' I said.

'How naïve are you? For an intelligent young lady, you do not even see the world around you. I have tried to protect you, as a promise to your parents...' He stopped, clenched his fists and walked away.

I had the urge to chase after him but left it. I turned around and punched the wall. What was I doing? Why was it hard to forgive him? I walked back out into the garden.

'There you are, Faith,' I heard Sebastian say as my eyes were adjusting to the difference in the light.

'Yes, my king,' I said, still waiting for them to adjust. I felt his hand around my waist, pulling me towards him.

'Is it true, Your Majesty, that there will be a union between you and the Bouchard heir?' an elderly man asked. He looked important. His clothes were fresh, his grey hair was tied back and he was roughly the same height as me. He was wearing black pants and a brown tunic. It was rather bland and boring but still looked as if it cost a lot of money.

'Yes, but not until Faith has adjusted to the customs of Hisadalgon,' Sebastian said before kissing the top of my head.

'Was she not born here?' the man asked again.

'I have no memories. I may have met all of you but yeah, sorry, none of you look familiar in the slightest,' I said smugly.

I could feel Sebastian's eyes piercing into the top of my head. I knew I should not have said anything.

'Yes, there still need to be some refinements,' Sebastian said. I noticed a lot of the people around him looking disapproving and I remembered what Aleksander said.

'Yes, and I look forward to learning them and becoming a part of your country and to being your loving wife and to having the honour of carrying your children,' I said, smiling and looking up at Sebastian.

All the faces changed from disapproving to little smiles. I could win over this crowd easily; the only problem was how much of myself would I lose in the process?

*

The rest of the afternoon was a blur; I stayed beside Sebastian for the remainder of the day, trying to charm the people. The grand hall was set up for the feast; there were four tables set up around the room. Sebastian had asked for me to walk into the hall with him to show the upcoming union. I agreed. We were standing outside the door; I looked at him and all I could think of were Aleksander's words running through my head.

He turned towards me and put his hand on my cheek. I closed my eyes and opened them again.

'I could look into your eyes forever,' Sebastian said and kissed my cheek. I grabbed his face and made him kiss me on the lips. I wanted to know if I would feel any semblance of a spark between us. I felt his tongue massage mine inside my mouth and his hands move behind to play with my hair. I could feel no spark, just an emptiness during the kiss. I had no feelings for him but I needed to fake it. This was the problem: I would never be safe because one day he would realise that I did not reciprocate his feelings.

The trumpets sounded and Sebastian pulled back and put his arm up for me to put my hand on top as we walked in together. The whole room erupted in applause as we walked in and I smiled and nodded to people around the room. *Keep the smile going,* was all I kept saying to myself. I was looking for Aleksander's face in the crowd; I knew I needed to forgive him. He was my only ally – my only hope and my only true friend who was born of this land. What had I done?

Sebastian stopped walking and turned to face me. I closed my eyes and knew I needed to concentrate on this dance. Everyone was still standing. The trumpets and violins started playing. Sebastian put his hands up and I followed. We walked around each other before he stepped before me and we started dancing. I remembered Aleksander's voice in my head.

'Let the man lead, follow his steps.'

I did exactly that and there were no mistakes. The crowd erupted in applause after we finished. Sebastian bowed and I curtsied; he led me to my seat right beside him. His mother was on the other side and looked unimpressed with where I was sitting.

I sat down and looked for Annie and Harley. I found them and smiled. I wished they were beside me. I ate and sat quietly; I wanted to get up and walk around but I was too scared to move. I looked at Sebastian.

'Excuse me, my king. May I please walk amongst the guests?' I asked him.

He nodded. I got up from the table and tried to walk gracefully over to Annie and Harley. Miguel was sitting beside Annie.

'Since when did you know how to dance? I was waiting for you to trip over,' Harley said, showing the shock on her face.

'Thanks for the vote of confidence and I had dancing lessons,' I said, smiling. I was still looking around for Aleksander's face but I couldn't see him anywhere. I started walking around the room smiling at people and nodding at them. I almost bumped into a servant.

'Oh God, I am so sorry. I almost bumped into you – that would have been embarrassing for both of us,' I said, chuckling a little.

'No different to how Crystal was as a child: always bumping into everything and never keeping quiet when she was asked to,' the man said.

I looked at him. His dark hair was short, and his beard was longer than his head hair. I looked at his eyes; they were blue like mine but duller in colour. He looked familiar; he smiled and walked away. I turned around and watched him walk away. He turned around and smiled back at me. I knew him. I chased after him.

'Wait, I demand for you to stop,' I said sternly.
He turned back.

'Bröak,' was all he said before walking out of the castle. Who was he? What was bröak?

The night was coming to an end. I was in my chambers but wanted to see Aleksander to apologise for my behaviour before he left tomorrow. I ran out of my room and down the hall to the other side of the castle to his room. I knocked and knocked and waited for a response. I opened the door but he was not in his room. I knew he would leave at first light and could try to catch him then. I went back to my room but diverted to Harley's room; I knew she would have snuck Aidan in. I didn't knock just opened the door and covered my eyes.

'Harley, is Aidan in here?' I asked. She laughed.

'Yes, but we are dressed. You can uncover your eyes,' she said. I removed my hand from my eyes.

'Where is Aleksander?' I asked, looking at Aidan.

'I do not know,' he responded.

Harley asked, 'Why do you need him?'

I ignored her question and thought I would try the same in Annie's room. I covered my eyes.

'Annie, do you have company?' I asked her.

'Yes, but we are dressed.'

I opened my eyes and shut them instantly again. I saw Annie and Langford with no clothes on.

'That was fucking funny. That image is burnt into my brain, you bitch. Langford, have you seen Aleksander?' I asked, turning around and shaking in disgust.

'No, milady.'

Fucking hell, where was he? I went back to my room; I did not want to leave him a note but swore that I would wake up at the crack of dawn to see him.

CHAPTER TWENTY-FOUR

Aleksander

I escorted Rohesia back to her room.

'Would you like to come in, my lord?' she asked, looking at me seductively.

'Not tonight – when we are wed. Goodnight, Rohesia,' I said and turned to head back to my chambers. I changed direction and walked in the direction of Faith's chambers. I knocked on the door but there was no answer. I walked to the roof to our spot and she was nowhere to be seen. I wanted to see her and apologise before I left in the morning. I sat down at my desk, pulled out a piece of paper and decided to write a letter to Faith.

> *My dearest Faith,*
>
> *I want to apologise for my actions over the last two days. I was wrong...*

I scrunched the paper and threw it into my fireplace. I pulled out another piece and started again.

> *My dearest Faith,*
>
> *I apologise for my actions over the last two days.*

My intentions were admirable but they were incorrect for our friendship. I waited to tell you of your parentage until you were comfortable in Zilanta. I hoped you would remember some parts of your childhood before I told you to soften the surprise. I was wrong in my actions.

I swear on my life that from this day hence, I will never mistreat you again. My sword is yours; I will protect you till my dying breath.

I discovered information relating to your family I would like to share with you before I depart in the morning. You are not the only remaining Bouchard. I will await your presence in the stables before the light rises over the mountains.

Forever yours,

Aleksander Marchés

I folded the letter, picked up the wax and melted it over a flame, carefully dropping it onto the crease before picking up my seal and sealing the letter. I kissed it for luck and headed out. I could not face her tonight and called on the messenger to pass on the letter.

'Please, it is of an urgent matter and to be given to Lady Bushanti,' I said before hesitantly handing it over. I felt uneasy in handing it over and prayed it would reach her safely.

I removed my tunic and pants; I felt along the scar on my torso that she healed for me. I climbed into bed and sighed. I hoped she would forgive me. I was sincere in my apology but she was even more stubborn now than as a child.

I awoke to the sounds of the castle. The lady's maids were awake and preparing food, clothes and items that were needed. I put on a fresh black tunic and black pants before attaching my belt to my pants. I swiped my hair off my face and wandered down to the stables. I was looking forward to seeing her face. I opened the door to Dmitirov.

'Good morning, Lord Marchés. We are almost set for our travels,' he said formally. Someone important was in the room for him to use such formality in my name.

'Thank you, Dmitirov...' I leaned in to whisper. 'Are there any guests for me?' I asked.

He shook his head.

'Are we expecting someone, my lord?' he asked.

'No, not at all. Just ensuring the king did not want to see us before we departed,' I said loudly before walking around the stables. I saw Faith's horse and walked over to him. I fed Milo some oats before rubbing his mane and walking back to my horse.

'We are ready, my lord,' Dmitirov said.

Aidan, Langford and a new face were my men for this journey. I was not ready to leave – had she not forgiven me?

Miguel walked over.

'Is there an issue, Aleksander?' he asked before introducing the newest member of my company.

'Jaksinsun Thrammer, he will be joining your journey.'

I looked him up and down. He looked to be a little over the age of sixteen and terrified. He was as white as the clouds and shaking slightly. I extended my hand.

'Pleasure to meet you, Jaksinsun. We will train you in no time,' I said, leading him to a horse.

The poor boy had no hair and no muscles. He was a stick with no meat to him. I doubt he had been given sustainable food to eat lately. I turned and looked towards the door that led back to the castle. There was still no sign of Faith; the sun was rising in the sky quickly. I resigned myself to the idea that she was not coming. She did not forgive me. I hoped the two months of separation would ease her hurt before I returned. I needed to assist Jaksinsun onto his horse. Aidan and Langford sniggered in laughter.

'I do not believe either of you were skilled at mounting a horse at his age.' I spoke towards them. They instantly stopped.

I mounted my horse and turned once more; Miguel had left the room.

'Are you waiting on someone, Aleksander?' Dmitirov asked. I turned towards him.

'Apparently not,' I said, clicking at my horse to begin trotting. We reached the hill and I looked back at the castle, hoping to see her standing on the tower. She was still nowhere to be seen.

'Farewell, Faith,' I said under my breath. I would miss seeing her face and magnetic eyes.

'Come now, men,' I said, making my horse begin to gallop. It would be two months before I saw her again.

CHAPTER TWENTY-FIVE

Aleksander

Two months later

I awoke to the sounds of my men shuffling about. The journey had been longer than expected with the accompaniment of a lady. I did not recall Faith, Annie and Harley complaining about heading to the castle but my new wife Rohesia was vocal in her dislikes. I placed my thumb on my new wedding band and moved it around. It was a simple iron band. Sebastian had given me a ring for Rohesia. It was gold with an emerald gem in the centre of the design. I felt Dmitirov kick my foot.

'Are you getting up, Aleksander? We need to make tracks to get to the castle before nightfall.'

I knew what he was saying; we needed to get going now before she started complaining and we would have to stop again. I got up, folded my blanket and packed it into my horse's saddle. I walked over to assist Rohesia, who gladly accepted and waited for me to help her get on the horse. I smiled politely and helped. I mounted my horse and we were off.

I was wary on returning; I had heard no correspondence

from Faith. I had hoped a separation would ease her into forgiving me. Aidan spoke of Faith searching for me on the night before I left but she never found me. Langford had received a letter from Annie and he had been quiet the entirety of the journey. He had yet to reveal the news. Dmitirov rode up beside me.

'How are you, Aleksander?' he asked.

'I am well,' was my only response.

'No, Aleksander, you have not heard from her. How are you feeling on the return to the castle?'

I looked at him and shook my head. Rohesia was in earshot.

'I am eager to show off my new wife,' was all I said and he dropped the matter.

Rohesia requested that we have a brief stop. I declined her request and said it was more important to reach the castle today than risk another day on the road. I was eager to return home; the hills before the castle were in sight. The sun was in the middle of the sky. We would return home before nightfall. I rode up the hill quickly and stopped at the top and looked at the castle. I asked Marcus if I could stay within the castle walls with my new wife as I wanted to continue to serve the king. He accepted but Rohesia was not happy at the decision. I was not happy about being forced to marry her and to complete that ridiculous ritual. Our wedding night was witnessed by his family and the priest – I found it to be barbaric. That was the only time I had lain with my new wife. I did not understand how some people enjoyed it. Dmitirov had said that it was amazing when it was with someone you loved.

We reached the town's walls.

'Men, dismount. We will walk through the town,' I said. I walked over to help Rohesia down from her horse.

'No, I want to continue riding,' she said defiantly. I looked over to Dmitirov who shrugged his shoulders.

'Sure,' I said, turning around and leaving her to walk through the town on her horse. I grabbed my horse's reins and started walking through the town.

'Lord Marchés,' several civilians were saying as I walked past. I nodded my head in acknowledgment.

I looked back at Rohesia; she looked uncomfortable. I ignored her and kept on walking. We finally reached the stables. I opened the door and put my horse away before walking over and helping my wife off her horse. I put my arms up and grabbed her as she fell into my arms. I kissed her on the forehead. I heard the doors open and shouting. I put my hand on my sword; Toby ran into the stables and Faith followed behind.

Annie and Harley followed. I saw Aidan and Langford go to move towards them. Faith shouted, 'What, could you not keep up, Miguel?' as he came riding into the stables.

'I believe it is proper to allow a lady to win,' he said, jumping down from his horse.

'No, you just do not want to admit defeat,' she said, sliding off her horse. She seemed so confident.

I looked at her and smiled. She closed one eye at me. I was confused by this action.

'Oh, look, it is Lord Marchés and his men back from their journey. Late, as usual. Quite incompetent, in my opinion.' She looked back at Annie and Harley.

'Yes, indeed.' Annie spoke, looking towards Langford who

was taken aback by this comment.

What was I missing? Faith walked her horse back to his spot. I looked at Dmitirov.

'Lady Marchés, please, I will escort you back to your new chambers,' he said.

I stepped to walk over. Faith raised her hand for me to stop. Annie was entertaining Miguel and Harley walked over to speak to me.

'Faith says later in your spot,' she said and walked away.

I nodded and left. Faith did not sound like herself and her general demeanour was unusual. Langford went to walk after Annie, looking rather distraught at Miguel placing his hands over his lady. I grabbed his arm.

'No,' I said sternly.

'Aleksander, Lady Wakchter is my lady. I demand an answer on why there is another man placing his hands on what is mine?' Langford spoke through his teeth.

'I am positive there is an explanation. For now, I suggest staying away,' I said, looking at Langford and Aidan. Aidan did not seem as distraught as Langford about the ladies walking off.

What had happened for the snide remarks from Faith? I slowly walked back to my chambers. I opened the door and had forgotten about Rohesia. She was unpacking.

'This room is not sustainable for a lady of my stature. All of my objects will not fit in these cupboards,' she said, pointing disapprovingly.

I smirked and walked over to wipe my face down.

'I shall look for some cupboards for you,' I said, walking out of the room again.

Dmitirov appeared from around the corner.

'I did not believe marriage would be this difficult. Rohesia never seems to be content. Your wife seems to always be filled with joy,' I said, shaking my head. Dmitirov laughed.

'I was given the opportunity to marry for love, Aleksander. You and Rohesia will find some common ground and build a friendship, which will in turn blossom into love,' he said, walking with pride, his hands behind his back.

'Bullshit,' I said and chuckled to myself.

Dmitirov seemed taken aback.

'Apologies. I believe that was Faith's influence but I perceive you to be lying to me,' I said, smiling. Dmitirov laughed.

'It is not wise to copy the language of Faith. It is not appropriate even if it is comical,' he said and walked off ahead of me.

I stopped after hearing her laughter through a door; I peered through the door. I saw her throw her head back while laughing and a large smile spread across her face as she struggled to form words through the laughter. I had missed her smile and her ability to seem so carefree and the sound of her laugh – it had the uncanny ability to make me smile. Dmitirov appeared.

'There you are,' he said, pushing past me to see what I was looking at. 'Aleksander, may I speak candidly?' he asked, seeming unsure of my reaction.

I nodded.

'Is it possible that you are judging the lovely Lady Rohesia based off your softness towards Faith?'

I looked at him, stunned. 'No, Faith and I are not matched or suited to one another. We have had this discussion before, Dmitirov. I enjoy her company but have no attraction towards her,' I said sternly and quickened my pace to walk away from him.

I heard Dmitirov whisper under his breath, 'Bullshit,' and chuckle to himself.

I had admitted to him, I found her beauty to be beyond words but there was no attraction between the two of us. We only enjoyed each other's friendship.

I found a spare cupboard for Rohesia and ordered two young slaves to carry it to my chambers. When I returned to my room, I discovered Rohesia had taken all my clothes out of the cupboard and was sorting through them. My mouth was open in shock before I could ask what she was doing.

'My husband must wear appropriate clothing. I request some money to order some items with more colour,' she said, standing there with her hand out.

I took the key out of my pocket and unlocked my chest where I kept what little gold I had hidden. I collected ten coins and placed them into a coin bag. I turned and handed them to her. I needed to freshen up before dinner; I undid the string on my tunic and took it off. Rohesia assumed this was an invitation.

'No, I am freshening up before dinner with the king,' I said, brushing her hand away. I saw her face.

'Do you not find my beauty acceptable?' she asked, looking devastated.

I did not know how to answer.

'I find you to be rather pleasing to the eye but I believe in love and I want for us to try to find love for one another,' I said, grabbing her hands and kissing them. She took them back and placed one hand on my face.

'I do love you, Aleksander,' she said. I doubted her sincerity.

'Love does not happen that easily,' I said, moving away from her and taking my cotton top off.

'It does if it is real love,' she said before leaving the room.

I looked back to the door after she left. I sat down on my bed and put my head in my hands; maybe I was wrong.

I quickly washed myself with rose water to ensure I did not smell of my journey. I grabbed a fresh cotton top and shuffled through my clothes for my blue tunic with black embroidery. I put it on, brushed my hair back and waited for Rohesia to return to escort her to dinner. I lay back on the bed and pulled my necklace out. The blue quartz. It was a gift from Crystal when she found out we were to marry when we came of age. I smiled and remembered the day she gave it to me.

'A trinket for my future husband,' was all she said and ran away giggling. 'You still need to chase me – I am not yours yet.'

She had such spirit and it made me smile, thinking about her. I heard the door handle move and sat up, putting the necklace away.

'We must head down for dinner with the king. Are you in need of assistance to change or will you stay in the same attire?' I asked, motioning my hand up and down. She looked at herself.

'Would you like me to change?' she asked, unsure of what I was talking about.

'No, you look very lovely and I think the king will accept what you are wearing,' I said, putting my arm out for her to hold on to.

We started walking down the stairs towards the dining hall.

'Lord Marchés.' I heard someone speak my name. I stopped and turned; it was Faith. It did not sound like her. It was too formal and sweet.

'Hello, Lady Bushanti. Have you had the pleasure of meeting my wife?' I said in the same tone.

'Yes, we met at the coronation but now it is more appropriate to call you Lady Marchés. How is married life?' Faith asked but the question seemed hollow and without any meaning behind it.

'Aleksander is an amazing husband and I look forward to bearing his children in the future,' Rohesia said.

'Yes, because there is so much to do as a woman apart from having children. I wish you both all the best and future happiness.' There was Faith – I understood what she said but Rohesia looked at me, confused.

'She wishes us well and hopes we have many children together,' I said, lying through my teeth. It was the first sign that she was not still annoyed at my actions before the coronation.

She walked in front of us at a much quicker pace. I strolled and tried to look lovingly at my wife. We arrived at the dining hall. Faith was in Sebastian's arms and she leaned up for a kiss. Sebastian saw my face and Rohesia's and pulled away from her.

'Lord and Lady Marchés, welcome. Aleksander, is she with child yet?' Sebastian asked.

I heard Annie cough on the other side of the room. I shuffled uncomfortably and smiled.

'Come, come, Lady Marchés, you will sit beside me,' he said, escorting her to her seat.

The conversations were light and Sebastian spoke to Faith and Rohesia for the entirety of the night. I attempted to catch Faith's eye to determine her attitude towards me. She avoided all eye contact with me. I felt someone kick my leg. I looked up and Harley was glaring at me.

'Stop,' she mouthed but I did not understand her actions.

Why was Faith different?

All of the courses had ceased and Sebastian spoke. 'Aleksander, can I request you stay behind?'

The ladies all stood up and walked out. Faith kissed Sebastian on the head and Rohesia put her hand out for me to place a kiss upon it. Faith looked back before leaving the room; I wasn't sure if it was towards me or Sebastian but she smiled sweetly.

'She is immaculate, is she not?' Sebastian said as the door closed behind her.

'Yes, she is rather pleasing and quite a prize for you, Your Majesty,' I said.

'She has agreed to marry me but when the time is appropriate. I believe in a few months, after she has completed all of her lessons and is behaving in a manner appropriate for a future queen. I have witnessed some change but some actions are still not befitting for her new role,' he said sternly.

'Yes, she must behave appropriately otherwise it will be detrimental to your role,' I said in agreeance.

'How was the journey? Did you encounter any disturbances?' he asked, taking another drink of his wine.

'No, Your Majesty. The snow has just melted over the mountain and the forests are of moderate temperature. If you leave within the week, it will be safe. I would recommend fifty men to accompany you. Are Lady Wakchter and Lady Gelden joining Lady Bushanti on the journey?'

'Yes, fifty men indeed and that includes your company. Yes, Faith has requested they join us as she does not want to be separated from them. She can be rather persuasive,' he said with a sly smile and took another drink of his wine.

'I am sure you are aware how persuasive a lady can be now that you are married. It is imperative that you impregnate your wife soon. It will strengthen my contract with the Arundel family,' Sebastian said.

I shifted in my seat. 'Yes, Your Majesty,' I said nervously – I did not want to have intercourse with my wife again until I felt more comfortable in her presence.

Sebastian rose from his seat.

'It is a good feeling to be a man, is it not? After being with a woman, it is quite satisfying. Faith has not opened her legs for me but I am positive it will be soon. I am showering her with gifts,' he said, grabbing my shoulders as I sat.

I did not want to hear this discussion.

'Yes, that is pleasing news. I had best be off for the night to rest. I have had a long and tiring day,' I said, standing up from my seat and heading towards the door. Sebastian drank the last of his wine.

'I may venture into Faith's room tonight,' he said, laughing.

I smiled and left the room. He had consumed too much and was speaking too openly; it was confronting. I was not sure whether to head back to my room or to head to the tower. I walked to my chambers and found Rohesia asleep in my bed. I closed the door and headed for the tower. I walked up the stairs, wary of what she would be like. I stood at the door with my hand ready to open it. I was afraid of her attitude and her behaviour, how she was around others but she was soft towards me.

I pushed aside my fears and opened the door. I did not look up to see if she was there until I reached the top. Her arms wrapped around me and held on tight. I wrapped my arms around her and smelt her hair. She smelt as sweet as I remembered with the soft scent of roses. I closed my eyes and did not want to let go of her. She pulled back and slapped my face gently.

'You know you are an idiot,' she said, smiling.

I rubbed my face.

'That hurt slightly,' I said.

'Not compared to the punch I gave you the first day we met,' she said, laughing.

I smiled.

'I have missed your smile so much,' she said and ran over to embrace me again. I would not let her go easily this time.

CHAPTER TWENTY-SIX

Faith

I sat down and waited for Aleksander. I knew the king would be talking to him for a while. I wondered if he knew about the letter. Sebastian had not mentioned it over the past two months. Only his mother Yelena, who was blackmailing me with the contents. Aleksander had made it difficult but I doubted he was aware of how. I had forgiven him after realising my own stupidity. He would have been so confused about my actions this morning. I portrayed the perfect princess in front of the important people but behind closed doors I was myself – if I wasn't, I think I would lose what little sanity I had left. I took my headpiece off; it had been rubbing behind my ears and they were so sore. I pulled out the band that held my hair up and let it fall;it had grown so much over the last two months but so had my stomach. I had put on a little bit of weight – let's hope no one had noticed. What I wouldn't do for a nice juicy cheeseburger though. Yummmmmy.

I closed my eyes and thought about the dream I kept having. I needed to remember to tell him when I saw him. I was a little girl running around the garden outside the castle with my two brothers (I assumed) but I heard my mother scream and would turn around and see her covered in flames. I was always waking up sweating, nearly every night now. I was chasing them around the garden and struggling to keep up with them but I was determined to try until I heard her piercing scream. I heard someone climbing the stairs and stood up, waiting for him to come through the door. I was standing there waiting patiently for what seemed like forever. I heard the door creak and when I saw his face, ran over to hug him. I had missed him; two months without seeing his handsome face. I pulled back and slapped him softly on his face.

'You know you are an idiot,' I said, smiling at him.

He rubbed his face.

'That hurt slightly,' he said.

'Not compared to the punch I gave you the first day we met,' I said, laughing at him.

He smiled back. It was good to see him smile; I really had missed his face. I stupidly opened my mouth and said what I was thinking.

'I have missed your smile so much,' I said and before I knew it, I hugged him again. I felt as if my protector was back to save me again. I did not want to let go of him. He did not have his usual smell but what did I expect? He had been on the road for over two months. I did not think showers were a top priority. I went to move backwards but Aleksander's arms did not budge. I think he may have missed me as much as I missed him.

'Aleksander, can I have my own personal space back?' I said in a squeaky voice so he would realise to let go.

He stood back and straightened his top. I sat down and

patted the ground beside me. He sat down beside me and looked at me.

'Are you aware that Sebastian would like to—'

I cut Aleksander off mid-sentence. 'What, fuck me?' I said crudely.

Aleksander creased his forehead.

'Right, sorry. It is a way of saying that two people have intercourse but in a rather crude way.'

Aleksander nodded.

'I am happy you understand,' he said, patting my hand.

'Yes, I am aware he would like to take my lovely lady flower but he knows it is non-existent and I am close to convincing him of waiting to consummate our love until marriage,' I said, looking up at the stars.

'Your love?' Aleksander curiously asked.

I looked at him. 'No, Aleksander, I do not love him. Unfortunately, I have no inkling of feelings towards him. It is all an act – I think I should win an award for my skills,' I said, giggling to myself.

'That is a dangerous game,' Aleksander said, sounding very worried about my plan.

'Yes, I am aware... Luckily, I have you to protect me in case it goes bad. Hang on, I forgot... How was your first night with your wife?' I said, poking his arm playfully.

'It was awkward. I am not sure if you know but on the first night of a marriage of importance, the consummation must be watched by members of the family and the priest who married us. It is to prove honesty on the female's behalf. If she bleeds, she is pure – if not, the husband can question the validity of his wife,' Aleksander said.

'Wow, that is barbaric and a rather ancient ritual. That is not the practice anymore back home, thank God. Wait, hang on. Will I have to do that with Sebastian? You changed the subject as well – how was it?' I asked him. I already knew the answer but needed that confirmation.

'Yes, you will and it was not as pleasant as I was told. I expected it to be life-changing. Does it depend upon the person?' he asked me with a sad look on his face.

'Yes, with some people it is better. It is the best when it is with someone you love or care about. You and Rohesia will grow with one another and it will get better. I mean, I would volunteer to show you how fun it is but um, yeah, I am not that type of girl,' I said, smiling cheekily.

He seemed shocked by my comment.

'Sorry,' I said.

'Faith, did you receive my letter?' he asked, lying down on the ground. I lay down beside him but moved on to my side so I could see his face.

'No, but I am intrigued by what you put in that letter because it managed to find its way into Yelena's hands. She has made it quite difficult with the contents and now I spy on Sebastian for her. She is just a lovely person all round,' I said and Aleksander started laughing.

'So not funny,' I said, poking him again.

'The letter contained my deepest apologies for hurting you, my promise to never hurt you again and that I pledge my sword to you for the rest of my life. I discovered information about the spell that sent you away. The witch informed me that you are not the only living Bouchard.'

I felt my heart sink after he finished his sentence. My mind was spinning. I stood up and started pacing.

'I met someone the night of the coronation. It was strange – he seemed familiar like I had met him before. I felt that when I met you but with this person it felt closer to home. His eyes were blue but a duller blue compared to mine and he had dark hair and features like me. I chased after him and he said some word – bröcke or something. I cannot remember. It was not English but he mentioned Crystal as well.' I was slurring my words – I must have confused him.

'Bröak?' Aleksander said.

'Yes, that's it. That is the word he said. What does it mean?'

Aleksander stood up.

'Are you certain this is the word?' he said, grabbing my arms.

'Yes, one hundred per cent. That is it! Aleksander, what is it?' I was beginning to raise my voice and freaking out.

'That is what your brothers used to call you. It means little one.'

I stepped back. I met my brother and didn't even recognise him. I smacked myself on the head a couple of times.

'Faith, stop.' Aleksander was worried about me and I could tell.

'No. Why do I not remember? I met my own brother and could not recognise his face. I want my memories back. Bloody hell.' I was still smacking myself on the head. Aleksander grabbed me and pinned my arms in his embrace. I started crying.

'Shhhhh,' he whispered in my ear. He kissed my cheek.

'I just... want... to remember,' I said between sobs.

He let me go and wiped my face clean. 'I am working with the witch to find a way for you to get them back. Everything I have done has been for you and will continue to be for you. I will always protect you.'

I nodded my head after he spoke and shook it off.

'Come now to bed, you need sleep. We can talk at another time. Keep up the pretence that you do not like me and I shall do the same.'

I nodded to what he said again. I was out of words and just wanted to sit down and cry.

Aleksander dropped me at my chamber door and put my head between his hands and kissed my forehead. He did not say goodnight but just kissed me and left. I opened my door and saw Annie sitting on my bed. I didn't look at her.

'Annie, can this wait until the morning? It has been a long day and I think my head may explode from what I just discovered.' I turned around and looked at her. I ran over – her face was stressed out and blotchy. I sat down on the bed.

'No, it can wait.' Annie spoke softly. I grabbed her arm.

'What's happened? Did Langford end it? I will kill him if he did. Prick.' I was getting increasingly annoyed.

She looked up through her tear-streaked face. 'Faith, I'm pregnant.'

Oh, shit!

CHAPTER TWENTY-SEVEN

Aleksander

I did not wake to the normal sounds of the castle shuffling about. I awoke to the feeling of Rohesia stroking my fiddle. I felt her hand around its neck, moving up and down. It was a shock but an overwhelming feeling; I did not ask her to stop. I lay back and enjoyed the feeling. I felt my breath quicken as she sped up her pace. I let out a small moan of pleasure; she was leaning half on top of me.

I decided to take Faith's and Dmitirov's advice and let it happen. I raised my hand and placed it on her cheek. I pulled her in for a kiss. I closed my eyes and felt her lips against mine. They were warm and wet. I kissed her gently before moving my hand around her back and moving my body on top of hers. I lifted her nightgown up slightly and slowly lowered my body on to hers. I pushed my way into her; she let out a small groan. I opened my eyes and saw Faith's face. I stopped in shock and shook my head before I closed my eyes again and continued to kiss her. I was glad when it was over. I stood up and walked over to the bath and hopped in. I did not say any words to her and she did not speak to me. I was doing my duty that

Sebastian ordered and that was all.

Rohesia brought up a tray of food; it was filled with fruit, black bread and goat's milk. I drank the goat's milk but instantly spat it back into the cup.

'Do you enjoy the taste of goat's milk?' she asked, while still drinking from her cup.

'No, it is rather sour for my tastes,' I said, putting the cup on the tray. 'Thank you for breakfast. I will not be able to spend time with you until dinner,' I said softly while getting dressed for the day ahead.

She was smiling sweetly; she was attractive and seemed genuine.

'What are you smiling for?' I asked, turning my head to look at her.

'I discovered that you do not like goat's milk. I will know not to retrieve it for you again.' She still smiled as she spoke.

I walked over and kissed her forehead. I was trying but I understood it was going to take some time. I picked up my belt with my sword attached and buckled it to my hips.

My duty for the day was to organise a suitable convoy by the week's end. I was cheerful this morning and ran down to the training area. 'Dmitirov, my good man. It is a beautiful morning,' I said, smacking my hand on his back.

'You are cheerful this morning, Aleksander.'

'Yes, I feel fresh this morning. I need to discuss something with you in private,' I said quietly, close to his ear.

'Langford, Aidan, continue with the training,' he said, turning around.

'I adhered to your advice and lay with my wife again but when I opened my eyes, it was not her face but Faith's. Is it standard to picture another woman?' I asked. I was new to this and he had been married for many years now.

'Aleksander, I know you do not want to admit it but you picturing another female while lying with your wife is not good. You have underlying emotions for Faith and you will need to be honest with yourself if you want to open your heart to Rohesia.' He spoke softly and walked back to continue to train the men.

Honest with myself? I pondered what he had said – I was honest.

'I have errands to run in the town,' I said to Dmitirov and left.

I had heard no correspondence from the witch Millicent since I departed for two months. I walked into town to find out if she had discovered a solution to Faith recovering her memories.

CHAPTER TWENTY-EIGHT

Faith

I woke in the morning with Annie in my arms. She was crying for most of the night. I was worried – how could I protect her? My one suggestion to just sleep with Miguel did not go down very well because she had already been trying for over a month with no success. He was not easily swayed by her charms. By her calculations, she was almost two months along. I had no idea how to help her. No man was allowed to touch any of us and if Sebastian found out, he had threatened to kill us. I opened the door and spoke to Sonny.

'Can you tell the king that Annie, Harley and I will not be attending any lessons today as we are not feeling well and think it would be best to have a day of rest?' I did not give him a chance to respond and closed the door. When I heard his footsteps disappear, I ran over to Harley's room and knocked on the door.

'We have a problem,' I said and she ran over to my room. She jumped into the bed with us and cuddled Annie.

We all lay together and did not move or speak for hours. We had no words and I could not think of any solutions. Harley hopped up.

'The only solution I see is for you and Langford to run away because abortion is not an option. Your life and Langford's are both at risk and if you leave the castle and find somewhere else away from Sebastian's grasp, you can be happy together.' She was smiling at her suggestion.

'There is only one problem with that. What impacts will that have on us and Aleksander? What if they are caught? Do you want to witness her beheading? I have sway with the king but not that much just yet because I am holding out on the one thing he bloody wants.' I paced the room with Harley.

Annie sat up in the bed and leaned over for my bucket. We both left her to vomit because we could not stand the smell.

'If you are two months along, we have two months before you really start to show – only your boobs are noticeable right now. God, I have no idea. I need to speak with Aleksander but I can't.' I slammed my back against the wall and dropped down to the ground.

'What is Aleksander possibly going to be able to do? And just go speak with him, this is serious,' Harley said raising her voice.

'Do not raise your voice. We are ill,' Annie said to Harley as she glared at her.

'Aleksander knows these lands. Maybe there is something we can do... and I cannot speak to him because Yelena is blackmailing me with a letter he sent. It contained him pledging his sword to me and the existence of another Bouchard that has been alive and here all along. We have agreed to avoid each other and pretend we hate each other for our and your protection,' I said, not getting up from the wall.

I sighed and put my head into my hands. I wanted to cry.

I would not lose another person I cared about. Harley headed towards the door.

'Go into my room and wait,' she said, leaving the room. I walked over to Annie to offer a hand. She pushed it away.

'I am not disabled nor do I have a broken limb.'

I laughed and we ran over to Harley's room without being detected. Annie jumped onto the bed and I walked over to her mirror; it was smaller than mine. My hair was all over the place. Some days I enjoyed my natural waves; others were like today and just crazy. I picked up her brush and combed it through before grabbing a ribbon and tying it up in a ponytail.

'Annie, I'm sorry. I feel as if this is all my fault deep down,' I said, looking at her. I felt hopeless and did not know how to help her.

'It is not your fault. Yeah, so we may be here because of you but I chose to sleep with someone and I chose to stay when you gave us the out. It isn't your fault and I don't blame you but start sleeping with the king already so we have more protection.' She started laughing.

'Yep, whore me out to get pregnant as well. No, thank you.' I smirked. I put my head on the table and pushed the chair back. I had not even put any clothes on yet. I was still in my nightgown. I thought I was due for my period soon; I disliked bleeding here more than back home. At least they had tampons and sanitary pads. Nothing here except a cloth to catch the bleeding. I felt so clean all the time. NOT!

I heard the door open. I did not look up as I assumed it was just Harley.

'Faith, Annie. Harley has explained the situation.' It was Aleksander. He was glowing today.

Someone had sex last night. I felt my stomach twist. Aleksander looked at me.

'You look drained,' he said.

'Long night, brain exploding from what to do.' I banged my head back down on the table. He chuckled.

'I believe Harley has the only viable solution but it is also the most dangerous one. I have people who can protect you but they may not accept the risk for no reward.' He walked with his hands behind his back.

He looked really good today – yep, I was definitely coming into my period. My mind was dirty around this time and my thoughts were good but not at the same time. Couldn't he be ugly or gay at least? I avoided looking at him.

'I will have to endeavour to get in contact but this plan will take time to devise. It will not happen until after the royal tour.' I stood up.

'No, it needs to be sooner. She will possibly start to show next month. We cannot take the risk that someone notices.' He looked at me.

'Wear dresses of a bigger size.' I scoffed and sat back down.

'Not that easy, Aleksander.'

'Faith, stop hating on him and just listen.' Harley glared at me.

I rolled my eyes; I stopped paying attention. I rested my arm on the table and dropped my head into it. I closed my eyes and my mind started drifting. I felt Aleksander's hand on my shoulder and he whispered my name.

'Faith, Faith.'

I woke up suddenly and so quickly that I fell back on the chair. My legs went up in the air and I hit my head on the ground.

'OWW,' I said while laughing at myself. Typical me falling backwards on a chair. I erupted into a fit of laughter; this is what happens when you get no sleep and worry too much – your brain cannot cope and just starts laughing.

'Is Faith unwell?' I heard Aleksander ask, looking worried.

'Define "unwell" because I still cannot believe we came here from a normal place to like the Middle Ages and I am some apparent princess with a right to the throne and one of my best friends is now pregnant and her only solution is to run away with a person she barely knows. I think I have seriously lost the plot. I am going to bed. Goodbye,' I said, still laughing as I left the room.

I entered my chambers, jumped on the bed and fell asleep instantly. Toby started barking at me.

'Go away, I am tired,' I said, pushing him away while he was barking and licking my face. I put my head under the pillow. 'God, you can be an annoying little shit.'

I heard someone clear their throat behind me. I froze as I hoped I was hearing things.

'Hello, Faith.'

Oh no, it was Sebastian. I did not look presentable enough for a king at the moment.

'Hi,' I said from beneath the pillow.

'I request to see your face,' he said so sensibly. Seriously, could he not drop the formalities sometimes? I was really in a grumpy mood today.

'Nah, I decline your request. My face is not the best today and I sent the message that I was not feeling well. Did you not receive it?' I was still hiding under the pillow. Sebastian sat on the bed. I put both of my hands on either side of the pillow. He would not get his bloody request today.

'Faith, I am in no mood for your childish games.'

I sighed deeply and lifted my hands away from the pillow. I turned my head in the other direction. Sebastian cleared his throat. I turned my head towards him. I did not smile.

'Where is my Faith?' he asked, looking rather concerned.

'Faith is tired and just wants to sleep and requests that you leave her be unless you want the face of nasty Faith,' I said, turning my head away.

'I am your king and I demand a change in attitude.' Sebastian spoke sternly.

I knew that I needed to be pleasant with him. I turned around and sat up with a fake smile on my face.

'Are you well enough for a walk in the garden?' he asked, moving my hair out of my eyes. I looked down at my nightgown.

'I need to change.'

'Yes, absolutely. I will wait outside and give you some time to change into appropriate attire.' He kissed my forehead and walked out of the room.

I stuck my head back into the pillow and wanted to scream. *No, you must be pleasant and gracious even though you would rather tell him to piss off.*

I thought I should look presentable and grabbed one of my more elegant dresses rather than my bland ones. Makenzie was not around to tie it up. I opened the door; Sebastian was speaking with Sonny.

'Begging your pardon, Your Majesty. I seek your assistance with an important matter,' I said and stepped back from the door.

He walked in. 'What is the matter you seek assistance with?' he asked, looking around.

I turned my back to him and swept my hair away.

'My lady's maid is not around and I cannot tie this myself. I am assuming you have some experience in this matter.' I tried to sound seductive.

'Yes – argh, yes.' He sounded uncomfortable.

I smirked to myself. *I still got it,* I thought.

I felt his hands on my back, pulling the strings.

'You are making me feel uncomfortable,' he said while tightening my dress.

'My apologies but there is no one else around to assist me,' I said as I shifted my shoulder slightly to look over it at him. I heard him mutter to himself. His hands came around my stomach and he moved in closer, kissing my neck.

'These are not appropriate actions for a king,' I said, giggling sweetly. He pulled back.

'Faith, I would like us to be intimate with one another. I wish to enter your lady garden.' He spoke so sincerely and looked down towards the floor. I wanted to laugh at his mention of a 'lady garden'.

'I believe it is appropriate to wait for marriage, considering the ritual that must be completed on the night of our wedding,' I said as I walked over to the mirror and put on some jewellery.

'Yes, it is custom for those of a high ranking.' He spoke softly and with a tone of concern.

'Well, we may need to get rid of that custom because we both know my lovely lady garden has been entered before. The purity ship has sailed.' This was incredibly awkward to bring up to someone.

'May I ask how many have entered your garden?' he asked.

Could he seriously not call it a vagina or say 'How many

people have you slept with?'

'Only two, Sebastian. One was willing and the other was not so willing but let's not get into details,' I said as I changed the subject as that number was not correct and headed towards the door. I was ready for our trip to the garden.

I opened the door and saw Aleksander standing there about to knock. My other hand was out of view of Sebastian. I looked at him sternly and moved my hand in a way that said 'move now'.

Aleksander quickly snuck around the corner and out of sight. Sebastian walked in front and held out his arm. I put my arm around his arm and we walked down the stairs before heading to the garden. Sebastian escorted me to a different area I had never been to before. We walked through the tall blue-green hedges until we reached a little pond. The pond was covered in lily pads and a mixture of purple and pink flowers. I bent down and moved some of the lily pads to uncover a multitude of colourful fish. Grey, gold, blue, black and many more. My mood softened with a smile coming over my face. It was the small things that always cheered me up. I looked up from the pond and saw all the different flowers. There were tall pink rose bushes, purple tulips, blue gladiolas with a touch of purple in the centre and one random sunflower. It looked to be about a metre and a half tall. I hadn't seen one in ages. I walked over to it and looked back at Sebastian and smiled.

'What is this place?' I asked him, loving the smells coming from the plants.

'It has always been called the royal retreat. I would like to give it to you to tend to the garden and your own personal space.'

I looked at him. 'But—'

Before I could continue talking, he cut me off. 'There is to be no discussion. I want you to feel comfortable in your new home.'

I walked over and hugged him tightly and kissed him on the cheek. 'Thank you.'

I walked back over to the sunflower.

'Is the yellow flower your favourite?' he asked, walking closer to me.

'It is called a sunflower and no but I am trying to see if it has any seeds to eat.' I chuckled to myself.

'That seems unwise.' He placed his hand on my back.

'No, I used to do it when I was young with one of my foster families. They had about fifty in their backyard. Oh, there we are,' I said as I picked out two seeds from the flower. 'Here, try it.'

Sebastian looked really confused.

'Watch me. You need to bite the outer shell and spit it away and just eat the part in the middle.' I bit the shell and spat it out – very unladylike – and ate the middle. I forgot what they tasted like. It had been years. I think I remembered the taste a little differently but still ate it.

Sebastian copied what I did. 'That is a strange taste but not unwelcoming.'

'Yeah, you generally feed them to birds but humans can eat them.'

Sebastian spat it out. I laughed so hard, I accidentally snorted.

'Faith, you amaze me,' he said as he moved hair from my face.

'Why? Because I am so special?'

'Yes, special indeed.' I giggled.

'Faith, it is my name day on Thaffdae and I will be hosting a ball the next day before we depart on our royal tour.'

'Sounds spectacular. Is it a normal ball or a masquerade

ball?' I asked him, looking down at where I was walking before sitting on the granite bench.

'I do enjoy the idea of a masquerade. Yes, masquerade it is,' he said and clapped his hands together in joy.

'Shall we match in clothing and masks?' I asked him.

His face lit up. 'Yes, indeed. I shall or—'

I cut him off this time. 'No, it is your name day, which I assume means your birthday possibly or something special. I shall organise our clothes for the night. I will need to venture to town to see Lord Carmelide to discuss what to wear.'

Sebastian nodded. 'I shall organise for you to do that tomorrow.'

While Sebastian was busy discussing other important details, I tried to remember what day Thaffdae was. Was it a Tuesday or a Thursday? I kept leaning towards Thursday because it started with 'th' but I could be wrong. I knew nearly all of the others except for Terndae and Thaffdae. Today was a Monday equivalent, which meant I had five days to organise what to wear for the both of us. I shuffled down the bench and lay down, resting my head on his lap and listening to him talk. He was so excited about the ball; it was as if he had no other troubles.

We spent the rest of the afternoon together in the garden talking. We escorted each other to dinner and Sebastian spent the entire night discussing the upcoming ball.

'Aleksander, I believe there should be twenty men standing guard. I request that you attend with your new wife and not be on duty for one night. The Marchés family needs to be recognised and old wounds should be closed.' He spoke so regally and graciously. He turned into a proper king and didn't sound so much like a young man struggling to find his feet.

'With pleasure, Your Majesty,' Aleksander said. It was hard to avoid eye contact with him.

I quickly looked up and noticed him staring in my direction. Aleksander instantly blushed and looked down. I smirked to myself.

'Faith?' Sebastian looked at me questioningly.

I looked up with a fork in my mouth. It must have been a rather attractive face.

'Yes...?' I asked.

'Why were you smirking?' he asked.

Wow, he was like an eagle: he saw everything.

'I was just remembering the garden from today, Your Majesty,' I said. He nodded.

'Yes,' he said and continued eating.

I looked at Annie; she was barely touching her food. I was worried about how we were going to hide this for another two months.

I walked with Annie and Harley back to their chambers.

'I know it is hard but you need to find a way to eat or try and pretend to eat. I can keep his attention on me but what if someone else starts to notice? We cannot take that chance.' I was worried about her safety over mine. Langford appeared behind us.

'Maybe it is not the wisest decision for you to meet so frequently. We do not want to arouse suspicion.'

Harley put her hand on my shoulder. 'Leave them be for a night,' she said.

I looked at her and walked back to my chambers. I closed my door and leant against it. I would not cry; we would get through this. I didn't change out of these clothes but headed up to our tower.

I beat Aleksander up here tonight, as I did the night before. It was chilly tonight. I sat down and huddled up with my knees and rubbed my arms to keep them warm. I felt a blanket being draped over me. I looked up. 'Thank you.'

He sat down beside me.

'Long day, hey?' I said to him.

'Indeed, you were acting stranger than usual.'

'Yeah, that is what happens when I am very tired. I become a bit delusional and quirkier than usual. Sorry about that,' I said.

'No need to apologise – that is who you are,' he said.

I lay down. I wanted to talk about my brother again and what he knew about him but was too scared to bring it up after last night.

Aleksander turned to his side to look at me. He took a deep breath.

'What's wrong?' I asked him, turning onto my side and holding my head up in my hand.

'I...' He closed his mouth again.

'Come on, spit it out,' I said, looking up into his brown eyes and placing my hand on his knee for comfort. He stopped and looked back into my eyes.

'I ventured into town to discuss the solution for recollecting your memories. Millicent, the coven leader, believes there is no spell that can be cast but rather a kiss from your betrothed.'

I was speechless.

'Who is my supposed betrothed? It cannot be my dead fiancé and it is not Sebastian. I have already kissed him. Who is my betrothed?' I asked, scratching my head. Aleksander shifted.

'I am not aware of who your betrothed is. The only solution I believe may be suitable is...' He paused briefly. He was incredibly uncomfortable – my mind suddenly clicked, like a lightbulb going off.

'Like you, because, we... um... we were... our parents organised for us to marry one another. Um, wow, that got awkward real fast.' I moved away from him slightly.

Aleksander smiled on one side; he was fidgeting with his hands.

'Alright, let us just bite the bullet,' I said to him and sat up.

Aleksander looked at me confused at what I just said.

'If what this Millicent said is the truth and we were engaged from like the age of five then we should just do it.' I crossed my legs. My knees touched his and we both looked so awkward. I grabbed his head and gave him a peck on the lips; it lasted about ten seconds. I pulled back and Aleksander's face was so shocked and he did not move a muscle for about a minute. I was waiting patiently.

'Yep, there is nothing coming back. I think she is full of it. Go get your money back or the waste of minutes you wasted talking to her,' I said, standing up and fixing my dress. It was still extremely awkward and I just wanted to leave this situation. Aleksander had stood up and was still wearing the same face.

'Yep, alright, goodnight. See you tomorrow.'

I put my hand out for him to shake it and took it back. I turned around and just walked off the roof of the tower and back to my room. I closed the door; Toby was asleep on the bed. I changed out of my gown with difficulty. Sebastian had tightened my dress too much and I was struggling to get out of it.

It took me over ten minutes; I finally put on my nightgown and hopped into bed. I snuggled into the wolf fur blanket and looked up at the roof. It was the first time that I had noticed the roof was not brick like the walls and floor. The roof was exactly the same as the floorboards in the same colour of teak. I put my hand on my head and sighed; I was hoping I would never have to kiss him again. It was annoying that the witch had lied, and I was no closer to the return of my memories.

It was stupid; I felt as if the day I got my memories back, everything would change. The sinking feeling in my stomach that something horrible was about to happen would disappear. I would be more confident instead of feeling as if I didn't have feet on solid ground. The other lingering question in my mind was, what if I remembered and it was not what I expected? What if my memories of my family were not pleasant? What if my life was just as horrible and I was cursed to always struggle? I know they say God tests you in life; he puts challenges in front of you and he would not put them in your path unless you can survive them. I felt a tear trickle down my cheek while my brain was going into overdrive. I wiped it away, rolled over, closed my eyes and wished for sleep.

I felt the warmth of the sun on my cheek. I rolled over and put my hand on Toby's hand. There he was in my bed again; it had been so long since I had seen his face.

'I miss you,' I said to him.

'I know you do. I am always with you and I always will be. I always believed you were destined for more than a classroom. Stop doubting yourself. I love you,' he said, leaning in and kissing me on the lips. I closed my eyes; I felt his warm lips on mine and felt his hand brush across my face to wipe the tear away. I moved back and rested my head on the pillow before opening my eyes again. It was Aleksander. He smiled at me so genuinely and beautifully.

'I love you,' he said as I woke up suddenly.

I sat up in bed instantly, and Toby barked. I picked him up and cuddled him. 'I do hope my real Toby is within you because you are my little protector. I mean, you have grown but you are still so small. Hurry up and get big.' Toby licked my face. I put him down and got out of bed.

Makenzie walked into the room. 'Good morning, Faith,' she said, curtsying.

'Hey Makenzie, what is with the formality?' I asked her, brushing my hair.

'You have company,' she said.

I noticed that her face was not usual; there was worry written across it. My door swung open.

'Morning, Lady Bushanti. I request your presence this afternoon,' Yelena said, not looking at me as she walked around the room, inspecting it.

'May I ask what this is about? I do have other plans to head into the town to see Lord Carmelide,' I said, not looking directly at her but continuing to brush my hair.

Makenzie fiddled around the room; she was eager not to leave me alone with her. She opened the cupboard and folded some fresh clothes and placed them in the cupboard whilst taking out my gown for today.

'I have a special task for you to complete,' she said as she raised an aging eyebrow at me. I needed to make sure I did not show any emotion or reaction on my face.

'Yelena, you have yet to discuss the contents of this letter. I will complete no more special tasks. I am not your spy – if you want information about your son, talk to him yourself. I am done,' I said, walking over to the door and waiting for her to exit.

'We are not finished, Lady Bushanti. I shall see you this afternoon.' She turned and looked at me before walking through the door.

'You are not aging gracefully, Yelena,' I said and closed the door on her. I ran over to the table and grabbed a piece of paper to write a letter to Aleksander. I paused; I could not write one. What if she intercepted it? I stopped. Makenzie watched.

'Yelena has been blackmailing me with the contents of a letter that Aleksander sent to me before he left two months ago. I now know what was in the letter. She cannot blackmail me anymore. I will not stand for it,' I said and stepped into my dress as she held it open. There was no elegant gown today but a simple dress. It was red with a black stripe across my midriff that turned into a small bow at the back. It also had a thick black stripe on the trim at the bottom and at the end of the sleeves. I liked it; I did not always wear the colour red but it was growing on me. Makenzie lifted up some gems for me to wear.

'No, I want to be plain and simple today,' I said to her before I headed towards the door. I was in a good mood. I stopped outside my door and looked in the direction of Annie's. I decided to leave her. It was early in the morning; she may not be well.

I took a step and looked back again towards her room. There were very few times I felt helpless and this was one of them. I had no idea how to comfort her. I knew I needed to suck up to Sebastian more than usual in case her secret was discovered. I turned back round.

'Faith, wait up.' It was Harley.

'Hey, how are you? How's Annie?' I asked her when she caught up.

'I am good and Annie is well but not well.'

I understood what she was saying and simply nodded.

'What happened to you yesterday? I was worried about you and knocked on your door but there was no answer. I didn't want to walk in because I was worried I would see something I didn't want to,' she said, smiling and bumping me.

'You're funny. Yeah, I was a bit tired and you know me. I get slightly delusional when I am that tired. I was either asleep or Sebastian was taking me to the royal retreat. I must take you there later, it is stunning. A little garden in the maze and it takes your breath away,' I said to her.

'Sounds beautiful. Cannot wait.'

We were entranced in our conversation and suddenly bumped into Aleksander.

'Good morning, Lord Marchés. How are you?' Harley asked him.

'Um...well... and yourself?' He was so scattered, I could not even look at him.

'Good thanks,' she said and Aleksander walked away.

'What happened there? Isn't he normally together and not that scattered?' she said, looking at me.

'Yeah, normally. I don't know.' I avoided eye contact with her.

'You know what I love? I love the fact that I know you so well. Especially the fact that something happened and how obvious you are when you want to avoid talking to me about it. It is fine,

I will just imagine what happened between the two of you last night on top of the tower. Hmmm, let my imagination fly.'

I looked at her and bit the side of my mouth. 'Really?' I raised my eyebrows at her.

I pulled her into a spare room.

'Alright, drop it, please,' I said.

'Not until you tell me. That was some serious awkwardness up there. What happened?' She was being persistent. She crossed her arms at me. She did this when she was not going to quit. I rolled my eyes and turned away from her.

'Aleksander has been speaking to the leader of the witch coven to find out why I have no memories. She came back with a suggestion because there is no spell to help. She said a kiss from my betrothed would trigger the memories. I said well, it isn't Sebastian or Toby. They are two people I have already kissed – maybe we should try because our parents had organised for us to be wed when we grew of age and we did. It was horrible and after it ended, I kind of left straight away. That is it. Now can we drop it?' I said, heading back towards the door to continue walking down for breakfast.

'One question though...' she said.

I turned around and glared at her. 'What?' I said through gritted teeth.

'Did you kiss him or did he kiss you?' she asked.

I hesitated in responding. I thought back to last night.

'I kissed him. Why does it matter who kissed who?' I asked her, throwing my arms up in the air.

'The leader said a kiss from your betrothed. Maybe he was supposed to kiss you,' she said, sounding rather cocky and tapping her foot, waiting for my response.

'I do not think she was speaking that literally, Harley. Can we drop it please?' I begged her.

'Alright, alright,' she said, heading to the door and opening it.

I did not want to tell her about my dream and I did not want to analyse the meaning behind it either. I walked into the kitchen and saw the maids preparing a fruit platter for breakfast.

'Oh, hello, yeah.' I grabbed Harley's hand and ran over.

'Hi,' I said shyly to the lady cutting into them. She walked over and grabbed two plates and filled them up.

'Thank you,' we said in unison and ran away giggling.

We ran into Sebastian.

'Your Majesty,' Harley said and curtsied. My mouth was full and I just curtsied.

'Are you incapable of speaking, Lady Bushanti?' he asked with a slight smirk on his face. I swallowed my food down quickly.

'Sorry, Your Majesty. My mouth was full of fruit.'

Harley and I both started giggling.

'Faith, we spoke yesterday about having matching gowns for the upcoming ball. I have organised for you to venture into the town with Aleksander and your personal guard Sonny. I do not believe Sonny is sufficient enough to protect you alone,' he said with his hands behind his back. He looked around before he grabbed my face for a kiss.

Harley grabbed the plate out of my hands and Sebastian moved closer and kissed me deeper. Even though there was no spark, he definitely knew how to kiss. I felt my head getting light as his tongue massaged mine. I could feel him smiling as we kissed. My body wanted more than just a kiss right now, damn hormones. Harley cleared her throat and handed the plate back to me.

'Yes, absolutely, Your Majesty,' I said and he grabbed a grape off my plate and walked off.

'Wow, that was intense. I feel like I need a shower.' I nudged into her and smiled.

'Yeah, I may not be attracted to him but I do certainly enjoy kissing him,' I said with a smile.

We walked back up to our rooms. I still had fruit on my plate and so did Harley. We knocked on Annie's door; there was no answer. I bent down and opened it and peered inside. Harley peered in over the top of me. We both started laughing; we were acting like children today.

'Go away,' was all we heard from Annie. We walked into the room.

'Can you two grow up and go away?' she asked, not facing us but still lying in bed.

'Um, grow up, never, but going away is a possibility,' Harley said cheekily.

'I remember the days you were innocent and not so sarcastic. We ruined her Faith,' Annie said, turning around to face us.

'Now to clarify, did we ruin her or did we make her more awesome? To match our awesomeness? Yeah, that is totally a word,' I said laughing. I handed her the plate of fruit.

'Eat,' I said to her. She looked at it.

'Can I eat later?' she said.

I nodded. 'Yep, I will be checking on you though to make sure that you do.'

She rolled her eyes.

'God, I feel like death.' She put her head into her hands.

'Yeah, the only downside to having sex is that one day you may need to push this massive thing out of your vagina. There are no caesareans here and no epidurals. Wow, you are going to be in so much pain.' Harley laughed her head off.

Annie pushed her off the bed.

'Glad to see you're not weak, at least.' I snorted and avoided her hitting me too.

Harley was still on the ground.

'In other news, Faith kissed Aleksander and the two of them are so awkward right now. It is to die for. I mean, they will not even look at each other,' Harley said, not getting up from the ground.

'And that is my cue to leave,' I said heading towards the door. 'I have more important people to see,' I said as I poked my tongue out and left the room. I walked towards Aleksander's room and knocked on the door. His wife answered with her red hair flowing down her shoulders.

'Hi, is Aleksander here?' I said quietly.

'What do you need to speak to my husband about?' she asked shortly. I was taken aback by her attitude; I thought she liked me. Obviously, I was wrong.

'Sorry to bother you, Lady Marchés. The king spoke to me earlier and said he was to accompany me to the town. I just wanted to tell him his services are not needed.' I spoke very properly and graciously.

Aleksander came to the door. He was not wearing a shirt. He definitely was nice to look at; he quickly pulled one on.

'No, the king demanded that I come and there is no reason to argue, Lady Bushanti. I will be bringing my wife Rohesia to explore the town as well.' He was rather blunt and had a different attitude. He put his arm around his wife. I looked and felt an anger build up. She was lucky to sleep next to him every night.

'Sure thing,' I said with a certain amount of sass and walked away. I did not want to spend any time with him today but apparently, life had other plans in store for me.

CHAPTER TWENTY-NINE

Aleksander

I had wanted to avoid seeing Faith after last night's encounter. She was a beauty there was no denying that but we had developed a strong friendship and I was married. Although I did not love my wife, I could not betray her trust or the alliance between the Marchés, Faulcon and Arundel families.

'Aleksander, it is normal for her to visit your chambers?' she asked while fixing her hair in the mirror.

'Yes, on occasion, when she has questions or assignments from the king,' I said as I buttoned up my tunic. I did not want to discuss Faith and opted to change the topic of discussion.

'While in town, it would be wise for you to shop for some clothes for yourself for the upcoming royal tour,' I said, checking the amount of gold she had spent from the day before. There was still plenty left for her to buy more dresses and a few nice tunics for myself. Rohesia draped herself in fine gems and placed her hair up off her face.

I knew that I would have to collect Faith from her room. I walked over.

'Sonny, how is Faith this morning?' I asked when I already

knew the answer to the question.

'She is as cheerful as always, my lord,' he said, standing completely still with his hands behind his back. He settled into his role well. I was not needed for this venture into town but I must do as the king bids. I knocked on the door and waited for Faith. She answered and put one finger up to me.

'One second.'

I peered into the room.

'Sorry, I am just trying to tie this necklace but my fingers keep slipping.'

I looked in the mirror as she struggled. I walked into the room. She could not fasten the tie from the cross I had given her; it was the first time I had seen her with it since our fight two months ago.

'Allow me.' I walked in and grabbed both sides of the ribbon. I felt her soft skin on my hands. My thoughts were beginning to wander; I quickly tied the ribbon and stepped back.

'Thank you,' she said and headed towards the door.

I could now grasp what Dmitirov was trying to convey. It was difficult to let Rohesia into my heart and to open it up to her because I had already given it away to Faith. I found her beauty to be intoxicating; I just wanted to be around her. It was not to protect her but rather to just be in her presence.

'I shall meet you at the entrance,' I said to her and walked away from her. I saw Rohesia waiting outside the door. I held up my arm to escort her to the door. I did not speak; there were no words. Faith stood at the entrance, conversing with Sonny. I saw her smile and laugh and poke Sonny playfully; her smile had the ability to light up the entire room. She had the uncanny ability to soften me. She changed me and I was not fighting it.

Rohesia let go of my arm and walked over to Faith. They were conversing quietly and giggling; Rohesia was holding onto Faith's arm and it did not bother her to be perceived as a male. Faith looked over her shoulder.

'I approve of your new wife. She is adorable,' she said as she flashed a smile.

I could not take my eyes off her luscious lips. I was contemplating whether to discuss my feelings towards her.

CHAPTER THIRTY

Faith

I was glad to finally arrive at Lord Carmelide's establishment. Aleksander and Rohesia went into another designer's house. I could tell by the way Rohesia spoke that she did not like me and was possibly jealous of my friendship with Aleksander. I would play nice with her in hopes of not making it uncomfortable for him.

'Lady Bushanti, it is a gift to look upon your beauty again,' he said, walking up and kissing my hand. I pulled it away quickly and wiped it on my dress.

'Yes, it is lovely to be in the presence of an amazing designer, Lord Carmelide. I have a request from myself and the ever-gracious king. He is hosting a ball for his name day and we would like matching gowns and tunics,' I said, looking around his shop.

'Yes, Lady Bushanti.' Lord Carmelide walked around his establishment, showing me different things. I raised my hand without speaking and he instantly stopped talking. I had that much power. I felt a shiver down my spine.

'Do you have paper and pens?' I asked him.

He snapped his fingers and a lady brought over the items.

I did not take any notice of her but she seemed rather young to be working. I walked over to the counter.

'I would like a blue and black gown for myself, something to really make my features stand out. Like... um... a black top and a blue bottom to my gown. For King Sebastian's tunic, well, I am not good at men's fashion. I want them matching so I shall leave that up to you. Are you able to possibly lift the dress in one corner and reveal a black underskirt? Oh, and with the mask, I want something like this,' I said to him, drawing quickly with the charcoal a mask in the shape of a butterfly with little jewels in the corner. He looked at the paper and looked back up at me.

'I can see it clearly, Lady Bushanti. Do you have a preference for gems?' he asked, walking over to his cabinet.

'Whatever you pick, I shall wear. I trust your instincts, Lord Carmelide. The ball is on Frashdae. I look forward to seeing your creations,' I said to him.

He kissed my hand again and I left the room. I felt like I needed Dettol after his kisses. I was still clean but it was hard to be as clean as you were back home. Cleanliness was not high in importance on the ladder. The sun shone down on me; I stood in it and felt it soak into my skin. I closed my eyes and just breathed.

'Come, Faith.' I felt Sonny's hand on my back. I looked at him.

'Thank you.' I saw the carts of fresh fruit. I stopped.

'How much?' I asked the old man standing next to the cart. He was barely able to stand. He needed a walking stick; I wondered how his family could let him come out daily.

'For you, milady. No charge.' He had a thick accent; it

reminded me of a French or Italian accent.

'Not necessary, please.' I looked at Sonny who held my coin bag.

He handed it over; I grabbed out three gold coins. I knew it was too much. I placed them in his hand and closed it before walking away.

I handed the fruit to Sonny while I reached up my dress to grab my little dagger. I had been holding on to it since I got here.

'Where were you hiding that?' Sonny asked, looking me up and down.

'You will never know,' I said with a laugh. I put my hand out for the fruit. It had been a while since I had eaten guava.

Sonny put his hand over. 'Careful.'

He was worried. I chuckled.

'I will be alright; I always did this back home. The knife is slightly larger and sharper but hey, I am confident in my ability.' I cut into the fruit and handed Sonny a piece while balancing it on my dagger. It was so juicy; I missed the taste. I loved the pink colour of the fruit. One of the pips got caught in my tooth.

'Ow.' I kept moving my tongue around to get it out. I was not having much luck. I handed the knife and fruit to Sonny and turned away so he didn't see me put my hand in my mouth to get it out. 'Ah, ha, gotcha. You little sucker,' I said out loud.

I turned around and saw Rohesia standing there with Aleksander.

'That is not an appropriate way to behave as a lady with a title,' Rohesia said as she held her head high and looked down on me. I wanted to be a smartass but decided against that.

I opened my mouth to speak but Aleksander got in before me.

'Rohesia, do not judge her actions. She was not raised the same way as us. She is adjusting to her new life; it is important to be patient. She will discover the consequences of her actions,' he said.

Consequences of my actions? Was he talking about me sticking my hand in my mouth or was he talking about last night? I just smiled sweetly, squinting my eyes and showing my teeth. I grabbed my dagger and fruit back off Sonny and started walking back towards the castle. I turned around.

'Oh, by the way, I will never be a normal lady to the standards that are expected of me. I am me, get used to it,' I said and smiled before continuing walking. Sonny was walking beside me.

'Faith, do not change. You are refreshing.'

'Oh, thank you, Sonny,' I said, putting my arms around him in a hug.

It was an awkward hug because it was just his torso. He raised his arm and smirked at me. I wanted to glare back at Rohesia but I chose to remain pleasant towards her. She was a member of one of the founding families; it may not be wise for me to cross the Arundels.

I heard shouts grow louder behind me and I was frightened to turn around and look. I noticed Sonny looking behind and moving closer towards me.

'Never fear, milady,' I heard Sonny say and I looked up at him. After he said that line, I was beginning to worry. The riot was growing behind us. Rohesia had appeared by my side between Sonny and I. Aleksander had appeared on my other side. We were all huddled together.

'Just walk straight. We shall reach the castle gates shortly,'

Aleksander said not looking at anyone and not showing any emotion. His face was blank but his hand was resting on his sword. I think he saw the fear written over my face; he looked at me and winked. It was not comforting.

'You there,' a man shouted from behind.

'Keep walking,' Aleksander instructed and we all kept walking.

'I SAID YOU THERE,' the man shouted even louder.

I put my hand across to Aleksander. I knew he wanted to stop but the group's size was larger than expected.

'It is the king's whore,' another person shouted.

I closed my eyes and knew I could not stop him after that remark. Aleksander stopped and turned around. Sonny grabbed my arm to drag me. I pulled it out and looked at him.

'Get Rohesia to safety,' I said to Sonny. I knew even though there were two of us, he would do everything he could to protect me from getting hurt.

'My, you are a pretty thing,' the man said.

I finally had the chance to inspect him. He was in his late forties, his dark hair was receding and he was almost fully bald on top. His shirt was covered in dirt and his pants were split open. He shouted but looked rather ill and weak. I scanned the rest of the crowd and saw the same. They all looked weak and angry. I stood beside Aleksander. He put his hand on my stomach and pushed me back behind him.

'I believe you owe the lady an apology,' Aleksander shouted in response.

'I will give her something but it will not be an apology,' the man said as he licked his lips.

'The castle guards have been informed of your presence and are on the way. I recommend you disperse and return to your homes before any harm comes to you.' Aleksander spoke so elegantly.

It was one of the few times he had sounded like a royal. He would not back down. Aleksander slowly stepped backwards and I followed; his hand was still firmly on his sword. The gang was erupting in shouts. It was hard to understand them.

'We want food! We are starving! Why is the king punishing us?' That was why they all felt ill – they were hungry and poor.

'Aleksander, what can we do?' I asked him.

'Nothing, it is not our place,' he said, not looking at me.

'Get them,' the leader of the group shouted.

Aleksander turned around and shouted, 'Run.'

He grabbed my hand and we ran. I struggled to run in this dress – fruit was getting thrown at us and narrowly missed us. We could see the castle in our sights; there were archers on the wall.

'No,' I said under my breath. I looked at him and let go of his hand. I knew I would be sorry for doing this.

'STOP,' I shouted at the gang.

The leader stopped in front of my face. His breath was gag-worthy and he smelt of human faeces. I stood my ground.

'You are the king's whore,' the man said in my face as the group surrounded me. Aleksander drew his sword.

'No,' I said, putting my hand up to him.

'You are misinformed, good sir. I am not the king's whore,' I said politely and looked him in the face. He spat at my feet; I took a breath. Aleksander said the Bouchards were highly respected and loved. I was hoping this would help.

'I am Crystal Bouchard. My life was spared many years ago and I have returned home.' I tried to sound regal and gracious

– I was worried I sounded like an idiot. The man stepped back.

'I am not the king's concubine or mistress. I am a simple lady. I understand you are hungry and I swear on my life that I will speak with the king on this matter,' I said as I stared him down, careful not to break eye contact. I knew if I dropped my eyes that it would be a sign of weakness or that I was lying. He inspected my face.

'I shall hold you to your word out of respect for your parents.' The man bowed in my direction. He took a step back; many of the other faces were not satisfied with what I said.

I felt for Aleksander's hand. He grabbed it tightly and I felt him pull for me to step backwards. I slowly stepped and smiled at each of the faces. I looked up; the archers were still on the wall. I could hear the crowd murmuring; the hairs on my arms were beginning to rise. I knew something was about to happen. I held his hand tighter – if now was my time, I was happy it was beside him. My equal, we were both as equally stubborn and obnoxious as one another. Something hit me in the back. It became a blur. I was on the ground and Aleksander was on top of me as he shielded my body. I heard the sound of the bows springing after each of the arrows was let loose.

'No, no, no,' I said.

'Shhh, I have you,' Aleksander said. His entire body was on top of mine. He protected me by sacrificing himself.

'Clear,' a man shouted.

Aleksander lifted himself off me and moved the hair out of my face.

'Are you hurt?' he asked. He was so close to me. I looked into his deep brown eyes and was overcome. I was lost. I felt his hand on my face. 'Faith, are you hurt?' he asked softly.

I shook my head. No words came out but he understood what I was saying.

He stood up and offered his hand. I grabbed it and he helped me up. He winced in pain.

'Aleksander, you are hurt.' I saw an arrow sticking out of his left shoulder. 'Come, I shall fix it,' I said to him.

We got through the castle gates. Rohesia ran over and embraced Aleksander. He cried out in pain. She started to cry and put her hand over her mouth in shock.

'Don't worry, I will fix him up,' I said confidently. I brought him to his chambers and asked for some warm water and a needle and thread to stitch the wound up. I sat him down on the bed.

'This seems familiar,' I said, chuckling. So much for wanting to avoid him. He smirked and winced at the same time.

'Alright, first step. Honestly, I am not sure whether to snap the arrow or pull out the whole thing now. Hmmm.' I wondered what would be best. I still had to undress him to get to the wound.

'You are not displaying much confidence, Faith,' he said.

'Alright, I am going to snap it first. It is going to hurt,' I said, getting in a comfortable position to be able to snap it.

'Like a motherfucker,' Aleksander said and laughed but stopped instantly from the pain.

'Aren't you cheeky?' I said before I snapped the arrow without telling him. Aleksander groaned in pain and grabbed the blankets on the bed.

'That was the easy part. I now need to get you out of these clothes to pull the rest out and stitch it up,' I said, throwing the arrow on the ground. I started to undo his tunic. I only wanted to pull out the one side but Aleksander had removed his right arm from his tunic and his shirt.

I raised his left and pulled them off slowly. He was wincing and groaned in pain. I felt sorry for him. I looked down at his toned torso and wanted to rub my hands on it. He was insanely attractive and sexy but after he looked at me, I snapped back.

'Well, it does not look too deep on the plus side,' I said and brought the bowl of water over to the bed and sat it in his lap to hold. I wiped away some of the blood.

'I need to remove the rest of the arrow; do you want something to bite down on?' I asked him. I had my hand around the arrow.

He looked at me and put his other hand up to my face. He brought his face closer to mine and I felt his lips on mine again. I pulled the arrow out quickly while he was distracted. Aleksander shouted in pain. I did not mention the kiss. I wiped the wound quickly and cleaned it.

'Hold this please,' I said as I got the needle and thread ready to stitch him up.

'You won't get another sneaky peck like that while I stitch, mister,' I said, playfully trying to remove the seriousness of the situation. Rohesia walked in.

'Just in time – I am about to stitch the wound. If you wanted to hold his hand and comfort him, it will hurt,' I said to her.

She ran over and knelt on her knees and grabbed his hands. I breathed and gathered the skin before running the first stitch. He groaned instantly and shifted but after the first, he did not move. He was trying to portray strength because I knew this would hurt. I finished and wiped it over one final time before wrapping some cotton around his shoulder and under his arm.

'It will need to be cleaned again before bed,' I said to Rohesia and wiped my hands on my dress before I left his room.

I walked back to my chambers and stopped outside the door. I walked over to Annie's room and looked in. She was asleep; she was not handling this well at all. She was not even close to the safe point of twelve weeks yet. I hoped some of her symptoms would settle down soon; she could not be in her room forever. I needed to find some natural remedies but I had no access to a library. I could possibly talk to Farak Jwanak but I did not know if I could trust him. I walked over to Harley's room to discuss what her thoughts were. I did not knock and walked in; Harley was reading on her bed.

'Hey, how is Annie?' I asked her and closed the door behind me. She finished and folded the corner of her page before responding.

'She has a fever. Is that a good thing or a bad thing?' she asked.

'I honestly couldn't tell you; I have never been pregnant,' I said to her.

'Yes, you have.'

I shifted on the bed. I did not like talking about it.

'Harley, please. That was different – it was an ectopic pregnancy and I had no symptoms,' I said as I looked away from her. I was in hospital for a couple of weeks after I lost one of my tubes and was told the chances of myself becoming pregnant again were quite slim.

I changed the topic before she could continue asking questions.

'I had an idea – you know our tutor, Farak Jwanak. He should have some books or knowledge on natural remedies. She needs to get out of bed to avoid suspicion. I have Sebastian's eye at the moment but he is growing weary of my lack of intimacy.'

Harley sat up and leaned against the wall in her room.

'How do we know we can trust him?' she asked.

'That was my exact question,' I said as I scratched my head and crossed my legs on the bed.

'What if we say a lady's maid is expecting or something? But even then, it will be sus if we ask that question for a maid,' I said as I contemplated what to do.

'Faith, you are paranoid. These people are more simple than us and of course of lesser intelligence.'

I snorted and laughed.

'That is so true. I feel as if I am Albert Einstein sometimes because they do not understand the tiny little things.'

We both started laughing.

'We should introduce them to algebra and calculus,' Harley said, falling on the bed in front of me, lying down and crossing her arms under her chin to prop herself up.

'Oh, God, that would be like us trying to create a computer program. Surprisingly, do you miss Facebook or Instagram? I don't. Is it not more peaceful to not be so connected to the world?' I asked her.

'Yeah, at first I did but now I don't – but I have wondered. Do people know we are missing? We literally disappeared into thin air,' she said, looking upset.

I knew her parents would miss her dreadfully; I adored her parents – they cared about her so much and you could see it.

'I know; if we ever get home, how will we explain where we have been?' I asked her, lying down on my back with my hands behind my head. She didn't say anything. I saw a tear slowly descend down her cheek.

'Would you take Aidan with you?' I asked her.

'You know, I am not sure. I care for him but I could not say that I love him. He is merely a distraction.'

I was upset for Harley. I wished she loved him. I wanted all my friends to be happy. I knew Annie had fallen for Langford.

'Harley, I know it is your life. I will only say this once. If he is simply a distraction, let him go.'

Harley sighed. 'I know, Mum.'

I slapped her on the head.

'Have you seen Aleksander?' she asked as she looked at me to determine whether I was lying or telling the truth. I looked back at her.

'Yes, he was with his wife and it was fine,' I said to her, opening my eyes at her to show that I was not lying. I did not want to mention what happened this afternoon.

'What are you hiding from me?' she asked, squinting her eyes at me shadily.

'Harley, can you be honest with me?' I asked, turning around and looking at her. She nodded and waited for me to continue.

'This may sound stupid and rather vain... I know I am attractive but I have never thought I was drop-dead gorgeous.' I waited for her to respond.

'What? Do you want me to rate you on a scale of one to ten...' She paused, waiting for my answer. I nodded.

'Oh God. Yeah. You would be a nine out of ten. Your stubbornness makes you drop down in points but honestly, you are quite irresistible. Your eyes are hypnotising more than anything and against your dark features... WOW!' she shouted at the end.

'Alright, alright, I get it. Thank you.' I got up from the bed.

'Faith, why are you asking? What happened? Did Sebastian do something untoward?' she asked, creasing the lines around her eyes in worry.

I was fidgeting with my dress.

'No, not Sebastian. Aleksander, surprisingly. It wasn't anything too bad but just not him, per se...'

She waited for me to explain.

'We were attacked this afternoon – I am fine, he is fine. Everyone is fine but he was shot with an arrow. I fixed it for him but when I went to remove the arrow, he kissed me. He had never been that forward before and it has just thrown me. But after our discussion this morning, he kissed me this time and still no memories,' I said while I picked at the skin on my hands.

'Bloody hell, Faith. You can be blind sometimes. Annie and I noticed from the first week that Aleksander had a soft spot for you. Did you think we were just playing around? He likes you and obviously that little peck last night triggered him and he wanted another.'

My mouth dropped open in shock.

'I knew he was attracted to me because, well, it is obvious when I catch him looking at me but saying he likes me is a reach,' I said back to her.

'Well, at your meeting tonight, ask him. He cannot lie to you,' she said confidently.

I smirked. 'I am not going to meet him tonight. I thought it would be best if we spent a night apart after last night and earlier today,' I said to her and sat back down on the bed with my back to her.

'Faith, I have one final question for you. If Aleksander does indeed have feelings for you, are they reciprocated?' she asked slyly.

It would not matter what answer I gave her, she had already made up her mind on what my answer should be. I did not turn around and face her to give the answer.

'No, he is rather attractive and if I had met him under different circumstances then yes but no. He is obnoxious and totally not my type,' I said defiantly.

'Yes, a strong, silent type who always protects you and is insanely handsome and has a wicked body. Not at all your type – nothing like Toby.'

I turned around and glared at her.

'You can be a real shit sometimes, you know that?' I got up. 'I am going to request a meeting with Farak Jwanak,' I said before leaving the room.

It was getting close to dinner time. The days seemed to go by so quickly. I wanted to see Sebastian about my request but I was unable to find him and I could not find Miguel either. Where was everyone? I felt the pit in my stomach grow – what had happened? I went to the next best room to get answers.

KNOCK, KNOCK.

Rohesia answered the door.

'Lady Bushanti, you again,' she spat at me.

Ouch, that was harsh.

'I was looking for the king. Has Aleksander seen him?' I asked her politely.

'Aleksander is not available,' she said as she closed the door in my face.

Wow, rude bitch! I walked away and wondered where he was. I went back to his room and decided to wait inside it.

I opened the door and no one was there. I lay down on the bed. It was bigger and more comfortable than my own. I started twiddling my thumbs and waiting for him. I wished I still had a watch. I got up from the bed and walked around his room. I looked at some of the books – they were not in English. I wished my tutor taught me some of the language of this place. I sat down in front of the lit fireplace and watched the wood burn and the embers fly around before landing somewhere and dying out.

I was still sitting by the fireplace hypnotised by watching the flames. I heard the door handle turn and got up from the floor to greet him.

'Your Majesty,' I said, curtsying.

Sebastian was not alone. Yelena and Miguel were with him and Yelena had a smug look across her face.

'Faith, are you hurt?' he asked, seeing the blood on my dress and rushing over.

'No, Your Majesty. It is not my blood,' I said, worried about the other two still being in the room. Miguel cleared his throat. Sebastian took a step back.

'We must discuss an important matter.' Sebastian's voice turned cold. I suddenly felt rather cold next to the fire. I waited for him to talk.

'The Queen Mother has brought to my attention the existence of a letter with crucial information.'

I could not say anything without implicating that I knew about it. I decided to hell with it, if Yelena wanted to throw me under the bus, I was bringing her with me.

'Your Majesty, I am aware of the existence of a letter but it never reached my hands. It was intercepted by your mother who has been blackmailing me with the contents that I am still unaware of. She has asked me to spy on you for the past two months.' I stood straight and held my ground. Sebastian walked over and slapped my face. I fell to the ground.

'She is the Queen Mother, you will respect her. You should have conversed with me instantly.' He held up the letter in fury.

I was still on the ground; my eyes were fuzzy and my arms felt weak.

'I have had concerns over the friendship between Lord Marchés and yourself and this letter shows that he has been lying and there will be punishment. You are mine,' he said as he lifted my face to his. 'Do you not understand that at any moment I can remove you from this castle? You live by my favour and generosity. Do you understand?'

Tears were welling in my eyes.

'Yes, Your Majesty,' I said, not moving. I was too scared.

'You may leave,' he said and moved out of the way. I got up slowly and walked out as I held back tears. Yelena may have won this round but I was determined to remove her from the castle forever. I wondered what the consequences were for Aleksander's letter. I could not risk going to see him or even passing a note. I would always be watched now.

CHAPTER THIRTY-ONE

Aleksander

The pain was bearable; however, in an effort to move, I could not. I was in the room alone and thinking about Faith. I was overcome with desire when I kissed her; she brushed it off. I would have to be upfront with my feelings towards her. I desired her more than I wished to admit. I wanted to wake up next to her and close my eyes looking at her. She was challenging for a female but I enjoyed the way she made me feel. I had not smiled for many years before she appeared. Rohesia walked back into the room with a tray of food. She did care for me and was pleasing to the eye but I did not desire her. It was unfair for her and I disliked myself for not putting in more time and effort as she deserved.

'Come now, up,' she said, placing the tray of food on the bed.

'I am not famished presently,' I said to her.

Her face dropped.

'I shall eat when the pain subsides.'

Her face was bright again. She moved the tray to the drawers and sat down beside me. We did not speak; she just watched me and was brushing my hair with her hand while humming.

It was irritating but it gave her joy.

KNOCK, KNOCK.

I sat upright and groaned in pain. Rohesia sprang off the bed and answered the door. It was a messenger; she ripped the seal and read aloud.

'Your presence is requested by King Sebastian Faulcon,' she said.

Her face was worried.

'I am sure it is just to discuss the riot,' I said to her as I moved my legs slowly to sit up. I took shallow breaths. Rohesia appeared before me.

'Do you need assistance?' she asked caringly.

'No,' I said sternly.

She was persistent today. I did not put on an undershirt. Rohesia helped to dress me in a presentable tunic. I left the room; I saw a glimpse of Faith and wanted to see her face. Her head was down and her shoulders were drooping. I felt nauseous in the stomach. She always presented herself with pride and grace; something must have occurred for her to be quite dejected.

I was wary on the visit with the king. I knocked on his door and waited patiently for it to open. Yelena opened the door.

'Queen Mother, I have a request from the king,' I said graciously.

She did not utter a word but moved aside to allow my entry into the room. I walked in slowly, smiling at Yelena. I noticed Miguel sitting on the chair with a superior look on his face and Sebastian was leaning against the fireplace. I could see the frustration on his face.

'Your Majesty.' I bowed in his presence. I waited for him to respond; he sighed and took a drink.

'Aleksander... I have grown to trust you and respect your counsel but it seems I was immature in my decision. You have disrespected me with your lies...' Sebastian held up the letter I wrote for Faith.

I looked towards Yelena and her face was full of delight.

'You discovered information on another living Bouchard and I was NOT informed.' He began to raise his voice. 'You pledged your sword to Faith but not to YOUR KING. THERE WILL BE CONSEQUENCES FOR THIS.' Sebastian was furious and I was worried about the consequences. I did not utter a word.

'Do you have any words for your actions?' he asked, finishing his glass and pouring another.

'I had the intention of informing you but I sent the correspondence before my two-month sabbatical. I had every intention of telling you when I had returned. I pledged my allegiance to Faith because she will be the future queen. I have continuously informed you of the lack of respect that Faith and I share for one another. I find her obtuse and obnoxious.' I spoke with a lack of finesse in my voice; it was blunt and smooth to reinforce my point.

Sebastian shook with anger. 'I will take your words into consideration while I confer with my advisors on your punishment. You may wait outside.'

I bowed and left. I leaned against the wall, waiting for my punishment, for no crimes. I grabbed my dagger out of its sheath and tossed it in the air and caught it again. I now understood why Faith was so dejected when I witnessed her in the corridor. I could hear raised voices in the room and they were not Sebastian's. I heard the door open again.

'Lord Marchés, the decision awaits,' Miguel said.

I did not respond but walked into the room past him. King Sebastian was sitting in his chair, looking defeated.

'Aleksander, the decision has been made...' He paused, shaking his head and looking at his mother. 'You are valuable within the castle and are able to keep your head. But blood must be paid. Your mother Lady Victoria Marchés will pay the price and the earnings for your role will be reduced.' Sebastian did not look at me while he spoke. He stared at the ground. He waved his hand when he finished speaking.

'Thank you, Your Majesty,' I said and left the room. I never had strong emotions towards my mother but she was to be killed for my imaginary actions.

I knew in that moment that Sebastian was like his father; he was never able to make the appropriate decisions without counsel. He would never make a great king. I would stand behind Faith in hopes of her overthrowing Sebastian. I could not face Rohesia. I walked with haste to the stables. I mounted my horse and rode slowly out of town. I could not ride quickly; it made my shoulder ache. I reached Dmitirov's home and jumped down. His house was tiny and quaint with a door and two windows on either side. It was covered with mud bricks and it was something that I desired one day for myself. Dmitirov was outside tending to his garden with his little boy. He was the image of his father at such a young age.

'Aleksander,' he bellowed. His little boy ran towards me. I scooped him into my uninjured arm.

'My, how you have grown, Charles. Almost as strong as your father now,' I said, rubbing his head and putting him down.

'Charles, inside. The men must talk.' Dmitirov put the rake

down and walked over, leaning on the wooden post in his garden. 'What is the nature of your visit, Aleksander?' he asked.

'The letter I wrote to Faith was discovered by Yelena and she revealed its contents to Sebastian. He was livid at my actions and has ordered the death of my mother.' I was strong enough not to reveal any emotions. I was upset that my mother would suffer for my actions.

Dmitirov did not speak; he knew me so well as to wait for my continuation.

'I want to overthrow King Sebastian and put a Bouchard on the throne,' I said.

'Aleksander, that is treason and you will lose your head at the idea of this,' he said, worried. He paced in his garden.

I uttered Bouchard knowing that a brother, a rightful heir, was in line for the throne but believed that Faith would be a stronger ruler when she found her voice.

'We cannot know where the male Bouchard heir is. You were informed on Trikeque Island but from the evidence Faith gave you, that is not true. How do we...?' He stopped short in speaking. We both had no inkling of where to start looking. He nodded and we parted ways.

I knew I could not witness her death tomorrow. I would attempt to say farewell tonight under the cover of darkness. I heard Dmitirov's wife call out.

'Aleksander, come eat supper before you leave.'

I knew never to turn down her invitations without her wrath. She was persistent and I was in no mood for an argument.

CHAPTER THIRTY-TWO

Faith

I sat down on the other side of my bed, out of sight, as I cried. I was annoyed with myself; I should have told Sebastian instead of falling into Yelena's trap. I had asked for Sonny to bring me some wine. I was not going to dinner. I made the decision to cry and drink the tears away; it was not a solution to the problem but it would momentarily make me feel better. I had been sobbing for about an hour, my face was throbbing and there were no icepacks to make it better. The bruise would be phenomenal. I would not run away like I did last time but rather make it hell for Yelena and Sebastian. If they wanted to ruin me, I could not care less. I knew who I was as a person and I would do everything to make sure they would not defeat me. My dress was annoying me so I grabbed the dagger and cut it shorter.

'Oh God, that is so much better, isn't it, Toby? Yeah, you don't care,' I said to Toby who was almost asleep on the bed.

I needed music but also needed some people around. Annie would not be very fun at the moment. I walked and half-stumbled over to Harley's room. I knocked and leaned against the door. My eye felt a little swollen and would look like I had a lazy eye.

Harley answered the door with a smile and her face dropped.

'Wow, I look that good,' I said with a laugh. 'I need a drinking buddy. I have consumed almost a whole bottle and have another on the way. Join me?' I said as I held up my glass and drank from it.

'Whoa,' Harley said as she grabbed my glass and finished it for me. I knew even while I was inebriated that this was for my benefit.

'That's my girl.' I grabbed her hand and pulled her back to my room. I closed the door behind me when I heard a knock again. Sonny had brought another bottle of wine.

'Can you bring one more?' I asked with a sweet smile.

He shook his head.

'Maybe without the judgment,' I said after he closed the door. I was giggling at everything I said. I knew I was on the way to being quite intoxicated, drunk, fucked up. Whichever word you would prefer to explain my current situation.

Harley poured herself a glass.

'Now, what happened?' she asked.

'You know, I have just thought of a great drinking game. Every time you ask what happened, I shall finish my entire glass,' I said while I laughed at my own joke.

'I get the picture,' she said as she finished her glass.

'Are you trying to catch me?' I turned on my side and looked at her with a cheeky grin across my face. I ran over to my side table and grabbed my phone.

'I think this current situation warrants some music with dancing and singing,' I said and turned my phone on. It was down to forty per cent; I made the conscious decision that I would waste it on this night. I put the phone on shuffle. Harley and I started to sing and dance around the room. We erupted in laughter and had fun like we used to. She grabbed my phone and started looking through the photos; she held up the photo of Aleksander and me.

'Yeah, I had better delete that,' I said as I reached for the phone and fell over. I hit my face on the ground. I could hear Harley laugh in the background. We had finished another bottle. I think Harley consumed more than myself on this bottle.

KNOCK, KNOCK.

'Sonny is back with another bottle,' I said as I ran over and opened the door.

It was Miguel. I closed it instantly in his face.

'Wow, I may regret that,' I said to Harley and started to laugh once again.

Harley spat out her wine.

'Who was it?' she asked with a giggle. She was getting worse than I.

I mouthed 'Miguel'. The door knocked again. I rolled my eyes and opened the door as I leaned my arm against the other side of the door so he was not able to enter.

'Yep, you knocked,' I said as I looked at the multiple versions of him and tried not to poke my tongue out at him and just annoy him.

'The king requests your presence for dinner,' Miguel said.

'Yeah, nah. That ain't happening but thanks anyway,' I said as I closed the door.

Miguel pushed the door to stop it from closing. I shot a glare back at him.

'The KING requests your presence for dinner, Lady Bushanti,' he said sternly.

I spun around and crossed my arms.

'Yes, I heard you the first time. I am not deaf or ill. Whatever the hell you call it. You can tell the king I heard his request and I am declining. You can leave now,' I said, turning around and raising my eyebrows at Harley in my own little proud moment.

Miguel had still not left the room.

'You cannot deny a king's request,' Miguel said, unknowing of how to respond to my attitude.

'Alright, I shall put this simply: I request the king suck his own cock and then I shall fulfil his request. Sound good? Now, GET THE FUCK OUT OF MY ROOM,' I said as I raised my voice and he left with his mouth open.

'Shit, Faith,' Harley said, shocked as well.

'No, the king does not deserve to request anything from me in this moment. He can seriously fuck off to hell. I am done playing nice in this place. I am me, get used to it,' I said as I jumped onto the bed.

There was another knock at the door; I looked at Harley. She got up and answered the door. Sonny had returned with another bottle of wine. I ran to the door.

'Sonny, we are preoccupied. If Miguel returns, you can tell him we are not having any visitors for the rest of the night, yep... awesome.'

He nodded his head and I tapped his chest. I closed the door and headed back into the room. We turned the music back up and started dancing around doing ridiculous dance moves: the lawn mower, shopping trolley, sprinkler and the old 1970s dance moves. We could not stop laughing; we were having fun like we used to before all this shit happened. In that moment, I was exceptionally happy and there was nothing to break my mood.

There was another knock at the door. We turned the music up louder and kept dancing and singing, ignoring whoever was at the door. Jon Bon Jovi's *Living on a Prayer* was blasting. We were dancing and singing at each other. We had almost finished another bottle of wine. That was two bottles for me and Harley was catching up with almost two bottles.

'What is the meaning of this?'

I turned around and it was Sebastian. Harley stopped and curtsied instantly. I spat my wine out and it narrowly missed him.

'Just a few girls having some wine and dancing,' I said like a normal person.

'Lady Gelden, you may leave.' Sebastian looked at her – he was not asking, she was being told.

'No, I forbid her to leave. After today, you have no right to come in here and bark orders. You can leave,' I said as I crossed my arms at him.

He grabbed my arm. 'I am the king. You will respect my orders or—'

'Or what? You can strip me of my title and send me away. I will gladly leave – you can even kill me, at least I shall be rid of you,' I said bluntly. I stood my ground.

'I think I shall leave,' Harley said as she snuck out of the room.

I could see Sebastian's vein in his neck throbbing. I knew I had annoyed him. I was glad too, I wanted him to hit me again with no one else in the room. Watch me fight this time. I just continued to look at him. He closed the door and covered his mouth with both his hands. I picked up my glass and went to finish it. He took it from my hands.

'Excuse me?' I said as I reached over to grab it back.

'I believe you have had too many glasses tonight,' he said as he put it on the table beside him.

'Who are you to tell me when I have had enough? You are not even man enough to make your own decisions. You need snivelling people like Yelena and Miguel to back you up. You are a weak king and your father would be turning in his grave at your actions today. A man does not hit a woman, a coward does.'

It was a low blow but I did not care. I had liquid courage and my mouth was running before my brain could catch up and comprehend what it had said. Sebastian stepped back and sat down on the bed. I would not apologise for that comment. I noticed the vein in his neck had disappeared and his eyes became glassy.

'I apologise for my actions, Faith. You are correct. I was wrong to strike you and seeing your face—'

I cut him off from speaking. 'No, you do not get to apologise for this. You are a fucking asshole, dickhead, little bitch. The only thing I want to do to you right now is smack you so hard in the mouth that I knock some teeth out.'

He opened his mouth and closed it again.

'That is not ladylike,' he said.

'Hello, I am no bloody lady. I may have been born here but I have no remnants of how I was raised to act in the correct manner. This is regardless of your princess lessons – take me as I am or let me go,' I said as I pleaded with him. Sebastian started to laugh.

'You speak as if you are not the same person but the way you are speaking, all I see is your mother and her strength. Faith, please sit,' he said as he tapped the bed beside him.

I did not want to sit down; the room was spinning and I was worried I would sway if I sat down. He raised his eyebrows at me. I walked over and sat as far away from him as possible. I crossed my arms and did not even look at him.

'I expect less candour when we are in front of the people but I never want you to change. You are refreshing; I enjoy you. I desire you and despite my counsel voicing their opinions, I believe our union will be strong and a defining moment in history. I apologise for my actions and wish I could change them. I shall make up for them in any way I can,' he said and left the room.

I wanted to argue more but I was left speechless on his apology and his agreement with what I said. I decided to leave it for the night. I was dumbfounded.

CHAPTER THIRTY-THREE

Aleksander

Night had fallen. I snuck to the castle prison. I reached her cell; she was praying to the gods and looking out the window at the moonlight that was streaming in. I cleared my throat to alert her of my presence. She stopped and stood up.

'Hello, my only son,' she said, looking sincere.

'Mother, I am sorry. This is my fault.' I felt the guilt rise as I looked upon her face.

'Aleksander, I do not blame you. This was always the plan but Yelena lost the hooks she had in her husband. I accept my death because it will not be the end.' She spoke so calmly.

A tear rolled down my cheek. She reached through the bars and wiped the tear away. I put my hand on top of hers.

'I could not be prouder of my son.' She was beginning to cry.

'Guards, open the gate,' I ordered them; they ran over. I pulled my mother into my arms and I felt the tears as they rolled down my cheeks freely.

'Aleksander, you are on the correct path. Help Faith reach the throne and the uncertainty in our country will soften. The alliances will strengthen but be wary of who you trust. Yelena had an alliance with a family that was never discovered. She is sly, witty and deceiving but she can be outwitted.'

I had not let her go. She pulled back and wiped my face.

'Do not be upset that I am gone – remember that I was here. I am the proudest mother and despite our differences, I know we have always loved one another. Do not attend tomorrow. I do not want this on your conscience.' She walked back into her cell and closed the door.

'Mother,' I said as my voice wavered.

'Hush, my little Aleksander. I shall be with your father and look over you forever.' I sat down. I could not bring myself to leave her.

I sat with my mother for hours as we discussed in hushed tones my admiration for Faith and how to overthrow the Faulcon family without having the Marchés line wiped out.

'I love you, Mother,' I said before I left.

I did not quite love my mother but I knew she needed to hear it before I left. I turned and walked away, not looking back. I would not watch her death tomorrow. I headed towards the tower but Faith was not there. I walked down to her chambers and stood with my hand on the door as I tried to bring myself to knock. I wanted to tell her of my desires and my wish to see her face every morning. I opened her door; she was asleep. I walked over and brushed her hair away before I kissed her on the forehead.

'I love you, Faith,' I said before I left her room.

CHAPTER THIRTY-FOUR

Annie

It had been three days that I'd been waking up unable to move and the simple smell of food was making me nauseous. Langford had been generous and caring; he snuck in every day to see me and made sure I ate something. The stress from not knowing my future and the fact that I had not eaten a proper meal in over a week were taking their toll. I knew Faith and Harley were caring but they also knew there was not much for them to do to help me. I saw the light come in the window; I heard music and terrible singing last night. I think Harley and Faith had too much fun. I needed to get out of bed. I pulled off the blanket and put my feet on the ground beside the bed. I lifted my body slightly off the bed and my legs began to shake. I was so weak but needed to show my face otherwise I knew the king would become suspicious soon. I had asked Ivy, my lady's maid, to draw me a bath. I attempted to get up from the bed again but my legs shook. I grabbed the post at the end of the bed and held on to it.

'Just breathe,' I said to myself and focused on walking and not on the noise my knees were making from banging against each other.

I pulled off my nightgown and grabbed on to the sides of the bath and dragged myself into the bath.

'Milady Wakchter, I am pleased to see you up and about. I was worried you may be gravely ill if this continued,' Ivy said as she fixed up my bed and grabbed out fresh clothes for the day. The bath smelt like lavender and I rested my head against the side of the wooden bath and just enjoyed the smell. I was finally relaxed and I was beginning to feel my nausea subside.

'Ivy, could you please bring me some bread?' I asked her before I would attempt to get out of the bath on my own.

'Yes, milady,' she said and left the room. I was grateful that she was gone. I just wanted peace and quiet.

KNOCK, KNOCK.

'Go away,' I shouted at the door. I heard it open.

'Hello, hello. Someone is out of bed,' I heard Faith say before she closed the door.

'I am surprised you are up so early after all the noise I heard from your room down the hall,' I snapped back at her. I was a little shitty that I was not invited but I knew why they didn't and I was glad.

'Oh, is my Annie finally back?' Faith said with a big smile on her face.

God, she was an annoying little child. I sometimes wondered how she was a teacher because she could be so incredibly immature sometimes. The other times she was so strong and mature; it was as if she had a split personality. I looked over to her; she was standing on one leg and poking her tongue out. I laughed.

'Alright, I get it. Can you help me out of the bath, please? I have, like, nothing left in me,' I said to her.

She pulled a face in disgust. 'I have to see you naked – my eyes, I can feel them burning already. No, no, please. The horror.'

'SHUT UP and help me,' I said as I snapped at her. I'd had no food for three days and had not had a proper meal in general for over a week. Faith ran over and put the towel over her shoulder before standing on one side with both arms stretched out. I put my arms up and she grabbed them so tight, it hurt my skin. I was not going to complain.

She lifted me out of the bath.

'Annie, this is bad. You have lost too much weight this last week. It cannot be healthy for you and for the baby,' she said as she wrapped the towel around me.

'I am alright. I feel better after the bath.'

She rubbed her hands down my sides to help dry me. This was the other side to Faith – the most complicated girl you will ever know, and that was why I loved her. She had the uncanny ability to make me feel at ease when I should be really worried. She calmed me and she did not only do it with me but she had the same effect on Harley. I even noticed the same attitude change when Aleksander was around her; it was hard not to adore her. She walked me over to the bed and sat me down. I still held the towel around me. She grabbed the gown that Ivy had gotten out and looked at it.

'Yuck, this is hideous,' she said and headed to the door. 'Don't move. I have a better one for you.' She left the room. She was back in a flash and held the dress up in front of me; it was stunning.

'Wow, I love it,' I said and was excited to see what it looked like on. She held the dress open at my feet and I placed them into the middle.

She lifted the dress up and I put one arm into the sleeve and waited for Faith to lift the other. She didn't tie it up too tight; she knew I hated that and preferred my clothes a little looser. I looked down at the dress – it was a beautiful reddish, maroon colour with a black trim the entire way around. I looked like a princess. A smile spread across my face and I saw Faith's face.

'What?' I asked her.

'It is about time I saw your pretty smile again,' she said and wrapped her arms around me.

KNOCK, KNOCK.

Faith looked up and was worried.

'It is probably just Ivy bringing me some food,' I said to her.

I did not want to sit back down because I was worried that I would never get up again. Faith answered the door; she grabbed the food from Ivy.

'Thank you, you're dismissed for the day,' she said and closed the door on her. She could be quite blunt sometimes but it was comedic to witness. She broke the bread in half and handed it to me. I offered her some but she grabbed her stomach and laughed.

'I might avoid food for a little bit today. Slightly hungover but it is my own fault,' she said.

I finally had the chance to look at her face and she was hiding half of it behind her hair.

'Faith.'

'Hmm?'

'What are you hiding? I asked her as I tried to look at her face.

'Nothing, I am fine. It is nothing for you to worry about,' she said and picked up my nightgown and put it on my chair. I walked over to her and put my hand on her shoulder. She turned and she had a bruise on the edge of her right eye. It was purple; I accidentally touched it and she flinched.

'I am fine. Please do not worry yourself.' She fixed her hair to cover her eye back up.

I crossed my arms and was swaying slightly as I stood.

'Sebastian found the letter from Aleksander and assumes there is something going on between us. Fucking Yelena. If it was not for her this would not have happened.'

I walked over to my one window and looked through it before I leaned against it.

I walked over and leaned against her; I grabbed her hand in mine and we were quiet together.

'Aleksander and I have kissed twice now,' she said with her head against the wall and looking up at the ceiling.

'Do tell,' I said as I waited for her to continue.

'I cannot remember if I told you or not but the witch Millicent said my betrothed would bring my memories back. So I said technically that is you because it was organised for us to wed when we aged. I kissed him and nothing. After yesterday and pulling the arrow out of his shoulder, he moved in and kissed me.' She stopped talking and I could see her brain turning.

'What's the matter?' I asked her. I knew she came in here for a reason.

'I had a dream. I woke up and Toby was there and he told me to stop doubting myself before moving in for a kiss and when he pulled back, Toby wasn't there anymore – it was Aleksander. Is my consciousness trying to tell me something? I mean, I think Aleksander is incredibly good-looking and like sex on a stick but really annoying personality-wise. I hate to admit this but I would like to kiss him again because there is no spark with Sebastian whatsoever. It is kind of like kissing your cousin,' she said, still looking at the roof.

I chuckled.

'You like kissing your cousin?' I said teasingly and she pushed me gently. I think she may have been scared I would fall over.

'In all seriousness, I think you and Aleksander have a connection that cannot be explained. You complement each other but I will not say anything else because you need to discover your feelings yourself. I will not influence you,' I said and stood up from the wall. I was going to fall asleep again.

'I wish you were not like that sometimes but thank you,' she said with a big smile.

KNOCK, KNOCK.

'You're popular today,' she stated as she looked at me.

'I have no idea who this is now.' I was confused.

'Can you answer it? If it is Sebastian I am not here.' She walked over and hid behind the door, out of sight. I opened the door.

'Your Majesty, how are you?' I curtsied and looked him in the eyes.

'Lady Wakchter, I am eager to be in the presence of Lady Bushanti but I am unable to discover her whereabouts.' He sounded genuine; he did care for her but I think the darker side of his personality was not sure how to act in a normal manner, per se.

'Apologies, Your Majesty. I am not aware of where she may be. I saw her earlier but she left to find some peace and quiet, she said.'

He scratched his head.

'Yes, thank you,' he said and he walked away.

Faith mouthed 'fucking asshole' as I closed the door.

'He had better not come back and see that you are here. He may kill me for that alone,' I said and felt my anxiety rise.

'I will never let anything happen to you. If you or Harley die, I will kill myself as well. Then he will not be able to have any of us,' she said cockily as she plonked onto the bed.

KNOCK, KNOCK.

'Are you fucking serious?' she said, a bit too loudly, for anyone to hear. I turned and scowled at her to be quiet. I opened the door.

'Lord Marchés, to what do I owe the pleasure of your company?'

I could see Faith mocking me as I talked.

'I would like to discuss some information with you,' he said formally and bowed to me. I glanced at Faith.

'Are you not alone?' he asked as he tried to look around the door.

'No, I am but...'

Aleksander pushed the door open further. Faith continued to try and hide. Aleksander stepped around me and saw her hiding; he smiled and shook his head. I closed the door.

'Sure, come in,' I said to him.

'Faith, you always astound me with your peculiar actions,' he said as he removed his gloves and looked around the room.

'Annie, I have been in contact with allies and they have agreed to help you get settled where it will be safe and you can hide from the king's grasp,' he said confidently.

I ran over and embraced him. He took a while to put his

arms around me but patted my back.

'I am overjoyed at your change today. Langford was beginning to worry; I shall tell him of your recovery,' he said. 'Faith, may I speak with you in private?' he asked as he looked upon her with want.

'I do not th—'

'My mother will be executed later today. I cannot bear to watch and would ask if you could possibly go as a substitution.'

'Aleksander,' I said, worried about his emotional state.

'Of course,' Faith said, walked over and held him tightly. She put his head on her shoulder and stroked his hair. I could tell she cared for him but I think she was scared to admit her feelings for him because of the hurt from the death of Toby. I smiled as I watched him put his arms tightly around her and take a breath of her scent. She stepped to move back but failed and waited for him to let go. His eyes were full of water and she wiped his face; it was a touching moment to witness between the two of them. I smiled when I saw them looking at one another.

'Thank you, I am indebted to you,' he said as he stepped back and put his hands behind his back.

'Not at all, it is my pleasure.'

He walked out of the room. She watched him leave.

'I had best be off anyway. I shall see you later,' she said, kissing me on the cheek goodbye.

I was happy there was now a plan in place to keep me safe. I rubbed my stomach and smiled.

'We will get out of here safely, little one,' I said. Ivy had taken Buddy for a walk. I sat on the bed and grabbed a book to read before wandering around the castle. I still had bread to eat and continued to munch on it.

CHAPTER THIRTY-FIVE

Sebastian

I had spent tireless hours in search of Faith within the castle, with no success. I felt it imperative to convey to her my deepest apologies. I could not undo what I had done; I would try. My mother was wrong and I was blindsided by her evil nature and her snake-like tongue. I was disappointed in my actions. I felt that Faith had cured the darkest parts of my soul and without her presence I would become a person that was not fit to call themselves a king. I questioned Lady Wakchter and Lady Gelden but to no avail; had they known the existence of her whereabouts. I scoured the castle, ignoring more important matters to emphasise my concern for my actions.

'Mother, how are you this morning?' I asked as I deeply wished she would remove herself from my presence.

'My son, it is imperative that you sign the treaty. Why are you wandering the castle walls?' she asked with a frown that creased her brow.

'I...'

'Lady Bushanti is not important at this moment. We need to strengthen the castle, not make it look weak with a love-sick king. Come along.' She grabbed my hand and dragged me to the private headquarters. She opened the door and led me in.

'Your Majesty, as discussed with the Queen Mother—' General Arthur Murtflire was speaking when I turned to my mother.

'You may leave, women are not needed in men's talks.' I stared her down before she finally left.

'General Murtflire...' I said and scanned over the document. 'We must discuss a new treaty. I want ten thousand soldiers for half of the agreed price. I shall offer protection and a new bride – you may pick from either Lady Wakchter or Lady Gelden. They are pleasing to look at and young enough to bear you plenty more sons.' I was happy with the new offer I had given.

The general fiddled with his aging beard before he agreed to the new terms. He stood proud after his many years of service. He was renowned by many for his battle skills and the scars on his darkened skin proved it. His dark hair had sprinkles of age throughout it but his dark eyes revealed the darkness inside him.

'I must lay eyes upon the beauties before signing the treaty,' he said confidently.

My mother had met the general on Somneri land and they were not to be trusted but had always been the richest and one of the most powerful families.

'Yes, I am hosting a ball on Frashdae. I shall introduce you on that night.' I extended my hand to seal our deal and he responded in kind. I had no thoughts of where he would acquire ten thousand men; I knew it would be under less-than-desirable circumstances.

'Make yourself comfortable in the castle. One of the guards

shall show you to some quarters where you may rest after a long journey.' I snapped my fingers and left the room.

There were two days before the ball and there was plenty of planning to do. I felt it imperative to find Faith and continued to search around the castle before I headed to the gardens.

CHAPTER THIRTY-SIX

Faith

After leaving Annie, I walked down to the royal retreat that Sebastian had graciously given to me. I sat on the ground and watched the fish swimming in the pond. I picked up a flower that was growing beside me. It was one of those yellow weedy-looking flowers that always grew in the garden. I started picking each petal off one by one.

'He loves me, he loves me not, he loves me, he loves me not...' I continued and lost count before throwing the flower into the pond. I felt myself changing in this place and I did not like it.

I was a strong person but here I was weak and could be overpowered by the men. I saw the fish swim up and try to eat the flower; I chuckled to myself. It was peaceful being here.

I heard footsteps approaching. There were two entrances to the royal retreat: one that was easy to get to from the castle and the for other, you had to enter the maze. I broke a branch from the hedge and held it up. I should not have left without Sonny, especially after yesterday's riot. I held it above my head ready to attack. I could now hear which direction they were coming from. I prayed it was not Sebastian; I would prefer the townspeople over him. I stood beside the entry out of sight, waiting for the mystery person to appear.

I closed my eyes and swung the branch. The person grabbed it before I opened my eyes. It was Sebastian; I dropped it. I was not going to apologise to him. I rolled my eyes and walked away.

'Oh, it is just you,' I said as I slumped down on the chair. It was a childish act but I seriously did not care presently. He cleared his throat and sat down next to me.

'I have been looking for your beauty all morning,' he said as he tried to wipe my hair out of my face. I moved away from him and stood up, walking to the other side.

'What, did you want to see the mark you put on my face? You bloody... mole.' Honestly, that was the best insult I could think of. I was ashamed that my wit had failed me this time. He raised his eyebrows.

'I could have you hanged for insulting your king,' he said smugly.

'Please, don't bring me joy and make my day.' I smirked. I was coming back. 'If you expect forgiveness, go to church because I honestly do not want to forgive you. You meant your actions, despite your lacklustre apology.' I started to walk around the garden, not making eye contact with him.

'I am aware that you do not accept and have come to bargain with you,' he said as he picked a flower from the garden and walked over to me.

I looked at him, not accepting it but he was bringing it closer and closer to me. I grabbed it and threw it into the pond (yep, childish but stuff it).

'I am listening,' I said curiously, wondering what the bargain was.

'I overheard your speech to the townspeople about talking with the king for more food. All of the gifts I receive on my name day will be used to buy more food for the townspeople.'

I looked at him, shocked. He overheard but didn't come rescue me, the little pussy. No wonder he was jealous of Aleksander who was lying on top of me at the time – he probably wanted to switch places. I contemplated his bargain.

'Okay, I get something out of this deal but what do you get?' I asked, worried about what his terms would be.

'My terms...' He looked at his nails and smiled. 'You forgive my actions and forget they occurred... and we marry after the royal tour where we shall consummate our love.' He seemed incredibly proud of himself.

My first thought was, *wow that escalated.* I knew Annie was planning on escaping after the royal tour; my wedding would be a distraction to help her leave.

'Deal,' I said as I extended my hand to shake on it. He looked at my hand and shook his head.

'Tsk tsk,' he said as he licked his lips.

I moved forward and kissed him on the cheek. He grabbed my head and pulled me in for a kiss. It felt like an invasion, as he shoved his tongue into my mouth. I pushed him back and slapped his face.

'Seriously, what, did you want your tongue to come out my arse?' I wiped my mouth from all the excess saliva and spit.

He seemed rather proud of himself.

'We have a deal, happy? I have somewhere I need to be,' I said as I left the garden.

I needed a toothbrush, floss and some mouthwash. It was almost time for Victoria Marchés' execution. I would watch it for Aleksander. I headed back to my chambers and grabbed my cloak. Sonny looked unimpressed that I had slipped past him again; it was not my fault I was a ninja in disguise. I walked down the hall and saw Aleksander. I could see the worry across his face. I wanted to comfort him again especially after earlier with our embrace that he did not want to end. I smiled at him and as I passed him grabbed his hand and squeezed it. He held on tight and let go. I looked back and could feel his pain. He never spoke of his mother but losing any family member is hard enough.

We exited the castle, with only slight delays. Apparently, I should have received permission before leaving but I just pushed my way through the men and Sonny followed. I sometimes questioned whether I needed him but he saved my life and I like to think I helped save his. I was yet to ask Sebastian about bringing his love Stresina to be with him. I had every intention but I needed more leverage over the king. I put on my cloak and kept my head down. Sonny was alert and scanned the crowds. I kept telling him to relax and blend in. He was tall and imposing and easily someone who stood out in a crowd. We almost reached the town centre when someone pushed through us.

'Excuse you,' I muttered to the person who turned around and I noticed a familiar face.

'Faith, is that you? I see the king found you.'

'Lizzie?' I had not paid her back like I said I would. I needed to add that to my list of things.

'Hi, how are you?' She embraced me.

Sonny grabbed his sword.

I whispered, 'It's alright, I know her.'

I would not say how I knew her but she did help me when I needed it.

'Are you witnessing the execution?' she asked. I nodded my head.

'I am guessing you are too,' I said.

'Oh yes, I love them. It is so fulfilling to see someone else losing their head and I get to keep mine,' she said with a sly smile. Wow, that seemed dark and unwarranted but she was not aware of why I was here.

'Yes,' I said, smiling.

She wrapped her arm around mine and we walked along together. I had ventured into the town quite a few times but never to the centre. It was massive – there were masses of people, roughly from one hundred to one hundred and fifty. They were all cheering. Lizzie grabbed my arm and pulled. I reached for Sonny and pulled him along as well. We were in the second row from the front.

'If we are lucky, we will get some blood splattered on us.' She was like a little girl, all excited.

I was worried to be standing beside her. I looked around and all I could see were faces and houses; people were watching from windows and standing on stalls to get a better view.

I looked up and saw the executioner with his face covered in a black leather mask. His clothes were covered in blood and he sharpened his axe, which had a metre-long handle. The axe looked to be the size of two of my hands laid beside each other. He had a smile across his face. I wondered if the executioners back then in the medieval times were silent serial killers. I shook at the thought.

The executioner bellowed, 'Lady Victoria Marchés has been

charged with witchcraft and treasonous acts against the king. She shall be beheaded for her crimes. Does anyone object?'

The audience went quiet and everyone looked around. Would anyone actually object? Hmm, that would be interesting. Nobody objected.

'Bring out the prisoner,' he yelled.

I looked around for her. She was being brought through the middle of the crowd. They threw food and spat on her. She never lifted her head but looked at the ground as she walked. I was not close enough to give her comfort. She was dragged onto the stage – she was not fighting the guards but she was not making it easy on them. The executioner moved the wooden block into the middle of the stage; it was quite high and had a dint in the front where the neck would be sitting.

'Any last words?' the executioner asked.

She scanned the crowd as they went silent. She may have been looking for Aleksander. I pretended to sneeze to bring her attention to me. She looked over and I smiled at her. I held up the cross in hopes she would recognise it. She smiled back at me.

'I apologise to the former king Charles Bouchard for not fighting for them when the Faulcons took over. They were the rightful rulers and I pray someone destroys the Faulcon family as they have done mine. Long live the Bouchards!' she shouted to the crowd.

No one cheered but they looked stunned that she wished ill upon their king. I grabbed Sonny's hand; I was not sure if I was strong enough to witness this. She bent down and adjusted herself to the wooden block and took off her necklace. She looked at me and nodded.

I turned to Sonny. 'Catch the necklace.'

She threw it into the crowd and it was lucky he was tall; he was able to grab it and hold it tightly.

'Look after my son.' I could hear her voice breaking. She was ready to die but still scared.

The executioner moved her hair out of the view of her neck and lined himself up. I closed my eyes and held my hands together, saying a silent prayer in my head.

'Our Father, who art in heaven, hallowed be thy name; thy kingdom come, thy will be done, on Earth as it is in heaven. Give us this day our daily bread and forgive us our trespasses, as we forgive those who trespass against us; and lead us not into temptation, but deliver us from evil. Amen.' I opened my eyes as his axe fell down and she was gone.

The crowd erupted in cheers as her head rolled around the stage and her lifeless body was still on the wooden block. I was appalled at the way they loved this entertainment. I felt something warm on my face; her blood had splattered. I wanted to be sick. The bells on the tower close to us rang out.

'Lizzie, why are the bells ringing?' I asked her.

'To let others know that someone has been executed,' she said, looking happy and watching the head roll around.

The executioner grabbed the head by the hair and lifted it up, shouting.

Victoria's face was covered in blood, the eyes had rolled into the back of the head, her mouth was open with blood coming out and blood was dripping from her neck. I could not hold it in any longer. I bent over and vomited from the sight. I wiped my mouth as I stood up again. Sonny whisked me into his arms and carried me out of the crowd.

I didn't get the chance to say goodbye to Lizzie but I doubt she would have cared; she was too engrossed in the beheading. I still felt faint and Sonny carried me all the way back to the castle before allowing me to find my feet. Miguel walked over.

'Where have you been?' he snarled at me before he looked me up and down. He must have noticed the blood and dragged me to King Sebastian. I was going to be sick again but I could not break his grasp.

'Your Majesty,' he said as he showed me to him.

'Faith, why are you covered in blood?' he asked before realising he already knew the answer.

I could feel the vomit rising in my throat. I put my hand over my mouth and ran over to a corner before vomiting again. It was quite acidic and burnt my throat coming up.

'Miguel, leave us,' Sebastian ordered.

'Your Majesty, this—'

'This means I ordered you to leave the room. Send a cleaner in to clean the mess.' Sebastian rubbed my back to comfort me. I looked at him.

'You wanted to be there because you care,' he said.

I nodded and a tear ran down my face. My legs began to shake. He picked me up in his arms and carried me to my chambers. Sonny opened the door and Sebastian laid me on the bed.

He ran over and grabbed a cloth and water to wipe the sweat off my face. I wanted to explain.

'Shhh, I understand. Aleksander could not stomach witnessing another death and asked for your presence at the execution so his mother was comforted. I do not agree because a lady should not witness such atrocities.'

I nodded my head and listened to him tell a story of his first execution. I must have fallen asleep; when I woke, there was an arm around my stomach as I lay on my side. I slowly moved to see whose it was. Sebastian was asleep behind me. I shifted on the bed to get away from him. He was a twisted person but I tried to see the good in him. He was just taking care of me while I was unwell and did not want to leave until he knew I was better. I grabbed a glass of water from my table and drank it slowly, watching him sleep. I could not remove the image of Victoria's head in the executioner's hand as he shouted in joy. I shook my head and walked over to the other side of the bed. I poked Sebastian gently until he woke.

He turned around quickly and saw me standing with a smile.

'Water,' I said as I offered him a glass. He shook his head.

'Are you feeling better?' he asked, getting off the bed.

'Yes, I am. Thank you for tending to me,' I said as I moved away from the bed.

He walked over and kissed me sweetly on the cheek before leaving. As he left, I turned to Sonny.

'You must warn Aleksander now,' I said, ordering him to move instantly.

Sonny handed me Victoria's necklace. I hid it in a drawer in my table before heading over to my window and looking out. At least she was with her husband now and was no longer in prison. I could imagine the two of them walking along the beach together, holding hands. I hoped they were proud of their son and all he had achieved after being dealt a rough hand in life. I hoped Sonny got to him in time to warn him the king was to visit his chambers. I was watching the waves crash against the sand and retreat back into the ocean before I heard...

KNOCK, KNOCK.

CHAPTER THIRTY-SEVEN

Aleksander

I heard whispers of Faith after she witnessed my mother's beheading. I wanted nothing more than to check on her but it was too dangerous for us to be seen with one another. I prayed Sebastian had not punished her further. Yelena's spies watched her night and day. I knew who they were as I had witnessed them watching me at every corner within the castle.

I watched Dmitirov teach the new recruits the proper way to hold a sword and the correct stance. Dmitirov was running the training session as my mind was elsewhere. A young boy fell over.

Aidan walked over. 'You just killed your fellow soldiers,' he said and stepped back.

I was disappointed; I had trained my men that they were all important to one another and when one falls, another must help or you lose your strength as a group. My father taught me the same as a child. Your fellow soldiers are your family and you protect them as if they are your own blood. I bit into my apple and watched; they were so weak and needed to be fed correctly but with the shortage of grain, it was difficult for them to be fed correctly.

Sonny appeared beside me.

'Lord Marchés, I have an urgent message from a friend,' he said as he looked around for a listening ear. I knew it was from Faith.

'I was sent to warn you that the king knows that you sent her to witness the beheading of your mother. She is worried about the repercussions from His Majesty.'

I did not say a word or even look at him. I nodded my head and he left. I was not worried the king was discussing his grievances with me on this account. I witnessed Yelena sneaking out of the gates of the castle in a cloak. I whistled to Dmitirov and nodded.

'I shall follow,' I said to him.

Langford followed. We were careful enough not to be spotted as we headed into the darkest area of the town. It was where the most crimes were committed – even my men did not venture into this part of town. I looked towards Langford; we were not wearing the proper attire and would stand out to the townspeople. I could not risk losing her tail.

'Langford, stay behind. If I do not return before sundown, inform Dmitirov,' I ordered.

'No, my lord. We shall go together or not at all.' He had grown so much in the last year and I was proud of his accomplishments.

We shook each other's hands and continued to follow Yelena. I dared not look upon the faces of the people in the streets. I held my hand on my dagger in my back pocket. Yelena disappeared into a cottage at the end of the row. Yelena would recognise my face easily so I waited closer to the cottage, out of sight. I watched the sun to grasp the time that had passed; it had moved out of sight – this was an indication that night would fall soon.

Yelena exited the cottage and snuck away. Langford proceeded to follow and I shook my head. I wanted to lay my eyes upon her visitor. Yelena was out of sight. Langford and I approached the door. I did not bother to knock but kicked the door in.

The man was lying on the bed with only a shirt on his body. He looked no older than myself. He had bright red hair and an eager-to-please face. Langford walked over and threw him some pants. He pulled them on.

'Sit,' Langford ordered.

I grabbed a chair and turned it around before I sat. I swung the dagger in my hand in an attempt to frighten answers out of the young man.

'Why was the Queen Mother visiting you?' I asked.

He shook his head in fear. I looked at Langford. He struck him across the face.

'I am a generous man when I get what I want. I am not to be trifled with.' I balanced the dagger on my finger. 'If you do not give me the information I need, it will not end well for you. I shall ask you again: why was the Queen Mother visiting you?'

I stood up from the chair to be an imposing figure. The young man shook his head. I did not want to punish him but if Yelena was visiting this area, it was for something important.

'Search the place,' I ordered Langford. I walked over and sat beside the young man while Langford searched the house. I put my hand on his knee. 'What is your name?'

'Jeffrey Lakitys.' He quivered.

'Do you know who I am?'

Jeffrey nodded his head.

'Now that we are acquainted...' I said while I applied pressure to his knee. 'Won't you inform me of why you are conversing with the Queen Mother?'

Jeffrey opened his mouth and grimaced in pain. Langford found papers.

'Aleksander, you had best look upon these,' he said with a worried look on his face.

'Watch him,' I said and grabbed them from his hands.

I looked upon them and was abhorred by the contents. They were letters between Yelena and the head of the Somneri family; they were paying her for information on Sebastian and Faith, and any treaties that were being discussed in secret between other founding family members. I folded the letters and hid them in my shirt. I put my hand over my mouth and smoothed my beard – how could I approach the king with this information? I was not on his good side and his mother was.

'Jeffrey, you realise she is committing treason and you are helping her. Do you wish to die so young?' I asked. My temper rose.

He shook in fear. I punched him twice in the face. Blood dripped from his nose.

'I can offer you sanctuary if you talk,' I said and struck him again.

I nodded to Langford. He ripped his shirt open. I threw my dagger at his head and it narrowly missed and lodged itself in the wall. I walked over to his fireplace and grabbed a log of wood.

'Talk or burn,' I said.

Langford grabbed both of his arms and held him down. I slowly walked towards him, holding the log of wood at arm's length.

He was trying to break out of Langford's grasp when he yelled, 'I will tell you.'

He sobbed in fear. I looked at Langford who let go slowly. Jeffrey slunk off the bed and held his head in his hands and sobbed.

'My name is not Jeffrey. I am the cousin of Prince Somneri. Yelena spent her exile with our family and had an intimate relationship with the prince. They have been planning on launching an attack on the castle and taking control of Zilanta and ruling the families. After the whispers of the existence of a Bouchard, the Somneris have halted their plans and are waiting for leverage.' He stopped talking.

Langford and I looked at one another and were shocked. Sebastian's own mother was going to overthrow her son.

'Yelena is trying to push the agenda ahead of schedule. She detests the Bouchard line and wants them gone. I am an outcast of my family and was sent here to spy.'

I knew I would have to end his life; it was too dangerous to keep him alive. I needed to find a solution to turn him.

'By the law of Hisadalgon, I should turn you over to the authorities.'

'No, Lord Marchés,' he begged.

'I shall spare you, if you become my spy on all correspondence between Yelena and Prince Somneri. If I find you have betrayed me'—I moved in closer—'I will cut open your torso and feed it to the dogs while you are still alive on the table. Do I make myself clear?'

He nodded.

'Yes, my life is indebted to you,' he said.

Langford and I left the home and started to head back to the castle. I was unsure whether to present this information to Sebastian now or to wait.

'Aleksander, all three of them are in danger,' he said and I saw worry cross his face.

'They have us, they will be safe,' I said.

Sebastian waited at the gate of the castle with his arms crossed, looking livid. Langford looked at me.

'Good luck,' he said and walked in the opposite direction.

'Your Majesty, you look displeased,' I said to him.

He turned and walked away. I knew that was an invitation to follow. I was about to be scolded for my request to Faith. We walked into the dining hall.

'Close the door behind you, Lord Marchés,' he ordered with his stiff voice.

I knew I would have to play the fool to protect Faith from her secret message. 'Your Majesty, I am unaware of what actions have insulted you,' I said with a soft and gentle tone, trying to portray my innocence.

'You requested that Lady Bushanti watch the execution of your mother,' he said, raising his eyebrow at me. I could not deny my actions.

'Yes, Your Majesty,' I said, looking towards the ground and clenching my fists in frustration.

'What would possess you to request that of a lady? She did not need to bear witness to something that horrific. Were you aware that she became unwell after witnessing it?' he asked.

I could tell his temper was rising.

'No, I was not aware that she was unwell. It was a selfish request on my behalf. I was a coward and I could not stomach witnessing my mother's death but I wanted her to see a familiar face. I knew Victoria would recognise Faith from her eyes that are like her mother's. I apologise for harming your future queen and I shall apologise to Faith.' I bowed after I finished speaking to show my respect for the king. He watched me carefully and nodded his head.

'You may leave but I shall pass on your apology to Faith,' he said, turning his back towards me. It was rather tempting to grab my dagger and throw it at him, ending his minimal reign.

'Your Majesty, I have come across some disturbing information that I believe is important for you to look upon.' I opened my pocket and removed the letters, holding them tightly in my hand. Sebastian sat down and moved his hand as a gesture to tell me to continue.

'I witnessed the Queen Mother leave the castle in an inconspicuous manner and my intuition tingled. I followed her with a fellow soldier. She ventured into the dark area of town and stayed in a house for a rather long time before leaving. I headed into the house and discovered a young man who was undressed. We discovered the presence of these letters. I shall let you lay your eyes upon them,' I said, handing him the letters and stepping back.

He read one and put it down, read another and slammed it on the table. He read another and stood up.

'WHAT?! That devious woman. I shall hang her for this treason. Trying to steal my throne. FIND HER NOW,' he ordered.

'Your Majesty, if I may speak candidly before I leave?' I asked.

His face turned red but he allowed me to speak.

'The messenger has now agreed to deliver messages directly to me after some persuasion. Would it not be useful to have an inside man?' I asked. I saw him ponder my suggestion. He stood from his chair.

'I understand your suggestion but I believe it is imperative for her to be removed from society and placed back into exile,' he said.

I felt my rage rise.

'Did you not just speak of your desire to hang her for her treason?' I raised my voice at him.

'You forget yourself, Aleksander. I am the king. I make the decisions!'

'You killed my mother but cannot bring yourself to end your mother's life for treason against you?'

'You may take your leave Aleksander,' he shouted and I stormed out of the room. I did not ask what would become of the young man who called himself Jeffrey.

I headed to my chambers. I walked into the room and removed my belt with my sword and threw it on the bed. Rohesia was not in the room. I washed my face and wet my hair. I sat on the bed and got up; I did not expect Sebastian to pass on my apology. I hid my dagger in my boot, drank a goblet of wine and headed to her room. I knew if we were seen together, there would be dire consequences. I arrived at her door. Sonny was not around. I heard her laughter from behind the door; I could see her smile through the door. I felt myself calm and realised I could not and would apologise to her later in the evening. I looked around to make sure I had not been seen. I headed to Annie's room and knocked.

'Annie, I would like you to pass on a message to Faith. I would like to see her tonight at our place,' I said and walked away.

Annie had no time to respond and I left before anyone witnessed where I was.

CHAPTER THIRTY-EIGHT

Faith

Annie told me about the message from Aleksander and I had decided not to go to the tower. I thought it best that we kept away from each other for our safety. Dinner with Sebastian was quiet. I was still annoyed at his actions but we made a deal and I would honour it.

I sat, ate and smiled often towards him but behind every smile was a grimace and a glare and a secret wish to slap him across the face. I finished dinner and excused myself early, using the excuse that I was tired after today's events and left for my room. I opened the door and changed into my nightgown, sat on the bed and tried to remove the image of Victoria's bloodstained face and eyes rolled into the back of her head. I put my arm around Toby and tried to relax my brain. I walked over to my table and looked at the necklace from Victoria; it reminded me of a rosary. They were black pearls; even back home they were rarely seen in a jewellery store. At the bottom was a locket with a cross on it. I wanted to open it but felt that would betray Aleksander and his mother. I put it back in my drawer and went back to my bed.

I grabbed a handkerchief from the cupboard and started playing tug of war with Toby. He was in a playful mood with two paws on the bed and his bottom up in the air. He growled and barked. I remembered earlier in the afternoon when someone knocked on my door but nobody was around just a note sitting there. I had no idea what it said because it was not in English; all it said was, 'Erki wredin tykun litck Bröak.'

Whoever sent it obviously thought I had knowledge of this language. Sadly, I didn't. I was frustrated and looked through some of the books on my nightstand but none spoke of the language. I knew there was a library – I was about to leave the room when I realised what I was wearing and quickly put on another dress – my favourite boring brown and red dress. I opened the door and left the room, heading for the kitchen where I believed Makenzie may be.

I reached the kitchen and avoided Sebastian and Aleksander. I looked in the kitchen and Makenzie was not around; I did see Ivy who was Annie's lady's maid.

'Ivy,' I called over to her. She wiped her hands on her skirt and walked over.

'Yes, Lady Bushanti.' She curtsied.

'Please, no need for formality. Do you know where the study is...' I realised she would not know what this was. 'A library – a place where books are,' I said, dumbing it down for her. She nodded.

'Follow me.' She walked and I followed. It was on the other side of the castle.

'Thank you,' I said before I knocked on the door and made sure that no one was in the room.

There was no response; I opened the door and stuck my

head in. It was empty. I snuck in and closed the door behind me. I walked over to the shelves; the room was dark in a way that you would not expect a library to look like. The fire was barely lit in the fireplace. I grabbed another log and threw it on, trying to bring it back to life and to illuminate the room. I grabbed a two-pronged candle holder and tried to light it in the fire. I burnt my fingers slightly. I started sucking on them to try and cool them down; it was not working. I kept shaking them but was trying to forget about it by looking through the books.

I had no idea where to start. I hummed to myself and rubbed my fingers across the leather-bound books. They were either black or tan with gold or black writing on them. I secretly hoped one said 'dictionary' on it. The top row was too high. I started from the bottom.

I sat down on the wooden diagonal flooring. The majority of them were discussing tales of different family members. There was one on a Bouchard. I wanted to pull it out and look through it but I couldn't bring myself to do it. I knew I was recognised as this Crystal but at the same time, I was not her. Moving up a shelf, they were still different tales. I stood up and the titles of the books in the middle shelves were hard to read from being so faded. I grew frustrated. I grabbed the chair and pulled it closer to the shelves. I put one leg on it and lifted to the other to make sure it could hold my weight. I was unsteady on my feet; the books were dusty and very worn. I rubbed the spine of a book and dust flew everywhere. I could feel a sneeze coming. I was trying to step down from the chair but could not find my footing.

'ACHOO.' I sneezed so loud it could have caused an

earthquake. I lost my balance and wobbled.

'Whoa, shit.' I fell backwards and closed my eyes. I knew I shouldn't put my hands down to break my fall. The last thing I needed was to have a broken arm, hand, shoulder or any other body part.

Arms wrapped around my stomach and under my knees. I took a breath and opened my eyes. I looked at my saviour and wrapped my arm around his neck.

'Thank you,' I whispered. I felt my body shake with adrenaline and fear. Aleksander put me down. I stumbled at first but found my feet shortly after. I clicked.

'Wait, how did you know I was in here?' I asked him as I sat as I tried to calm down.

'I heard your humming from the corridor and came to investigate,' he said, leaning against the shelves in front of me. I stood up.

'You know, back home this is called stalking. I could have you arrested and sent to jail,' I said.

He was confused.

'Stalking is when someone keeps following you and you don't really want them to.'

He nodded that he understood.

'To protect you, I must stalk you.' He nodded his head and sounded proud of himself.

'Anyway, did you want something or did you just come in the room to gig?' I asked as I turned back around to the shelves of books to inspect them.

'I... er...' he stuttered.

'Well, spit it out,' I said as I continued to look at the books.

'I was looking for you earlier to apologise,' he said, looking down at the ground.

'Apologise for what?' I asked, confused, and frowned at him.

'I heard that you were unwell from witnessing my mother's execution.' He looked sincere and worried about me.

'Oh, right, that. Yes, well. It was certainly an eye opener but it was just the shock. I am fine. Thank you for your concern but you needn't have apologised for that. I did a favour for a friend,' I said, turning back around to look at the books.

I did not want to ask him for help. I wanted to find the answer on my own. I was too independent sometimes. He sat there like he had something else to say. I turned around and looked at him, waiting for him to talk.

'I am uncomfortable with what I am about to discuss with you,' he said and walked to the other side of the room. I sat down on a nearby chair and crossed my legs.

'Take your time. No one knows I am here,' I said, speaking with my hands and adjusting my dress.

'Faith, I feel it is important to tell you that... I have struggled with feeling emotions towards my wife. I do not feel the same level of affection towards her that I do you, after our moment on the tower...'

I put my hand up.

'Please, do not finish that sentence.' I stood up from the chair in frustration.

'I feel it is imperative to finish my sentence,' he said and straightened himself.

'No, you cannot put that back in the bottle when you say it. Do not ruin this.' I grew emotional. I did not want to hear him say those words. It would make it difficult for me to look at him knowing how he felt. He started toward me. I moved the chair in front of me as a form of protection.

'Faith, I grow weary when I am not around you. I feel empty when I cannot lay my eyes on you. I only wish to lie beside you every night and wake up with you. I wish for us to never be apart.' He was still trying to come closer to me.

I kept shaking my head and repeated, 'No, no, no, no, no.' I did not want to listen. 'Aleksander, stop. You cannot say that. Do you understand what you have said and what will happen if anybody finds out?'

I walked away from him, putting my hand on my forehead and looking at the wall. He grabbed my arm and looked at me.

'Do you reciprocate my feelings?' He searched my face for the answer.

'No,' I said sternly and pulled away from him.

'Do not lie. I can see it and feel it when we are together.'

I slapped his face.

'I said no. Do not accuse me of lying. You can leave.' I turned away from him. I felt ill at his admission and my actions. I heard him close the door as he left. I remembered Annie's words that I needed to discover how I felt without any influence.

I turned around and was glad to see that he had left the room. I was not sure how I should feel about this. Guilt, worry, anxiety, frustration and so many other emotions – I was all over the place. I opened the door and left the room; I knocked on Harley's door.

'Girl time, now,' I said, turning away and leaving for Annie's room.

She followed with haste; she knew I was serious. I knocked on Annie's door and entered. Langford was giving her a back massage. I smiled sweetly.

'Langford, Harley needs some girl time. Can I request that you leave for the night?' I was being sugary sweet and lying through my teeth at him because I was worried that he would report this back to Aleksander. Langford left and Annie sat up.

'This had better be important, I am feeling alive today and was looking forward to fucking him. We slept together once before he left and haven't been together again.' She was pissed. Oh hormones – this was the beginning; she was only going to get snappier and moodier.

'Really? You had sex once and got pregnant? Sure,' Harley said, looking happy that she still had her contraception.

'Regardless of the fact that you want sex, I need help. I am unsure of how I am feeling.'

Annie's face changed drastically and Harley walked over to the bed and sat down.

I sat on the chair and leaned down with my hands in my lap clasped together. Tears were stinging my eyes.

'Fucking hell, why am I emotional? Can I not be normal for once?'

Harley was worried. 'Faith, what is the matter? You are scaring me.'

I could see the fear in her face.

'Argh... Aleksander told me...' I took a breath and looked up at them.

Annie spoke. 'He told you how he felt, didn't he?' she said.

I nodded as tears trickled down my face.

'You don't know how to handle it because you feel a sense of betrayal from him and from yourself.' Annie understood me.

Harley ran over and hugged me; the tears were falling quicker.

Harley whispered, 'It is okay to let go and feel. You don't always have to be our rock and show your strength – you can show your fear and emotion.'

I chuckled between my tears.

'When did you grow up?' I said to her.

She let go and stepped back. 'Faith, we have watched you grow into a different person here. You flourish more here than back home. Aleksander brings out that part of you that you have buried for so long now. You can admit how you feel and you will not be betraying Toby. He would want you to find someone again; remember your dream. He told you to stop doubting yourself. You are doing it now.' She stopped and grabbed my hand and pulled me over to the bed.

I sat in between them. I grabbed both of their hands and held them tight. They put their heads on my shoulders.

'I don't blame you. He is incredibly hot – I would tap that if I could.' Harley laughed.

I chuckled with her and kissed her forehead.

'I am too scared to say it as well. When I do, it adds so much danger to all of us,' I said.

'But no one else needs to know,' Annie said.

'That is easier said than done. Will the pit in my stomach ever disappear? The hardest part of losing him is the fact that I never got to say goodbye or tell him how much I loved him,' I said, feeling the tears in my eyes again.

'He knew – he still knows now. A piece of your heart will always love him and that is okay,' Harley said.

I held their hands tighter.

'Say it out loud, Faith. Let it out,' Annie said, kissing my hand.

'I do like him. I feel incomplete when I don't see him. I would love to push him up against a wall and just kiss the hell out of him.'

'Well, that escalated quickly,' Harley said cheekily. We all started laughing.

'Slumber party?' Annie asked.

Harley and I looked at one another and nodded. We ran to our rooms to change into nightgowns and ran back to Annie's room. I was on the end, Harley in the middle and Annie on the other side. We chatted and giggled all night.

'It is Sebastian's birthday tomorrow. Yay!' I said before closing my eyes and letting sleep take me away. It was the best sleep I had had since getting here. I felt freer and more open. I had no idea how I was going to tell Aleksander or even if I would. After all, he was married.

CHAPTER THIRTY-NINE

Aleksander

I was abhorred at Faith's actions. I believed I understood her. I was unable to sleep or rest that night. I ventured to the tower and sat watching the stars in the night sky. I felt the warm breeze on my skin. I wished I had not left the room; she was scared to admit her affections towards me.

I took off my necklace and held it in my hands. I clenched it into a fist and struck the ground. How could I have been such a fool? Sebastian delivered a message earlier in the evening; Yelena had been removed from the castle and placed into exile. I lay on the ground and sat for hours. I watched the moon rise in the sky and begin to descend again. I walked past Faith's door and paused. The girl who handed me the necklace was gone. I leaned against the door and breathed, wishing I had not revealed my affections. I headed back to my chambers. Rohesia was awake.

'Where have you been?' she asked, looking annoyed with my absence.

'I was unable to rest and walked through the castle to get some air,' I said, taking off my shirt and lying on the bed.

'Do you take me for a fool?' she said.

I was not aware of what she was talking about.

'Rohesia, I do not take you for a fool. Can you enlighten me about what you may be referring to?' I asked, turning on my side to look at her.

'You were with another lady – a beauty with crystal eyes and a seductive personality.' She spoke with such anger.

'I was not and I am offended at your remark. I am forever faithful to you. This discussion is finished,' I ordered her. I reached over her and blew out the candle. I shut my eyes and wished for sleep to wash over me.

I awoke to an empty room. Rohesia had left for her morning duties. It was Sebastian's name day and as was custom, there was a special ceremony at the chapel to celebrate among the gods. Rohesia had placed my clothes on the chair and the bath was drawn. I de-robed and washed myself, remembering the moment that Faith walked in and was shocked and unable to leave. The mere thought of her brought a smile across my face. I dressed in the appropriate clothing and kissed my necklace.

'I know you have affections and I shall wait for you,' I said.

I felt a connection with her and prayed that she felt it too. I looked at the attire Rohesia had chosen for the day: black leather pants and a dark blue tunic with white stitching. It was new and must have been a recent purchase. I looked at my finger and saw my wedding band. I would never forgive Sebastian for negotiating a marriage out of spite and jealousy.

I waited for Rohesia to return before we headed to the chapel. I watched Faith walk in the chapel on the arm of Sebastian. I watched her smile and could see the act she portrayed. She walked past me; I could smell her sweet scent and breathed it in deeply. She looked over her shoulder, in my direction. I could see her pain and how she wanted to show emotion but eyes were watching her. She turned back and smiled at the king and placed a sweet kiss on his cheek. I became overpowered with the feeling of holding her hand in mine and wanted nothing more than to be beside her. I could hear the laughter of the girls and see the glares that everyone was giving them.

CHAPTER FORTY

Faith

I knew what Sebastian wanted from me today. I would play the part I was given and give a loving performance but it secretly had nothing to do with him.

I entered the church on Sebastian's arm; the entire venue turned and looked at us. I smiled and nodded at every person in acknowledgement. The church was beautiful. There were stained glass windows in blue, red and green. Various images I had never seen. The five gods were displayed in the windows at the front of the church. One window for each.

The God of the Sea was displayed in a blue-stained glass with green plants, I believed, around him. The God of the Land was displayed in a desert-type landscape. The God of the Sky had the sun behind him and a beautiful golden staff in his hand. The God of the Underworld was displayed in, yep, you guessed it, flames. How original. The last god, the God of the People, was different: he had a feature from each of the different windows. From what our tutor Farak spoke about, he was the leader of all the other gods because it was believed that without people, there would be no need for anything else.

I was in love with the surroundings of this church, the carvings in the wooden posts and the marble table at the front with gold drawings etched into it. The ceilings were so high, you would need a crane to reach the top. They were covered in drawings of angels and the gods. It could seat possibly two hundred people. There were just rows and rows of benches to sit on. I saw Aleksander and did not want to look in his direction for fear that another may witness and spill to the king. I could not shake the feeling that I needed to.

I peered over my shoulder to look at him and smiled. I was scared to hold his gaze for fear that others would see and I noticed Rohesia glare at me. I turned back and smiled at the king before sweetly kissing him on the cheek to show the people my affection towards the king. We sat at the front of the church with Annie and Harley standing beside me. I tried to take a sneaky look and find Aleksander's eyes but had no luck. The priest came out from behind the table; he was wearing a bright red robe and a golden cross hanging from his neck. He started speaking. I was in shock. I had no idea what he was saying – he sounded ridiculous. I heard Harley snort and I shot her a look – all eyes were on us and we needed to be respectable.

Annie whispered, 'What are they saying?'

'How the hell should I know?' I said back, trying not to move my lips, like a ventriloquist. Sebastian turned in my direction. I pretended to be paying attention.

Harley snorted again and I heard Annie starting to giggle.

'Would you two stop it?' I snarled under my breath.

'Sorry, he sounds like he is drunk,' Annie said.

'Listen to him.' I ignored them and kept watching the priest and tried to be respectful.

He did sound like he was intoxicated but when you don't understand the language, of course it sounds different. I was trying to pick out any words that sounded familiar. I could speak a little Italian and knew some words of Latin from the nuns but I would never claim to be bilingual. I heard Sebastian's name in the middle of the priest talking; the two priestesses came over and grabbed the hands of Sebastian and dragged him to the centre of the room. They were wearing a similar robe but it was different when it came to the style. Their robe was more Grecian; it was one-shouldered and was tied around the waist. They looked immaculate and so happy to be doing this; the smiles could not be wiped off their faces. They danced around Sebastian with a tree like plant in their hands. I hoped that there were not going to be any sacrifices or anything weird. After the dance, everyone in the hall shouted some words. I could not understand them and all the people bowed or curtsied in Sebastian's direction.

Sebastian raised his hand for me to come and stand by his side. I walked over with poise and elegance and placed my hand upon his. We started to walk together. I walked past Aleksander as he grabbed my spare hand. I clasped my hand on it quickly before letting go. I felt comforted by this and knew he was not annoyed with me, after I slapped him across the face after his revelation.

We left the church and the people filed out behind us. I kept the smile on my face; I had not given him a gift nor had I bought him one. I was adamant on not getting one for him because of how he had treated me for the last couple of days. We continued walking until we reached the castle. I finally stopped with the fake smile and tried to relax my jaw. I felt like a statue stuck in that position. Like the old wives' tale, if you hold your face like that and the wind changes, it will stay like that forever.

Sebastian let go of my arm and I began to walk away from him.

'Faith, I have one final request,' he said in an arrogant tone.

I turned around, rolled my eyes and when I was facing him, pulled on another smile. 'Yes, Your Majesty. I was going to venture into town and pick up our matching gowns for tomorrow's ball,' I said, sounding really sweet and sincere.

'I understand that you do not want to be intimate before we are properly wed but I would like to lie with you tonight. As a gift from you for my name day.'

Sebastian was pushing me into a corner. I did not want to but I knew that I had no choice. 'But Your Majesty, will that not tarnish my reputation?' I asked, trying to sound genuine and worried.

'I shall endeavour to avoid any witnesses,' he said in a flirty tone. I had no response and just nodded before I walked away from him again.

I wanted to see Aleksander but I had noticed a new person following my every move. He was careful to stay out of sight but if I was fast enough, I could catch a glimpse of him. His pitch-black hair and pale skin made him stand out; he looked gravely ill with skin that white. They were the only features I could see before he would disappear from my view.

I arrived at my room and turned to Sonny.

'Can you deliver a message to Aleksander directly please?' I asked him.

He nodded. I walked into the room and grabbed some paper and the feather ink pen.

Aleksander,

I am venturing into town to collect my gown.

Would you like to escort me?

Give your answer to my messenger.

I did not leave my name as he would know who it was from and if it was intercepted, it would be hard to determine who it was from; at least, I was hoping that. I folded it and handed it to Sonny before closing the door. I sat on my bed, biting my nails as I waited for him to get back. I was nervous. Toby watched me on the bed.

'Stop looking at me like that. It wasn't a stupid decision... or was it? God, it was. Shit, someone got the message from Sonny. I just risked our lives again. I really can be an idiot sometimes, can't I? Fuck!'

KNOCK, KNOCK.

I ran over to the door; it was Sonny and Aleksander.

'Hello, gentlemen, how can I help you?' I asked, playing slightly dumb.

There were butterflies in my stomach as I looked at Aleksander; he looked so handsome in his navy tunic and his hair was brushed back off his face. The scruff on his face had grown longer but his eyes were still a warm, beautiful brown. I could stare at them all day.

'Sonny requested that I assist in your venture to town,' he said smoothly. My skin tingled and not in a bad way.

'Of course, after the last venture, I believe it is important to have extra protection,' I said loudly on purpose to ensure others would hear but I said it with a smile for Aleksander to understand that I was happy with this decision.

I walked back into my room to my drawer and removed his mother's necklace and my coin bag. I headed to the door and put my hand in his as I walked past and handed him the necklace. I did not look back at him but kept walking; I knew I would have to inform Sebastian.

I walked to his room and knocked on the door. Miguel answered.

'Miguel, I would like a word with King Sebastian,' I said, looking over his shoulder.

Sebastian appeared instantly after I finished my sentence. 'Faith, I did not believe that I would see your face so soon. Please, come in.' He moved aside. I glided into the room and was sure to stay close to the door.

'Your Majesty, we have important matters to discuss,' Miguel said and looked me over. I rolled my eyes at him and smiled in a sarcastic way.

'Faith, please...' He grabbed my hand and led me to his desk. 'I am drawing up a peace treaty for all the nations.' He indicated for me to read it over.

'May I offer a suggestion, Your Majesty?' I asked, still reading it quickly.

'Yes, we shall be ruling together.'

'It is my belief that if you want peace, it is important to leave a space for a counter offer. What if one of the families wanted something specific from you?'

He nodded and grabbed my arms and kissed me quickly. 'Miguel, change this at once. I want peace and if peace is to be sought, there must be a compromise. Thank you, my future queen.'

I cringed when he finished his sentence. Miguel snatched the paper and began to roll it up.

'Your Majesty, as I informed you earlier, I was to venture to town. I would like for Aleksander to accompany me after the riot. I would feel safer with more guards.' I placed my hand on his face. He put his hand on mine and pulled it away before kissing it.

'Miguel, can you accompany Faith, Aleksander and Sonny to town? The more protection, the safer you shall be,' he said.

My stomach dropped. I understood his reasoning behind this move. He did not trust Aleksander and wanted an eye to be kept on both of us.

'As you wish, Your Majesty,' he said before he walked out.

Sebastian followed. 'Aleksander, Sonny. I have requested that Miguel accompany Faith for more protection. I would feel safer knowing the future queen is in capable hands,' Sebastian said, standing with pride.

Aleksander raised his hand to speak.

'Your Majesty, considering the state of the townspeople and their annoyance towards the king, I believe it is important for the townspeople to look upon your face and that of the future queen and witness the affection between the two of you.'

He finished speaking and I turned to glare at him and mouthed, 'What are you doing?'

He avoided me and smiled. I turned back to look at Sebastian and saw him contemplate what Aleksander had said. I looked down at my hands in frustration and tried to stop my face from showing emotion.

'Yes, I shall,' he said and placed my arm on top of his.

'I believe it is important to remove the formalities during our venture to show you are one of the people,' Aleksander said quickly.

I bit the inside of my lip, hiding a smile. He had asked for him to join us but didn't want to see him touching me.

Sebastian and I walked beside each other through town.

'Would you like some fresh fruit?' I asked Sebastian and he gestured and followed behind me.

'Hello, can we have five of the green apples?' I asked the elderly lady, who seemed ecstatic that I spoke with her.

Her face and clothes were covered in dirt. She looked to be in her early eighties but was still really mobile and scurried to collect the fruit. I handed her more coins than what was needed and she smiled as she threw her arms around me. 'Thank you.'

I could see her eyes well up. I looked at Sebastian and smiled – he had a glow across his face from watching my interaction. I knew he was still grooming me and he seemed proud of how I was acting. I saw Aleksander standing behind him, smiling and watching me intently. I wanted nothing more than to speak with him. We continued to Lord Carmelide's humble abode. I entered without knocking. He ran over and bowed before taking my hand and kissing it. Sebastian cleared his throat in disapproval.

'My apologies, Your Majesty. I am humbled to be in your presence,' he said nervously.

Aleksander stood by the door next to Miguel; they were chatting with one another but Aleksander's face was harsh and Miguel's looked pleased.

'Lady Bushanti, your gowns are complete and I pray you are

pleased with them.' He snapped his fingers at one of the ladies to collect them. He walked behind the counter and grabbed a black velvet box to hand to me. 'Your mask, to the design you wanted with some sparkle attached,' he said.

I opened the box. It was stunning and immaculate. I removed it from the box and placed the box on the counter. I heard a noise behind me; Miguel had tripped over. I knew Aleksander would have contributed to this. The charcoal mask was in the shape of a butterfly with two blue gems in both corners and some lace over the top. The black string came together with a variety of gems: pearls, diamonds and sapphires. There were no words to describe the utter brilliance of the mask. I placed it gently back into the box and closed it again. I was not letting go of it. Lord Carmelide placed a wooden crate on the counter that had our clothes for tomorrow. I did not want to open it until tomorrow. Sebastian waved his hand; Miguel proceeded to walk over but Aleksander placed his hand on his chest.

'I do not want you to injure yourself,' Aleksander said. Was he gaining more of my sarcastic wit? I turned my head away and smirked.

'Faith, are you well?' Sebastian asked.

'Yes, Your Majesty. It is rather dusty and I was going to sneeze,' I said, looking back at him.

Aleksander grabbed the crate between us and poked his tongue out, luckily with no one else looking. I had to bite my lip again to hide a smile. Where had this confident Aleksander come from? He had changed from a quiet endearing person to this confident and witty one.

'Thank you for the lovely gown and mask, Your Majesty. I look forward to dancing the night away with you tomorrow.'

I placed my hand gently on his arm in an affectionate way. He placed his arm around my waist and planted a kiss on my cheek.

'To see your smile, I will endeavour to always please you,' he said, smiling down at me.

We walked back to the town. There were rows of townspeople outside Lord Carmelide's establishment. I smiled but Sebastian looked uncomfortable.

I grabbed his hand and said, 'Smile and wave. They are happy to see you.'

I smiled and waved. I let go of Sebastian's hand and walked over to the people, shaking their hands and saying hello. Aleksander was careful to walk closely beside me. I turned and looked at him.

'I hope that your shoulder is not hurting,' I said, worried that it may be too heavy for his wound.

'I am capable,' he said and kept watching the crowd.

'You are as lovely as your mother,' one lady commented. I smiled at her.

'Thank you for your kind words,' I said and kept moving on. I saw Aleksander watch the lady as we walked away. A little girl was standing with a bunch of red roses. I bent down to her level. She had the cutest chubby face with short brown hair, green eyes and freckles galore. She would have been around the age of five.

'For you,' she said and handed them to me.

'Thank you,' I said, pinching her cheeks.

She smiled and pinched mine back.

'Oh, you are cheeky. I like you.' I tapped her nose and stood back up again.

She grabbed my hand and pulled me down and said, 'Erki wredin tykun litck Bröak.'

I opened my mouth. 'What does that mean?' I asked her but she ran through the crowd. I stood up to follow her but Sonny grabbed my arm to stop me.

'Not safe,' was all he said.

What did that mean? It was the second time I had heard those words; I knew that the last word meant 'little one' and it was a message from my brother but none of the other words made any sense to me. I kept looking back for her; I noticed a piece of paper hidden in the flowers. I pulled it out and snuck it between my cleavage.

Sebastian walked over and placed his hand on my hip.

'Come now, we have final plans that need to be assessed,' he said as he dragged me away from the people.

I waved and smiled goodbye – after the riot a couple of days before, they seemed so much happier. I saw Aleksander's face; he was wincing in pain from his shoulder but too proud to admit it. I turned to Sonny.

'Can you offer Aleksander some help? He has an injured shoulder,' I said, knowing he would not accept and possibly take the offer for help as an insult. He shook his head at Sonny and continued with a look of pain on his face. We arrived through the gates of the castle. Sebastian kissed my hand.

'I look forward to spending the night with you,' he said before walking away. Aleksander appeared beside me.

'Spending the night?' he queried, looking at me. I did not bother to look at him.

'It is his name day present apparently. He requested and I had no choice.'

I could see worry cross his face. There was nothing I could say to make him feel better; he followed in silence to my room where he left the crate on my bed. I reached for his hand and wanted to talk to him but pulled it back. He must have felt the air brush past his hand.

'Faith, I know and thank you for the necklace,' he said and closed the door behind him.

The rest of the day was a blur with people in and out of my room discussing where I must sit tomorrow and how I shall enter the room, who I must speak with and who I must avoid. I had been writing all of this down to make sure I remembered. I had a throbbing headache from information overload and probably because this was the hardest it had worked in a while. I was no longer planning lessons or doing brain teasers; I was essentially playing dress-up. During the two-month royal tour, I was going to pack some books to read up on the culture and hopefully keep my brain active. I was not hungry and asked for Makenzie to try bring a small amount of food to my room to eat. She brought black bread and a selection of vegetables. I ate it and changed into my nightgown before slipping into bed to start turning my brain off. There were no headache tablets here and I did not know of any natural remedies – water and rest were the best I could think of.

KNOCK, KNOCK.

I knew who it was at the door and I was so nervous that he would try something.

'Come in.' I was not going to get out of bed for him.

The nightgowns were baggy and in some instances, you could see straight through them. Sebastian walked in with a black coat over his nightgown. He smirked like he had won some prize.

'Faith, I appreciate the gift.' He removed his coat.

He wore a similar nightgown to my own but it was shorter and I had to look away as I could see his package through it. I could feel myself blush; I could sometimes be a prude as much as I was a perve. Toby was lying in the middle of the bed and I was not about to move him for the king. He lifted the blanket and noticed where Toby was lying. Toby yelped as Sebastian picked him up and placed him on the ground.

'Was that necessary?' I asked, upset that he had been moved. He always slept beside me on the bed.

Sebastian climbed into bed and moved over to come closer to me. I knew what he was expecting; he was lying on his side looking at me intently. I kept looking away. His finger was tracing around my stomach. I brushed it away.

'I made my feelings quite clear, Sebastian,' I said, shifting over and away from him.

'I request a kiss goodnight,' he said. I knew I would have to.

I rolled over to my side and placed one hand under my head as he looked at me. He moved closer, placing his hand on my hip and shuffling closer. His face grew closer to mine and I closed my eyes. I felt his lips on mine and tried for a peck and pulled back but that was not what he had in mind.

He placed his hand at the back of my head and pulled me closer again. I kissed him, opening my mouth and feeling his tongue massaging mine. His hand was shifting around my back as his body weight began to shuffle on top of me. I would play along until I knew the appropriate time to stop. His hand began to move down my leg as his fingers grasped my nightgown as he attempted to lift it up. My body wanted to continue and was enjoying the way he was kissing my neck.

'No,' I said, pushing him off forcefully and jumping out of bed. 'I am not a fucking whore and I said I would not until we were properly wed. If you cannot respect that decision, I recommend you get out now.'

I was jumpy all over. I wanted to but not with him. He got out of bed and came over to comfort me.

'I apologise for my actions but I find you alluring and cannot contain myself around you,' he said, placing his hand on my face and pulling me closer – I assumed for an embrace but I was wrong. He started kissing me again. He walked backwards slowly and before I knew it, he was on top of me again on the bed. I got up instantly.

'NO,' I shouted and slapped his face.

He dropped to the ground. I could not tell if he was angry or in shock. I stepped away, ensuring there was plenty of distance between the two of us.

'How dare you strike your king?' He stood up and I could feel his rage from across the room.

'How dare you disrespect your lady? No means NO. I have told you when I believe it is appropriate. If you cannot respect my decision, then you do not deserve my affection,' I said, sternly standing my ground. I would not let him overpower me this time; I was in charge. I was not going to lose my voice.

He took a step back in surprise at the rise and change of my tone. He opened his mouth to speak. I raised my eyebrow, waiting for his retort. He stopped and climbed into bed quietly. I was anxious about hopping back in, but I did after a few minutes. He slept on my side and I slept on the other. I awoke and he was no longer in the room. I sat up and brushed my hair off my face. I bent my knees and put my head on them and wrapped my arms around them. I would avoid seeing him and portray a different person later tonight at the ball.

CHAPTER FORTY-ONE

Aleksander

The day was filled with haze as I leaned on the balcony outside the grand hall, taking the occasional sip from my goblet. I could hear laughter and music. I had not seen her face or heard her sweet voice. I desired to discuss her true feelings and to feel the touch of her soft skin. The hall went quiet. I finished my goblet, replaced my mask and headed back into the hall. I searched for Rohesia's face and searched for the reason for the quiet.

I stopped suddenly when I saw her; she was the reason the hall had fallen silent. Her beauty was beyond words. I could see the desire in every man. Her charcoal and blue gown was unlike any people had witnessed before. It emphasised her enviable waist and enhanced her luscious breasts; the gown flowed in sky blue from her waist. Her hair was curled to perfection with the mask fitting perfectly to her face. She glided through the hall, smiling and nodding at everyone. They were in awe of her beauty, many even beginning to bow and curtsy. Her gown was lifted in one corner with the shape of a rose and was the same charcoal as the top.

She glided past me and smiled; her eyelids had been powdered darker to enhance the colour of her blue eyes. From behind, the mask was joined by a selection of gems that wrapped around a tail in her hair. There were blue gems, clear gems and pearls. Rohesia appeared by my side and I smiled at her; she looked well-dressed but could not compare to Faith and the elegance and grace that she displayed. I placed my arm around her waist and watched as Sebastian stood to greet her. She smiled and placed a gentle kiss on his cheek. Faith raised her small hand above her head while holding a goblet.

'Everyone, raise your glasses in celebration of the king's name day,' she said, toasting before taking a small sip of her wine.

I could not take my eyes off her; she was perfection. I watched as Sebastian and Faith ambled through the hall, greeting important lords and ladies. She smiled and laughed. She had her father's grace and her mother's beauty. She would become the perfect queen and she embodied all the appropriate qualities.

She looked in my direction and displayed a big smile, showing her teeth and looking happy. I could feel Rohesia's eyes on me and I looked in her direction and gently kissed her forehead.

'Lords and ladies, I would like to show my appreciation for your attendance at my celebration. I swear by all the gods that I shall become the king you deserve, with the most beautiful queen in the entire land. I am overjoyed to announce the return of Crystal Bouchard and that she has agreed to become my queen. We shall rule as the most peaceful rulers in history.' Sebastian spoke while looking at Faith and smiling.

I could see the worry behind her smile. Everyone cheered

and raised their goblets. I was not happy and I knew Faith would not be either. She disliked being trapped and with this announcement, she was. I saw her look towards the floor and bite her lip before looking up again with a smile. Sebastian grabbed her hand and led her to the people. She searched the crowd for my face. I stayed in her eye line for comfort; I was always here for her.

Sebastian clapped his hands together and the music stopped.

'In honour of the return of the Bouchard line, we shall dance the Brokad,' he said, leading her into the middle of the dance floor.

She stumbled trying to keep up with him. I grabbed Rohesia's hand and pulled her in and ensured I was close enough to have the chance to dance with her once partners were swapped. She was trying to speak to Sebastian who put his hand over her mouth to silence her. She frowned at him and looked displeased. Sebastian clapped again and the music started.

Our hands entwined and I placed my other hand on Rohesia's waist. She smiled. We glided around before she spun out and came back with her back towards me while we spun with my hand on her stomach. She spun out and I danced with another lady; she was rather large and one of the poorer ladies of the region. Her dress did not fit her appropriately; it looked as if it would rip open. The music's pace quickened and so did the dancing.

I danced with two more ladies before Faith reached my arms. She smiled at me but quickly hid her face and whispered, 'I have yet to mess up my steps.'

I smiled at her.

'You are the most beautiful lady here today.' I leaned in closer. 'My only desire is to hold you all night and show you how much I want to be with you.'

I pulled her close and smelt her overpowering scent of flowers. She blushed. I felt a connection with her being this close. I knew she was feeling it too; she struggled to breathe. I could feel her body trembling from my touch. She twirled out and twirled back in with her back to me. I was overcome with desire and placed a few gentle kisses on her soft neck; she turned her head to look at me. I could feel her breath on my face. I wanted nothing more than to spin her around into my arms and kiss her passionately and never let her go.

She twirled away to dance with another before finishing with the king. She clapped before she whispered in the king's ear and walked away. She did not look back at me and left the grand hall. I waited before leaving after her and not telling my wife. I exited through the doors and could not see her; I wiped my hand over my face in frustration before hearing a noise. I walked around the corner and there she was, leaning against the wall, struggling to breathe.

'Faith,' I said, walking over to her with haste.

She put her hand up. 'No.'

I walked closer to her, not adhering to her warning. She slapped my face.

'How could you be so stupid as to do that?' She spoke with annoyance.

'I was overcome with your beauty. Did you not enjoy it?' I asked her, slowly taking step by step to get closer to her again. I could not take my eyes off her lips; they enticed me.

She did not answer but turned away and held her stomach

and bent over before standing back up and turning to head back towards the grand hall. She attempted to walk by me but I stepped in her path and smirked. She stepped around me before turning back and pausing. I reached for her hand. She grabbed mine. I pulled her closer, placing my hand on her face. She turned to kiss it. I was stepping into her until she landed against the wall. I pushed my body against her and felt her arms wrap around me and her breath quicken before I looked up at her and...

CHAPTER FORTY-TWO

Faith

I was so nervous as I walked down the stairs towards the grand hall. Makenzie had spent over an hour doing my hair and colouring my eyes to make them stand out behind my mask. She wrapped the gems around a tail in my hair that was surrounded by my curls. I hadn't realised how long my hair had gotten; it had now passed my bra strap and was getting close to my bottom. I would have to ask Makenzie to cut it a bit shorter soon. I hadn't seen what Annie and Harley were wearing and was anxious to see them. I arrived at the door and the two guards moved to open it.

'No, wait.' I turned back around. I was feeling sick in the stomach, light-headed and sweating like crazy. I was so nervous to walk into the room, like I was going for a job interview. I did not like being the centre of attention and I had a feeling from how I looked that I was going to stand out.

'Are you alright, milady?' one of the guards asked. I saw the concern on his face.

'Yes, I am ready,' I said and he opened the door. I plastered a smile across my face.

The entirety of the grand hall had fallen silent and everyone's eyes had fallen on me. I kept the smile on my face; those closest were either bowing or curtsying. I just nodded in appreciation.

I was looking around for a familiar face: Annie, Harley, Aleksander, Dmitirov, anyone? The hall was still silent. I continued walking through slowly, trying to be the picture of grace and poise. My eyes finally found Aleksander's; he was stationary in the middle of the room just staring at me. I wanted to extend my smile when I saw him. His face said it all. I looked good. I mean, like I said, I was not a girly girl but sometimes every girl wants to look like a princess for a day. I reached the king and produced a bigger smile for display. He stood to welcome me and I pecked his cheek. I grabbed a glass of wine and tried to speak with joy to deceive everyone here.

'Everyone, raise your glasses in celebration of the king's name day,' I said and took a sip of my wine after toasting. I looked at him to try and show some sort of affection. I looked back out to the people and saw Aleksander. My smile extended to the point where my teeth were now showing; I was so happy to see him after not being able to see him all day. I saw him look towards his wife as jealousy tickled my system.

I looked back at the king as he started to speak to the people.

'Lords and ladies, I would like to show my appreciation for your attendance at my celebration. I swear by all the gods that I shall become the king you deserve, with the most beautiful queen in the entire land. I am overjoyed to announce the return of Crystal Bouchard and that she has agreed to become my queen. We shall rule as the most peaceful rulers in history.' Sebastian looked at me and smiled.

I was so annoyed. I knew that I was Crystal but, in my eyes, I was still Faith and did not agree with being announced to a room full of sycophants, even though I said it to a group of strangers in the town. The people cheered and raised their glasses. I bit my lip in annoyance and nerves before displaying my confident persona and looking at Sebastian again. Sebastian reached for my hand and I allowed him to grab it and lead me to the swarms of people. I was looking for Aleksander's face for comfort; he was always in my eye line. I knew he was doing it on purpose.

I smiled and said, 'Lovely to meet you,' to everyone Sebastian introduced me to. After plenty of introductions and males trying to kiss my hand, I needed some anti-bacterial cream to sanitise my hands. Some of the men were using tongue – I mean honestly, dirty old men. I shook and felt like I needed a bath.

Sebastian clapped his hands suddenly; even I was shocked as the music stopped in the middle of a song.

'In honour of the return of the Bouchard line, we shall dance the Brokad,' he said, grabbing my hands and rushing to the middle of the dance floor.

Which dance was the Brokad again? I struggled to breathe because the corset on the dress was really tight. I opened my mouth to speak but Sebastian put his finger up to stop it. I was pissed at him and frowned, glared, gave him the bitch face to show how annoyed I was. Sebastian clapped his hands and the music started again. I was trying to remember the steps and count the music.

I closed my eyes and remembered what Aleksander said: 'Let the man lead.'

I opened them again and started dancing. I did not stumble and was doing well to remember the steps. Sebastian twirled me out and spun me back in, placing his hand on my stomach and walking around. I could feel his breath on my neck and wanted to move away instantly but smiled and let out a girlish giggle. I was looking around for Aleksander; I wondered if I would get the chance to dance with him. I saw him dancing with a rather large woman and his face said it all. He was not impressed but the woman looked so happy to be dancing with such a handsome man.

I finally reached Aleksander; with all my twirling, I was shocked I was not dizzy just yet. I smiled at him but looked down to hide it from others. He looked very handsome today; the scruff on his face was longer than usual and added to his rugged look. He was wearing a red tunic with black lace around the collar and cuffs. He had washed his hair and brushed it off his face, showing his widow's peak. I had never noticed that before.

He was wearing new leather pants and black boots. His tunic was not buttoned to the top like usual and I could see some of the hairs on his chest and a little definition. My mind was beginning to wander to the day I saw him naked in the bath; he was delicious.

I shook my thoughts off and whispered to him, 'I have yet to mess up my steps,' and he smiled back at me before speaking.

'You are the most beautiful lady here today,' he said before he leaned in closer to keep talking. 'My only desire is to hold you all night and show you how much I want to be with you.' He pulled me in closer and I could feel my own desire rising, knowing I would love to leave the room with him.

I could feel my cheeks growing warm; I was blushing. I was so comfortable being this close to him, my breath became ragged. I twirled out and back into his arms. I could feel my body trembling from being this close to him. I could feel his breath on my neck and his hand on my waist. I was feeling a fog in my head and passion overtaking me but I needed to stop it. I was in a room full of people. His lips were on my neck; he kissed me softly, and I turned my head to look at him and wanted nothing more than to pull his face to mine and kiss him. I was thankful that I twirled away and danced with another partner. I couldn't look at him. The dance finished with me back in Sebastian's arms.

I clapped my hands together and raised them to my mouth and whispered to Sebastian. 'I am short of breath. I am going to step outside for some air. I shall be back shortly,' I said before leaving the grand hall. I walked around the corner and leaned up against the wall, trying to catch my breath again.

'Faith.' I heard Aleksander walk over to me.

I put my hand up to stop him.

'No,' I said sternly.

He was still walking near me in all his sexiness. I slapped his face to stop myself and him from doing something stupid out here in the open.

'How could you be so stupid as to do that?' I was really annoyed with him.

'I was overcome with your beauty. Did you not enjoy it?' he said smugly.

I noticed he was staring at my lips. I knew what he wanted and I wanted it too, more than anything. I turned away from him, trying to catch my breath and holding onto my stomach.

I needed to head back to the grand hall and I turned away and went to walk past Aleksander.

He stepped in front of me, smirking. Where was all this confidence coming from? He was being rather persistent. I stepped around him and turned back to look at him one more time. He reached for my hand. I hesitated before grabbing his – that was all I wanted to do, just grab his hand and let it go again. He pulled me closer and put his other hand on my face. I leaned into it and turned to kiss his hand.

He was stepping into me and pushing me backwards towards the wall before the hardness hit me. He pushed my body against the wall. I wrapped my arms around his shoulders. He looked at the floor before he looked up at me and smiled, slowly edging his face closer to mine. A smile spread across my face and I closed my eyes, waiting for his lips to touch mine. He paused gently and after kissing them, he pulled back to look at me.

He touched my face and brought it closer, rubbing my cheek with his thumb. Now he was smiling and his warm lips were on mine and I opened my mouth and felt his tongue on mine. He was pushing his body harder against mine. I could not stop myself from smiling as he kissed me. We both wanted more. His hand ran down my side and behind my back. He moved it over my bottom and lifted my leg up and around him. It was getting hotter and I wanted to rip off his shirt and I knew he wanted to undress me as well. I bit his lip and he pulled back.

'You are...' He didn't finish his sentence but kept kissing me.

'Where is Lady Bushanti?' we overheard someone say and he let me go and walked away.

Seriously, he disappeared into the darkness. What was he,

a ninja? I pretended I was still out of breath when Sebastian came around the corner. I was hoping I did not look flushed after what just happened. I was so flustered right now and in a really good mood.

'Faith, how are you?' he asked, looking concerned and he was hesitant to place a hand on me.

'I am better. I just needed some air. My dress is a bit tight and the dancing did not help.' I giggled a little.

'No more dancing. I have some guests I would love to introduce to you.' He took my hand and led me back inside.

I stopped and planted my feet.

'Sebastian, wait,' I said not letting him pull me.

'Yes?' He let go of my hand and turned to look at me.

'I am annoyed with you for your introduction of me. I am aware of who I am but I did not appreciate being identified at Crystal Bouchard. I may be her but my name is Faith and I don't want to feel like I have to become this other person that I was before. I do not want others to see me that way. I want to—'

His arms were crossed but he dropped them. 'Faith, I understand and no one shall perceive you as Crystal if you do not want to be. The only person I want you seen as is my queen. Now, come, we have plenty of important guests to meet.'

He somewhat understood what I said and I was not going to push the matter. I followed Sebastian and looked back towards the darkness for Aleksander. I could not make out any figures. We entered the hall and I realised I had yet to see Annie and Harley – where were they? I scanned the crowd, looking for their features but it was hard with all the masks. I saw Aleksander laughing and standing beside Rohesia. How did he get back into the room? He looked over and raised his glass at me. I smiled and looked away. I was like a giddy little girl and was enjoying the feeling; I had not felt like this in a long time.

Sebastian introduced me to a variety of different nobles. I could not remember their names; I was a little distracted. I was talking to a lady.

'Yes, Princess Bouchard. You are as gracious as your mother,' she said.

'My name is Faith. Thank you for your kind words,' I said and walked away.

I took a sip of my wine and realised I was getting a headache. I felt the dull ache in my left temple. I started massaging it, hoping it would go away. I had yet to eat and wandered around looking for some of the trays of food. I found the food table and scanned it for something that was not sweet; the wine had enough sugar and could be contributing to this headache.

'Lady Bushanti, I have yet to inform you of how lovely you are looking this evening.' It was Aleksander. He said it too smoothly.

'Thank you, Lord Marchés. You look nice this evening.' I was trying to contain my smile.

'If you keep smiling like that, I shall find a dark corner.'

I cleared my throat.

'You are naughty. Go away before we get into trouble,' I said, not wanting to look into his delectable eyes.

He grabbed my hand and kissed it. 'Anything for a lady such as yourself.'

I giggled and he walked away.

I snacked on some of the meat and vegetables on the table. My headache was not going away but rather getting worse.

I turned around and looked once more for Annie and Harley. I was annoyed I hadn't found them. I looked for Sebastian.

'Your Majesty, a word?' I asked nicely, smiling while he was amongst other guests.

'Yes, milady,' he said.

We walked out of earshot.

'Sorry, Sebastian, it has been a long day and I am getting a nasty headache. I am going to retire for the evening. I hope you enjoy the rest of your night.' I kissed him on the cheek, not giving him the option of telling me no.

I left the grand hall; the headache had progressed to a migraine. I was struggling to see out of my left eye. I ran my hand along the wall to make sure I was going in the right direction.

'Faith, wait up.'

It was Annie. I felt her grab my hand.

'Are you alright?' she asked, looking at me.

'No, I am getting a migraine and the pain behind my eye is excruciating,' I said.

'Come on, I'll help you get back to the room.'

I felt another hand on the other side. Harley was there as well.

'What, have you been poisoned again?' Harley asked.

'No, Yelena has been exiled – I think I am safe. It is just a headache or migraine,' I said to her.

'Did you guys enjoy your night? I couldn't see you anyway and I would say you look nice but my eyes are a little fuzzy,' I said to them. It was too dark to see what they were wearing. Annie had her boobs out.

'I made out with Aleksander outside the hall before

Sebastian interrupted us. I would say it was a fun night, no?' I said just as we arrived back at my room.

Their mouths were open.

'Goodnight, girls. I will talk to you tomorrow. I need a dark room to close my eyes and rest. There's no Nurofen here.' I closed the door. I laughed at myself and started undoing my dress before slipping on my nightgown and jumping into bed. God, my head was getting worse. What was happening?

I closed my eyes, hoping it would make the pain in my eye go away. I could feel my body temperature rising and the sweat was beginning to fall off me. I pushed the covers off and lay on top of the bed. I thought I could hear someone talking. I sat up and saw a figure in the corner of the room; the pain was getting worse.

'Who are you?' I shouted at the person in the corner. They were still whispering.

I wanted to get out of bed but I couldn't move without more pain searing through me. I could feel liquid falling from my nose and it landed in my mouth with the disgusting metallic taste of blood; I needed a towel.

KNOCK, KNOCK.

'Go away,' I shouted to whoever was on the other side.

I stumbled for a towel for my nose; it was hard to walk while tilting my head and pinching my nose. I stumbled and fell on the floor; the door opened. I couldn't make out his face as both of my eyes were fuzzy. I was more scared than I had been in a while. I felt the man's hands grab my underarms and lift me back up to the bed. I caught a scent of his smell; it was familiar but I couldn't decipher whose it was.

They moved away and I felt the towel being held to my nose.

They pulled me into their chest; I was still upright. The pain slowly subsided as this person relaxed me.

'I have you, sleep,' was all I heard before I passed out.

I dreamed a man was holding me tightly, so I couldn't run. I was screaming at the top of my lungs.

'Mummy, Mummy, Mummy, no.' I watched a chapel being burnt in front of me.

I turned around and looked at the old man.

'Why?' I asked him.

'To protect you,' was all the man said.

Another flash. I played in the garden with the lily pads before falling into the water and bursting into a fit of laughter. I finally saw my mother's face as she pulled me out of the water.

'Crystal, you are always so silly.' She smiled.

I had my mother's eyes and beautiful long hair but the darker skin must have come from my father.

'Charles, look at your daughter.' She turned and the man came into view and I raised my arms for him to pick me up.

He was about six feet tall and broad; he was a strong man and I had all his dark features, his dark chocolate brown hair, olive skin, his nose and the softness of his eyes.

'Now, Crystal, one day you may become queen. Is that an appropriate way to act?' he asked, smiling but pretending to tell me off.

'Hmmm, I would say yes, Father, because I shall be the queen who brings laughter to the world,' I said with a smile.

He tickled my stomach and threw me into the air before catching me.

'Charles.' My mother was not happy and he put me down.

Another flash; it had been announced that Aleksander and

I were to be wed when we both came of age. Thank God that had not occurred – I would have been fourteen and married, no thank you. I gave him the necklace.

'A gift for my future husband,' I said, tying it around his neck. 'You are not allowed to take it off, ever,' I said to him sternly.

Aleksander was a chubby little boy with longer hair than he had now. I could see his mother and father watch as I handed it to him.

'But I am not yours yet and you will need to catch me,' I remembered saying as I ran away laughing.

He never caught me. I was too quick. I remembered my brothers, Edgar and Victor. They could almost pass as twins; I was a happy child and loved playing the piano and being mischievous and causing trouble wherever I went. I remembered how I got my scar from falling into rose bushes and when I met some important lord or lady, I was always the proper princess. Many of their young sons wanted to dance and I would turn them away. My parents were apologising for my actions probably too much.

The last memory was of the day before my mother was killed. She was in my room sitting on the bed. I could see the fear in her face.

'Crystal, it is important that you remember this. I apologise for what I am about to do to you but it is for your safety. I have hidden a letter among my gems for when you return home again. I shall always be with you. I love you.' She pulled me into her arms.

I could feel myself crying before I woke up. I could still feel the pain behind my eye but it was not as severe. I got out of bed; it was still dark but it wouldn't be long until the sun came up. I ran over to where I had hidden the note from the little girl.

'Erki wredin tykun litck Bröak.' I remembered what it said. It said 'meet me by the lilies'; I assumed he meant in the garden. I quickly threw on a dress and hoped I was not too late. I wrote a note and put it on the bed for Makenzie for when she came into the room.

I ran down the stairs and out into the garden. Some of the guards saw me but I ignored them and snuck out of sight. I could remember the way around here and the secret passageways to get out. I ran into the garden, careful not to fall on any rocks or plants. I reached the pond with the lilies and there he was standing with his back to me near the sunflowers...

CHAPTER FORTY-THREE

Aleksander

I felt like a new man after last night. I wanted to see her face but knew that time was on my side. I was to be with her for the next two months on a journey. It was dangerous for us to admit our true feelings but I was unable to keep them contained. I dressed and ventured to the stables to ready the horses and carriage before leaving on the royal tour. I ran to Sebastian's room to organise any final steps that needed to be taken. I knocked on his door.

'Your Majesty, do you need any assistance? I am organising the carriages before we depart,' I said with my hands behind my back.

'Aleksander, you are chipper this morning. I have no need of assistance. You should check on the ladies,' he said before he closed the door.

I smiled and turned; I knew this was an opportunity to see her again. I walked with haste to her door and knocked. There was no answer and Sonny was not outside. I knocked again and pressed in closer to hear any noise behind the door. I opened the door and Makenzie was packing a crate with gowns.

'Where is Faith?' I asked, worried about where she may be.

'She left a note this morning and I have yet to see her.' She handed me the note.

Makenzie,

I am in the garden and I shall be back soon.

Faith.

Her handwriting was rushed; I put the note down.

'Thank you,' I said before I turned to the door.

'Wait, Lord Marchés. It is not wise for you to be looking for her,' she said with worry on her face.

I nodded in agreeance but chose to ignore her advice. I headed towards the garden. I reached the garden and could hear her voice. My foot crunched on a twig and the voice stopped. I overheard a male voice.

'I must go,' he said before Faith spoke, sounding distressed.

'No, wait, please. There is more to talk about. Please.'

Whoever this person was, she begged them to stay. I quickened my pace before I rounded the corner and saw Faith facing the secondary exit that very few people knew how to get in and out of. She held her head in one hand and was shaking her head. Her shoulders drooped. I stopped and did not want to disturb her; she sighed in frustration before turning around.

'Ahhh,' she screamed in fright. She grabbed her chest. 'Holy shit, you scared me. What are you doing here?'

She was out of breath and looked as if she had jumped out of bed.

'Who were you speaking with?' I asked as I walked around to the second exit.

'What? No one.' She sounded defensive.

'I heard you,' I said as I noticed fresh footprints. 'Who do these belong to?' I asked, frustrated at the avoidance in her answers.

She looked around and walked over, cupping my face and pulling me in for a kiss. I raised my arms and wrapped them around her. I wanted nothing more than to always hold her and smell her. She pulled back and grabbed my hand.

'We must get back to the castle.' She walked away from me.

Sebastian was at the castle doors and Faith walked up to him and embraced him and placed a kiss on his lips. I looked away in irritation.

'Thank you, Lord Marchés.' She turned to smile at me and turned back. 'I got lost in the garden. I went out the other exit and got lost. He must have heard me yelling from the stables. I got so scared,' she said and she embraced him again.

'You are safe now, Faith. Thank you, Aleksander.' He kissed her on the head and nodded in approval of my non-existent actions.

'Well, I must pack.' She could be deceiving when she needed to be. I had just remembered that she did not answer my question.

I walked up the stairs to Faith's chambers and decided to leave the matter and headed to Annie's room. I knocked and Langford answered the door, holding the crate in his arms.

'Yes, thank you for helping. Has Harley's crate been placed with the carriage?' I asked and he shook his head. I walked over to the corridor to Harley's room and knocked before entering. She had finished packing and was brushing her hair.

'Thank you, Aleksander. You are positively glowing today. Did you enjoy your night?' she said with a big smile on her face.

My face grew red and I picked up the crate. It was no shock that she had informed her closest friends. I placed the crates on the carriages and secured them with rope. I was wary of this journey as the families would have the chance to meet Faith and they would believe what I had informed them of many months before. The guards were dressed in their armour and were standing in their appropriate positions. There were three carriages with one guard on each, five guards at the front and five guards at the back with my men spread on the sides evenly.

Sebastian walked around to inspect the men and nodded as they bowed in his presence. Annie and Harley entered the stable with their arms interlinked, smiling and giggling amongst themselves.

They curtsied to the king and Annie asked, 'Your Majesty, where are we to sit?'

She sounded so polite. Had the girls changed or had they educated themselves on the proper way to behave in a crowd of people?

'In the first carriage place, Lady Wakchter and Lady Gelden,' he said and looked displeased as they walked away. He did not want them to accompany Faith and the king on their journey but knowing Faith, she was not going to accept no as an answer. I turned around and faced Dmitirov.

'How upset is your wife?' I asked him.

'I only hope she is happy when I return again.' He shrugged his shoulders.

I felt her walk into the room and turned to hide my smile when I laid eyes on her face. She peeked in my direction and turned towards Sebastian.

'Where am I to sit? Oh my, you are bringing Milo.' She

rushed over and ignored Sebastian. She looked so happy and the smile lit up her face in a way that amplified her beauty beyond what words could describe. I felt a kick on my ankle.

I turned to Dmitirov and said through my teeth, 'What was that?'

'You are too obvious,' he said and he was right.

I avoided looking in her direction again. I heard her laughter and wanted to turn to look at her again but Dmitirov pulled a face that warned me of my actions. I looked ahead and watched her climb into the second carriage with Sebastian. I was yet to see my wife and was about to dismount when she appeared. I smiled and watched her climb into the first carriage. I moved my horse closer to the second carriage and attempted a glance to see her. The wooden carriage was in the shape of a square with red and blue fabric covering the windows. The curtain moved and there she was.

'Are you going?' I heard Sebastian ask from behind me and she smirked and pulled a face before sitting back beside me. I saw him grab Faith's hand and kiss it tenderly. I believed he genuinely cared for her but doubted his feelings were as strong as my own.

'Let's go,' I shouted to the men in the front and we all started moving.

*

The first stop on the journey was to the Arundel family in Nharabalu; it was a week-long journey. The first few days were easy before we reached the deep forest. I could hear Faith arguing with Sebastian.

'Yes, I understand your fears but I believe it is important for me to experience the land before arriving and meeting this royal family. I do not have memories of this place and would like something that I can converse with them about.'

I heard Sebastian grunt in frustration.

'You are an incredibly difficult woman and frustrate me beyond belief. I want to keep you safe and you are choosing a dangerous path. I care for you beyond words, Faith. Why can you not just listen to me?' He raised his voice.

'Yep, sure, absolutely. Let us do whatever you want, Your Majesty,' she said and I saw the carriage move; she changed sides to be further away from him. She opened the curtain and saw my face.

'Why do we not ask Lord Marchés what his thoughts are on this predicament?' She turned smugly back towards Sebastian. The curtain was drawn back to be closed.

'What, is he not your most trusted advisor?' I heard her ask.

I turned to Dmitirov who said, 'Ride ahead,' and I did as he instructed, moving closer to my wife's carriage.

'Rohesia,' I called out to her. She drew back the curtain.

'Yes, Aleksander?' She smiled. She was a beauty and I felt guilt at not feeling anything towards her.

'Are you comfortable? Can I do anything to assist you?' I asked, caring for her all alone in the carriage.

'When shall we be having a break? I would like to stretch my legs when we have a chance.' She did look exhausted from sitting. We had been travelling nearly all day.

'A few more hours, my dear. I promise,' I said before looking up at the sun to determine how long until it went down.

A few hours had passed and the sun was on its way down.

'Your Majesty.' I knocked on the carriage and his head appeared. I could see his face smiling from laughter and Faith was laughing as well.

'Yes, Aleksander?' He looked displeased at being disturbed.

'I request that we stop and set up for the night.'

'Make the call then.' He drew back the curtain and I could hear Faith burst into laughter.

I was frustrated at her being alone with another.

'Halt, we shall make camp just ahead in the trees,' I shouted to the men.

When we stopped, I dismounted and helped Rohesia out of the carriage as I offered my hand to her. I watched as Sebastian lifted Faith out of the carriage and placed her on the ground. She smiled and laughed before leaving his presence and heading towards Annie and Harley. He watched her and walked over to her, wrapping his arms around her and pretending to bite her neck affectionately and she giggled like a little girl. How could she bear to be in his arms?

'Lord Marchés, where shall we set up the tents?' a man asked. I kissed Rohesia's hand.

'Stay with Faith and the other ladies.' I left her to help the men set up.

CHAPTER FORTY-FOUR

Faith

I was ecstatic that we had stopped travelling for the day and I could get out of the carriage. My legs were cramped and my back ached. As much as I despised Sebastian, I knew I would have to try and form some type of friendship as he was dead set on being my husband. He lifted me out of the carriage and put me down. He could be cute sometimes. I skipped over to Annie and Harley.

'Is it me or are the carriages rather uncomfortable?' I said with a smile on my face, knowing that Sebastian was watching me.

'Why are you still smiling?' Harley asked, raising her hand at me in confusion.

'Because he is watching us.' Annie answered the question and put a smile on her face.

Sebastian walked over and wrapped his arms around my waist and started to affectionately nibble on my neck. I giggled like a little girl but rolled my eyes in the direction of Annie and Harley.

'How are you enjoying the journey?' he asked them.

'It is a beautiful country, Your Majesty, and I cannot wait to see more of it,' Annie said politely as she held her hands in front of her.

'Sebastian, my dear. May I request some alone time with my friends to venture a little bit?' I said, sickly sweet, and rubbed my hands on his, which were still holding onto my waist.

'Yes, I must see to other details. Be safe.' He kissed my cheek and left.

'God, I feel like if I have to keep smiling like that, my face may change. It hurts my cheeks.'

Harley laughed and I playfully pushed her. I looked around; there was grass as far as the eye could see. The castle was no longer in view. There were sporadic trees for shelter every couple of kilometres. I grabbed their hands and walked into the trees. They seemed as tall as the sky; the dead trees covered the ground with moss and bugs. There were mushrooms, flowers, shrubs and spider webs. I was glad I had my memory and knew that they had no freakishly large spiders here. I desperately wanted to climb a tree and see as far as I could but this dress was not helpful in doing that. I stopped short when I realised we had possibly strayed too far from the camp but I knew we would be out of earshot.

'Okay, I have two things to tell you and you must not react too much in case we are being watched. You got it?'

They didn't move.

'Well, you can nod your head to acknowledge that I spoke,' I said as I pretended to slap them.

They nodded their heads.

'So, Millicent, the leader of the witch coven, wasn't lying. Aleksander and I... um... were overcome with passion and well, you know how it goes. Yes, he is rather good at kissing and likes to take control. I am not going to complain about that but we were interrupted and luckily the king did not see us together. We kissed again this morning but that was only to distract him from something else. Anyway, moving on, after that happened and as you saw, I got a horrible headache or migraine. Well, I found out that was because it was my brain remembering, like, everything. I saw my parents being burned in the church; I remember them sending me away. I remember Aleksander. He was such a cute little chubby kid – you know, the one with the cheeks you just want to squeeze. I remember the old language and I met my eldest brother this morning.' I finished speaking and sat down on the ground in front of them. The grass was cold and a little bit wet but I didn't care too much.

They looked confused – maybe I should have slowed down while I was speaking.

'Wait, so...' Annie said. She stopped and looked deep in thought.

'Yeah, I am with you on that one. So, it is official. You are legitimately Crystal Bouchard but how did you... and we... and your brother. Oh my God, my head hurts.'

'Yep, that was mine last night. Who knew magic was actually real because I never believed in it – well, I used to but I do now because I saw it growing up. Wow, that is weird to say.' I looked up into the trees. It felt like home and I closed my eyes and felt the breeze on my skin and felt it blow through my hair. I breathed it in; I could smell the grass and the smell of the bark and the flowers around me.

'Holy shit, you are a princess. Does that mean you are

technically queen anyway now?' Harley asked.

'No, because her parents were overthrown and she has an older brother. She is technically a princess by birth but that's it, yeah?' Annie looked at me to check she was right.

'Yep, my family was overthrown and are no longer the rulers but in the hierarchy, we are pretty much at the top; it would go something like Bennett, Bouchard, Faulcon, Marchés, Somneri, Arundel, Fitzhugh and Ladislas – not including the other families who were wiped out, similar to mine. There is always someone who wants more power but yeah, I am a princess. Now, where is my tiara?' I pushed my nose into the air and laughed.

'I cannot believe Aleksander is technically a prince but why did your family pick him over Sebastian?' Harley asked.

'How the hell should I know the answer to that question? I was like five or six when they picked. I wasn't given the choice.' I was annoyed they did not ask about my brother.

'Wait, wait, wait. Take a step back, your brother is still alive... how?' Annie said as she crossed her legs and threw her hands into the air.

'His name is Edgar and he said our mum paid off someone to switch places. Which is wrong to think about but someone took him to Trikeque Island and he only left when he heard about the possible existence of his little sister. He knew as soon as he saw me who I was. We had met a few times apparently but I didn't remember until the night of the ball when we bumped into each other. He doesn't want anyone to know he is alive and he wants to hang around just to protect me because I am not safe but he would not go into detail about whom I was not safe from and then Aleksander interrupted us. He says he will try and see me again soon but he is so mysterious and gives very little away. He is darker than I remember – a lot has changed in twenty years.' I remembered his wariness on divulging any information.

'How are you?' I asked Annie as I looked at her stomach.

'Getting better; some days are better than others but my boobs are becoming really sore and tender...'

SNAP.

We heard a branch or twig snap behind us and we all stopped talking and looked around. I slid my hand up my dress to grab the dagger just in case. I knew it would not do much to protect us but something was better than nothing.

I saw a green dress through the trees and saw a glimpse of red hair. I pulled my hand out.

'It is Rohesia.' I rolled my eyes.

I would be nice as I always was.

'Rohesia, over here,' I called out to her and stood up so she could see me. I was waving my arms above my head. She saw me and I sat back down to cross my legs.

'Hello, Rohesia,' Harley said.

'I would prefer to be called by my proper name,' she said in a rather snobbish tone.

I turned and looked at her but Annie shot me a look to say no.

'Of course, Lady Marchés. Forgive us. We are not used to such formalities and prefer to be casual around one another when it comes to titles,' I said with a subtle tone.

She stood up; it was becoming rather uncomfortable and no one was speaking.

'Soooo...' I said as I pulled grass out of the ground and threw it into the air.

'How is Aleksander as a husband?' Annie asked, trying to make conversation.

'He is well but I... we are disappointed that I am not with child,' she said flatly.

I coughed uncomfortably.

'Lady Marchés, would you not rather sit down?' I asked her, looking up and catching the sun in my eyes and squinting.

She looked down. 'It is dirty, I shall not.'

I suddenly felt I was being judged by her and stood up. 'Well, I am out.'

I stood up and walked away.

I had met plenty of people in my life and I knew I had the charm to soften people but apparently not her. I found another log near a small stream. I picked up a leaf and allowed some water to gather in it before drinking out of it. I sat down.

'I mean, why are some people so boring? Could she not be civil to other people?' I said out loud to myself.

I crossed my legs and lifted up my skirt, looking at my legs. They were in desperate need of a wax. I rubbed them and put my skirt back down. Before I left the castle, I found my way into the room where my parents' items were being stored. In my last memory of my mother, she told me about a letter that was hidden in her jewellery box. I had yet to rip open the wax when I felt someone's hands on my shoulders and pulled out my dagger quickly and spun around.

'Bloody hell, do you not think of introducing yourself before touching someone? You gave me a fright.'

I lifted my skirt back up and placed the dagger in the leather holder on my thigh.

'By the way, your wife is lovely and so full of conversation,'

I said to Aleksander and extended my hand for him to help me back across the log.

'No, I disagree. I find her to be full of conversation,' he said. I looked at him suspiciously and I saw a smirk line on his left cheek.

'Were you just using sarcasm and being cheeky like me?' I said, poking him and laughing. 'You are not allowed to do that. I forbid it.'

Aleksander offered his hand for me to come back over the log.

'What were you reading?' he asked as I was hiding it in my cleavage.

I opened my mouth to tell him that I could remember and heard my brother's voice in my head, telling me not to trust anyone.

'Um, it is nothing. Just some scribbles I wrote down to remember stuff.' I lied through my teeth, avoiding eye contact to ensure he did not suspect my falsehood.

'Rohesia is over here,' I said leading the way.

We walked in silence. His hand brushed mine as we walked together. I saw him look in my direction but I did not want to look at him. I was worried about not only what I would do in a forest alone but what he would do as well. We both knew how we felt for one another but we also knew the importance of hiding our feelings from others' eyes. He reached for my hand once more and clasped his around it; he lifted it up and kissed it. I pulled back quickly.

'Lady Marchés, Aleksander has been looking for you,' I said with my hands in front of me. He looked at me.

'Lady Marchés?' he questioned, creasing his eyebrows.

'She said she preferred the formality. She is a very proud

wifey.' I walked over to stand beside Annie and Harley.

She did not speak any words but walked over and kissed him on the cheek.

'ROHESIA,' he said loudly to prove a point, 'the tents have been assembled. I do need a moment to speak with Lady Bushanti alone.' He kissed her hands.

I watched all three of them leave, as did he before he spoke.

'I am not sure if you are aware but Sebastian has organised for him to share a tent with you.' He looked annoyed and uncomfortable.

'I was not aware, no. Sneaky bugger,' I said, pretending as if it was nothing.

'I am not comfortable with the idea of this,' he said, showing the worry behind his eyes.

'Aleksander, I will be fine. It is not the end of the world. I shall sleep on the bed and he can have the floor or vice versa. Trust me, it is all good.' I walked past him.

'I do not understand how you can be so cavalier on this matter. I worry for your safety.'

I stopped and sighed deeply before turning around. He was upset.

'Are you more worried that I am sharing a tent with him rather than you or that whispers shall arise from us sharing a tent?' I posed the question to him.

I could see him thinking about what I had said.

'My point exactly,' I said, walking away from him. I could hear him running to catch up. He grabbed my hand.

'Can I not care about your safety?' he said and pushed me into a tree.

'I never said that. My point was only to point out your

jealousy. Which is bullshit and hypocritical,' I said and pushed him off me.

I was walking back to the campsite when I turned back around in frustration.

'You are married – or have you forgotten that? She wants to have your child. Do you not feel guilt for yesterday? Because I do.' I was annoyed with him but I could tell I was upsetting him. 'I do not know how this is going to work, Aleksander. If you do not fulfil your duty as a husband, will you be safe?'

He shook his head.

'I can't talk about this now. Don't stop me again,' I shouted back to him, walking away.

I arrived at the camp; there were four tents up and plenty of beds all around the firepit that Aleksander's men were making. Dmitirov walked over.

'I hope you did not kill him in the forest,' he said smugly.

'No, although it was quite tempting.' I smiled at him to show that I was not serious.

'He means well, milady. He is just unsure about his intentions. On one side, he is married to benefit the crown. On the other, he would prefer to spend every day in your company but he cannot. He is torn between his duty and his heart,' he said.

I looked at the ground, knowing exactly what he was saying. It was impossible for us to ever be together.

I heard Aleksander's feet march on the ground with the sound of crunching leaves and breaking twigs. I did not turn to look at him.

'Dmitirov,' he said as he walked past me. He did not look back at me.

It hurt me to know that I had hurt him but I knew I was correct in what I had said. I breathed out deeply and headed over to Sebastian who was cautiously watching my interactions.

'Should I be worried about your time alone in the woods with Aleksander?' he asked, pulling me into his arms. I put my head on his chest and snuggled in.

'No, not at all,' I said, feeling emotional but burying my feelings by snuggling deeper into him.

The sun had almost disappeared behind the mountains. The fire was now lit and I could see the men wandering around, doing various chores. I walked into the tent and sat on the bed. I wanted desperately to read the letter from my mother but had no time to myself. I heard the cloth door move and Sebastian walked in.

'Faith, you are not yourself.' He looked worried.

'I am just tired. It has been a long day and I am sure there will be plenty more like it.' I raised my eyebrows at him.

'Come eat,' he said, raising his hand for me to grab it.

'I shall later,' I said and lifted my legs onto the bed as he left the tent.

I could hear laughter and chatter. Annie and Harley were cracking jokes and telling stories of what cars and aeroplanes were, and how people no longer rode horses to get to locations. They were quiet as they listened to the differences in the worlds. I stripped out of my dress and into my nightgown. I hid the letter in my crate, hidden underneath the red fabric. It could not be seen unless someone went searching for it. I pulled the covers up to my shoulders and brought my legs up to my stomach. I closed my eyes and let myself drift to sleep. I woke up suddenly during the night after seeing another vision of my parents burning. I heard the screams as they could not escape and watched as the chapel was engulfed in flames. There were tears in my eyes. Sebastian had snuck into bed with me and was lying beside me as I woke.

'I'm good,' I said without turning and put my hand on his.

'I need some air.' He moved to follow me.

'I'd prefer alone.' I exited the tent.

I could see several men sleeping close to the fire, which had dimmed; it was almost extinguished. I sat on the outskirts of the encampment and stayed in view of the guards who were still awake. They nodded in my presence.

I sat down and closed my eyes. All I could see was the chapel burning and I heard the sounds of my family's screams. A tear ran down my cheek. I wished that I hadn't received my memories. I sat there until I saw the sun begin to emerge over the mountains. The red glow before it changed to the orange hue and the smallest peak of the sun. I re-entered the tent and went through my crate to find what to wear today. I grabbed my trusty brown and red gown and quickly put it on before Sebastian awoke to see me naked. I brushed my hair and put it into a ponytail, then pulled the letter out of the crate and placed it securely between my cleavage. I heard Sebastian stir and exited as I heard more chatter from the men outside.

'Morning.' I nodded to all the men who passed me. I walked over to Milo and started stroking his mane. He whinnied and nodded his head. 'I have missed you and I am glad you are coming with me.'

He put his head on my shoulder and started nibbling on my hair.

'Hey, not funny, you.' I pulled back, laughing, and heard someone laugh behind me.

'It is not normal for a lady to speak with a horse.' Dmitirov stood with his hand on his sword and watched the surroundings.

'Yeah, I have always said I am not normal.' I turned back around and Milo pushed my back to move me. I shook my head. 'Is there an issue, Dmitirov?' I asked, running my fingers through my ponytail and removing the horse saliva.

'Yes, there is food and you did not come out to eat last night. I will not have you faint and see the worry on my lord's face and the king's,' he said sternly and was not accepting any resistance from me.

'Yeah, yeah.' I walked away from Milo but paused. 'On one condition: you speak to the king about allowing me to ride the horse instead of sitting in the carriage.' I crossed my arms smugly and raised an eyebrow at him.

'Your spirited attitude does not charm me,' he said and grabbed my arm to pull me.

'Come on, Dmitirov. I want to see if I remember something. Would it not be better if I was outside seeing the sights?' I lied but it was a good point. He let go of my arm.

'Deal,' he said.

We walked back to the firepit. He watched me sit down before speaking.

'Your Majesty, may I request a moment to converse with you?' He spoke so formally; it was the first time I had heard him use this tone.

Aleksander looked on, confused. I just smiled. He turned his head in my direction quickly and I turned away, trying to make the smile disappear. He was trying to get my attention. I turned back and he shook his head and mouthed something I could not understand and I squinted my eyes and shook my head in confusion. Sebastian and Dmitirov walked out of earshot of the people and I saw them conversing. I could see Sebastian nodding his head in agreement and raising his hand to stop him from talking.

They walked back over and Sebastian walked over to whisper in my ear. 'You are relentless but it is truthful what he says and you get your wish.' He kissed my cheek.

I smugly smiled and clicked my tongue in joy.

'Only if you are happy, Your Majesty,' I said without looking at him.

'Your Majesty, it is dangerous for her to be out. I must utter my worries. I cannot protect her if she is seen by any enemies.' Aleksander stood his ground.

'You forget your place, Aleksander. The decision has been made.' Sebastian shut him down instantly.

Aleksander put down his bowl and walked away. I moved my legs to stand up but Annie put her hand on my knee to stop me. I shot her a look.

'Not wise with so many eyes watching,' she said.

I stopped and pretended I was stretching to hide my true intentions.

'Well, I had better make sure my horse is saddled correctly.' I placed my bowl down and watched Harley and Aidan clean it together. I walked over to Milo; he was tied to the tree. I made sure it was buckled correctly on one side before walking around to the other.

A hand grabbed my arm and pulled but before I could yell

out, a hand covered my mouth. I was pushed against the tree.

'Shh.' It was Aleksander.

I tried to talk over his hand but he moved it and put his finger to his lips to tell me to be quiet.

'What did you do that for?' I whispered, confused about the secrecy.

'The king is always watching. Why did you betray me and speak to one of my men?' he asked, upset about what I had done.

'I told you, I wanted to ride and I knew you would not agree and chose to speak to someone who could put emotions aside.' I tried not to raise my voice. He looked frustrated but walked over, putting his hand on my face as he pulled me in for a kiss.

'I only want you safe. I cannot bear the thought of losing you again,' he said so close to my face that I leaned in for another kiss. He wrapped his arm around my back and pulled me closer. I put my hands up and pushed him away.

'What I said yesterday still stands.'

He came in to kiss me again. I could not resist him. He moved from my lips to my neck, slowly kissing down my neck. I was out of breath.

'We need to stop,' I said, unable to move as my body did not want him to stop. He took a breath and looked at me.

'Tell me to stop and I shall.' He paused momentarily.

I jumped on him and wrapped my legs around him. I had not felt passion like this ever, even with Toby. I could not resist him; I felt so close and connected with every kiss and touch.

'Ahem,' we heard and he let me go instantly. I opened my eyes and saw Annie smiling and clicking her tongue and looking rather pleased. I sighed in relief that it was not someone else.

She looked down at Aleksander's crotch. I shoved her.

'Hey, not necessary.'

I walked away. He brushed his fingers through his hair and stood with his back to us, trying to regain his composure.

'Um, he looks like a decent size.' She raised her eyes and smiled at me to get more information.

'That is something you do not need to know.'

She stopped. 'You haven't done anything yet? After that display in the woods and the passion between you two... wow.' She was shocked.

'Um, hello, when have we had the time? What, you want me to sneak away into the woods and just jump him?' I said.

'Well, yeah, and then give me all the details.'

I laughed and looked away. Sebastian was discussing important matters; the tents were packed onto the different horses.

'Your Majesty, when will we begin our adventure?' I asked him politely.

'Soon, my dear.'

The following two days dragged on with more mountains, grass and sporadic areas of trees for shelter. I tried my best to get a spare moment to read my mother's letter but was not having any luck. I had been avoiding all contact with Aleksander and tried to always have someone near me to not fall into the same trap as before. We could not risk being seen in that way otherwise he would lose his head; for myself, I did not want to think about what Sebastian would do to me. I was granted permission to continue to ride my horse but it had to be within view of Sebastian. Annie and Harley chose to ride a horse as well. It got uncomfortable sitting in the carriage all the time. I watched Aleksander pay close attention to his wife in the company of others but when she was not around, his eyes were always on me.

CHAPTER FORTY-FIVE

Aleksander

There was only a day's journey left before we reached Nharabalu. I could already feel the warmth growing in the air. I saw Faith ride in front of me; her hair flowed down her back. She wore one of her favourite gowns again. The brown on her skin made her complexion darker and the red simply added colour to the dress. I watched the surroundings for any movements but I knew we would be safe.

The lands between Hisadalgon and Nharabalu had always been the safest. The trek over the mountains had always been the most dangerous. She leaned in close to the carriage and spoke with Sebastian. I did not enjoy the nights knowing they were to share a bed. She had no affections for him but I worried for his actions may not be true. I felt I must always protect her and could not bear to be without her. There was something different about her in the way she spoke and acted. I wondered if she was regaining her memories from the past but knew she would inform me but she had yet to tell me of any such memories. We rode over the hill. I knew what was on the other side. At the top, she must have seen the beauty of the field. She rode ahead without thinking.

'Faith,' I shouted after her as I kicked my horse to catch up to her.

She had ridden down the hill and stopped. She jumped off her horse and stared at the lavender field. It was purple as far as the eye could see and the smell was overpowering. She ran into the field and bent down to smell them; she stood upright and jumped in the air; she continued to run through the field, screaming in excitement. I dismounted my horse and watched her with my hand holding onto my sword. I had never seen her look so happy. The rest of the men caught up. Sebastian jumped out of the carriage and looked furious.

'LADY BUSHANTI,' he shouted at the top of his lungs.

She did not care; she twirled around in circles with her hands by her side to stabilise her. I caught a glimpse of her face when she twirled and her face was so bright and the beauty radiated off her. I watched with a smile on my face and looked at Sebastian. His face was covered in rage.

'Your Majesty, there is no harm. She is admiring the land around her. She does not need to act in the appropriate manner right this moment. No one is around to witness her unsuitable actions.' I tried to soften his mood.

He still did not seem impressed.

'Your Majesty, look at her face. Admire the beauty of her,' I said as he looked in her direction. I witnessed his face soften as he watched her and a smile curled across his face.

I let go of my sword and watched her. I wanted to walk over but felt Rohesia slide her arm around mine. I placed my hand on hers and smiled; I remembered Faith's words that I was failing in my duty as a husband. We were a day away from the Arundel family and knew they would be eager to hear of a child with the Arundel and Marchés bloodline. I watched Sebastian walk over to Faith. He grabbed her hand and she twirled into him, throwing her head back in laughter. I saw his hands all over her and looked away; I knew we had less than a day's journey left till we reached our destination.

'Men, we shall set up here for the night,' I shouted and they began to unpack the tents.

I kissed Rohesia's hand and moved to help the men. I could not bear to watch their interaction. I heard her laughter growing as she ran back towards the carriages. I heard Sebastian laugh.

'Faith, you have spirit and energy that many cannot duplicate.' He was out of breath from chasing her.

'I am going back into Harfvilloa and I am going to lie on the ground and smother myself in that smell.' She looked so happy.

'Your Majesty, did you tell her the name of the field?' I asked as I realised she had proper pronunciation.

'No, didn't you?' he asked.

'Yes, I must have.' I wanted to throw off suspicion. She had remembered but why had she chosen not to tell me?

I watched her closely for the rest of the night and every little thing she did. She was more gracious in her movements and delicate in how she walked. I could not deliver a message to Faith directly. I saw Annie head into the tent. I walked over to outside the tent.

'Annie, may I enter?' I asked as I waited for a response.

'Yes, I am dressed,' she said.

I wondered why she felt the need to tell me that information. I entered the tent.

'Annie, I would like you to deliver a message to Faith.' I felt it was important not to ask but rather advise her to do so.

'There is no request in that, Aleksander. Is it wise for you to be close to one another after what I witnessed earlier in the week?'

I looked at the ground; I knew she was right but chose to ignore her warning. 'Regardless of your thoughts, I ask that you tell her to meet me at the first tree in Harfvilloa when all others are sleeping.' I knew this would test her and show if her memories had returned. I left the tent before she could give any more warnings.

I waited until I felt Rohesia sleep. I chose to lie with her tonight in hopes of creating a child. I left my shirt open and just pulled on a pair of tan pants. I grabbed my belt and sword for protection and snuck into the field. I found the first tree; it had a thick trunk unlike the others. I leaned against it and waited. I heard footsteps in the dark before I heard her voice.

'How did you discover my secret? I thought I was doing quite well hiding it.' She spoke softly.

I was still unable to see her face but I could see the outline of her body. She appeared and I could see her smile.

'The name of the field. Neither myself nor Sebastian told you the name,' I said confidently.

She sat down opposite me.

'Dammit, I was trying hard not to show anything.' She sounded frustrated but I couldn't see her face.

'Yes, I watched your movements and you are not as rough but are more delicate.'

She huffed in frustration. 'Please, do not tell the king. That is the last thing I need – for him to find out.'

She lay down on the ground. I wanted her to rest on me but

was too afraid to ask; we had avoided each other's company.

'Your secret is safe with me. Do you remember—'

'We came here as children with our parents and picked off stalks and would throw them at each other. Yep, and I would always tell you to—'

'Catch me if you can.' I finished her sentence and heard her chuckle.

'I am surprised the necklace didn't trigger my memory. I gave it to you as a gift because you were going to be my husband in like possibly ten years. Thank God that did not happen – wow, to be like fifteen or sixteen and married.' She went quiet after she spoke.

'Yes, we would have had plenty of children by now. I have always wanted a handful.' I put my head back and looked at the stars.

'A handful? Yeah, I am lucky we aren't married already. Have that many children running around?' she said quickly. I was hesitant in what I wanted to say but felt it necessary.

'Faith, I have been lying with Rohesia in hopes of fulfilling my duty as a husband and keeping the alliance for the crown.'

She did not speak but remained silent. I wished I could see her face but was unable to as she lay on the ground. I lifted myself off the tree and moved over her. She stared at the sky.

'Faith, please,' I begged.

'I do not know what you want me to say on this matter. It is something I cannot stop like how one day I will have to marry Sebastian and be with him. I don't want to but I know I must to save my life, pretty much.' She sounded so sad. I tried to look into her eyes; I could see her pain.

'We could leave the castle. We could find a small farm and

live out our days there. We could be happy.'

She sat up and shook her head.

'No, I can't do that. To do that would be to risk Annie and Harley's lives. I could not live with myself if they were harmed. Do you now understand what I have been trying to say? Now is not our time... maybe in another life.' She stood up and went to walk away.

I jumped up and grabbed her hand and pulled her in close.

'I don't believe that. The day you arrived, I saw the star shoot across the sky and I was thinking about you at that moment. Is that not a sign?'

I could feel her shake in my arms. I brought her head to mine and I could smell the salty tears.

'I have hope for us one day,' I said and brought my lips to hers. She kissed me back. I wanted to hold on to this moment forever.

'Stay the night with me,' I begged and tightened my grip on her. I felt her nod her head.

'For a while.'

I leaned back against the tree as she cuddled into my arms, rested her head on my waist and wrapped her arm and leg around me.

'I want to remember this always. This was the last place we spent time together before everything and it will be again. Harfvilloa will always be ours.' She pulled me in tight and held on.

We fell asleep in each other's arms. I heard the birds singing and saw the sun was almost up. I shook Faith to wake her; she stirred before she opened her eyes and realised it was later than either one of us had intended. She jumped up, fixed her dress and headed back to the tents. It was not long until Sebastian exited his tent looking for Faith. She pretended to pick some lavender and bent down to smell it. She was good at distracting people from what they should have seen. I did not want to sit up; I was worried Sebastian may see me. I waited until she was in his arms.

I stood up and walked back; she turned him around to avoid him seeing me. I looked at her and knew she was right. I could not betray my wife.

I assisted the men in packing up when I felt Rohesia place her hand on my back. I turned to look at her. She grabbed my hand and pulled me away.

'What is wrong?' I asked her, worried as she was not speaking.

'You left and did not return last night. Are you loyal?' she asked.

I could not be offended by that question and chose to answer honestly. She looked at me with her green eyes; they were filled with worry. I placed my hand on her face lovingly and kissed her lips.

'Always, you are the only woman I have ever lain with. I shall try to be a better husband to you.' I pulled her into an embrace.

Faith was right; it was not our time. I closed my eyes and remembered her in my embrace last night. I shall always cherish that moment.

Shawline Publishing Group Pty Ltd
www.shawlinepublishing.com.au

SHAWLINE
PUBLISHING
GROUP